Amanda Jennings lives just outside Henley-on-Thames with her husband and three daughters. *Sworn Secret* is her first novel, and she is currently writing her second.

SWORN SECRET

Amanda Jennings

Constable & Robinson Ltd
55–56 Russell Square
London WC1B 4HP
www.constablerobinson.com

First published in the UK by Canvas,
an imprint of Constable & Robinson Ltd, 2012

A copy of the British Library Cataloguing in
Publication Data is available from the British Library

ISBN: 978-1-84901-969-9

Printed and bound in the UK

3 5 7 9 10 8 6 4 2

For my three graces: Ella, Beth and Lexi

Acknowledgements

My thanks go to Krystyna Green, Becca Allen and the rest of the talented team at Constable & Robinson for turning this book into a reality. To my wonderful agent, now friend, Broo Doherty, whose unfailing encouragement and belief is only outshone by her humour and enthusiasm. To those friends and family who read various drafts of this book and sustained me with their generous comments. To Rebecca Dixon for helping me text like a teen. To Charlotte Moore, Janet Howard and my darling Sian Johnson whose input and suggestions were invaluable. To my sister and parents who have been a constant source of love and support. To my patient, beautiful daughters who never complained when it was sandwiches for supper again. And, finally, to Chris: husband, best friend, soul mate. Without your unerring love and faith this book could never have happened.

Almost a Year Before

The stuff coming out of his mouth was lies.

She stared at him. A gust of wind whipped her hair across her face. She tucked it back behind her ear. Then, not knowing what else to do she grabbed hold of his shirt, raking her fingers against his chest through the soft laundered cotton. The smell of it, the washing powder, the sweet musty sweat, a hint of his deodorant, sent a shiver through her. His smell, them together, him inside her.

She looked up at him but he turned his face away from her. Why wouldn't he look at her?

'I don't believe you,' she said.

But he didn't move a muscle, his eyes stayed fixed away from her, and she wondered whether she'd said the words loud enough or if they'd been carried away by the wind unheard. She snatched at his hand and thrust it against her breast, holding it hard against her until she felt him stop resisting. He looked down at her then and she saw his eyes had that strange glazed look they always had before they did it. His fingers closed around her. Relieved, she smiled and lifted her other hand, ran the tips of her fingers down his cheek.

'No.' The word was sudden and harsh and hit her like a sack of lead. He pushed himself away from her. 'I can't do this.'

But she could see the lie in his lusting eyes and suddenly felt angry. Angry that he wouldn't kiss her, that he was wasting his breath on words he didn't mean, playing some stupid game. She needed him to take her seriously; to know the games were over. She looked around her, at the flat roof bare of anything but those shabby old cushions and the empty bottle of vodka. Then she knew what to do. She went to the edge, climbed up onto the ledge, wobbling a little as her drunken head spun. She faced him.

'If you don't kiss me I'll jump,' she said, thrusting her hands hard against her hips. 'I will. I'll jump because without . . .' Her voice trailed off then. She was surprised to find a lump in her throat, and her eyes welled. 'Because without you,' she whispered, 'I don't want to live.'

'Get down,' he said.

She shook her head and a handful of tears tumbled down her cheeks.

'Get down off the wall.'

She shifted, feeling the rough brick beneath her bare feet, the edge pressing into her heels. She glanced down at the playground below, cast a deep blue in the moonlight, and wondered at the picnic tables and benches, how small they seemed, small enough to be from a dolls' house. The tables blurred in fresh tears and she looked back at him. Why hadn't he stopped her? Why was he standing so still, like a stupid, impotent statue? This wasn't what she'd planned. This was the opposite of what she'd planned.

'Say you love me!' she suddenly screamed so loud it hurt her throat. 'Say you'll be with me *for ever*! Or I'll do it. I will . . . I'll jump!'

'No. I can't. It's over.'

'*But I love you!*'

As she screamed the words she felt a pain, as if a fist with broken

2

glass for nails had torn into her body and ripped out her heart, and she began to sob, proper, wrenching sobs, because at that very moment she knew it was true.

'I love you,' she whispered.

She saw his hesitation and for a second she thought it might be all right, that at last he was going to walk over to her, lift her off the ledge, kiss her, and hold her tightly against him. But he didn't; he turned and began to walk away from her.

'If you don't,' she said then, 'I'll tell them. I'll tell everyone your secret. They'll all know about you and they'll all *hate* you.'

Then something happened, maybe a strong gust of wind, or perhaps she just stumbled. Had she imagined the thump to her chest that took her breath? All she really knew was that she was falling, hurtling through the hot summer darkness towards the ground, and then, before she could think of what to do next, there was nothing.

Superdad: A Present-Day Hero

As always she heard the buzzing first and, as always, an instant panic froze her. Only her eyes moved, flicking from side to side, desperate to find it. When she finally did her fists clenched and she gasped. It was enormous. Not a bee but a hornet. A wasp on blinking steroids.

Lizzie took a couple of deep, slow breaths, and then as calmly as she could, with her eyes locked on the hornet, she reached for her bag. Her heart stopped. It wasn't there. Her hands patted up and down her chest and over her shoulders in a frantic search. It never left her; it was always looped over her head and one shoulder, ready and waiting. Just not today, the day she needed it, the day she found herself sharing their tiny bathroom with a hornet the size of a spaniel. She tried to remember where it was, but as her mind raced faster and faster towards blind terror, her thoughts blurred to an indecipherable mess.

Focus, she told herself firmly. *Focus on the bag.*

She closed her eyes and pictured it, hoping this would trigger her memory. The patchwork squares in a rainbow of Indian silks, some of their edges beginning to fray, a black cotton strap, her name stitched inside, a folded piece of paper with instructions on what to do with its precious contents if the hornet turned nasty. But there was nothing. Blank. She could only hear the humming.

Then the noise stopped. Lizzie's heart leapt again. No noise was way worse. Without the damn noise how did she know where the stupid thing was? She was aware then of a thick dampness creeping over her body. Sweat. She wanted to cry. Bees could smell sweat, couldn't they? No, she told herself, you made that up. It was sharks that smelt sweat. No, that wasn't it; you didn't sweat in the ocean! She shook her head to keep her thoughts clear. It was definitely wee. Sharks went for wee. And blood. So did that mean it was bees that went for sweat? And if they did, did hornets too? A white fug fell over her, muddying her vision and clamping her lungs.

'Come on, Lizzie, be brave,' she whispered aloud. 'Don't be such a wimp.' It wasn't unusual for her to speak to herself. She did it a lot. Especially when she was nervous. She'd always done it, though perhaps more so in the last year.

She forced herself to move. 'You've got to,' she whispered. 'Just walk.' She began to edge towards the door. One tiny step. Then another. One more. 'You're nearly there. Keep going.'

But as she crept, images as clear as day began to play in her head like an old slasher flick. She saw the hornet, still and waiting; an ominous silence hung about it. Without warning it dropped its head and fixed a ghastly eye on Lizzie. Its feelers stroked its thorax as if rubbing evil hands. It licked whatever stood for lips. And then it fell. Direct as a dart. Straight for her.

'Mum!' Lizzie screamed. 'Mum!' She screamed again and again. 'Mum! Mum, quick! Please!'

The door to the bathroom flew open and Lizzie fell into her mother's arms and buried her face in her chest, breathing her in: Persil, Dove, white spirit.

5

'Where is it?' her mum said urgently, knowing immediately what was wrong.

Lizzie could feel her mother searching over her shoulder as she backed them out of the bathroom to the relative safety of the upstairs landing. Her dad appeared at their side, his face tight with concern as he pushed past them. He paused for a moment or two at the bathroom door. Don't go in there! Lizzie wanted to cry. Don't take another step! But no noise came out of her mouth. She closed her eyes as he went in.

'It's a hornet,' he called back. 'It's on the shower curtain.'

'Can you get it?' her mum asked.

'Yes, it seems quite sleepy.'

Lizzie kept her eyes tightly closed and listened to the noises of the execution: some grappling, muttered cursing, a bang, then another, one more. Then silence. She pictured her father breathing heavily, beads of sweat on his brow, adrenalin surging through him.

'It's over,' her mum whispered, kissing her forehead. 'It's dead.'

Lizzie exhaled. Despite shivering like a little match girl she felt a sharp stab of sympathy for the squashed hornet.

Her dad appeared and scruffed her hair. 'That was quite a biggie.'

Lizzie tried to smile. 'I didn't have my bag,' she said weakly.

'The hall table,' her mum said. She took her arms away from Lizzie. 'You put it there because the strap was coming loose. I was going to fix it for you. I forgot.' She made a sucking noise as if to say how lax she'd been.

'Are you OK now?' her dad asked. His brow was crinkled with deep anxious furrows, and his hair, a thick and soupy mix of brown and grey, was messed up from his tussle. She wished he didn't look so worried.

'I'm fine,' she nodded. 'Sorry. I'm so pathetic.'

'You are *not* pathetic, you daft thing. That was the biggest hornet I've ever seen. But,' he paused and grinned at her, 'luckily, no match for Superdad!' He stretched a balled fist in front of him and sang his superhero jingle: 'The dad all stingers dread to meet!'

Then he laughed.

Lizzie laughed too, albeit with less enthusiasm, but she stopped when she felt her mum's thorny quiet beside her. She glanced at her dad and caught the last ray of his smile before it set behind his eyes. He cleared his throat and her mother sniffed loudly.

Lizzie couldn't read minds, but she was ninety-nine-point-nine per cent certain that theirs were soaked in her sister, memories of a few years back, when laughing was OK and smiles held on. Lizzie knew that Superdad popped out by accident. She also knew her dad would be beating himself stupid for the slip, desperate at the thought of upsetting her mum, of flaring her heartache. He just didn't get it; her mum's heartache was flared to the max already. She couldn't *be* any sadder. None of them could. Tiptoeing through this crazy minefield of spoken words was pointless. What happened had happened, and no amount of pretending there wasn't a before would help. She didn't understand them. If it were up to her they'd talk about Anna teasing her dad every day. She closed her eyes and saw her immediately.

'Here he comes! Like a flash of light. It's the one, it's the only . . . family drum roll . . . iiiiiiiiiitttttttsssss *Superdad*!' Anna cried, her smile wide across her face, as she held their dad's arm aloft like a boxing champ.

Looming Tuesday

Jon seemed about to speak to her, so Kate dropped her eyes and turned away from him.

'Are you coming down for breakfast, Mum?'

Kate briefly looked up at Lizzie and forced a smile. 'In a minute,' she whispered, still trembling from the aftershocks of Lizzie's scream. Though the frantic fear that filled her had begun to ebb, she was still finding it terribly hard to breathe.

'Come on you,' Jon said to Lizzie. He walked over to their daughter and took her hand. 'Let's get some toast on.'

Kate waited until they'd gone down the stairs and then covered her face with her hands. She felt queasy. Unnerved and shaken. How on earth would she cope with meeting Stephen now? And she had to; this was her last chance to stop Tuesday. She'd been over the words again and again. She thought she'd mustered the strength to tell him she just couldn't go through with it. That he'd have to cancel. She was sorry. Really sorry. She appreciated everything he'd done, but there was no way. But now, standing shivery and faint on the upstairs landing, she knew she wouldn't get those words out. She should have told Jon how she was feeling. Stopped trying to be brave. She should have told him as soon as the doubts had begun to darken and gather. Jon would have understood, and he would have had no problem telling Stephen. Maybe she could even have painted while he did it, her thoughts safely tucked a million miles away, and when she emerged the threat of Tuesday would be gone. But instead of confiding in her husband, instead of being honest, she'd tried to be strong, pretended she was, and now, because of it, she was struck dumb with sick fear.

Kate was halfway down the stairs when the phone rang. Her immediate thought was that it was Stephen calling to cancel the meeting.

'Oh, God, please, please, please,' she muttered, running the remaining stairs two at a time.

Between a Rock and a Sad Face

Jon was buttering the toast when the telephone rang. He balanced the knife against the pot of butter and went to answer it just as Kate appeared at the door and grabbed for the phone.

'Hello?' she said urgently. Then a muted: 'Oh.'

He guessed who it was. Kate bowed her head and held the receiver out towards him.

'Hello, Mother,' he said.

'Jonathan . . .'

Her voice was weak and unsteady. His stomach turned over.

'Is everything all right?' he said.

She didn't reply. He could hear she was crying. He asked her again what was wrong, but she still couldn't speak as quiet sobs stifled her words.

'Mother? Speak to me. What's wrong? Is it Dad?'

'I'd like . . . to see you,' she managed. 'Can . . . you come now?'

'Of course,' he said. 'What's wrong?'

No words, just soft gasps of breath.

'Mother,' he said, as calmly as he could. 'Sit down and wait for me. I'll be with you as quickly as I can.'

His knees gave a little as he replaced the phone. 'That was my mother,' he said to Kate, who was leafing through the pile of post, her eyes locked on the middle distance, her mouth set. Ignoring her lack of response he began to rifle through the collection of keys in the wooden bowl on the side. 'She, um, needs to see me. Shit!' He emptied the contents of the bowl in frustration. 'Where are the car keys?'

'What's wrong with her, Dad?'

At last he found his keys. He turned to Lizzie and tried to smile. 'I don't know yet, sweetheart. She couldn't really tell me.'

'Poor Granny.' Lizzie stood up from the kitchen table. 'Shall I come with you?'

'No,' he said. He smiled another tight smile. 'Thank you. I'm sure she's fine.'

'You can't go.'

He reached for his jacket, which hung on the back of a kitchen chair and made for the door.

'Jon,' Kate said, stepping into his path. 'Didn't you hear me?' She paused and shook her head. 'You can't go.'

'I have to. You heard the conversation.'

'No,' she said. 'I didn't hear the conversation, I only heard you say you'd be there as quick as you can.'

'What if it's my father?' Jon said, more to himself than to her.

He rubbed a hand across his mouth as his question echoed over Kate's silence.

'You didn't hear her,' he said. 'If you had, you'd tell me to go. She was so upset, distraught even.' As he spoke, the dread in his stomach thickened. 'When is she ever distraught?'

'Maybe if it was more often she'd be more understanding of it in other people,' Kate said with stale apathy. She went back to the post and picked up an unopened envelope.

'I know you're angry with her—'

Kate snorted and shook her head. He saw her eyes well. She

11

pinched the bridge of her nose: her tried and tested way of stemming tears.

'Something's wrong and I need to go over there.' He put an arm through his jacket. 'She never cries,' he said under his breath.

Kate walked over to the swing bin on the other side of the room and deposited the mess of junk mail and torn envelopes. 'Stephen's coming.'

Jon swore silently and stopped in his tracks. He turned to face his wife, but her eyes dropped away from him.

'I'd forgotten.'

She gave a nod, heavy with I-expected-nothing-more, which rankled. He clamped his lips shut to stop himself snapping.

'What time?'

'Ten.'

Jon looked at the clock on the wall. 'Half an hour. That's OK,' he said. 'I'll be back for him.'

'You won't.'

'I will. Ten minutes there, ten back. I'll spend ten minutes with her, make sure she's OK and then get back for him.'

'Jon,' she said, looking directly at him, any challenge now gone, her eyes pleading with him. He had to look away.

'I have to go,' he said.

'Jon . . . I can't . . .'

'I'll be back,' he said, glancing up and catching her injured look square on. 'I—' He stopped, interrupted by the memory of his mother crying. 'What if it's my father? She couldn't even speak, Kate.'

They held each other's gaze for a few moments. Her eyes searched his face. He knew she was waiting for him to change his mind. He stayed silent and watched her eyes harden to a familiar glaze. She nodded once and turned towards the sink. He watched her roughly put the plug in, turn the taps on, squeeze too much Fairy into the water.

'It's fine. It doesn't need both of us.' She forced the words out of her like a stubborn splinter.

He hesitated, but again he heard his mother's crying. 'I'll be half an hour. OK?'

Kate fixed her eyes on the suddy water and didn't say anything more.

The Fourth Chair

Lizzie grabbed an apple from the fruit bowl, went through to the living room and sat in the armchair beside the window to watch the rainy street for her dad's car. It was three minutes to ten and there was no sign of him. He was usually pretty good at keeping promises, but even she knew he was going to struggle to get to her grandparents' and back in time, especially if her grandmother was as upset as he'd said. She hoped it wasn't anything too serious. She was pretty sure it wasn't her grandpa, not dead anyway; her dad would definitely have called them by now.

She sighed and took a large bite out of her apple. She didn't want to be there, but she couldn't let her mum be alone for the meeting with Dr Howe, even though she couldn't bear the thought of it.

'Come on, Dad,' she whispered, craning her neck to look down the road.

He wasn't going to make it. She lifted her apple but hesitated before she bit, then decided against it. She put it on the window sill and then pulled her knees up to her chest, listening to the sounds coming from the kitchen – the boiling kettle, clinking crockery, biscuits tipping onto a plate – and tried not to let the living room get to her. She hated the room. So miserably gloomy. It never used to be; just another thing morphed by crippling sadness. Ironic, she

14

thought, that it was called the living room, when it felt like the complete opposite. She was never comfortable in the room now, not even on those rare evenings when the three of them sat and stared at the television make-believing they were spending quality time together. It was that spot on the mantelpiece. The new and hideous heart of the room. Lizzie never looked anywhere near it, terrified in case she saw the urn still there.

She rested her chin on her knees and felt the rough graze of the large scab she had. She lifted her head and looked down at it, deep and crusted, the surface beginning to crack with healing, new skin beneath literally itching to break free. She was far too old for scabs. This wasn't even a grown-up version, a graze from tripping in the street or falling up a step, no, this was falling off a swing. She'd tried to jump off when the bell rang for the end of break, and landed right on her knees. It was the most painful thing ever, totally made worse by a couple of Year Sevens who laughed and pointed like idiot hyenas. At least she'd managed not to cry. Now Lizzie picked at the edge of it with a tentative fingernail, which was a welcome distraction from the chill around her.

'Do you want me to get that?' she called, when the doorbell rang a few minutes later.

There was no reply, but she heard her mum's footsteps in the hall, so stayed where she was and looked back out of the window. There was still no dad to be seen, and a heavy weight fell down on top of her.

When Dr Howe came into the living room she was polite enough to say a brief hello to his, but didn't engage any further. It felt too weird. It was bad enough that her mum and dad were on first-name terms with the man, without her having to endure his forced chat. It wasn't that she didn't like Dr Howe; in fact, she wished she felt warmer towards him, especially given the support he'd been to her parents. She just would have preferred he didn't constantly pop up in her actual home like some sort of bizarre, besuited jack-in-a-box. Violated was too strong a word, but she definitely felt compromised by his visits.

Dr Howe was tall, very tall, and his tallness made their living room feel even smaller than it was. There was just enough room for the two-seater sofa, the armchair, TV and the small circular table with four chairs, but not really enough for the glass coffee table squished into its middle or the sideboard that held the CD player and a vase of immortal silk sweet peas, and with Dr Howe looming in the doorway the room felt like Lilliput. He was also broad, with the air of a retired Olympic rower. His eyes were Swedish-blue, his teeth too white and too straight, and his dark hair was grey only at the sideburns. He always wore a navy suit, which that day went over an open-necked shirt that looked uncomfortably casual. Lots of the girls at school said they fancied him. She'd even heard Anna call him *kinda hot*. But they were talking in tongues. He was their headmaster; he couldn't be any sort of hot, and he shouldn't be in her living room.

'Goodness me,' he said, brushing rain off his shoulders. 'Cats and dogs out there!' He smiled at them both.

'I'm afraid Jon can't join us,' said her mum. 'There's been an emergency.'

His eyes hooded with concern and he stopped brushing off the rain. 'Nothing serious, I hope?'

Her mum ignored his probe. 'Lizzie's going to join us instead. She had a bit of a shock this morning.'

'I'm fine,' Lizzie mumbled, wishing her mum hadn't mentioned her.

'Delighted for her to sit in.'

16

Dr Howe gave Lizzie a wide smile showing all of his teeth. She felt her cheeks flush.

Her mum sat down at the small table with the four chairs where they used to eat their meals. Lizzie couldn't remember the last time they had. Eating was mostly a routineless mixture of standing in the kitchen or on laps in front of the television. The problem was the fourth chair. As soon as they sat it screamed loud as a klaxon, far too loud for them to enjoy a conversation. Or even eat. The fourth chair made swallowing difficult, which left over-chewed food in her mouth like lead. Of course, it wasn't just the fourth chair. There were stacks of reminders: the ever-closed door of her bedroom, their old and rusted swing in the garden that creaked with the memories of childhood games, her name carved into the damp plaster on the garage wall, and the spot behind the compost (two steps to the north, one to the west) where a box was buried with some Jelly Tots, a pair of tiny Barbie shoes, a cotton hankie and a book of matches from Bertolli's down the road, all waiting patiently for a lucky prospector from the future. It was an endless list of foghorns all shrieking: 'She's gone! She's gone! She's gone!'

Dr Howe sat on the fourth chair and Lizzie closed her eyes as the two of them began to engage in empty small talk, with Dr Howe asking inane questions and her mum delivering clipped one-word answers. Then the discussion appeared to run out of steam. Lizzie opened her eyes and turned to look at them. Dr Howe was watching her mum, waiting for a reply, it seemed. He cleared his throat, but her mum just stared through him, her eyes glazed. Dr Howe glanced downwards at the open file in front of him.

'So,' he said, clearing his throat. 'I think we're almost there. There's just a few final—'

'Actually, Stephen,' interrupted her mum quietly. 'There's something I need to say.'

He rested his hand on the open file. 'Yes?'

'Well . . . it's . . .' Lizzie looked up in alarm; her mum was about to cry. 'I . . .' Her voice trailed off to nothing.

'Is everything OK, Kate?' Dr Howe's voice was creamy with concern.

Her mum looked up at him. Her mouth opened then closed a couple of times.

'Mum?'

Her mum turned towards her and seemed surprised to see her there. Lizzie smiled. Her mum looked down at her lap. 'Nothing,' she whispered. 'Carry on.'

They started talking again, their voices low, his laced with efficiency, her mother's muttered syllables distinctly reticent.

Lizzie started to pick at her scab again and tried to think of her sister, tried to magic up a gorgeous memory of the two of them together. Maybe it was being in the ghastly living room, or her mum and Dr Howe's soft, serious voices, but there were no gorgeous memories at all. All Lizzie could think of was her lack of Anna, the lack of her that sat in the fourth chair, that creaked the swing, that made her mum cry and her dad look shattered. The lack of her that set those strangers whispering whenever Lizzie walked past.

'That's her,' the strangers whispered.

'Who?'

'That girl's sister.'

'Which girl?'

'*You know . . .*'

Those whispers drove her mad, poisonous hushed tones that groaned beneath the weight of suspicion, judgement and aspersion. They made her want to turn and yell at the strangers, tell them *that girl*, her sister, had a name. Her name was Anna, and they had no right to whisper. No right to wonder. No right at all. Because she knew what most of them thought. That Anna didn't fall. It was Lizzie's worst nightmare, a dark, skulking thought that she banished to the back of her mind where it prowled night and day.

Lizzie breathed deeply, moved Anna firmly out of her head, and made a concerted effort to concentrate on her mum and headteacher. They were finalizing arrangements for Tuesday. Her mum's voice cracked a couple of times, the words too heavy for her to carry. She looked so drained, and it yanked at Lizzie's heart. Her lips were drawn tight over her teeth and recurring tear tracks trailed her sallow cheeks, but even so, pale and unmade-up, with delicate features, blanched skin and fine dark hair tied loosely back, her mother possessed an almost consumptive beauty. If it were possible, Lizzie would have spirited her away to convalesce somewhere remote and safe where Dr Howe and Tuesday and that noisy fourth chair weren't.

'We've chosen a tree,' Dr Howe said, a note of triumph in his voice. 'An apple tree. I hope that's OK.' He stopped talking and looked at her mum, who was doodling on the empty sheet of paper in front of her.

'Kate?' he asked. He laid a hand on hers, the one that was drawing, and Lizzie saw her land in the here-and-now with a heavy thud.

'Sorry?' Her voice was vague and faraway, and mirrored her eyes. She moved her hand from beneath his.

'The tree we've bought,' he said. 'It's an apple. We thought it might be nice to grow some fruit. Maybe the home economics club can make some chutney. There'll be a plaque on it, engraved with Anna's name.'

Her mum didn't say anything. She just kept on with her doodles. Even without looking Lizzie knew what she was doodling.

19

Straight lines. Lots of them. She'd Googled doodles and found a site called *Doodling and the Inner You*. Apparently, straight lines show a suffocated doodler and shading shows an anxious doodler. Lizzie used to shade, but when she read that shading meant she was anxious she decided it was better to doodle stars. Stars show an optimistic doodler. When Lizzie told her mum about the doodling website, though, she said in no uncertain terms that you doodle what you doodle, and doodling lines and shading doesn't mean anything more than that you doodle lines and shading. But Lizzie felt she'd missed her point about the Inner You.

'And you've thought about music,' said Dr Howe.

Her mum didn't reply and he stared hard at her, making Lizzie's heart beat a fraction faster, nervous in case he decided to say something sarcastic about the importance of paying attention, which he did all the time in assembly.

'Why don't we let Mrs Goldman handle it? I know she's prepared something.'

No reply.

Anxiety spiked again and Lizzie stood to go to her mother's side, but as she did her mum suddenly jammed the biro into the paper and turned her doodling face down.

'I think we're done, Stephen,' she said.

Lizzie looked nervously from her mum to Dr Howe and back again.

'Ah. I see. Well . . .' Dr Howe looked down at his red file, flicked forward a couple of pages, and then shut it.

Lizzie caught sight of her sister's name in bold black capitals across the front of it.

ANNA.

She still loved the look and sound of it. She always had. It was fabulous, simple and feminine, and . . . a palindrome! Anna had teased her and called her a geek when she pointed this out.

'It's not just that it's a palindrome,' she'd said to her sister, smarting a little. 'Elizabeth is so blinking dull. Just queens and stamps and some fancy cruise ship. Anna is romantic. Anna floats. Anna twirls. Anna gets kissed by Prince Charmings. Elizabeth chops people's heads off and pays for postage.'

'I don't float and twirl!'

'You get kissed by Prince Charmings.'

Anna smiled at her. 'Most of those need their heads chopping off.'

Then they laughed.

Lizzie missed her terribly, and seeing her name on Dr Howe's folder, yet another black reminder, was a punch in the stomach.

'Yes,' Dr Howe said, roughly interrupting Lizzie's sadness. 'I think we can leave it there. If there's anything else,' he continued. 'I'll telephone.'

Her mum nodded and then, without even a mumbled goodbye, she walked out of the room, leaving Lizzie and Dr Howe in an awkward, sticky silence.

'Um . . . she's . . . um . . . pretty tired,' Lizzie mumbled. 'You know . . . not been sleeping well . . .'

She turned towards the front door, praying he wouldn't try and talk to her. They almost made it, but then she heard him clear his throat to speak. Her stomach clenched.

'So, Lizzie, tell me,' he said, sounding a lot like the kind but useless bereavement lady she was sent to after Anna fell. 'How are you *feeling* about Tuesday?'

Lizzie reached to open the latch. 'Er . . . fine,' she mumbled.

This seemed to be the wrong answer, as he didn't smile but gave her one of those teachery looks that said there was a far better

21

answer floating about in the ether somewhere. Lizzie stared at the empty patch of space above his head and searched for it.

'I mean, well, I'm sure it'll be hard.'

She shot him a look to see if this was closer to what he'd wanted. It appeared so. His frown softened, and the corners of his mouth curled into a smile.

'Yes, it will be hard. But, I think, once it's over we'll all feel so much . . . better.'

Then he nodded.

Lizzie nodded too, even though she knew full well that planting an apple tree for the home economics group and singing some songs chosen by her unstable music teacher wouldn't make losing Anna any better at all.

They stood in silence for a moment or two. He stared at her so hard she felt as if she were standing on a metal sheet heated up as hot as it could go. She avoided his eyes and shifted her weight from foot to foot like one of those dancing desert lizards.

'You know you can always talk to me if you need to,' he said. 'My door at school is always open.'

Lizzie breathed a massive sigh when she was finally able to close the door behind him. She wandered back to the living room and sat in the armchair to pick her knee and wait for her mum to come back down.

With the scab finally gone, flicked in tiny bits onto the carpet and her knee all pink and bloody, there was still no sign of her mum. She went to the bottom of the stairs and leant against the banister and waited a few minutes. Twice she nearly called her, but didn't. If she was in her studio, the room in the loft with dusty Velux windows and cork tiles that lay unglued across ply, she wouldn't disturb her, because, even though her mum never said so aloud, Lizzie knew that this was where she was happiest.

The Wrong Type of Tree

An apple tree?

Kate closed the door of her bedroom and rested her forehead against it. Why on earth didn't she tell him they couldn't possibly plant Anna an apple tree? Anna didn't eat apples. Not unless Kate peeled and cored them and cut them into eighths, and she'd stopped doing that for her when she turned twelve.

'You can peel your own apples,' she'd said to her. 'Honestly, you're the fussiest child I've ever met. Lizzie doesn't need them peeled and she's younger than you.'

Kate hadn't said this nicely.

She'd been tired. It was one of those days when nothing had gone right. She was hormonal. She and Jon had argued about who should have remembered to put the bins out. She got a parking ticket because she stopped to help a frazzled new mum whose carrier bag split on a zebra crossing. The warden was writing it out as she ran back to the car, and while she tried to explain he pretended she wasn't there. When she got home and unpacked the shopping she realized she'd forgotten the milk. Then Anna had asked for an apple and Kate had told her to get one herself.

'Can you peel it for me?'

You can peel your own apples.

The words tumbled out, hard, unbending, exhausted. Just a peeled apple. What would it have taken to peel that apple for Anna? Thirty seconds, tops. Instead she spoke unkindly. And then a little over three years later, maybe, what, a thousand days at the most, Anna was snatched away from her. A thousand days. It sounds a lot. It's not; not if that paltry number of days is all a mother has left with her child. If only she had known. If she had, she never would have snapped. Or told her to peel her own. She would have smiled and kissed her. Taken the apple and peeled it, careful to take off every bit of skin. Then she would have cut it into the neatest eighths and arranged them on a plate to look like a flower. And she would have given her the plate and smiled and maybe kissed her forehead gently.

If only she had known.

If only she had known, Kate would have peeled and sliced her an apple every day they had left together. Every one of those thousand days. One thousand apples. Just for Anna.

The Tortoiseshell Comb: Part One

'Is everything OK?' asked Jon, as soon as his mother opened her door. Her eyes were puffed and reddened, and he guessed she'd been crying for quite some hours.

She tried to smile but her skin seemed too taut to allow it. She didn't say anything, just turned and walked down the hallway, her shoes tapping on the chequerboard tiles on which he and Dan used to play toy soldiers – Jon's small regimented army always on the lookout for Dan's renegade snipers. He hovered, unsure, on the doorstep. He had no idea of what waited, and worry dripped steadily into the pit of his stomach as he willed himself over the threshold. He wiped his feet on the sisal mat and shook the water off his jacket. Just running the short distance from the car to the front door had been enough to soak him.

In the kitchen his mother leant against the sink. She wore immaculate black slacks and a pink cashmere sweater, her white hair put up, as it always was, in a neat bun held in place by her tortoiseshell comb. Her back faced him. Both hands gripped the stainless steel, but there was a slump in her body, a looseness to her limbs; she looked beaten. It was the first time he'd seen her anything other than stoically composed, with the starched upper lip that defined that certain sector of her generation. But now she was shattered like a mirror, broken and tear-stained, barely recognizable. It unnerved him. He looked around for hints of what was wrong, but nothing seemed amiss; the kitchen looked exactly the same as it always had. Of course it would do; as far as he could remember, nothing in the house had changed in forty years. The upright Bechstein in the corner topped with books and papers. The copper saucepans hanging above the antique butcher's block. The collection of china jugs lined up in height order on the window sill. All unchanged for as long as Jon could remember. The oak farmhouse table – so out of place in their detached townhouse in the smarter part of Chiswick – still held his father's disorder (piles and piles of papers, a collection of obscure works by eminent French economists here, dog-eared paperbacks of unknown Russian literary geniuses there) organized by his mother as best she could. Every room in the house, including the kitchen, was essentially overflow from the room his father called a study and his mother called the library. He smiled to himself. How had two such contrasting personalities spent so many years living in such apparent harmony? It never ceased to amaze him. Everything about her screamed order, cleanliness and aspiration; everything about his father was bookish, distractable chaos.

Jon rested a gentle hand on his mother's. She was so warm, just as he remembered her as a child. Always warm. Like a splendid hot-water bottle, his father used to say with a grin.

'Is it my father?' Jon asked her.

Even as the words came out of his mouth he wished he could haul them back in. What if she nodded? What if his father was dead and he had to deal with the aftermath? He wasn't sure he had sufficient energy for that today.

She turned to face him; her eyes were soft beneath a film of tears.

26

'He's fine. It's just . . .' She hesitated. 'I'm just so tired.'

Then she shook her head.

The shake dislodged her tortoiseshell comb, and as it slipped her snow-queen hair came loose. She closed her eyes and pulled the comb fully out and placed it between her lips. She began to smooth her hair back into its proper place, but then she seemed to run out of steam, and her trembling hands fell to her sides. Without a word, Jon stepped towards her and took the comb from her mouth, then rested it beside the sink. He turned her around. She moved without resistance. He stroked her hair, which had aged to the finest strands of bleached silk, and gathered a new ponytail with the experienced hand of a father of daughters. He twisted the ponytail up against her head and pushed the comb into place. Then he lightly touched his fingers to the tortoiseshell. He had always loved the comb. His mother told him often how it had been passed down to her by her grandmother, and to her from an allegedly wild and unknown great-great-grandmother.

'How this comb could tell stories,' his mother used to say. 'Palaces, castles, even a prince's bedchamber.' And Jon would beg her to tell him. He would sit next to her, gazing at the comb, listening to those tales of passion and daring, fascinated by the way the light caught the milky mother-of-pearl inlays, setting their green and purple glinting. He stared at the comb now; all those decades and barely a scratch.

'Thank you,' she said.

She turned back and he stepped closer and tentatively put his arms around her. The last time they'd held each other was the morning after the night Anna fell. Standing there, trying to give her comfort, he was suddenly overcome with memories of that morning. Breaking the news to his parents, his mother's stoicism, his father's lack of comprehension. Jon gripped her harder, not for her but for himself – he felt weak, as if he might crumple and bring them both to the floor. He tried to stand tall, but even as he did, he felt the strength in his backbone seep out of him into the ground. Her body stiffened and she pulled away from him, a cool mask set over her face. She pressed the corners of her eyes with the neatly pressed handkerchief that nestled in the sleeve of her cardigan.

'Come on now. That's enough, Jonathan. Stop looking so terribly stricken.' Her voice was suddenly sharpened, stark in contrast to how feeble she appeared. It was instantly reassuring. 'Your father and I are fine.'

'I want to help.'

'There's no help needed,' she said. 'It's just the end of a silly cold I've had; it's run me down. I need a good sleep and a dose of chicken soup.'

He knew there was something else; his mother didn't get ill and even if she did she certainly wouldn't admit to it.

'I've not been—'

His sentence was cut short by shuffling and grumbling from the hall. She drew the handkerchief from her sleeve again and patted it over her face, smoothed her hair with her hands and straightened her shoulders.

She cleared her throat. 'He's not so good today.'

Jon wished they had time to clarify the not-so-good. As far as Jon was concerned, even good days were not-so-good. On good days there were still the staring eyes left empty by the lack of recognition, still the flaring temper, the sentences left unfinished and the aimless wandering and disorientation. Even on good days there was always the gaunt thinness and the muscle twitches and hands knotted into the arthritic claws of a man he didn't know who bore a striking resemblance to his father.

The man trundled into the kitchen in pyjamas and a plaid dressing gown with creases ironed the length of each arm, the yellow tint to his snowy hair emphasized by the neat rows left by his wife's combing. He was immaculate save for wearing only one slipper.

Jon forced a smile.

'Not those pipes again?' said his father gruffly. His glaring eyes floated away for a moment, but then darted back and fixed on Jon. 'Actually, don't I know you?' he barked.

Jon felt a flush of heat on the back of his neck. He tried to smile. His father flicked a gnarly finger at him.

'Yes, yes, you've been before.' He gave a couple of guttural tuts. 'Just you make sure you check your watch, Barbara. This is that one who charged me double. Disreputable bunch.'

Jon glanced at his mother, who raised a stern eyebrow. He swallowed uncomfortably. 'The pipes look fine,' he said. 'No charge today.'

The old man grumbled and shuffled past Jon.

'You've lost a slipper,' his mother said. 'Your foot must be cold.'

His father looked down at his feet. When he lifted his head the crusty glare had vanished and his face held the bewildered confusion of a lost child.

'Not to worry, I'll fetch it.' She patted his hand. He flinched and drew his arm close to his body.

Jon's mother left the room and Jon watched his father apprehensively. He felt sickened by the lack of affection he had for him. He might as well have been a stranger; everything familiar was gone. He thought back, desperate to peg his emotions to a fond memory: his father's smiling face across the dinner table, his patience teaching algebra, showing him and Dan how to light fires with flint, the soporific lilt of his voice as he read them *Moby Dick* by the fire while they ate an entire packet of chocolate digestives.

But looking at this ruined man, these recollections were as faint as rumours. Jon watched him float about the kitchen like a living ghost, walking from nowhere to nowhere, his hands fluttering at his sides with the memory of use, and racked his brain for conversation to fill the silence that drowned them.

'How was your trip to Kew Gardens?' he said at last.

The old man looked shocked. 'Excuse me?'

'You went with Mother last week. She took you to see the herbarium collections.'

'What the blasted hell are you on about?'

'The gardens,' Jon tried. 'Kew?'

'Why are you even talking to me? Just get on with your job!' His voice rose as his eyes filled with blind panic. 'Wasting time and filling air with nonsense about gardens and mothers!'

'Goodness me,' said Jon's mother, as she hurried back into the room clutching the missing slipper.

She went straight past Jon to her husband's side and guided him to a chair, cooing softly as she did. She threw Jon a look that spoke silent reproach.

'This man's talking nonsense! Going on like a stupid child. A dunce. I know what he's up to. He's creating some sort of . . . of . . . a smoke screen. He's trying to take my money. You should check his bag.' His father's eyes suddenly grew wide and flicked up to the ceiling and back. 'You know I can hear them upstairs again, Barbara. Can't you? Can't you hear them up there? How many are there this time?' His voice was now a whisper. He nodded. 'Lots. I can hear lots. At least ten. It's my watch they're after. They're trying to take my watch.'

'There's nobody up there, Peter,' she soothed. The softness in her voice seemed unfamiliar suddenly, and Jon tried to recall if she'd ever used this tone with either him or Dan. 'It's just those squirrels again. We've had so many squirrels this year. Remember? We were watching them out of the window, eating the nuts I put out for the blue tit. Try not to get yourself worked up.' She stroked his hand. 'Let's get this slipper back on before your foot turns to ice.' She bent down and cradled his foot, carefully sliding the slipper on as if both foot and slipper were made of glass.

'Now,' she said, leaning back on her heels and resting her hands on his knees. 'How about I make you a nice cup of tea?'

'What the hell do I want tea for!' he shouted suddenly. He leant forward until his face was only inches from hers and grabbed the tops of her arms. Jon could see his knuckles whitening as his grip tightened.

'Mother!' cried Jon. He stepped forwards, but she stopped him with a lifted hand.

'It's OK, Peter,' she said. 'Everything's OK. You don't have to have tea.' She turned to Jon, her face calm, controlled. 'You should leave now, Jonathan.'

Jon didn't move.

'Jonathan,' she said again with more force. 'It's upsetting your father.'

Jon nodded. 'Yes . . . yes, of course. I'll leave.' At last Jon saw the tension lessen in his father's arms, and his mother's face relaxed as he heard her exhale. 'I'm leaving right away.' His father released his grip and then he stood and began to shuffle out of the kitchen.

'He's slept late this morning,' his mother said to the empty chair when her husband had gone. 'He always wakes in a tetchy mood.'

'He hurt you.'

'No. He would never hurt me.'

Jon didn't say anything.

She went to the cupboard that held the china teapot. This, too, they'd had since Jon was a child. Over the years it had been

31

broken and broken and broken again, but each time, rather than throw it away, his father would mend it. He'd carefully lay the pieces out in front of him on a double spread of the *Sunday Times*, and set about rebuilding it with superglue, his glasses perched on the tip of his nose, his face the picture of concentration, so that now its white bone was tinged brown by the multitude of hairline scars that crisscrossed it. Jon and Kate had given them a brand new teapot several years back, Wedgwood Polka Dot, gold banding, dishwasher safe. They'd paid quite a lot of money for it, but it sat unused at the back of the cupboard. His parents thought the old one made the perfect cup of tea.

'He'll be better for some tea,' she said, still facing the empty chair. 'Will you have a cup?'

He hesitated and glanced at the clock on the oven, then felt a sharp stab of guilt from his now broken promise to Kate. 'I should get home. Kate's meeting the headmaster to talk about Tuesday.'

Her mouth set hard and her eyebrows lifted a fraction.

He drew a deep breath, wondering why on earth she couldn't forgive his wife. It wasn't as if she'd done that much wrong, not really, not if you took everything into account, remembered what she'd been through. Kate didn't need his mother's ongoing disdain; she needed her compassion, her support. He nearly said as much, but instead he kept silent. This wasn't the right time for that discussion. He looked at the oven clock again and wondered if he'd make it home before the meeting with Stephen ended.

'Would you like me to stay?'

'That's kind, but no thank you. I'm fine now. I don't know what nonsense got into me.' She tried to smile, but didn't quite manage it.

'Well, you must call whenever you need,' he said. 'I am always here for you.'

From the look on her face it was hard to be sure if she believed him, or whether she merely saw his sentiments as empty platitude. He couldn't blame her if she did – after all, he'd done very little for her recently. He tried to remember if he'd called her in the last week. A malevolent voice in the back of his head began to point the finger at Anna's death, but he silenced it quickly. Anna was too easy an excuse, and it wasn't fair on her. It certainly wasn't her fault he'd been a neglectful son. It had been a year now. Once Tuesday was over he would try and put her death behind them. It was time to stand tall. He would make Wednesday the start of a brand new chapter.

The Him in Her Head

Lizzie went back into the living room to get her half-eaten, browning apple from the window sill and went upstairs. She thumped her feet heavily so her mum would hear her and know she was there if she needed her. She waited briefly at the top of the stairs in case she appeared, but there was no sight or sound of her so she went into her room and closed the door. She sat on her bed and took a bite of the apple and stared out of the window. Dr Howe was right about the cats and dogs. It had been raining day and night for most of the last two weeks. Certainly it had been non-stop yesterday and the day before and the day before that. The newspapers said it was the wettest June in fifty-six years. This made her laugh because every June was always the wettest June in whatever number of years. As far as she was concerned, it would only be news when June was thirty days of anhydrous sweltering heat. Lizzie didn't care, though; she loved the rain. Mostly because bees didn't; then again, she pretty much enjoyed anything that bees didn't – rain, November through February, high winds, bonfire smoke, snowflakes that stayed on her nose and eyelashes . . . all just a few of my favourite things. She smiled to herself and hummed the tune quietly as she watched the pelting rain.

Gradually, the rain began to change and the sheeting frantic drops became fattened little balloons that exploded on the window ledge like water bombs. She threw her apple core into the waste-paper bin and stood up, leaning against her white-painted desk, so tidy, just as she liked it, with a neat pile of lined paper and a jar of pens and pencils, rubbers and a ruler and a stack of books on the floor beside it. She was about to spend most of the next twelve months glued to this desk. It wouldn't be too much of a hardship. Her friends at school were moaning continually about the loom-ing threat of their exams. She kept quiet. She liked exams. She'd always found work comforting, especially since Anna – such wel-come respite from both the crying and desperate silences that rung about the house, not to mention her own brooding. She loved the whole exam nonsense, making neatly colour-coded revision time-tables, organizing her notes into labelled sections, ticking modules off when she'd revised them thoroughly. She had worked really hard for the school exams she'd just done. Now, all those colour-ful notes and immaculate lists of key dates and names and capital cities were all tidied away, stored beneath her bed ready to appear in September when she began preparing for her mocks and then her GCSEs.

She leant over her desk and pushed her forehead against the window. She noticed the drops of water on the glass, wiggling their way downward, some merging with static drops, some not, some sliding to a halt, others so beefed up by snowballing they suddenly catapulted off at tremendous speed. Why did the drops zigzag? she wondered then. Why did some of them run out of steam, while others hurtled? Surely they should behave predictably, rigidly scientific, obey some water-on-glass formula that governed them from unseen mathsy heights. Their behaviour appeared totally ran-dom and as she watched the drops, irrational and unpredictable, the hairs on the back of her neck began to prickle and her heart started racing. She slid the latch open and lifted the lower half of the window so her room was filled by the unseasonal weather and the papers on her desk quivered in surprise. She breathed in the beautiful smell of rain on warm pavements. She breathed in again, convinced she could also smell mowed grass on Brook Green.

Lizzie moved the paper and pens to the floor and then climbed on to the desk, one knee at a time, trying to ignore its wobble. Then she carefully swung each leg out of the window, gripped the frame with both hands, and lowered her head beneath the sash to ease the top half of her body outside. Her heart pumped. She didn't look down. If she did she might think of falling, and she couldn't think of falling. She tried to distract her mind, tried to concentrate on herself, her body, the feel of the cool rain on her warm skin, anything to keep away her dark thought of Anna. But the dark thought fought back, pushed itself out of the shadows in her head where it prowled day and night. She closed her eyes and winced. Now it was here it wouldn't go away. She would have to indulge it, but only for a moment: any longer and its ugliness would begin to crawl beneath her skin. She took a deep breath and readied herself. Then she closed her eyes.

Immediately, Anna was there. She was standing on the edge of the roof. Her arms were outstretched. Lizzie could feel her sister's blood fizzling, little bubbles of adrenalin rising and bursting inside her like champagne. Anna wanted to fly. She wanted more than this world could offer her. There were tears. They glittered like tiny diamonds embedded in her eyes. Lizzie wanted to call out to her, but like in a dream her voice was muted. Lizzie had to watch, helpless to stop her, as Anna leapt like a glorious angel, her hair billowing out behind her, ecstasy shining out of her like the beam of a lighthouse. And then Lizzie felt the familiar sickness. The sky behind Anna turned a deep, gunmetal grey. Her luminescence faded. Lizzie shook her head. It was time to shoo the thought away. If she stayed with this imagining of Anna taking her own life, of leaving without a goodbye or even a note, unable to talk to her own sister, she'd feel too sick to breathe.

Your sister didn't jump. She fell. It was an accident.

Lizzie made herself think of the rain again. She turned her face upwards. The drops were falling harder now, almost tropical.

Your sister didn't jump.

Then as quickly as the thought had shown itself, it was safely hidden away and she was suddenly aware of how soaked she was, of how wet her shirt and jeans were, how the fabrics clung to her. She felt the rain running down her cheek and into her mouth, fresh and cold, down her neck and chest. How glorious! Her arms became peppered with goose bumps and she shivered. Then she smiled. She could feel it again, the change in her, Lizzie-the-Adult pushing out of her shrivelling childish cocoon like a spectacular butterfly. It was exciting. Exhilarating. The promise of so much unknown.

She eased herself back into her room and wrapped her wet arms around her body. She shivered again, this time from the cold alone. She rubbed her hands against the tops of her arms to warm herself, gripped herself, dug her fingers into her skin. Then she closed her eyes and imagined the hands weren't hers. They were his. They belonged to him. Her him. A him with no name, no face even, but a him who wanted her, who yearned for her. A boy who loved her so much he would do anything for her: sail seven seas, slay dragons, even die for her.

She squeezed her eyes tighter and leant closer to him, opening her lips just a fraction in case he was about to kiss her, hoping and hoping and hoping he would.

The Colour Grey

In the next-door room Kate sat on the bed and stared out of the window. She stared past the trailing raindrops and over the rooftops to somewhere much further away. Visions of a previous incarnation of herself flashed through her mind, numbing her. Visions of her young self, happy, sublimely unaware of the unfathomable sadness she would one day feel. A free spirit who skipped in the streets and laughed until she cried, who walked the city pavements barefoot in the sunshine, pavements of the very same city that all the while watched, passive and silent, as her life within its walls crumbled to nothing.

When she first arrived in London, centuries ago it felt like, she imagined she'd crash-landed in heaven. Seventeen, wrinkle- and cynicism-free, excited by the opportunities this place could give her. She was determined to make the most of every single one. It was like stepping into Wonderland. A kaleidoscope of characters bustled along golden paving, busying about each other like insects, scuttling from one corner of the city to another. Kate would lie awake those first few nights with blood pumping through her heart like she'd run a hundred miles. Sirens flew past on a road outside her window that growled like a thousand bees twenty-four hours a day. Drunken voices laughed and fought. An orange glow from the street lamps sent unidentifiable shadows dancing across the ceiling hand in hand with smells of the next-door kebab shop, of rubbish bins and exhaust fumes. Kate felt alive then, woven into the fabric of this magnificent, filthy, wondrous city. That first year so many things happened to her, each one revealing a little more of a self she wasn't aware of. She lost her virginity. Passed out from alcohol. Smoked marijuana on the top deck of the number thirty-seven. The following year she pierced three holes in her left ear, a few weeks later her nose. She marched against the poll tax and skinny-dipped in the Serpentine. These were the moments of Kate's youth. She unfolded like a rose, nourished by the smoggy vigour of London Town.

But staring across the rain-drenched buildings of Brook Green and Hammersmith, with Chiswick, Hounslow and Heathrow somewhere beyond, she could see nothing of the wondrousness that once held her so captivated. Kate's tear-blurry eyes searched for the honeyed colours, but all that was left were shades of grey. Losing a child will do that, you see. Losing a child turns everything grey, settles over life like a dirty shroud, sucking the joy out as it smothers every last thing.

Kate lay back on the bed and turned on her side, tucking her hands beneath her cheek, pulling her knees into her chest. She wished she'd been able to tell Stephen to cancel the memorial. But it just wasn't that easy in the end. He'd been to so much trouble, put so much time and thought into remembering Anna, and Kate knew how important it was to remember her. Remembering Anna bled her days dry, left little of herself for anything else, desperate as she was to keep Anna alive in her head. It wasn't always easy, and sometimes, when her memories were hazy, harder to come by, a panic consumed her, so violent she often passed out, only to wake moments later, weak and nauseous on the floor.

A knock on the door dragged her from her thoughts. She lifted her head from her hands and saw Lizzie.

'Hi, Mum,' her daughter said. 'Can I get you anything from the kitchen?'

'No, I'm fine.'

Kate laid her head back on the pillow to avoid the despondency in her daughter's eyes. She wondered what harm could have come from thanking her and asking for a drink of water or a ham sandwich. Lizzie was such a good girl. So soft and gentle. So caring. Kate knew she wasn't being fair. She found it too easy to withdraw herself from Lizzie, so much easier than engaging and risking seeing Anna in her sister's mannerisms, of hearing her echoed in Lizzie's voice, of glimpsing Lizzie out of the corner of her eye, having her mind trick her into believing she was Anna, alive, then the crushing realization when she looked again and saw it wasn't Anna, but only Lizzie. At times like this she had no choice but to walk away from her youngest child, for fear the sweet thing might see her disappointment.

'Thank you, though,' she managed.

Lizzie didn't move from the door. 'Can I lie down with you?'

Kate's stomach pitched and a lump grew in her throat. She nodded and lifted her arm. Lizzie lay on the bed and pushed herself into her mother, her back to Kate's front. Kate lowered her arm and held Lizzie to her, then she moved her head until her lips rested lightly against her daughter's head. Her hair was wet and cold.

'You've not been out in this rain, have you?' she asked.

Lizzie shook her head. 'No, I just had a quick shower.'

'Good,' Kate said, closing her eyes, and breathing Lizzie in. 'I don't want you catching pneumonia.'

'I know, Mum.'

The Stranger's Second Photograph

There were six people in the photograph: a man, the man's parents, his wife and their two daughters. They were on a rocky outcrop. In the Lake District. The sky behind them was navy blue with splashes of wispy cloud. Jon could hear the screech of the red kite that circled above them, unseen in the photo, but there nonetheless, searching beneath it for prey. The six people all looked happy. He could hear them laughing. He remembered putting his arms around each of the girls. Hugging them to him. Telling them to smile as the stranger pointed the camera hopefully at them. The stranger pressed the button. Then the stranger told them he would take another one *just to be on the safe side*. He heard his father thank the stranger and the stranger waved and rejoined his wife. They walked on while his family rearranged themselves, tied laces, unscrewed a bottle of water and passed it between them. Kate's jacket was around her waist. She wore trainers. His parents wore walking boots, of course, with thick khaki socks turned over their tops – mighty hiking warriors, Kate had whispered with a giggle when they'd appeared in the reception area of the bed and breakfast.

His father carried the rucksack and map, and his special walking stick, the extendable one that looked like a ski pole, which Jon and Kate had given him for Christmas. Jon remembered how happy his father had been with it. He walked around the garden in Chiswick in the wet snow that didn't stick, thrusting the pole in front of him, unaware he was being watched and affectionately mocked by the rest of them through the kitchen window.

Jon stared at the photo. Those smiling faces. Blissful in their ignorance of what lay in wait. He stroked the tip of his finger over the face of his dead daughter. Then his father, strong and dignified, so different from the frail man being consumed day by day by an illness that fed on that very strength and dignity. Jon looked at his mother. The comb in her hair – like the kite, out of sight but there. Her face was kissed brown by the sunshine they'd enjoyed that week. Seven days of dusty August heat. Jon remembered Kate asking his mother to hold her watch while she put sun cream on her arms and face. He saw her hands rubbing. He remembered feeling desire for her, remembered leaning close to her and telling her so, remembered her lifting her eyebrows and mouthing a promise of herself. His wife. Kate. Destroyed. And, lastly, he looked at Lizzie. His precious girl. Tossed into a world of misery and silence, all the happiness drained out of it, the people around her struggling to cope, her needs so poorly met. She deserved more.

He shut the album. Then straightened his tie and took a deep, full breath.

'It's time we left!' he called up the stairs.

He went into the kitchen and grabbed the car keys from the bowl. When he went back into the hall, Lizzie was at the bottom of the stairs.

'You OK?' he asked.

She nodded and smiled. 'You?'

He didn't attempt a reply, worried in case he found himself unable to speak. Instead he reached for her hand.

'Lizzie and I will wait in the car!' he called again. 'Is she ready?' he asked his daughter.

Lizzie shrugged. 'Your bedroom door was closed. I didn't want to disturb her.'

He handed her the keys. 'Go and get yourself strapped in. We'll be out in a sec.'

Kate was sitting on the end of their bed. When he got near her she looked up. She seemed terrified, her pale fragility accentuating her striking beauty, and as always he was surprised how she took his breath.

'Hey,' he said. 'I think we should leave, don't you?'

'Sorry,' she said. 'I'm not quite ready.'

'Don't worry; we've time yet.'

'This is awful, isn't it?'

Jon nodded.

Kate's red and puffy eyes pooled with fresh tears. She lifted a raggedy scrap of tissue and dabbed at them. 'I must look a real mess.'

'You look fine.'

She breathed deeply and sniffed. 'I'm not sure I can do this,' she whispered.

'You'll be fine. It's just a school service and it's only an hour. It's for the kids, her friends. It's a nice thing for the school to do.'

Kate shook her head and uncurled her fingers from his. Her eyes were fixed on the carpet. 'I can't go back there. I can't. I . . .' She shook her head, unable to finish her sentence.

He knelt at her feet and stroked her hand. 'You don't have to come, you know,' he said softly.

Then she shot him a look, suddenly accusatory, incredulous. 'I'm her *mother*,' she said, enunciating each word with deliberate restraint. 'Of course I have to come.'

He stood and nodded once. 'Lizzie and I will be in the car,' he said. 'Take whatever time you need.'

Chalk and Cheese

Lizzie found it hard to look at anything else but her music teacher, who was flinging herself around to the disharmonies of the school band like some drugged-up druid casting demons out of village folk. Anna wouldn't have approved. She hated Mrs Goldman. Most of them did. She was one of those teachers who was all at once ridiculous, humourless and ferociously hormonal, and double music was universally torturous.

Lizzie forced a glance at her mum. Her heart sank. She looked tranquillised, her eyes glazed and distant, no doubt desperate to protect herself from this day, the whining music, the dreary hall, the acrid smell of chip fat and pizza wafting in from the kitchens making the stuffy air almost unbreathable. Lizzie crossed both sets of fingers and prayed for the hundredth time that her mum kept a hold of herself. The possibility of repeating Anna's funeral turned her blood to ice. Though she'd mostly managed to block that day out of her head, there were always the occasional flashbacks that turned her stomach inside out. No, better her mum stayed safely tucked away wherever she was, somewhere mundane, with the week's shopping list, perhaps, or maybe beside the sea in a long-ago memory.

She looked away from her mum, drawn back against her will to Mrs Goldman who was mid-flourish, dragging the hotchpotch ensemble, squeaking and crashing, to their final note. The woman held quivering hands aloft and teased the discord to nothing more than an awkward silence during which the audience wondered whether they were supposed to clap. In unison they decided against it, and instead there was a rustling of paper as photocopied service sheets were consulted blindly.

Anna's memorial. An hour to think about Anna. It was laughable. Lizzie didn't think there'd been a single hour in the whole of the last year when she *hadn't* thought about Anna. An hour of oblivion might be more satisfying. Yes, how lovely, she thought, Anna's existence, past and present, obliterated by sixty minutes of blissful amnesia.

Her sister's face beamed out of a huge screen that hung at the back of the stage, the hum of the overhead projector underwriting her beauty. Lizzie marvelled for the umpteenth time how different they were. Beautiful, glamorous Anna, with her rosy cheeks and thick chestnut hair that shone like a varnished conker, her womanly curves and blinding self-confidence. On top of all that, she was popular and cool, the girl to know, whilst scrawny, freckled Lizzie, with blonde hair that stood in a permanent static halo around her head, was studious, flat-chested and forever referred to as 'Anna Thorne's little sister'. As far as she was concerned she was Anna's echo, arriving a little later, a little fainter. There were eighteen months between them but nobody would have been surprised if it had been double that. *How unusual*, people always said, *for sisters to look so different! Are you sure you're actually sisters?* Lizzie had never been a hundred per cent.

'We can't be, Mum, I mean . . . look at us!'

But her mum assured her they were.

Lizzie loved Anna deeply, idolized her. Anna was the funniest, most charismatic person Lizzie had ever met, and though it could sometimes be a bit chilly in Anna's shadow, Lizzie wouldn't have had it any other way.

Lizzie came back to earth with a jolt and realized that Dr Howe had started speaking. She focused on what he was saying, but quickly wished she hadn't bothered. His words made her feel somehow uneasy, melodramatically perched as they were on the edge of emotion. He called Anna an angel in Heaven, the epitome of everything one could wish for in a young woman, so much potential extinguished like a candle; the world was a desperate place for losing her. He knew she'd stay alive in the hearts and minds of all of those present. He knew she'd be in his. Lizzie couldn't believe he could even think up such pompous words, and what on earth gave him the right to speak about Anna like that?

She tuned his voice out, and as she did her thoughts settled on the night Anna died. It was still so vivid; she could recall every creak of the floorboards, the smells around her; she even imagined she could remember the sound of tiny insects scuttling in the boards beneath her carpet, the bed bugs in her mattress, the spider spinning a web in the corner of her room. She also remembered how hot the night was, the type of hot that makes sleep sweaty and fitful so that when the phone rang at two in the morning she might well have been awake already. Then the harrowing wail from her mum that she still heard in her frequent nightmares. A door banging. Her mum screaming. Her parents' feet thumping down the stairs. Her stomach fizzing with dread as she went out to the landing blinking in the harsh electric light. When she called to them from the banister they looked up at her as if she were an unexpected stranger, their faces drained of colour, both shaking like skeleton leaves in a storm.

'There's been an acci—' Lizzie's father's voice dried up before he could finish.

'What accident?' Lizzie asked.

Then her mum collapsed and a noise came out of her like she'd been speared, and that was pretty much the moment that Lizzie knew her big sister was gone.

Remembering Anna

It was worse than Kate imagined it could be. She felt faint and resentful, claustrophobic in this manufactured ceremony of grief and celebration. Stephen's voice sent surge after surge of nausea billowing up inside her. The sickly sweet tone of his voice, the politician's hand gestures, the pumped-up gravitas. She wished she could stop him talking. She wished that dreadful woman would start up the awful band again, anything to stop his voice.

Kate looked around the hall and the sickness thickened; a memorial peopled with children. It was so wrong. It didn't matter what you believed in – nature, science, God – the death of a child was against the rules. Death was for old people. The young should be left outside in the parks and playgrounds, laughing and running, all full up with being alive. She noticed how many were crying. Young girls huddled in twos and threes. Boys in groups or alone. Teenagers, each the centre of his or her world, utterly convinced of themselves, utterly convinced that nobody else felt the agony of grief like they did – until lunchtime, of course, when Anna would be all forgotten and they'd be giggling across plates of over-salted chips, playing football, beating each other up, bitching, lusting, teasing. She didn't blame them for that. They were no more than babies, babies with longer hair, scruffier clothes and self-absorbed, petulant, hormone-fuelled bodies. Babies like Anna. Babies who still needed protecting and shepherding, given help to negotiate the dangers in life. Protected against their own poor, sometimes fatal, errors in judgement. Kate squeezed her eyes shut and winced against the pain. What kind of mother was she to let her baby play on a roof? To let her get drunk. To let her die. How does a mother let her baby die?

Kate opened her eyes and for the hundredth time caught Anna's picture full-on. She flinched. Why hadn't he told her about the photograph? Was it supposed to be a surprise? Did he think it would make her happy? A six-foot image of Anna as she was. Every time she looked at it her heart stopped. How could she be dead? There she was, aged fourteen, not more than a year before she fell, her face shining, the deep brown of her eyes like polished stones, her smile almost a laugh.

Kate would have given her life to hear Anna's laugh just one more time. She closed her eyes and tried to conjure it. Almost immediately a rush of dread filled her as she realized she couldn't hear it. All she could hear was Lizzie's laugh. So similar, yet worlds apart. It was the inflection. The heaviness. Lizzie's laugh was a shade or two lighter; Anna's came from somewhere deeper. She concentrated. A couple of times she nearly had it, but then it was yanked out of reach by invisible rope. It was like chasing a carrier bag in the wind.

Kate's hands began to sweat. She tapped her toe on the wooden floor trying to ward off the sweeps of panic that came like contractions. Her vision faltered. She leant closer to Jon.

'I can't remember her laugh,' she whispered. She tried to keep her voice level.

'Of course you can,' Jon murmured.

Kate shook her head, trying not to cry. 'I can't. It's not there.'

'Try at home when it's quiet.'

'No,' Kate whispered back. 'It's gone.'

Jon reached for her hand and patted it twice. The double pat meant *be quiet*. Kate pulled away from him. *I'm losing her, I'm losing her, I'm losing her* was all she could hear in her head.

And then there was a fuss from the back of the hall.

At first Kate couldn't hear the words, shrouded as they were by the rumbling voices of people around as they craned to see. She moved left and right trying to see through the heads.

'Get your hands off me,' a girl's voice said. Then louder, 'No, I won't be quiet!' Then she started shouting. 'Get off me! This is bullshit! How can you listen to it? It's a fucking joke!'

In glimpses Kate saw Rebecca. Her lips were snarled into a grimace and angry tears poured down her cheeks. She saw two girls trying to calm her, a worried teacher useless beside them, a group of boys smirking. Everyone else was shocked, staring. There was the scrape of a chair to the side. Kate looked. It was Angela Howe. She was marching to the back of the hall, her heels on the polished parquet, clip, clip, clip.

'Who on earth is that?' muttered Stephen loudly, still on the stage beneath the picture of Anna. He looked to the back of the hall. His eyebrows lifted. His hand pointed, then gesticulated, his irritation thinly masked by his effort to stay in control.

Kate turned again to the back of the hall and saw Angela bustling out of the double doors pushing Rebecca in front of her. Then the doors closed. The excited murmuring in the hall continued. Kate strained to hear the muffled shouting as their footsteps hurried away.

Rebecca knew something.

Kate had known it since that night, as soon as she and Rachel had arrived on the scene. They had come as soon as Jon called, Rachel flustering around the place, shaking her head and making excuses, pleading ignorance, trying to make sense of her part in the tragedy. In some sort of hellish trance Kate had stared at the muted Rebecca, whose face was lit in blue flashes as the light of the ambulance twirled in its eerie dance. There was a look on her face, a muddle of guilt and fear and knowing, that, as a mother, she recognized immediately; it was the look that tells tales on children. Kate had gone to her side, taken hold of her limp hand, and struggled to ask her what happened, but Rebecca wouldn't meet her eyes. She insisted she knew nothing. Over and over again she shook her head. But she was Anna's best friend; she knew something. Kate was certain.

Kate started to follow, but Jon grabbed her wrist.

'Stay here,' he hissed.

She pulled herself free.

'Kate!'

She hurried away from him, to the back of the hall, out onto the corridor, past tatty displays of artwork, deserted classrooms, school bags that spat their contents across the floor. She heard their voices. Angela's high-pitched and furious. Rebecca's through tears.

Kate started to run.

She found them in Stephen's office. Rebecca was sitting on a chair. Her fingers pulled at each other and tears fell like drops of black paint on to her grey school skirt. Angela was picking up the phone. When she saw Kate, she replaced the receiver.

'I can only apologize for her,' she said. Her voice was at once a canny blend of blame directed at Rebecca and theatrical sympathy towards Kate. 'Please, go back to the hall, Mrs Thorne. I will deal with her. You don't need to be here.'

Though Kate got on well with Stephen, she and Angela Howe, who was brusque, direct and rarely smiled, were on different pages, and since Anna died they'd scarcely spoken. She often walked away from Kate and Jon rather than talking, though this wasn't an unusual reaction. Many of Kate's friends, and most of her acquaintances, found it hard to meet her eye or strike up conversation. Some people just found death impossible to deal with.

Angela was the deputy head. And a good one at that. She was a formidable character, straightforward and driven, who suffered fools neither gladly nor otherwise, respected at arm's length by parents and pupils alike. With her practical haircut, tweed skirts and comfortable brogues, her sexuality had been discussed in hushed voices by scores of parents. It had come as quite a surprise when the position of head teacher became available and the man who took the job – that most assumed would go to her – turned out to be the woman's husband. She even had an eleven-year-old son who then joined the school. Nobody thought this would be good for the school – working with your spouse never worked; the interests of the children would be compromised; they would be forced to look elsewhere for schooling. But the Howes proved them all wrong. Together they were an educational powerhouse, and suddenly the doubting parents couldn't believe their luck. Within two years of his appointment, Park Secondary became one of the most oversubscribed in west London.

'I have no idea what's got into the child,' Angela continued. 'The emotion of the day, I'm sure. The girls were close, of course, but the behaviour,' she glared at Rebecca, 'is unacceptable.'

Rebecca glanced up at Kate, caught her eye then quickly dropped her head, pulling at her fingers more frantically.

'Tell me,' Kate said. She dropped to her knees at Rebecca's feet. 'Please, Rebecca.' Kate's voice cracked in desperation.

'Please go back to the hall, Mrs Thorne. This is a matter for me to deal with.'

Kate leant closer to Rebecca. 'Rebecca?'

Again Rebecca looked up at Kate, this time holding her gaze for a few moments. She seemed so close to speaking but then, with a quick nervous glance at Angela, she lowered her eyes. Kate felt an irritated stab of frustration and her fingers clenched, digging into Rebecca's knee. The girl flinched. Kate was suddenly filled with an overwhelming urge to scream at her, demand she tell her what the bloody hell it was that she knew. She'd never liked Rebecca that much, not really. She certainly never understood why Anna was so fond of her. Familiarity, she knew, had much to do with it; they'd been friends since they were babies, when Rachel and Kate saved each other from a hair-wrenchingly dull NCT group. But as the girls grew, Rebecca turned out to be quiet and withdrawn; she didn't play sport or like drama, she wasn't bright or funny or even that pretty, and there was a permanent glumness about her. Her father leaving didn't help – she seemed to retreat even further into herself, sometimes unable even to say hello. But, like it or not, the two girls were inseparable, until that fateful night, of course, when Rebecca stayed safe in her bed and Anna didn't.

Angela began to dial. 'I'm calling her mother, Mrs Thorne. Go back to your daughter's service. You should be there. This young lady has much to answer for.' Angela lasered Rebecca with a terrifying glare. 'She will be dealt with appropriately.'

She held the phone to her ear, glowering, never once lifting her eyes off Rebecca, but when she said a terse hello to someone Kate assumed to be Rachel, Rebecca jumped up, shoving her chair so hard it fell backwards as she ran for the door.

'Don't you go anywhere!' bellowed Angela Howe, moving after her as far as the phone cord would allow. 'Come back here this minute!'

Kate didn't hesitate. She ran after Rebecca.

'Mrs Thorne!'

Kate had to get to her. If Rebecca knew something about Anna's death Kate was going to find out what it was, right there and then. 'Rebecca!' she called. 'Stop. Please!'

But Rebecca kept running.

She hurtled through the maze of corridors, with Kate desperate and gasping behind her, trying not to slip over as she threw herself around corners, ricocheting off walls, pulling work off display boards as she tried to keep up. Kate kept shouting at her to stop but Rebecca ran on. They banged through two sets of double doors. The air in Kate's unfit lungs was burning. Up ahead she saw Rebecca disappear through a door, and outside.

Kate shouted again.

'Rebecca, stop! I just want to talk!'

Kate followed her outside. It took a few moments for her eyes to grow accustomed to the brightness. When they did, however, and she realized where she was, she stopped dead in her tracks and a chill fell over her. She stared around her in horror, panting heavily, dizzy, her head swirling both with the effort of running and spikes of hideous recollection. There was a spindly apple sapling in a large plastic pot with an extravagant white bow tied around it like some sick present. The sight of it snatched her breath. Why had he put it in there? Surely not to mark the exact spot of vile concrete that had taken Anna from her? Kate struggled to breathe. Bile rose in her throat. This was hell itself.

From a distance away there was a despairing shriek that broke the silence in the deserted playground. Kate heaved her head, a leaden weight, in the direction of the noise. Rebecca was wailing and beating feeble hands against a wrought-iron gate in the boundary wall. Kate made herself breathe in and out. She listened to the sound of it, concentrated on her lungs filling and emptying, her heart rate calming. Then she took a step, then another, one foot in front of the other, slowly advancing on Rebecca, walking on autopilot. She didn't care now if she reached her or not. If Rebecca ran again, or made it through that padlocked gate, Kate wouldn't follow; she was ready to give up, ready to fall to the ground, defeated.

But Rebecca didn't run. She, too, it seemed, had lost her fight, collapsed as she was against the gate, wheezing and crying with exhaustion. She turned slowly to face Kate, who put her hands gently on the girl's shoulders, panting heavily, her lungs burning. Then, as Kate stood just inches away from her daughter's closest friend, mere feet from the exact spot where her daughter had died, she began to be bombarded with horrific images of Anna that she'd spent a year trying to wipe from her mind. Kate closed her eyes tightly and violently shook her head, desperate to block them out. Anna's twisted body. Rigid on the ground. The pool of blood that circled her head like a devil's halo, shining black in the moon-light. Her creamy skin spattered with grit. Dead eyes staring at the stars. Her blue-tinged mouth open as if calling for her mother.

'Not here,' Kate rasped.

Kate tried to drag her away from the shadow of the gymnasium, back towards the main school building. Rebecca started to pull and wriggle, digging her feet into the playground, yanking her arm back again and again. But Kate held on, desperate to get away from the recollections of Anna. When at last they began to fade enough for Kate to think, she turned Rebecca to face her, held the girl's hands in hers, and bent so she was level with her face.

'Now,' she said, flat and quiet. 'Tell me.'

Rebecca lifted her eyes and for a moment or two they held each other's stare, but then her face set hard, eyes narrowing, mouth clamped shut, surly, uncooperative.

Make me, she said silently to Kate. *You just try and make me.*

And then every emotion Kate had, everything that occupied her, the anger and frustration, the guilt, pain, hurt, the bastard unfairness of it all, swelled up inside like boiling milk. *Why wasn't it you instead of her? Why did she have to die and you get to live?* Kate would have sold her soul for sixpence to have the tragedy the other way round. Was it wrong of her to feel that?

'Tell me!' she screamed. 'For Christ's sake, speak!'

But Rebecca gave her nothing. Kate started to shake her, as those returning images of her dead daughter bit into her with every push and pull. Rebecca's head flopped back and forth like a rag doll's. There was no resistance from her, just blankness, acceptance and a glaze that covered her eyes like a scab with whatever she knew buried beneath.

'Why won't you fucking tell me?' Kate screamed. 'You stupid little girl! I know you know something!'

Kate kept screaming at her, on and on, and the more she screamed and the longer Rebecca stayed quiet, the angrier Kate became until everything blurred and all she could see was the six-foot photograph of Anna that hung over the stage, but instead of her glowing skin and breathing beauty, the face she saw was bloodied and deformed, flattened so there was no definition, a nose so badly broken it didn't protrude from her face, her teeth smashed, her skin saturated beneath the surface with blood, all swollen and bloated like a purple balloon.

Kate lost all control of herself then. She lifted her hands and began pounding them into Rebecca. Again and again she beat her fists against her, hitting out at all the pain she felt, begging Anna to be alive. Kate's hands flailed, smacking into Rebecca in a clouded frenzy, her sobbing mingling with Rebecca's and Stephen's speech on angels, and Angela Howe shouting from somewhere behind her, and then Jon, close to her, begging her to stop.

Blame and Reflection

'Please, God, Kate! Stop it!' He pushed himself between them, putting a hand on Kate's shoulder to distance her from Rebecca. 'Kate! Stop! Stop.'

Eventually Kate's exhausted hands stopped hitting and fell to her sides as if she'd run out of batteries.

'Kate?' he breathed.

He saw her eyes focus on him and as they did, the realization of what had happened, of what she'd done, slowly grew. With his hand on his wife's shoulder, Jon turned to Rebecca, who was hunched and shivering on the floor like a terrified animal. Her arms covered her face, a split lip just visible beneath the crook of an elbow. He reached out to touch her. She recoiled, and as she did the enormity of what had happened fell on him like a dead weight.

He looked then at Angela Howe, who was doing her best to control the gathering crowd. He frantically scanned the faces until he found Lizzie, her bewilderment and terror a reflection of his own. He was torn between going to her and staying with Kate and Rebecca, but when Rebecca made a soft whimpering sound, he dropped to his knees and gathered her in his arms, held her head to his chest, stroked her hair, told her over and over that she was safe. He ventured a glance at Kate, scared in case she caught his eye and saw his shock. But she wasn't looking at him; her terrified eyes were bolted to Rebecca.

For a split moment it was deathly quiet around them, but then the place erupted. There was a rumble of muttering, the odd scream, people were crying. Angela Howe shouted for some-one to call an ambulance. Voices started saying *police*. He heard Lizzie then, calling out for Kate, saying no, no, no, repeatedly. Jon searched the crowd again, but she'd gone. He called her name, then tried to stand, desperate to find her, but Rebecca clutched at his jacket.

'Don't leave me,' she sobbed softly.

He turned back to Kate. 'Lizzie?' he shouted over the noise. 'Where's Lizzie? Can you see her?'

Kate didn't move; she didn't even register she'd heard his voice.

'Lizzie!' Jon called. 'Lizzie!'

Then Stephen was at his side. He crouched next to him. Leant close to his ear. 'The police are on their way. You should go with Kate. They have to talk to her.'

'Rebecca doesn't want me to leave her,' he said.

'I think you'll have to, Jon,' Stephen said. 'Someone needs to be with Kate.'

Jon looked down at Rebecca, who stared back at him. 'I'm going to leave you with Dr Howe,' he said, as gently as he could.

Rebecca didn't let go of him.

Dr Howe held out a hand towards her. 'Come on, Rebecca. Mr Thorne has to go. You'll be OK. It's only for a few minutes; your mother is on her way.'

Rebecca recoiled from Stephen, tucking herself tighter into Jon's shoulder. 'No, I want him to stay.'

Jon looked at Kate and her eyes met his. 'I'm sorry,' she mouthed. 'I'm so sorry.'

He turned back to Stephen. 'I'll stay with Rebecca. She knows me.'

Stephen nodded. 'Then I'll accompany Kate.'

Jon's stomach clenched as he watched Kate walk away from him, the quietened crowd parting like the Red Sea to let her and Stephen Howe through.

He closed his eyes. There was a dreadful throbbing in his head. A sickening sense of foreboding filled him, as if he might never see her again. How on earth had he let this happen? Kate had done something awful and he couldn't bear to even consider the repercussions, not just from the legal point of view, but on their family, on Lizzie.

He stroked Rebecca's hair, holding on to her tightly, trying to absorb her shivering, wondering what he could do to make this go away.

Christ, he thought, *you idiot. What were you thinking? You saw it in her eyes. You knew she wasn't up to it. You did nothing.*

She'd even told him, straight out, said she wouldn't manage it. He should have been stronger. He should have insisted she stay behind. He should never have exposed her like that. He knew how she felt about the school, how it made her feel. She hadn't been back since the night Anna died. Not a parents' evening, or a Christmas concert, or even to meet Lizzie after school, like she used to occasionally, when they'd walk home via Costa for three caffè lattes and two-between-three chocolate brownies. How could he have been so stupid?

Once again all Kate could hear was her own breathing, rasping in painfully deafening spasms against a silent background. What had she done? What the hell had she done?

As she walked back along the school corridors, she went over every excruciating detail, desperate to pinpoint the exact moment she had lost it. Was it when she lifted her hand to Rebecca? When she followed her out of the school hall? With Anna's lost laugh? Maybe it was as early as sitting on her bed, trying to muster the strength to leave her room. She should have stayed at home. She'd known full well she wouldn't cope. She should have locked herself away until Tuesday was over. She was stupid. Stupid for trusting herself.

Stephen opened the door to his office and stepped to one side to allow her through. She wondered if he might say something, but he stayed quiet, his eyes on his feet. How unlike him. He was usually the definition of cool. Like the night Anna died, when he'd stepped into the breach, taken control, calm and collected. She often wondered what she and Jon would have done if he hadn't been there to help. He'd been such a pillar of strength and support. It was Stephen who had broken the news to them. He'd called from this very office. She looked around the room, at the bank of cheap metal shelving that held red, blue and black lever arch files. His desk, tidy and neat, in-tray, out-tray and pending, one of those executive toys with the suspended chrome balls that knocked against each other, pointless and perpetual. Then the phone, grey and cold, placed perfectly in the top right corner like a postage stamp. She pulled her eyes away from it, trying not to recall the words he'd used that night, unable to hear anything else.

'Mrs Thorne, it's Stephen Howe. I'm at the school. There's been an accident. A terrible accident,' pause, 'it's Anna.' Long pause. 'I'm sorry.' A final pause. 'I was too late here. She was already dead. There . . . there was nothing I could do.'

After that it was blank. No matter how hard she raked through the wreckage in her memory, there was nothing between those words and the moment she laid eyes on Anna on the concrete. She must have gone back upstairs after seeing Lizzie peering down from the landing, got out of her pyjamas, dressed, brushed her hair, thought to go to Anna's room to grab a cardigan in case Stephen was wrong and she was alive, and, fashionably underdressed as always, was now feeling the chill. They'd have got in the car, driven to school. Parked. Walked through the school. Been led to their dead daughter's body. There was no recollection of any of it; it was all blank.

She couldn't have done without Stephen that night. His familiar eyes were a lifeline in amongst all those of the silent, cautious paramedics and police, who looked at her with knowing, sympathetic glances. But Stephen's soft words, his hand on her lower back, his calm control. He'd been such a support, and not just that night, but following on, with Lizzie too. Hand-delivering the work she missed at school, checking up on her most days to see if she was coping OK, arranging for the counsellor to talk her through her grief. To see him staring at his feet, pale and twitching, unable to meet her eye, was agonizing. What she'd done to Rebecca, her inexcusable loss of control, was clearly a step beyond him, and calling the police to deal with her had apparently floored him.

Stephen cleared his throat when the two policemen finally arrived to break the dreadful silence.

'Dr Howe?' the older one asked. He didn't look at Kate.

Kate squeezed her eyes shut. She wouldn't cry. She couldn't. She wasn't the victim here and she deserved whatever was coming.

Musical Interlude: Number One

She watched the scene from the front of the group of people. They'd all run out of the hall when they heard her mum screaming in the playground then got stuck with shock at what they saw.

Lizzie was numb. She couldn't feel a thing. All she could do was stare at them both, her mother shaking uncontrollably, standing over a terrified Rebecca.

Noise grew louder around her, and as it did she felt herself smack into life. She started to shake too. She felt faint. Lost. She wanted her mum. She wanted to run to her, have her hold her and tell her it was OK and that she hadn't meant to hurt Rebecca. She began to cry and call out for her. She'd never seen anything so awful as her mum hitting Rebecca; the anger etched into Kate's face had terrified her.

Lizzie stepped backwards through the crowd, being jostled left and right as they all tried to get a better view. When she reached the back and found herself free from everyone else, she turned and blindly looked for a place to escape to. But where? She felt faint, sick even, and for a horrible moment she thought she might actually throw up. She leant forward, resting her hands on her knees, trying to breathe deeply, hoping her head would stop spinning enough for her to walk away.

Then Lizzie felt someone touch her.

In a daze she looked up to see who it was. Her vision was blurry and she had to squint to focus. The figure slowly began to make sense; it was Haydn. She was surprised to see him. She hadn't imagined he would come back for the service. Silly really; of course he'd be there.

Haydn didn't say anything. He just took her arm and guided her away from the people towards the picnic tables. He sat her down on a bench. She started to speak, but he shushed her with a finger on her lips. He smelt of cigarettes and his skin was rough as if he were made of sandpaper. She watched him reach into his pocket, moving deliberately, silently, as if in slow motion or under water. Then in his hand were headphones, small delicate wires of white, and without a sound he put an earpiece into each of her ears, all the while holding her gaze until he brushed his hand down over her eyelids, closing her eyes and blocking himself and the world around them out.

The music filled her head, muting the shocked gasps, the screaming and crying, flowing into her body like water to a dying man in the desert, the first notes of a tune she didn't recognize running along her veins to the tips of her fingers and toes, pulsing with her heartbeat, filling her head with colours. A man began to sing. His voice was soft and low, a mournful magic carpet that carried her away from the chaos around her, dissolving her broken mum and the quivering Rebecca into nothing but pinpricks far below.

Haydn's hand slipped something into her own, and then he squeezed her fingers closed around it. He held her hand for the briefest of moments and there it was again, the sandpaper skin, but this time it was safe and strong and knowing, as if it were the most familiar skin in her world.

She opened her eyes to see what it was he'd given her. An iPod. She looked at him. The music still played. It had wiped everything else out of her head – there was only him and her, like cardboard cut-outs, cut from the real world and stuck to a sheet of brilliant white paper. Just them and nothing else. Then he stood and smiled at her.

It was a simple, uncomplicated smile that needed no explanation or translation and required no reply. It was the sweetest smile she'd ever seen, and at that very moment something amazing happened. Something she could never have predicted. For as long as she could remember, the him in her head had been a faceless shadow, an indistinct silhouette without a name. She'd danced with and kissed and loved this mysterious stranger a countless number of times, waltzing around those spaces in her mind she'd so carefully furnished with candles and flowers and happiness. Never once in those hundreds of times did she ever imagine that beneath her lover's featureless mask was Haydn. Yet there he was, the him in her head smiling at her, suddenly, fantastically, with both a name and a face.

A Ghastly Accent

Jon stared out through the windscreen. He gripped the steering wheel, knuckles white as a corpse. Behind him Rachel unclipped her seatbelt. He didn't turn to face her; he couldn't stomach the thought of laying eyes on Rebecca, who was sitting beside her on the back seat. All he had were hows and whys. How and why repeated over and over.

It was grief. Grief was how and grief was why. Her grief and his. He'd let his out and it had got in the way, clouded his judgement, loosened his grip on her, allowed her to run after Rebecca. But he still couldn't work out why he hadn't followed her. Why it had taken so long for him to check she was OK. Why it was only when they heard that dreadful shrieking from the playground that he'd thought to find her. He'd just stood there, gawping through tear-blinded eyes at that blasted picture of Anna. He couldn't look anywhere else. From the moment he walked into the hall it was all he could see. Her smiling at him. Maybe if they hadn't put that picture on the stage he might have stopped Kate following Rebecca. But the picture pushed his grief out like volcanic lava. He'd worked so hard to keep it locked away, ever conscious that Kate and Lizzie didn't need his misery. They had more than enough of their own, and his was surplus to requirement. The only thing he could do was box and bury it. But that picture, which in an instant tore him open, exhumed that miserable box of sadness and missing, and now his wife was at the police station and the child she'd beaten was sitting dumbstruck in his car.

He cleared his throat, wishing there was something obvious to say. A way to apologize. But words were insubstantial, inappropriate.

Rachel opened the car door and moved to get out, but then she stopped, and sat back in the seat.

'What on earth possessed her?' she asked.

Jon turned then. He readied himself for the sight of Rebecca and then made himself look at her, still quivering, white with shock, her lip swollen. She clutched her arms around her middle. She was unable to look at him, avoiding his eyes as if he were the Devil, her eyes fixed, unseeing, on something outside the car window. Their moment of closeness, when she'd clung to him with every ounce of strength she had left, had gone.

He looked back at Rachel and considered her question.

'The day,' he said at last.

And yesterday, he thought, and the day before that and the day before that.

He thought of Kate. He saw her standing above Rebecca, her face clouded with alarm, her hand raised to her mouth, tears collected in her eyes. She had fixed her eyes to his, begged him to help her.

I'm sorry, she'd mouthed, *I'm so sorry*.

Jon's heart ached for her and he knew that he had let her down. Kate was the last person to hurt a child. She'd never raised a hand to their girls, and both of them, Anna especially, had certainly deserved it on occasion. His mother never understood why they didn't get a sharp smack every now and then.

'It never did you or Daniel any harm,' she'd mutter, disapprovingly, as Kate disappeared to reason with whatever tantrum blazed. But that wasn't Kate's way.

'Children don't need to be smacked. They're like flowers. All they want is some food and water, a bit of sunshine and lots of love, and they'll grow just right. If you hit them, you'll break them.'

She was a good mother. Sometimes, way back then, before Anna's death, he'd find himself watching her with the girls, in utter admiration. She was so young when she'd fallen pregnant with Anna, then Lizzie so quickly after, and then he was away with his job, leaving her for weeks at a time with the two small children. She never once complained. Instead, she made sure they didn't miss him, painting him love-you-Daddy pictures, making fabulous misshapen biscuits with fluorescent pink icing and too many silver balls, leaving incoherent messages on his mobile that he'd listen to over and over in those sterile hotel rooms in every lonely corner of Europe. Had he ever told her how much he'd appreciated that? He couldn't remember.

Rachel got out of the car and walked around to Rebecca's side. She opened the door and held her hand out and waited until her daughter took it. They stood next to Jon's window. Rachel's arm lay protectively around her daughter's shoulders; Rebecca leant against her mother.

'Will you be all right?' he said.

Neither replied.

'I don't know what else I can say, but if either of you need anything, you must call me, any time, day or night.'

'You know, it's her who needs help,' Rachel said. 'Not us.'

He dropped his head, but feeling Rachel's eyes needling into him he glanced up again. Her mouth twitched ever so slightly, then she reached through the window and laid her hand on his.

'It's not your fault, Jon.'

He stared at her hand. Her skin was creamy and smooth and peppered with tiny moles like the shell of a speckled egg, so different from Kate's, whose hands were dry and red in places, with paint ground permanently into them.

'And, I know this is probably out of turn, but from where I'm standing, it's not fair on you either,' she went on. 'You lost Anna too.'

Jon closed his eyes as she stroked him with her thumb, warm and gentle. He tried to imagine her touch was Kate's.

'I should go.' The words caught in his throat. 'I need to get back to Lizzie.'

'Poor thing,' Rachel whispered. 'Seeing her mum like that.'

Jon didn't reply.

He waited until the two of them disappeared inside the house before he started the engine. He drove in a numb daze, unable to distinguish one emotion from the next as they jostled inside him. He felt as if he were wading through glue. The amount of effort required to do simple things – shift gear, check mirrors, park – was exhausting. He sat in the NCP near the police station and tried to steady himself. What was he going to tell people? What would they think of Kate? He winced at the sound of his mother's voice in his head. *Well, of course*, she said tightly. *I'm not in the least bit surprised.*

Jon shook his head. 'You mustn't blame her,' he said aloud. 'Losing Anna turned her world upside down.'

He saw his mother's eyebrows arch. *Losing Anna turned all our worlds upside down*, she said. *But all she sees is her own tragedy. What the rest of us feel is of no concern to her. It's about time Kate realized the whole sorry situation doesn't simply revolve around her.* He saw his mother cross her arms and lift her chin, the tortoiseshell comb pushed firmly into her snow-white hair. He wouldn't agree with her. However fond he was of his mother his loyalty was with his wife, as strong now as it had been the first time he brought her home to meet his mother. He remembered how terrified Kate had been, juddering about on the doorstep while they waited for the door to open and, when it did, her hand squeezing his so hard he laughed. He pulled her along the corridor as she ohmygodded her way past framed doctorates, the photo of his father shaking hands with Neil Kinnock, the one of him in a crowd of eminent strangers with the grand red-brick façade of Harvard behind them, then proudly holding his knighthood, his mother beaming out from beneath the rim of her ridiculous pink hat.

'What am I going to say to them? Oh my God, they're going to think I'm a moron.' She paused. 'And I am a moron, by the way. I failed my maths O-level.'

'It doesn't matter.'

'Twice,' she whispered. 'I failed Maths O-level twice.'

Jon laughed and kissed her forehead.

'I've never met a Lady before. Shit. What the hell am I doing here?' She tried to pull back towards the front door. He held firm and pulled her on.

'He's knighted for services to economics, so really, she's only a Lady because he was such a swot at school,' he whispered with a grin.

She groaned. 'None of the swots at school could stand me. They thought I was a real pain in the arse.'

'They'll adore you, just like I do,' Jon said.

As they walked into the front room, or lounge as Kate called it, he crossed his fingers behind his back.

He was besotted. She was so different from the ones before, a samey-samey group of respectable girls who were headed for Oxbridge, and who dressed nicely, with parents who were solicitors or doctors or academics, and whom his mother grinned at while sipping sloe gin. But Kate, with her lace-up boots, nose ring and art school flair, was fire and frivolity and full to the brim with lust for life. She injected him with energy. She was his elixir. It was only when he met Kate that Jon saw how dull his life had become, typical eldest child, conservative, responsible, desperate to please. It shackled him. But then he found Kate and she had the key.

'So?' he asked, when he returned to the front room having put Kate in a taxi back to east London.

'Oh, Jonathan, darling, she is so *uncultured*,' his mother replied. 'Doesn't even play the piano. Not a single lesson!'

At that moment Jon decided against telling them about the pregnancy.

'And how *anybody* can think that the painting of the Sistine Chapel isn't an important moment in the history of art is beyond me. I mean, that's verging on the criminal.'

'She didn't actually say that,' said Jon, fighting to keep his voice level. 'She said she didn't class it as a catalyst of stylistic change.'

'She certainly did not use the word *catalyst*, darling. I doubt very much if she could even *spell* catalyst!'

Jon took a deep breath. 'Was there anything you liked about her?'

'Well, if you pushed me, I suppose she was occasionally amusing, though brash-amusing, not witty-amusing. But I do think it's rather tasteless that she used to be with Daniel. I mean, is it Daniel? Or is it you? These modern women have fewer morals than common street girls.'

'She had a couple of drinks with Daniel,' Jon said, trying to ignore a surge of jealousy. 'It was nothing more than that. We've been together for nearly three months and,' he paused, 'you know, it's actually pretty serious.'

His mother snorted.

'I thought she was rather delightful,' his father said, from behind the *Sunday Times*. 'And jolly pretty.'

Jon gave his father a grateful smile, but his mother's second scoff saw it off.

'Not *jolly* pretty, Peter. Pretty I'll give her, but she's too self-consciously avant garde to be *jolly* pretty. And, darling,' she said, wrinkling her nose against an undetectable smell. 'Where on earth is that ghastly accent from?'

'She doesn't have a ghastly accent.'

Jon's mother cocked her head like a toy poodle.

'Fine,' Jon said. 'Have it your way. My girlfriend's accent comes straight from the gutter of Bristol, her father left when she was no more than a baby, she can't play Für Elise on the piano, she says *ta* instead of *thank you*, and she failed her maths O-level, twice. But how about we pretend, just for one moment, that none of these things matter a jot in the real world, and acknowledge that we've all had the privilege of spending time with one of the most fabulous women I've ever met. I love her, and God help me if I won't do everything I can to make sure she marries me before some other lucky bastard nabs her.'

For a moment or two there was a stunned silence, and then his mother calmly laid both hands palm down on her lap and looked straight at him. 'The girl failed maths O-level *twice*?'

And with that he walked out and hailed a second cab to Dalston.

'They hated me, didn't they?' Kate said, as they lay tangled in the sheets.

'No. How could they?'

'I said "ta for dinner". That's wrong, isn't it?'

'You were being polite. That's anything but wrong.'

'But you call it lunch. I remembered that as soon as I said it.'

'It doesn't matter what you call it.' He kissed her perfect nose, small and upturned with freckles and a mole on one side that looked like a full stop. There we go, one beautiful girl with a perfect nose, he imagined whoever-made-us-all saying, as she was finished with that full stop and a flourish.

'Ta ever so truly very much for my super-duper delumtious luncheon, Mrs Lady Thorne, your ohsoloftyhighness, would've been best. You should have warned me.'

He laughed.

'They won't be happy about the baby.' She patted her washboard stomach.

'They'll be over the moon.'

'Liar.'

'If not, then, well, fuck them.'

'Jon! You swore!'

'Yes,' he said. 'Fuck them, fuck them, fuck them!'

'No,' she whispered as she leant in to kiss his neck with soft, lingering lips. 'I'll fuck you, ta very much.'

Jon's mother had eventually come round, and until the day of Anna's funeral, she and Kate got along fine, because as much as his mother disapproved of her accent and her views on the importance of Michelangelo, or her lack of mathematical prowess, when the baby-out-of-wedlock appeared, the two of them were immediately united. His mother loved Anna, and then Lizzie, nearly as much as Kate did, and that shared love was enough to cement them. It broke Jon's heart when he thought back to those days, all of them together, maybe watching one of Anna's countless dance shows in the living room, being presented home-made tickets, Lizzie at the CD player on music duty, his wife and mother both grinning with love and affection as Anna performed and Lizzie followed her with a bike-lamp spotlight. They had barely spoken for nearly a year, their only exchanges brief and perfunctory. Jon was at a loss. His mother's harsh lack of forgiveness and Kate's stubborn refusal to offer any apology or regret seemed to make the chasm unbridgeable.

Jon walked up the steps to the police station and saw Kate through the glass door, sitting on a chair beside the vending machine near the front desk. He stood for a moment or two outside the doors and watched her. She looked like a frightened child, a refugee, thin and pale, her fingers clutching her knees, her feet pressed together, shoulders stooped. She must have sensed him and looked up. As he walked through the doors he made himself smile. She didn't give one back. There seemed to be no emotion whatsoever on her face. She was usually such an open book, her thoughts and feelings displayed for all to see in both her eyes and body language. But right now he couldn't tell what was going on inside her and he found this disconcerting, perhaps worried that when she finally did try and explain there would be a lack of contrition which he'd be unable to take. As he approached her he felt like the young soldier charged with the job of defusing his first landmine.

She stood up as he reached her. They were no more than a foot apart but there was a stifling awkwardness between them. He knew he should hug her, but he wasn't sure how to instigate it. But seemingly this was something he needn't have worried about, for despite the stilted air she fell into him, pulling him into her so hard he felt momentarily alarmed. He closed his arms around her and felt her lambswool cardigan soft beneath his fingers. He breathed in her freshly washed hair, clean and familiar, and for a moment everything else faded to nothing. He wondered if they could stay like this for ever, in that needy embrace, but he knew it wasn't possible, that soon they'd have to split. When they did he turned and walked out of the police station with her following.

Despite the evening drawing in, the sunshine seemed to have grown brighter, too bright, perhaps, to do justice to the gravity of their situation. *A sky the colour of faded underwear would have been more appropriate*, Jon thought. And maybe some drizzle to make the air damp, the type of damp that cuts through to the bones.

'Will they press charges?' Jon asked as they stepped on to the pavement.

'They were vague,' she said. Her voice was thin and tired. 'It has a lot to do with—' She stopped talking suddenly and stumbled, collapsing on to her hands and knees on the pavement. His stomach turned over. He dropped to the ground beside her and placed a hand on her back, trying his best to ignore the looks from curious passers-by. He watched helplessly as she tried to breathe. At last her knuckles lost their whitish tinge and her body relaxed a fraction. She rocked back on to her haunches and faced him.

'It depends on what Rebecca wants to do,' she whispered.

They walked back to the car in silence. They didn't hold hands. Jon walked a step in front of Kate, leading the way, using his arms every now and then to guide people out of the path she walked blindly. He wanted to talk. He wanted to tell her that it was going to be OK, that Rebecca was OK, that she wasn't scared or hurt, and that when he dropped her off she laughed and said to pass the message on that she was fine. But of course he couldn't say those things, and saying anything else seemed pointless.

Eventually, though, when they were both strapped into the car and he'd put the key into the ignition, the silence became impossible.

He cleared his throat. 'Did the police treat you well?' It was all he had.

'Yes,' she replied. 'They gave me tea.'

'You must have been scared.' Jon meant to be sympathetic,

but the words came out too forced and he worried he sounded insincere.

Kate didn't answer.

Then without warning a sudden swell of anger hit him. He slammed both hands against the steering wheel so hard he felt Kate jump.

'Damn it, Kate, what the hell were you thinking! I mean, how? How could you do that?'

'I wasn't.'

'Wasn't what?' he asked, exasperated.

'Thinking.'

They didn't speak again.

He pulled up outside the house and she got out of the car. He watched her walk up the path to their front door then disappear indoors. He didn't make to follow; it was better where he was, alone in the car. The car was like a bubble, comfortable, quiet and protected. He closed his eyes and imagined many pairs of invisible hands sealing him inside, working quickly and quietly, before an enormous remote-controlled machine dropped the car with him inside into a large hole, then filled the hole, shovel-load by shovel-load, until he was buried and all that was left was a scar of freshly turned soil on the ground above.

The Shed

Lizzie hoped her dad was OK. She wasn't sure if he'd properly heard her when she told him she needed a walk. He hadn't replied, just gave a dilute smile through the gathered crowd, his eyes clouded, full of her mum and Rebecca.

She went straight to the shed. It was the first place she thought about. She kept her eyes on the pavement in front of her and didn't dawdle or look in any shop windows. She pushed her hands into the pockets of her school blazer and tried to keep her mum and Rebecca out of her head. She knew the shed would help. It always did. Even before Anna died it was a place where she felt safe.

The shed was at her grandparents' house, and though she and Anna had called it *their* shed for years and years, it was really her grandmother's. She'd given it over to them when they were small. Their mum and dad had gone away for the night – their anniversary or something – and Lizzie was missing them. Grandpa told them he would make them a special place at his and Granny's home, so that if they ever felt lonely or sad, they had somewhere to go. Their grandmother said she didn't need the old shed because she now used the lean-to conservatory, which was more convenient than traipsing up and down to the top of the garden anyway.

It took a whole day to clear out her clutter, a heavenly mix of terracotta plant pots, old-fashioned tools, almost empty bottles of gloopy black liquids and about a million spiders and their old torn webs. Then the girls swept it out, the clouds of dust making them cough and splutter. They found wooden crates for seats and a table, and an old tea towel for a tablecloth. They filled a jam jar with pretty weeds. And begged for tins of food and a few chipped ornaments to decorate the shelves and make it look homely. Even when they grew older they would go to the shed and sit and chat, away from the eyes and ears of grown-ups. Anna would light a Marlboro Light and the air would quickly become unbearable with smoke and dust, and Lizzie would stare at her delicate fingers holding the cigarette, envious of her perfect nails. Anna had always had perfect nails, even as a small child. They were long enough to look grown-up, but not tart-long, and neatly filed with a flawless white tip. Lizzie's own were bitten to the quick and red around the edges where she'd gnawed too low.

The shed was their special place and, just as Grandpa had said, she felt safe there. It was the first place she thought of when the end of Haydn's music dropped her back into the reality of the heaving, whispering playground. There was a gate straight into the back of the garden from an access road that ran parallel to the street on which her grandparents lived. It was narrow and made of wrought iron and was mostly covered with dark green ivy, and when Grandpa had been well it was where he had to take the rubbish because her grandmother said that bins at the front of the house looked shabby.

Lizzie paused at the entrance to the shed and looked down towards the house. Her view was almost completely obscured by leaves and branches, but she could just about see the kitchen window and behind it the ghostly figure of her grandmother coming in and out of vision as she moved slowly about. Lizzie imagined she was making a pot of tea, and perhaps putting some chocolate Bourbons on a plate because they were her grandpa's favourite.

She considered running down to see her. She loved her granny. She always knew the right thing to say, always had a hug and a kiss. She never tried to tell Lizzie how she should be feeling, but would listen and nod, and then, and only if Lizzie asked, she might offer some advice, concise and calm, as if she had a thousand years of wisdom. Lizzie had spent a lot of time with her in the weeks immediately after Anna's death. Her dad would pick her up late at night and apologize all the way home for not coming sooner, saying this was a transitory phase, that he and her mum just needed to find their feet, get back to some sort of routine. Lizzie didn't mind at all. At least her grandmother always had food in the house, and whenever she was there they would sit down together and watch *Countdown*, both with pen and paper and play along as if they were real contestants. Every other adult in her life seemed permanently wedged into a long meaningful silence, heavy hands on her shoulders, tissues at the ready, eyes full of irritating pity. Her grandmother's controlled company, Carol Vorderman and a plate of Bourbons had been a heavenly retreat. But Lizzie couldn't go to her today. She couldn't tell her what happened at the memorial. It would be like betraying her mum.

Lizzie sat on the upturned crate and collapsed forwards on to the little dusty table. Her thoughts were all Haydn. How had he known just what she needed? She would never have thought of music. But it was perfect. Amazing, even. The way everything nasty disappeared. Her mum, Rebecca, all the others, the staring and whispering girls and boys who looked at her like it was her that did it. And it was just the right music, too, and the right volume. It was incredible what he did, how he appeared out of nowhere and came to her rescue.

She hadn't seen him since Anna died. He didn't come back to school after it happened, which meant rumours about his involvement that night flew like wildfire with the other rumours – work-pressure suicide, heroin addiction, a jealous love rival from another school – there were so many it made Lizzie's head spin. Thankfully, the conspiracy theories fizzled out as quickly as they flared. People also seemed to forget about Haydn. Everyone apart from her mum. She blamed him for most of that night, for feeding Anna alcohol, for taking her up on the roof, for goading her on to the ledge. But she was wrong to blame him. It wasn't his fault. Anna wouldn't have done something because Haydn told her to; she was strong-headed and stubborn. Lizzie knew she would have climbed up herself, that Haydn was telling the truth when he said how worried he was, how he'd begged her to get down again and again, how traumatized he was when Dr Howe found him, shivering and huddled in a corner.

The police had confirmed how shocked he'd been at witnessing the fall. But her mum didn't care. She needed someone to blame, that's what her dad said. He said it made it easier for her. So Lizzie let it go and listened quietly to the mutters and rants about Haydn and Rachel and Rebecca and the man in the corner shop who sold vodka to children. She kept reminding herself that the police had confirmed Anna's death an accident, and as far as Lizzie was concerned an accident, by definition, absolved them all of blame, which totally suited her, because if it wasn't an accident, if Anna had done it on purpose, for whatever reason, then they were all to blame, and nobody more than the sister who wasn't enough to confide in, and that thought, that dark lingering thought, was the worst bit of any of it.

Lizzie lifted her head and rested her chin on the splintery wood. She brought his iPod into sight and stroked the side of her thumb against it. Then she pushed the earphones into her ears and pressed play. His music began again and she closed her eyes, remembering his sandpaper skin and his cigarette smell and the way his sad eyes lit up when he smiled.

Painting a Laugh

'Your laugh,' Kate said to herself. 'Where's your laugh?'

She'd gone straight up to her studio. She'd been desperate to get there ever since Jon asked her how the police had treated her. The police had treated her well. Better than well. The WPC who'd brought her a plastic cup of watery grey tea had been almost apologetic. Kate assumed she didn't know why she was there. That she thought Kate was the victim of some type of street crime, maybe an attempted rape, or domestic abuse. She shuddered when she imagined the moment the woman found out.

Really! she saw her exclaim. *All these years and you never can tell, can you?*

Jon's question had made her stomach clench. It was as if he wanted her to tell him how dreadful they'd been to her, how aggressive and rough. She knew that would have made it easier for him to be kind to her.

She needed to paint. She didn't want to think about Rebecca, or the police, or the fury with which Jon had hit his hands against the steering wheel; all she cared about was Anna's laugh. She picked up her paintbrush and breathed deeply as the heady mix of oil paint and white spirit stole into her blood like an opiate.

'Remember something funny,' she whispered.

As the fumes took hold of her, and the soft noises of people on the street below bounced along beneath her thoughts, she saw them all together. They were in that odd little hotel in Devon. It was July. The girls were eleven and twelve. Anna was dressed in a halter-neck top tied around her swanlike neck, graceful as a Sixties model. The outline of her budding breasts turning her from girl to woman were just detectable beneath it. Her legs and arms were tanned from playing on the beach, her hair tied up in a high ponytail. Everyone in the restaurant turned at some point during their meal, some subtly, some not so, to glance at the exquisite girl. Her daughter. Anna. With each look Kate had at once felt a burst of pride followed by a pang of sympathy for Lizzie, the haze of static hair hovering around her, so small and thin and plain in comparison. Kate prayed she didn't notice people not looking at her. She watched her youngest daughter, ready to give her some sort of compliment if needed, but Lizzie was oblivious, only concerned with what pudding to order. Kate remembered the swell of love she'd felt for her then – such an untroubled child, happy in her own place, the rest of the world something that happened around her.

So, they were looking at pudding – Kate was having cheesecake, Jon the brûlée, Anna the chocolate mousse – but as usual Lizzie was having trouble deciding. She'd spent nearly ten minutes flitting from one choice to the next like an anxious butterfly.

'Come on, slow coach,' sighed Anna impatiently. 'Just have the mousse like me.'

Lizzie nodded and closed her menu, but then a few seconds later she shook her head and opened it again. Anna groaned.

'What ice-cream do you think they have?' she whispered to Kate.

'How do I know, you silly sausage? You'll have to ask.' She smiled at Lizzie, who suddenly looked terrified.

'I'll ask for her,' said Anna.

'Let her do it, Anna.'

The waiter appeared and the rest of them ordered. 'And you, mademoiselle?' he said to Lizzie, in a French accent so overblown Kate was convinced it could only be dramatic affectation.

Lizzie went red and looked at the tablecloth.

'My sister would like to know what flavour ice-creams you have,' Anna said, loud and satisfied, with a smile that almost broke her face in half.

The waiter turned to face her. He beamed. 'Well, mad-a-mwa-zayll. Too-deh! On ze menoo! We 'ave strorberree, shockalah, vaneee-ya, and for zee sorbets zair is zee leemon, pinnyapple and . . . errrr . . . zee mongo!'

Anna started it. Jon went next. Lizzie and Kate gave in last. They laughed so much that tears streamed down all their faces. It was a painful number of minutes before they managed to tame their laughter and tuck it behind aching straight faces. The waiter, puce-faced and unable to hide his affront, turned to Lizzie.

'You would like?' he said curtly.

'I'd like,' she said, desperately trying to hold herself together. 'The . . . um, the . . . um . . . mongo.' And as she exploded, so again did the rest of them.

Kate concentrated on that final scene. She turned the other laughs down, removed Jon, then Lizzie, then herself, the noises of the people in the restaurant, the indignant huffing of the waiter, until all she could hear was Anna.

'There you are, my darling,' she whispered. 'I have you.'

She eased the laugh out of the story, careful not to let it slip away from her like a thread of silk in the breeze. When she finally had firm hold of it, she relaxed and breathed in the painty smells, and let the beautiful noise of her eldest daughter laughing ring about in her head as if she were savouring the very best chocolate melting over her tongue. Then she opened her eyes and touched her brush to her palette and began to paint Anna how she was that day, with her halter-neck top and her swan's neck and the end of the mongo-laugh creasing her eyes into pools of life.

All's Fair

'Hello Jon.'

Jon had no desire to speak to his brother at all, and wished he hadn't picked up the phone.

'Dan, this isn't a good time. Can I call you tomorrow?'

'Not good tomorrow,' said Dan. 'Look, I just wanted to let you know I'm flying over.'

'Why?'

'What on earth do you mean, *why*? Do I need a reason for coming back to see my family?'

'Yes, Dan, I would imagine you do.'

Dan laughed. 'Big brother Jonny, always so terribly cynical.'

'It's not cynicism. I just know you too well.'

'As you wish,' Dan said. 'On this occasion you're right. Mother asked me to come back for the old boy's birthday.'

'You don't normally,' Jon said, snapping back to life. He thought of his mother and her desperate tears. 'Why this year?'

'No idea. She said it was important, then she buttered on the guilt. Blah, blah, you never call. Blah, blah, you never visit. Blah, blah, blah.'

'I think she's finding it all quite hard.' Jon paused. 'She didn't come to Anna's memorial service because she didn't want to leave Dad.'

'Oh, I forgot about that. How did it go?' said Dan, as if he were asking about a job interview.

'Fine. You know, it was a school service.'

'And how's Kiki?'

Jon had been expecting this question, but even so he couldn't stop the familiar knife twisting in his gut. Jealousy, such a ridiculous, juvenile emotion. Until Kate, Jon had never felt it. From childhood onwards he'd watched Dan stroll through life, women knocking on his door, success falling at his feet, friends queuing up, money, looks, style, talent; Dan had it all, but not once had Jon been jealous. Until Kate.

They had met at Dan's twenty-first birthday party. Jon turned up very late. And alone. He had done everything he could to find a girl to take, but it had been a fruitless search, which peaked with a dreadful blind date. He'd been desperate; turning up to Dan's party without a girlfriend was unthinkable. He would never hear the end of it. To Dan, Jon was a pitiful joke. The invite had included a dress code – 'wholly inappropriate' – and told him to bring a girlfriend. Jon could almost hear the goading in those scrawled few words:

If there is one!

He imagined how much Dan had smirked as he wrote that. Dan the Stud. Dan the Player. Dan the bloody Man. But Jon's little black book of dead-end dinners, awkward kisses and (a pathetic two) one-night stands threw up nothing but flat *no-thank-you*s, and so there he was, outside the party, no girl and preparing for Dan's relentless destruction of his manhood. His dread thickened – parties were occasions to be endured, the only satisfaction to be gained was from surviving them – and it took him well over twenty minutes of nervous loitering before he finally felt able to face it. He pushed open the doors, went down the stairs towards the thump and hum of the basement. As he neared he was met by a thick fug of cigarettes and marijuana, and a wall of laughing, screaming and music so loud his ears rang. People spilled out of the party room ahead, lining the walls of the corridor like touting hookers. He walked past them, feeling them look him up and down, imagining them sniggering. Three times he nearly turned round, but each time he spoke to himself firmly. *It's your brother's twenty-first birthday party. You must at least show your face.*

He pushed through the throng of scantily clad women and men, squirming in his tweed suit and bow tie, which at the time of choosing seemed perfectly *wholly inappropriate* for a twenty-first birthday party in the basement room of the trendiest art school in London. The London in-crowd, however, clearly took *wholly inappropriate* to mean nearly naked, and now all he felt was ridiculous.

'I'm looking for Dan?' he asked a nearby girl, having to shout to be heard above the thunderous bass. She turned her head slowly, looked blankly through him, her eyes glazed and fixed on a vanishing point somewhere behind him.

Jon looked at a man next to her who wore nothing but women's suspenders, underpants and small rounds of tin foil stuck to his nipples. 'Do you know where I can find Dan?'

The man with tin-foil nipples gestured to the back of the room. Jon followed the direction of the man's point.

And that was when he saw her.

She was dressed in black PVC boots that reached up to her thighs and what appeared to be a black one-piece swimming costume, with a white band around her neck and a floor-length black coat with a scarlet satin lining. Her hair was cut in a short bob with a blunt fringe. She was the most striking thing Jon had ever laid eyes on. He was transfixed, and the rest of the party blurred around her. She caught him staring, but rather than look away she held his gaze, and he was drawn towards her like a sailor to a siren, his heart pumping louder than the music with nerves and excitement.

'Hello,' he said. How brave he was!

'Hello,' she replied.

And then she smiled.

The smile was something the like of which he never imagined could exist. It illuminated her face, showed her perfect teeth, wrinkled her nose, crinkled her gleaming eyes and bunched her cheeks. Not a single part of her face was left out of that smile. He was stunned.

'I like your outfit,' she shouted above the music. 'You look fabulous!'

He stared at her, unable to talk, scared that as soon as he did she'd lose interest and vanish.

'I love the tweed!' she pushed on, reaching out to run her fingers down his lapel.

He had to find his tongue. It was now or never. 'You're taking the Michael, I feel.' His heart sank at his dismal offering and he readied himself for her leaving.

But she didn't leave.

She laughed.

'Taking the who?' she said.

'Um . . . the Michael. It's the Mick really. But I say Michael instead. I don't know why, really . . . it's just . . . well, a joke. Anyway, it means you're teasing me.'

She laughed and touched his arm. He looked down and saw her hand on his sleeve, the skin covered in splodges of ingrained paint, neat nails, more paint beneath.

'I'm not! I promise!' she said. 'This is a bloody sweatbox. You're dressed in a stupidly hot suit that a toff would wear to do shooting, or whatever they do. You look wholly inappropriate. I tried to be too clever and I just look like a tart, which is what Dan wanted, of course, so is wholly *appropriate* and so, by definition, doesn't obey the dress rules. See my problem?'

He was smitten.

'What do you mean, too clever?' he asked.

She looked at him, then put her hands on her hips, smiled and posed, jutting a leg forward. He stared at her, thunderstruck with desire. She feigned irritation then pushed her hands together in prayer. He stared. She shook her head and grinned.

'You see? People should never try to be clever. Wholly inappropriate? A dog collar? I'm a vicar. A *woman* dressed as a vicar? At this godless party?' She lifted her leg, bent at the knee. 'High heels on a vicar? Inappropriate.' She opened her coat and he stared at the exquisite curve of her waist. 'Scarlet lining? Black boots? Not very holy!'

Jon laughed. 'Holy! Wholly. Yes, yes, I get it! You're right, that is clever.'

'Nope,' she shook her head. 'Just a tart, like all these other tarts.'

'Not at all,' he said. 'You're beautiful.' He paused. 'And very chaste.'

She smiled again then held out her hand. 'I'm Kate.'

'I'm Jon.' He took her hand. 'The toff.'

She laughed. Then someone came up behind her and put his arms around her, hands rising up over her breasts. He kissed her neck, then looked up and grinned at Jon.

'Kiki, you've met my brother, I see.' He lifted her hand to his lips and kissed it, his eyes staying on Jon. And there it was, the first stab of jealousy Jon had felt, cutting into him with its serrated, acid edge. 'Just be careful he doesn't bore you to death,' he said, then he winked at Jon as if that made it OK. 'Good to see you, brother.

Get yourself a beer, loosen up, maybe lose the dickie bow, not sure it does much for the ladies, if you know what I mean.' He winked again. 'And now, my little Kiki, let's see if we can't take this party up a gear.'

Kate smiled at Dan, all long lashes and moist lips, and then she and Jon watched him sashay away, kissing everyone warmly, men and women, as he passed, then lifting his arms and pumping the air in time with the beat. Kate and Jon turned back to each other.

'I don't think you're boring at all, by the way,' she said. 'And keep the tie. It's funky.' She smiled again. 'See you later.' And then she danced after Dan.

Jon was born again. Evangelical. It was love. His brother's girl-friend; wholly inappropriate.

Jon hung in a corner with a bottle of beer the whole evening, his eyes bolted to Kate, moving her back into his line of vision when she skipped out of it, or became obscured by others. The music raged around him, people jostled him, he became hotter and stickier, but he never let his eyes leave her.

By the early hours of the morning the remaining partygoers were a gooey drugged-up mess, locked in amorous pairs or passed out in heaps. If the scene was a modern-day Hogarth, then Dan was the ultimate rake. Nude from the waist upwards, his chest glistened with sweat, his hair flopped over his face. He held Kate up against a wall, his hands either side of her shoulders, kissing her aggressively, her hands around his rear. Delicate fingers. Perfect nails. Those painterly marks.

Jon drank from his bottle and seethed. He wanted that girl. She was too good for Dan, too good to be just another in his line of conquests. He watched as she drew her face away from his brother and ducked beneath his arm. She disappeared in the direction of the loos, and he walked over to Dan.

'Hey,' he said. 'Good party.'

'You still here, bro?' Dan's mouth was shiny with saliva. Hers.

Jon nodded. 'Kate's great,' he said.

'Kiki?' Dan smiled a drunken leer. 'Sure is. She's special. I think she's the one, mate. I really do.' He batted Jon on the shoulder. 'I'm in love.'

Jon shook his head. 'You're not in love. Think of all those women you'd have to give up.'

'She might be the one to change me. Anyway, she's cool; she'll let me sleep with other girls. Sex is one thing. Love is something else. They don't relate, man. You should try it.'

Jon stared at him. Dan winked again and Jon forced a smile.

'Hey, boys!' They both turned.

'Gotta take a slash,' Dan slurred.

Kate smiled at Jon.

Jon waited until Dan pushed out through the double doors. 'Have dinner with me,' he said quickly.

'What?' she laughed.

'Dinner. With me.'

'I'm going out with your brother!'

'No. Have dinner with me. Just dinner.'

'It's his birthday and you're trying to steal his girlfriend? How does that work?'

'He won't stay faithful. He can't.'

Her face fell and her eyebrows arched; the defiance in her, the sudden fire, the way it lit her eyes and set her mouth, magnified her beauty such that he found it difficult to speak.

'Ask him,' Jon managed. 'Ask him if he'll stay faithful.' He looked up and saw Dan staggering back into the room. 'If he says he won't, call me.' Jon passed her a piece of paper on which he'd already written his number. 'Just dinner.'

She called two days later. She needed a friendly shoulder. Was the offer of dinner still open? Jon held the phone away from his mouth and dropped to his knees, thanking the skies for the chance he'd been given. She'd found Dan in bed with a girl from their sculpture class. He wasn't sorry. He said life was too short to say no to these things. But he wanted her, too. He begged her to stay with him. She couldn't, and, as Jon pointed out that night over dinner, she was better off without him.

Kate had reassured Jon time and time again that she'd never loved anybody the way she loved him, but there was always a part of him that believed at some point she'd realise she'd chosen the wrong brother, and it was the handsome, wealthy artist who lived in a penthouse apartment in Manhattan she really should have married.

'So when are you flying in?' Jon asked, ignoring his brother's ask after Kate.

'Couple of days. Sunday, I think. I've got an opening on Saturday that I can't get out of. They need me there to smile and charm.'

'Would you like me to meet your plane?' Jon forced.

'Jonny, my man, that would be great. Maybe Kiki could make us some lunch. It would be good to spend some time with her, and you and little Lizbette too, of course.'

The Girl in the Cage: Part One

The day after the memorial Lizzie decided she had to see Haydn again.

Her dad was in the kitchen pouring a glass of orange juice. He'd just got back from work, his suit was crumpled, his tie loose, top button undone. He looked tired, as if he'd had a difficult day.

'Hi,' she said.

He turned and smiled a weary smile. 'Hello, angel, how are you?'

She shrugged. 'Fine.'

'How was school?' he asked carefully.

She shrugged again. 'OK,' she said. 'You know.'

In truth, school had been hard work. She nearly didn't go, but she knew she'd have to face the place sooner or later and, a bit like having a jab, it seemed best to get it over and done with. A couple of girls shouted across the playground that her mum was a loony and should be in the psycho ward; there was a degree of general whispering and pointing, and when she walked into the dining room, a few moments of loaded hush. The fact that she'd been unable to think about anything other than Haydn was actually very helpful.

'I know what you mean.' Her dad sighed heavily as he opened the fridge to put the juice carton back.

'I think I might go for a walk,' she said, as casually as she could.

'That sounds like a good idea,' he said. He drank his juice in one. 'Tell you what, give me a few minutes to change out of my suit and I'll come with you.'

Lizzie stopped in her tracks. 'Oh. Well, actually, do you mind if I go alone? You know, after yesterday, I feel like some quiet time . . . to think stuff over . . .' She trailed off, hoping she'd not upset him.

'Yes, yes, sure. You go on; it's a lovely evening. Perfect for thinking.' Lizzie could tell he was disappointed. She hesitated, wondering if she should stay, but then again, she was totally desperate to see Haydn.

'I won't be long,' she said. 'We could have a game of chess when I get back.'

'OK. You're on.'

'I'll beat you, so you better be ready.' She hung at the door, still unsure.

'Go on, you. Have your walk.'

'Sure?'

'Go!' He smiled and shooed his hands at her.

'Love you, Dad.'

She ran all the way to Haydn's house, worried she would lose her nerve if she didn't get there quickly. When she reached the front door she was so out of breath she had to stand panting on the doorstep, waiting to catch her breath before ringing the doorbell.

Mrs Howe looked shocked to see her and seemed unsure what to say. Her mouth opened then closed again.

'Can I talk to Haydn?'

'Well, I'm not sure—'

'He lent me something. I need to give it back to him.' Lizzie spoke quickly, her stomach tumbling over itself as her bravery seeped away.

Mrs Howe looked up and down the street over Lizzie's shoulder then crossed her arms; her eyes turned hard. 'I think you should be at home with your mother.'

Lizzie felt her cheeks grow warm. From the tang of judgement in Mrs Howe's voice, Lizzie figured she must be even more disappointed with her mum than she had imagined she would be. She looked at her feet and tried to steady her racing heart. She felt protective of her mother, wanted to explain how hard the year had been for her, make her deputy head realize she wasn't herself, but sort of semi-permanently out of normal operation, and that though she might well be existing on a day-to-day basis, she wasn't really living, because rightly or wrongly she didn't seem to see the point of it. Maybe hearing those things would take that nasty edge out of Mrs Howe's voice. But Lizzie couldn't say any of it, not because it wasn't true, but because if she said all those things then Mrs Howe might conclude that Lizzie wasn't enough to keep her mum going, that Lizzie being alive was pale in comparison with Anna being dead.

'Is Haydn in?' she mumbled.

'He's in his room. He won't want to come down. Just give me whatever it is.' She presented the flat of her hand and flicked her fingers. 'I'll tell him you dropped—'

Haydn's face beside her stopped her flow. She plastered a bright smile on her face, and when she spoke, her voice was lighter. 'Haydn, sweetheart, Elizabeth came to return something. I told her you were probably too busy to see her.'

Lizzie tried to speak but found she couldn't.

'Do you want to come up?' Haydn asked. His voice was almost too quiet to hear. He glanced at his mother. 'That's OK, right?'

Lizzie looked at Mrs Howe, who sighed impatiently. 'It's not a good time, Haydn. I'm not sure—'

'She won't stay long. Five minutes,' Haydn said, and then

looked at Lizzie and gestured with a jerk of his head towards the stairs. 'Come on.'

Lizzie didn't know what to do. Her deputy head clearly didn't want her to come in, but she was desperate to follow him. She hovered on the doorstep and braved another glance at Mrs Howe.

'Fine,' Mrs Howe puffed. 'Five minutes.'

Lizzie dropped her head so she didn't have to look at her as she passed, and followed Haydn, wordless, up the stairs. They reached a door at the far end of the corridor. It was covered in peeling black-edged football stickers, a *Keep Out* sign and scribbled black marker pen over every centimetre of exposed gloss paintwork. He disappeared inside, but she paused, suddenly self-conscious, worried about what she would say when they finally got to his room.

'You coming in?' he called from inside.

Lizzie told herself not to be so wet, and tried to invoke the spirit of her sister, who would have skipped in and leapt on to his bed, legs crossed, smile on.

Though not quite skipping, she managed to step inside. She was immediately knocked sideways by the smell, a mush of masculine sprays, stale cigarettes and sheets that hadn't been changed for maybe months, a giddy, unfamiliar cocktail that was both exciting and intimidating. The room, too, was like nothing she'd seen before. Like the door, every spare bit of wall was covered. Heaving leather-clad Neanderthals who bared their teeth and shook sweat-drenched hair rocked guitars next to photographs of bloodied animals with political slogans scrawled beneath. There were CD covers, train and cinema tickets, handwritten paragraphs surrounded by biro cartoons, flattened lager cans and beer mats and foreign bank notes. Lizzie felt her cheeks redden at the naked torso of a part-plastic woman who snarled scarlet lips, her hands clasped and tied with a leather strap, legs dressed from stiletto heel to thigh in black. She thought of her own bedroom. Of the white wallpaper dotted with tiny blue flowers, the coordinating curtains and bedspread that covered her neatly made bed, the three framed prints: Van Gogh's bedroom, Dali's clock, Klimt's kiss.

Her eyes took their time wandering the display, and when they finally came to rest, they did so on a drawing stuck to the wall by his pillow. It was a drawing she knew. She moved close enough to look at it properly, folding her arms protectively across her stomach. Described in black ink, the drawing showed a cavernous empty room. There was a cage in the corner with a naked girl crouched inside, who gripped the bars of her cage with both hands. Behind her was a pair of enormous folded wings, like an angel's, feathered in extraordinary detail. The girl's inked face stared back at her. Her eyes were full and watery, pools of longing, and the marks used to draw them were finer than hair. Her lips were opened as if she were about to ask something. Lizzie expected to hear her familiar voice at any second begging to be freed.

'It's one of Anna's,' she said.

She stared at it, biting back tears. Her sister was an amazing artist. She took after their mum. Lizzie was all maths and logic like their father. She wasn't dreadful at drawing, but her stuff lacked creative flair. Where her houses always had four windows, a front door and a neat spiral of smoke coming out of a rectangular chimney, Anna's would perch on rocky outcrops with windows made from irregular panes of rainbow glass.

'She was brilliant at art.'

Haydn didn't reply.

'She used to tell me all the time that she felt caged, that there was so much out there she couldn't get at.' Lizzie tore her eyes off the girl in the cage. 'I'd say there was life all around her, but she used to laugh at me as if I didn't get it.' Lizzie paused. 'She was wrong, though. I did get it.' They caught eyes for a moment and Lizzie flushed, suddenly self-conscious.

While they waited for the heaviness of Lizzie's words to lift out of the room, Haydn reached across the desk and picked up a bag of tobacco and began to roll a cigarette. Lizzie checked the door, suddenly worried in case his mother or, even worse, his father, came up and found him smoking. He offered her the cigarette, white and thin as a lollipop stick. She shook her head and watched as he put it in his mouth and lit it. Then he walked towards her, and as he passed he brushed her arm. Her heart started racing. Haydn leant over his chaotic desk and lifted the window open, then sat on his bed with his long lean legs stretched out in front of him and smoked. The cigarette filled the room in seconds and soon, despite the window, the charged air became thick and smoky. She closed her eyes to stop her head swirling.

Lizzie found it peculiar to be so close to the person who had last seen Anna alive. It was eerie and at the same time addictive. It drew her to him like iron to a magnet. Her head filled with questions she wanted to ask about those last few hours, irrelevancies that would embellish that final picture of her sister. It was as if Lizzie was umbilically tied to him and the cord was Anna.

She couldn't believe how much he'd changed in the year since Anna died. He was a boy back then, with a neat haircut and clear skin, quiet and shy, well behaved, the headmaster's son. Now he was grown up, he'd filled out, got taller. He was almost totally dressed in black, with jeans so tight they might be sprayed on, black T-shirt, greyed with washing, and a moth-eaten black cardigan with his fingers pushed through holes in the sleeve like he was wearing evening gloves. His hair was dyed black, too, and flopped over his eyes, and there were two rings in one ear. He was very good-looking. Beneath his fringe were deep blue eyes like his dad's, and he still had perfect skin, not a spot to be seen.

'So why did you come?' he asked, as he drew heavily on the cigarette, then squinted at her through the smoke. There was a hint of impatience in his bluntness that threw her.

'I've been thinking about you,' she muttered.

'What?' The look of amused surprise on his face caved her lungs.

'I mean . . . well . . . I . . .' Her voice dried up.

He didn't say anything. She knew he was laughing at her. Why did she tell him she'd been thinking about him? Now she looked like an idiot. A child. It was the type of thing a baby would say.

'I . . . it was . . .'

'It was what?' He drew on his cigarette and stared at her.

She didn't really have a reason why she'd come and now she wished the floor had a big hole that led right back to her bedroom. Her heart sank. 'Your iPod,' she managed to whisper.

She held it out towards him. He didn't move, so she took a couple of steps closer to his desk and placed it carefully on the corner. Then, so embarrassed she could hardly walk, she went to the door and reached for the handle. Now he thought she was a freak and she'd never see him again. *If you don't speak now*, she told herself sternly, *you'll have to live with the shame for ever.* She forced herself to turn. 'What you did . . . at the memorial . . . was . . . well, you really helped me. I don't know what I would have done . . . you know, if you hadn't come when you did. And . . . and, I . . . well, thank you, that's all. That's what I really came here to say. I wanted to thank you.' She turned again and opened the door.

'Wait,' he said. 'Don't go.'

Her stomach flipped and she stopped, turning back to face him, painfully aware of the way her hands were shaking and the fact she was only able to look at him in snatched glances. He flicked ash out of the window and leant forward on the bed to pick up the iPod. 'Did you like the music?'

'I loved it,' she said, grasping at his words with relief. 'I've never heard anything like it! The singer has an amazing voice.'

'*Had* an amazing voice,' Haydn said. He stubbed the cigarette out in an overflowing ashtray on his desk. 'He OD'd on happy tabs about thirty years ago.'

'Oh.'

'What kind of music do you listen to usually?'

'I don't, really.'

'Don't what?' he cried. 'Listen to music? What's on your iPod?'

She flushed.

'You *do* have an iPod?'

She didn't answer.

'You don't have one! Shit. Shit!' he laughed. 'Keep mine.'

'Keep it?'

Haydn nodded.

'I couldn't.'

'Why not? You need fucking music. I can't believe you don't have any music. How do you get through the day? Serious, have it.'

'It's yours, though.' Lizzie looked at the iPod through the prickle of tears. 'Thank you, but I really can't.'

Then he shrugged. 'Did you listen to the whole album?'

Lizzie nodded.

'What was your favourite track?'

'Um . . .' She wondered which was the one that should be her favourite.

'It's not a trick question,' he said, reading her mind. 'Just which one did you like the best?'

Of course she knew. It was the one he'd plugged her into when the world around her had crumbled into bedlam. 'The third one.'

'I like that one too.' Haydn reached for a guitar that was slotted between the bed and desk, sat back down on the bed and rested it on his knee. He looked just like a rock star. He began to play the tune she'd mentioned, very softly, slower than the original and not note-perfect, but mesmerizing. Lizzie was like a snake in a basket, hypnotized, spellbound. She thought of Anna up in this room, alone with him and his music, and wondered how often he used to play for her. If she'd been Anna she would have begged him to play to her every single day.

'Do you miss her?' she asked.

Haydn stopped playing, but didn't look up. 'No,' he said. 'Not any more.' He plucked a string and let the note sound to nothing. 'I think about her, though.' He closed his eyes and his face screwed up as if he was being cut into.

'I miss her,' she said.

Lizzie's voice echoed around the room, ringing in her ears, and she realized that even though she'd thought those words every day since Anna died, it was the first time she'd heard them aloud.

Thankfully, he began to play again, and this time he sang too. His voice was thinner than the other man's, with less resonance, but to Lizzie it seemed as if the lyrics were Haydn's own, his private thoughts for only her to know, and as the room filled up with Haydn's music, for the second time so did Lizzie. For what happened next she could only blame the man who'd written Haydn's song. He had clearly been a magician of some sort, and with his extraordinary powers he reached out long fingers that stretched through the decades and from beyond the grave to grab hold of her and drag her to the boy who played the heavenly tune on the edge of his bed. He made her kneel. It was he who put her hand on the strings to stop the music, and when the boy looked at her, he who made her lean in to kiss him, and, when the boy drew back in surprise, it was he who made her pull him in to kiss her again.

Eleven o'Clock Coffee

'It's after eleven. Would you like your cup of coffee?'

She hadn't heard him come into the kitchen. She was absorbed with watching next-door's cat asleep in the sun on the roof of their lean-to conservatory. It was a tabby mog, old and thin, with dusty fur that stuck up in all directions, but she thought it couldn't look happier curled on the roof up in the warmth with nothing to disturb it.

Kate wondered then, before Jon came in, if maybe the cat was actually dead. It was so still. So peaceful. Maybe it had passed away in its sleep. Its family would be sad, of course. She heard them calling it to bed every night. Always an excited greeting when it trotted out of the shadows and scooted into their kitchen, a *hello poppet, caught any mousies tonight,* or something similar. But when they called that night he wouldn't appear. The man might drive the streets, peering out of the car windows, desperate to return home with their pet, desperate to wipe the anxious look from his wife's face. In bed they'd worry about telling the children. Then, the next day, or the day after that, one of them might spy him on the conservatory roof, curled up, cold and stiff, and after they'd buried it they'd cry for a day or two, and every now and then after that they'd feel sad, but other than those occasional times, life would carry on as normal.

Kate sighed; she hated how much she thought about death. She hated how even looking at a contented sleeping animal would spark morbid thoughts inside her. Black thoughts, from anything. She didn't want to think like that but there was nothing she could do about it; she was an addict, morbidity her drug.

'Kate?' Jon said, breaking into her thoughts. 'Would you like a coffee?'

She turned away from the cat and looked at the clock. It was two minutes past eleven.

'Thank you,' she said. 'That would be nice.'

Two teas. One at seven. The next at nine thirty. Then, some-time in the hour between eleven and twelve – not a minute before eleven – she'd have her cup of coffee. Milk and half a sugar. White mug. Another tea at four thirty. A black decaff at six. The same at ten. This happened every day.

Before Anna died she frowned on routine. Routine was an afflic-tion of the uptight. Kate was fluid and spontaneous, chaotic, with double-figure late marks in the school register. Kate booked holi-days two days before they went, she ran out of milk, she conjured impromptu suppers for friends who only popped in to say hello.

'Stay for supper.'

'Are you sure?'

'Of course!' Laughing as she cracked open a bottle of wine. 'We'd love you to join us.'

'But we only popped in to say hello.'

'Well, now you're staying for supper!'

But since Anna, she found routine helped; it was routine that got her through the onslaught of dark days and nights that threat-ened to stretch out for ever in front of her.

Jon put the mug on the table in front of her. He rubbed her shoulder. She leant against him and closed her eyes.

'I'm sorry, Jon,' she whispered, wincing again at the memory of Rebecca in the playground.

'Sshhh.' He gripped her shoulder briefly.

'What's happened to me?'

He placed his own mug down and pulled a chair beside her. He laid a hand on hers.

'Your daughter died.'

Kate took a sip of too-hot coffee and burnt the tip of her tongue. She sipped again.

'I tried to go to the supermarket today,' she said. 'But I couldn't get out of the car. I couldn't stop thinking about what I did to Rebecca and trying to work out how I became this awful person.'

Kate circled her finger around the rim of the mug. Jon didn't say anything but she knew he was waiting for her to continue. He wouldn't interrupt her. Jon believed talking was therapeutic. He was always telling her she needed to paint less and talk more.

'I looked up,' she went on, 'and something caught my eye out of the windscreen. It was a key, just hanging there on one of those posts beside the walkway, on a red cord.' She rubbed her face and took a steadying breath. 'First, I wondered what it was for. A house or a bike, maybe. And then I thought of the poor person who had lost the key and couldn't get into her house, especially if she had things for the freezer that were melting. But then it dawned on me that the key was meant for me, that I was supposed to find it – someone had put it there for me to find – and that it was a magic key to a different world, like a portal or something.'

She searched his face for signs of boredom or confusion. But he was staring right at her, his eyes soft, understanding.

'I imagined,' she said, as she fixed her eyes back on the cup of coffee in front of her, 'that whoever had left it wanted me to get out of the car, take the key, find the lock and go into the other world. And while I was thinking this I saw the world.' Her eyes filled with tears that misted her mug out of sight. 'It was beautiful, really beautiful. It was like this one, only brighter and sharper and all the sounds were crisper and the smells sweeter and I felt at home. I closed my eyes and breathed it all in. And then I heard her voice, Jon. It was Anna. She was there. Alive.' She looked at him, but his face was lowered. 'I got out of the car.' She breathed deeply. 'And I took the key.' She breathed again. 'And then, oh my God,' she groaned quietly, covering her face with her hands. 'What's wrong with me . . . then I looked for the lock.'

'It's OK,' said Jon, touching her knee. 'It's fine that you did that.'

She began to shake her head. 'No! It's not fine. I searched for it for *over an hour*. Every nook and cranny in the brick walls, the tarmac, the recycling bins. Everywhere. I'm crazy, aren't I? I must be.' Kate remembered how the key had dug into her hands as she'd clutched it so tightly. The rising panic in her stomach as she realized she wasn't going to find the lock. The desolation she felt as she collapsed against her car emotionally spent, exhausted. 'I'm scared, Jon. I'm just so scared.'

Then she felt him. He leant forward, kissed each of her hands, so gently. He eased them back from her face and kissed each of her cheeks, then her lips. They stared at each other. His eyes told her he understood, about the key and the hidden lock and the parallel world where Anna played in the sunshine. He didn't think she was mad. And he loved her.

She needed him suddenly, her body aching to be close to his. She pulled him towards her and kissed him. It felt so good to kiss him, his lips, his softness, the way their mouths fitted, the familiarity of him. Then she felt his lust fire with a sudden desperation. His hand went behind her head. His fingers buried into her hair. He stood her up. Pulled her into him. Pushed himself against her.

She responded, kissed him back. His hand went under her shirt, fingers splayed across her chest and collarbone. He nuzzled his face into her neck and whispered words she couldn't hear. She threw her head back, indulging the desire that coursed through her veins. It felt good, right and comfortable, to want her husband, the man she'd loved for twenty years.

'Let's go upstairs.' His gravelly words shattered the spell and she remembered Anna with a thud that took her breath. The moment was gone like smoke in the wind. What kind of monster was she? How could she forget? Self-loathing and disgust erupted inside her. Suddenly and aggressively, she pushed him away. She felt faint and cold. Her hands shook.

'No!'

She couldn't look at him. He grabbed at her and dragged her back into his arms.

'Kate,' he moaned. 'Please stay with me.'

'Let go of me.'

He reached for her again, but she jumped backwards out of his way.

'I love you, Kate. Please, come here.' He moved to kiss her again, but again she stepped back. She straightened her jumper. Ran her hands over her hair and breathed slowly to calm her heart that raced with the remnants of her lust. He didn't move, shoulders hunched, hands hanging loose at his sides. Her heart spasmed. She wanted to take him in her arms. She wanted to hold his head against her chest, reassure him, show him, somehow, how much she loved him.

'How can I?' she whispered.

He was silent.

'How can I do that?'

'You're allowed to love me. You're allowed to make love to me,' he said. 'We're allowed to feel some happiness.'

'No,' she said. 'I'm not allowed to be happy again. How can I be?'

Everything has changed, she thought, *why don't you understand that?* But his body, his sadness, the defeat in his shoulders, told her he never would. He wanted to pretend nothing was different, as if Anna was upstairs listening to music or reading a magazine, or chatting to a friend on her phone. Her guilt and sorrow hardened into anger.

'Don't look at me like that!'

He opened his mouth, but then shook his head and closed it again.

'What!' she said. 'Speak, for God's sake. Tell me you understand what I'm saying!'

'You're letting her death kill our family,' he said then. His words stung and tears spiked. 'It's suffocating us.'

'And you'd like to carry on as normal?'

'No. No, that's not what I want.' He sat down at the table and stared at the wall. 'I know our lives will never be normal again, whatever the hell normal is.' His voice was flat. 'I just wish you wanted to fight for us. I need you. Lizzie needs you; she needs her mother. I need my wife. We're desperate without you.'

She stared at him. Hating him, not for voicing such a hideous truth, but for expecting anything else of her; when Anna died she took her mother's soul, and the empty shell standing beside him was all that was left.

'I'm sorry if that's how you feel, but this is the best I've got. Most of the time I want to curl up and die, but I don't, and that's *only* because of Lizzie and you. But life won't be the same. It can't be.' She stared at him, waiting for him to speak. He didn't. She clenched her fists and walked away from him. She paused at the kitchen door.

'Please don't touch me like that again.'

Untouched Croissants

'Thank you for coming to meet me,' Jon said, standing as Rachel approached.

She took off her jacket and sat at the table without meeting his eyes. 'If you mention dropping the charges against Kate I'm afraid I'll have to leave.'

He was taken aback by the harshness of her clearly rehearsed words that was so unlike the Rachel he knew. 'That wasn't my intention,' he said.

'So what was?' she asked. 'It must have something to do with what's going on.'

Sitting opposite her, it was hard for him to remember the precise reason he had for wanting to meet up. In part it was to make him feel like he was actually doing something. Kate wasn't talking to him. Since they'd received the letter informing them of Rebecca's decision to press charges she'd completely withdrawn, painting a lot, mostly waiting until he was in bed before emerging from her studio. He listened to her creeping in, holding her breath as she slipped under the covers beside him, keeping herself as close to her edge of the bed as she could. Perhaps he wasn't being honest with Rachel when he said it wasn't his intention to mention the charges. He had certainly hoped to influence her by getting together, hoping to remind her how close she and Kate had been, hoping nostalgia might help prompt Rachel to question whether twelve stony strangers sitting in uninformed judgement on Kate was really what she wanted. His own memories of their friendship were acid sharp. All those evenings he arrived home, tired and stressed, to open the door on their glorious laughing. Then hushed giggling as they realized they'd let time slip. He'd poke his head into the kitchen and they'd both look shamefaced, barefoot on kitchen chairs with glasses of sov blonk in their hands. Rachel would make an apologetic excuse, while Kate got up, kissed him and opened the fridge to grab him a beer. Then he'd settle down and join them, listening quietly to their gossipy patter.

A waitress appeared and asked if Rachel was ready to order.

'I'd like a cup of tea, no milk, and a croissant, please.'

'That sounds good,' Jon said. 'I'll have a croissant, too.'

'Another coffee?'

Jon shook his head and the waitress thrust their scrawled order under the pepper mill.

Rachel watched her leave then looked back at Jon. 'Before you say whatever it is you need to say,' she said, 'I'd like to speak first.' She took a deep breath. 'I haven't said this to you before,' her voice trembling, 'but I'm sorry. I hope you know that. I'm sorry about Anna.'

'You have nothing to be sorry about.'

Jon meant it. Unlike Kate, he laid no blame at Rachel's feet. Anna stayed at Rebecca's a lot. She'd returned to them safe each time. Just not that last time, the night she told Rebecca she felt ill, pretended to be asleep – snoring, as Rebecca recalled – then snuck out to meet her boyfriend. He and Kate had stopped fighting over it. There was no reasoning with her. As far as his wife was concerned, Rachel was responsible for the welfare of her daughter while she was under her roof. He'd heard it over and over. It was her responsibility, Kate said. She was in charge of our daughter, and Anna died because she let her leave her house.

But Kate was blinkered. It wasn't that straightforward. Anna knew what she was doing. She wilfully deceived Rachel and she knew it was wrong. After all, she was fifteen, old enough to know to stay in bed in the house as Rachel expected her to.

'Anna would have ended up on that roof if she'd been with us, or with her grandparents, or with another friend. It wasn't—' Jon's voice cracked. 'It wasn't your fault and you have no reason to apologize.'

'That's not what Kate thinks.'

'Just forget what Kate thinks. Kate blames everybody. Christ, she even blames me. You know what for?' He paused, but Rachel didn't speak. 'For *looking* like Anna.' He shook his head with bitterness. 'She sees her in my face and every day it breaks her heart. But what can I do?' Jon paused to allow a wave of emotion to sweep through him. 'And Lizzie? Well, she sounds like her. Kate finds it difficult to talk to her because all she hears is Anna. Does she think Lizzie doesn't pick up on that? You'd have thought the kid had enough to deal with without her mother bursting into tears and rushing out of the room whenever she asks for cornflakes.'

Rachel reached out, hesitating before taking his hand. He stared at her speckled skin for a moment or two and then he pulled his hand away and laid it in his lap.

'I don't mind you talking,' she said. 'Even if you cry, it doesn't matter.' She paused. 'It must be so hard living with Kate in the state she's in.'

Jon looked out of the window and watched the cars stop-starting down the Fulham Palace Road as he let Rachel's words roll gently around his head. Was it hard living with Kate? Yes, he wanted to say, it was hard living with Kate in the state she's in. Too hard, sometimes, and he'd certainly thought about leaving. Not because he didn't love her, not even because he thought she didn't love him. It wasn't about love. It was about statistics, the paltry number of marriages that weathered the death of a child. And he understood how those marriages crumbled, because just as he was a constant reminder of Anna for Kate, so she was to him, because Kate might think she could see Anna in him, but the truth was that it was Kate who was so agonizingly like their eldest daughter, and so neither of them could escape it, waking up with each other every morning, getting into bed every night. Every look. Every sigh. Every slammed door. A constant bombardment of sickening aides-memoire. It was only natural to wonder whether it might be less cruel to put their marriage out of its misery. But just the notion of this made him sick with despair.

Yes, Rachel, he thought, *living with Kate is hard, but it's the thought of living without her that freezes my heart. Whatever state she's in.*

'It's kind of you to offer to talk,' he said. 'You know, most people don't want to. They don't know what to say, you see. You'd be amazed how many friends would sooner cross the road than say I'm sorry for your loss, or how are you doing? My first day back after the funeral was the worst.' He turned his cup slowly in the saucer. 'I walked into the office, desperate for a snip of normality, and was met with this pin-drop silence. People looked away, dialled pretend phone calls, rushed off to meetings. Nobody said a thing. There were some flowers on my desk with a card I didn't open.' He smiled at Rachel. 'Death is worse then leprosy for popularity.'

Rachel nodded. 'When Rob left I felt that. No telephone calls any more, no invites, half the number of Christmas cards.

110

I presumed they didn't know what to write. To Rachel, Happy Christmas, try not to think of your husband shagging the receptionist. Lots of love, kiss, kiss, kiss.' She paused and studied her thumbnail for a moment or two. 'Except you,' she said.

'Sorry?'

'You always treated me the same. I'll always be grateful for that.'

'You were a good friend.'

She dropped her head.

Jon was quiet, aware the past tense had stung her.

'I know I haven't been around for her, Jon. I know that. I mean, losing a daughter, God, I can't imagine. But . . .' She took a deep breath. 'Kate made it so difficult for me to do anything else. She closed herself off from me. I rang all the time, sometimes five or six times a day, but she put the phone down on me every time. She never called back.' Rachel shook her head. 'Maybe I should have tried harder. I don't know. She just made it so clear she wanted nothing to do with me. Quite honestly, it broke my heart. I felt so helpless. I knew how much pain she was in but I couldn't do anything. For the first time in fifteen years she was going through something without me. All I wanted to do was hug her, to help you all, to help Lizzie. I've never felt so alone, even more than when Rob went. Those weeks after Anna died are some of my blackest.' She paused. 'And I went over it all. Again and again. Wondering what I should have done to stop it, filling my head with what ifs: what if I'd Chubbed the front door and hung the key in the cupboard, what if I'd heard her, what if Rebecca had been awake?'

Jon saw her eyes had filled with tears and handed her a paper napkin.

'We all have the what ifs,' he said. 'Nobody has more of them than Kate, believe me. She doesn't blame you any more than she blames herself. She just seems to need things to focus her sadness on. She's,' he paused to choose his word, 'struggling.'

Rachel pressed the corner of the napkin against both eyes and nodded in agreement that Kate was struggling. Jon was suddenly struck, feeling duplicitous. Kate would hate him using that word to describe her. Kate didn't struggle. She was a fighter, feisty and independent. Traits that had bewitched him all those years ago, but traits that had been altered by Anna's death, pushed off track and shifted in their line of trajectory. Feisty had become volatile rather than spirited. Independent was no longer unfettered but solitary, and though she was still a fighter, her fight was all taken up with just making it through to the end of each day.

'I can't forgive her for what she did to Bec. I have nightmares about it, horrible dreams in which Kate doesn't stop, but keeps on hitting until she kills her.'

They were quiet then, both staring at the croissants that sat untouched on the small white plates in front of them. Jon knew their meeting was over.

'Thank you for coming to see me today,' he said. He took the bill out from beneath the pepper mill, then pulled a five-pound note and two pound coins from his wallet and put them in one of the saucers. 'Please send my best wishes to Rebecca.'

Rachel dropped her head. 'Thank you for breakfast,' she said.

He stood, but as he did he had a flash of Lizzie's face. What on earth would she do if her mother was sent to prison? How would she cope? It would finish her.

'I know what she did to Rebecca is incomprehensible and I would never expect you to forgive her, but please, Rachel, if you can, put yourself in her shoes. That's all I'm asking. I know you've been hurt; I know she behaved dreadfully. But please think of what she's been through.'

Rachel lifted her head and he saw anger in her eyes. 'You think I don't do that? Of course I do! I put myself in her wretched shoes all the time. I loved Anna. I watched her grow up from a baby. Every day I thank Heaven I still have Rebecca, because God only knows how a mother copes with losing her child. But she attacked my daughter. An innocent child. You're right, what she did was unforgivable; I'm not a strong enough person to forgive it.' She sighed and rubbed her face with both her hands. 'Look, I told Rebecca it was up to her. I don't want to influence her either way, but,' she hesitated. 'But if it were up to me, Kate would be sectioned.'

Jon's head began to pound. 'She'll come through this,' he said. 'She will.'

'It's too late, Jon. She needs help.'

I'm trying! screamed Jon in his head. *God help me, I'm doing everything in my power to try and help her.*

Rachel stood and put her jacket on, then she patted his hand. 'I should go,' she said, gently. She waited at the table as if trawling her head for something else to say, but they both knew there was nothing. When she left, he turned to look out of the window again. There was a child right outside howling inconsolably, red in the face with livid tears streaming down his cheeks, his mouth circled in chocolate. His young mother, another baby in a pram beside her, looked fraught. Jon watched her duck briefly out of sight below the window. She reappeared, and in her hand was a dropped ice-cream. For a second the child stopped screaming and watched intently as his mother tried to flick bits of whatever off what was left of the ice-cream in the cone. Then she shook her head and threw it back on the ground. Her son started screaming again. She bent down and tried to talk to him. Jon wondered if she was promising another treat or threatening bed or counting to five for the crying to stop before she got really, really angry. Then she stood, glanced down at the child and raised her eyes to the sky, before grabbing hold of him with one hand, taking the pram in the other and starting off, the little boy kicking and fighting and pointing back at the ice-cream in the gutter.

Jon stood to leave.

'Do you want me to pop those croissants in a bag?'

Jon looked back at the table and then at the waitress.

'That's kind of you,' he said.

The waitress smiled and then took the two plates to the serving counter. Jon left before she returned.

Haydn the Eco Hero

It was hot. Sticky hot. Lizzie wore a long-sleeved cotton shirt, a skirt that reached her ankles and flip-flops. Her bag of allergy meds was, as usual, hung over her shoulder. It was Haydn who suggested the swings in the park. She'd agreed, terrified he'd think she was some kind of pathetic loony if she told him she felt uneasy outdoors in June, July and August. She held her bag like a security blanket and repeated over and over that there was nothing to worry about. The bees weren't out to get her. She was completely fine.

As she neared the playground gate the bees fell out of her mind and Haydn stepped into their place, and quickly her fear was replaced with frantic nerves. She'd thought about this meeting almost continuously since they'd arranged it, self-conscious and full of happy jitters, soon after their kiss on his bed. She hid herself behind a tree, peering around it to watch for him. She couldn't be the first to arrive. That would make her look desperate, not to mention put her at risk of being stood up, and though she'd experimented a hundred different ways to look nonchalant whilst she waited, she had yet to succeed. No, it was way better to stay hidden until after he arrived, then appear half-running and apologizing for being late. This would get three birds in one hit: she wouldn't look too keen, she'd be certain he was there and her apology would fill those first awkward minutes, the spectre of which loomed over her in all its stilted hideousness.

Everything clenched when she finally saw him.

She tucked herself tighter into the tree and watched him open the gate to the playground. He was too amazing for words! His slight swagger, the way he had his hands in his pockets, so cool, so confident. One earphone was in his ear, the other trailed over his shoulder. She felt a shiver of excitement as she remembered the way his lips had felt and tasted, all soft and smoky.

He sat on a swing and kicked himself back and forth while he reached into his jacket pocket for tobacco and papers. Her pulse hammered. She watched as a woman eyed him warily before pulling her son off the next-door swing, her arm protectively around the small boy, her eyes fixed on Haydn as she hurried them away. Lizzie was confused; the only thing that looked the tiniest bit scary was the top-to-toe black, and perhaps the fact his hair obscured his face, and, maybe, the convict-style smoking. It was a book-and-cover thing; if the lady knew what Haydn had done for her at the memorial or how gently he stroked the back of his fingers down her cheek after they'd kissed, she'd *never* have run away.

Lizzie smoothed her hands over her hair to calm the static, pinched her cheeks like they used to do instead of blusher, took a deep breath, then sidestepped out from behind the tree and ambled casually – she hoped – concentrating on each step as she tried to keep her pounding heart in check.

'Hey,' he said.

'Oh, hi!' she said, with feigned surprise.

'Y'OK?'

'Uh-huh.' She tried looking at him, but found it scrambled the monosyllables in her head, so she fixed her eyes on the church steeple that peeped over the trees that surrounded the park. 'You?'

'Yup.'

Lizzie perched herself on the vacant swing next to his and was immediately overwhelmed with dread. It was the painful silence; she'd forgotten all about the apology for being late, and now they were firmly wedged in the gloopy quiet she'd feared. He squashed his cigarette into the bark chips at their feet. Lizzie glanced at the mother who'd hurried her son away. The woman glared at her, which made Lizzie feel like poking her tongue out.

'So,' he said. 'What do you want to do?'

'Whatever you want is fine,' she mumbled.

Then he laughed, and Lizzie's cheeks flushed hot.

'Look, I'll be in charge today,' he said. 'There's somewhere I'd like to take you.' He jumped off the swing. 'You do next time.'

Next time.

A warmth spread through her and she allowed herself a fleeting smile. 'OK,' she said. 'I'll do next time.'

'Cool. The tube then.'

Talk was stilted as they walked, and Lizzie's heart quickly sank. She found it impossible to think of anything to say. She fired a couple of mundane questions into the quiet, but the single-word answers that came back only intensified the ugliness. When she mentioned the weather he didn't even acknowledge it. Of course, to make matters worse, everywhere she looked people were chatting – bustling cafés had set up on the sunny pavements, work colleagues shared cigarettes and gossip outside their offices, mums with barefoot babies nattered at the bus stop – all of them ramming her inadequacy down her throat with their relaxed and easy ways. Becoming desperate, she ventured music. It was a risk as they both knew she knew nothing about music, but at least it was interesting to him. Though it worked to a point, what resulted couldn't really be called a conversation. While Haydn talked, Lizzie could only contribute bland nods. What he was saying was gobbledegook. It was useless, and only a matter of hours before he realized they were as compatible as ice and fire. When he mentioned someone she'd heard of, Chris Isaak, Lizzie almost said something, but the words got jammed by the pressure. And what would she say anyway? Oh, yeah, I know his name, he did that song, you know, the one Anna played me that time. She hung her head and followed him down the station steps. They didn't say another word for the rest of the tube journey, and with each second of silence she cringed a little more. It wasn't until she'd followed him off the tube, up the escalator, crossed to the overground platform and then stepped on to the train, that she managed to ask him where they were going.

'Dalston,' he said as he scrolled on his iPod.

She hadn't even heard of it. If she could have spoken she would have suggested he carry on alone. This was a terrible mistake. She never should have kissed him. What a stupid thing to do! No thought for the consequences. It was so unlike her. She stared blindly at the adverts on the platform billboards of the stations they passed, hating herself for imagining this could work.

Finally, Haydn stood and moved to the doors. 'Come on then.'

Dalston station was decorated with splashes of graffiti and rubbish that lay in the sun like washed-up flotsam. Lizzie began to panic as she thought of her mum, who would have hated her in this part of London, what with all the guns and knives and terrorists blowing stuff up without warning.

'You all right?' Haydn asked. 'You look tight.'

'I'm fine,' she said. 'It's just, well, I haven't been here before.'

Then he reached for her hand. His fingers laced through hers. His thumb grazed the length of hers. Her stomach turned over and her pulse quickened. His grip was a shot of hallucinogen. When his thumb stroked her again she had to bite her tongue to stop herself shouting out in joy. Where his skin met hers she tingled, as if energy flowed between them, all her previous worry forgotten. The sun was warm on her face, she was floating, her feet dancing clear of the dirty pavement. She felt like laughing, not just happy, but ecstatic. She started to look around her – the colours had turned celluloid, the strange noises were sounding like music. Even the smell of the place – ripe fruit, old rubbish, cooking smells, musty sweat – was intoxicating. She took three deep breaths and enjoyed the feeling of her body relaxing.

As they walked, she noticed how many different places to eat there were. On just one side of the road they passed Turkish, Indian, Bangladeshi, Kurdish, Italian, Polish. Reggae boomed out of a parked car that overspilled with young men laughing and talking with West Indian accents so thick she couldn't make out the words. They passed a mosque, an Orthodox church and a man with sandwich boards who told her that without Jesus she'd burn for eternity. A rainbow of people flowed past them. Some laughed, others ambled or strode, some looked sad or angry while many seemed to drift along without purpose. A few sat in doorways with grubby sleeping bags draped over their knees, loosely holding misspelled pleas for help on torn bits of cardboard.

'I like Chris Isaak's music,' she said, suddenly.

'Really?' said Haydn, squeezing her hand tighter as he pulled her through a crowd of gathered people.

'Yeah, he sang one of Anna's favourite songs.'

Haydn smiled at her. '"Wicked Game".'

'She loved that song.'

'It was Anna who told me about him. I thought he was a bit of a prick, but then she played me this song.' He looked at her. '"Two Hearts"?'

'From *True Romance*.'

'Yeah! That's right!' He grinned. 'And she said I should watch the film and listen for the song, and then tell me if I thought he was still a prick.'

'She loved that film. She tried to make me call her Alabama for a couple of days, but I kept forgetting,' said Lizzie. She smiled, remembering watching it with Anna like it was yesterday. Someone had given it to her at school. It was an eighteen certificate, a pirate copy. Lizzie wasn't sure about it.

'Listen to your evil big sister,' said Anna, with a naughty lift of her eyebrows. 'You'll *love* it.'

They snuggled under a duvet in the dark, eating microwave popcorn and falling in love with Christian Slater. Lizzie recalled the worry she'd felt when any violence or sex came on to the screen. She'd pull the duvet up to her nose and cross her fingers, praying and praying their parents didn't walk in.

'You like it too?'

Lizzie nodded. 'That's one of the only similar things about us. We loved the same films.'

'And your voice.'

'Sorry?' Lizzie asked.

'Your voice. You have the same voice as Anna. Exactly.'

'I've heard that so many times,' she said. 'Lots at her funeral.'

'Really?'

'Uh-huh. When people ran out of the normal things to say, like "you must be so upset", and "what a shock for us all" or whatever. There'd be this awful silence and they'd mention our voices.' She smiled at him to break the tension that talk of her funeral had brought.

'It is weird though,' he went on. 'When you came to my house. I heard you from upstairs, and like, it could have been her.'

'It sounds different to me.'

'It would, wouldn't it? I mean, your own voice always sounds different in your own head, like when you hear yourself on a phone message or something. But to other people you sound exactly the same.'

'Weird,' she said.

'Yeah, really weird.'

'So,' she said, keen to change the subject. 'Where are we going?'

'Nearly there.'

They turned into Stoke Newington High Street. Almost instantly the faces began to whiten, the rubbish lessened and the discount stores and pound shops gave way to old-fashioned toy-shops and organic bakeries; Lizzie felt a pang of disappointment.

Haydn stopped walking, flourished a bow, then opened his arm in the direction of some imposing iron gates.

'Velcome,' he said, in Draculesque.

Lizzie didn't understand, and looked from the gates to him then back again. 'A cemetery?'

He gave a cartoon evil laugh. 'Don't you know zat all ze girlz love ze place of ze dead?' He raised an eyebrow. 'Ladiez virst.'

Lizzie peered through the gates at a couple of lopsided grave-stones.

'So? What are you waiting for?' He took her hand and pulled her after him. 'You'll love it. I promise.'

Within minutes her doubts had vanished. The cemetery was beautiful, the most unusual place she'd ever been. She even forgot about the dead people everywhere. It was like a spell had been cast. The noise from the street was lost behind towering yew, ivy crept in thick blankets over hunks of carved marble and birds sang. It was an enchanted forest. As they walked down an avenue of trees dappled in sunlight, hand in hand in a silence that was comfortable now, she gazed around and drew as much of the magic into her as she could.

'It's amazing,' she whispered. 'It reminds me of Anna.'

'How?' he asked.

'Like I imagine her now. Serene and at peace. I can see her asleep in her coffin; her face is like this, undisturbed, beautiful and sort of other-worldly.'

Lizzie thought then of her mum. Of how she'd lost it at the funeral. She saw Anna's alabaster face stir, her eyes flick wide open, riven with horror as her mother raged. Lizzie shivered.

Haydn stopped walking and pulled her towards him. He kissed her on the lips. If their first kiss was a ten out of ten, this second one was off the scale. Intense and gentle, her heart pounding, a moment of fear as his mouth opened and she panicked that his tongue would make the kiss awful. It didn't. It was better. She did the same, and soon it felt like this was what she'd been born to do, to kiss Haydn. He was the one. She knew it. She pushed her fingers into his hair, loving its softness, its unfamiliarity.

'I could do this for ever,' she murmured.

'Me too,' he said, between kisses. 'I think you're amazing.'

This was her best day ever. 'Come on,' she said, taking hold of his hand. 'Show me more.'

Every step threw her something else. There were stone piers with eagles perched ready to take off, praying angels gazing heavenwards, gleaming marble headstones, then ones so weathered they might be mistaken for odd-shaped rocks. There were flat graves with broken slabs that made Lizzie wonder if the souls within had forced their way out to wander the earth for eternity.

'It's like something out of a fairytale,' she said. 'How did you find it?'

'My grandad. He was from round here. He taught me all its history, showed me his favourite graves and stuff. You'd never know, but it's one of the most important wildlife areas in London.

Anyway, when he died a few years ago, I came back, you know, to remember him and that. And, well, now I volunteer here every week.'

'Volunteer?'

'Clear weeds, tidy the paths, help count the animals. It helps keep my mind off stuff.'

'What stuff?'

'The dark stuff. The things I shouldn't think about. Things about Anna, what I should have said or done. Wishing her back. Wondering what life would be like if she hadn't died.' His voice was quiet, but over the stillness Lizzie heard every syllable, every breath between, every heartbeat beneath.

It was the same in her own head. The thoughts she tried to stop. Useless, waste-of-time thoughts that could eat up hours and hours of the day. Her what-if thoughts, she called them.

'How often do you come here?'

'Most weekends. I'd come after college too, if it was closer, but by the time I get here they're ready to lock the gates. I've done the morning chorus a couple of times.'

'The what?'

'It's a walk. People come at dawn to listen to the birds. There are loads of different breeds nesting here. Butterflies too. It's got the largest population of Speckled Woods in inner London. And,' he went on – his enthusiasm bordering on the divine to Lizzie – 'it was the first European cemetery that would bury anyone, however poor they were, and there were no special closed-off areas for different religions, and there was nothing official to say it was a burial ground. It was just a beautiful place where anybody could end up.' He stopped speaking suddenly and looked at her. His face fell. 'God, I'm boring you, aren't I?'

'No, no. Gosh, no.' said Lizzie, horrified that he might really think that. 'You're the least boring person I've ever met, and I *love* it here. I love places like this. It's like these woods we used to go to when me and Anna were little. It'd be a treat, you know, on a Sunday afternoon or whatever, with lunch in a pub or fish and chips in the car, and then this long walk, kicking through leaves. I used to imagine there were fairies there, and sometimes I'd write these silly notes for them in the morning before we left and leave them in places I thought they would go. And we'd pretend we were fairies too.' Lizzie picked off the tip of a low-hanging branch and twirled it between her fingers. 'Anna would always be the fairy princess, of course, and make me be the evil goblin trying to capture her. I wanted to be the fairy princess, but she'd never let me. I used to get so upset.' Lizzie smiled at Haydn and dropped the piece of twig. 'Silly, huh?'

'Not at all.' His eyes stared at her so intently she tingled all over.

They walked the sylvan paths for over two hours, Haydn smoking and doing most of the talking, Lizzie holding his hand and listening. It was perfect. No bees, no parents, no sadness, just the heat of the sun and the feel of someone else's skin on hers.

They stopped at a ruined chapel, all broken windows and rotten wood and signs suggesting they keep out for their own safety. They crept through a gap in the chained gates and surprised a group of dozing pigeons that complained loudly as they flapped off their rafters. Then they kissed for ages. When Lizzie slid her hands underneath his holey cardigan, a flash of heat shot through her as she felt the hardness of his chest through his T-shirt. She breathed him in. Closed her eyes. Lingered over the feel of his hand on the back of her head. She thought about every movement, her tongue, his tongue, the way their heads moved, the way their kiss grew between them.

And then there was buzzing.

She stopped both kissing and breathing to concentrate. She willed the buzz to be in her head, but she knew it wasn't. The thing was real. She pulled away from him and scanned around her for the wasp or bee. Her hand flew automatically to her bag.

'What's wrong?' he asked, dragging the back of his hand across his wet mouth.

She shook her head and chewed on her lip, desperate not to look as scared as she was.

'You've gone white.'

'It's nothing,' she said, grasping her bag even tighter. She searched around them, still hearing the buzzing, louder then softer, as if it were circling her. 'It's, um, it's just. I—'

Then the wasp landed on her shoulder and she screamed.

'It's just a wasp. Keep still.'

'I can't!' Lizzie ducked and ran, but the wasp followed. She started crying and beating her hands.

'Stay still!' Haydn's voice – strong and unruffled – stopped her in her tracks. 'Let it settle.'

She held her breath and waited, trying to stop tears spilling out of her eyes. Why did they go for her? It was as if she gave off some irresistible pheromone. Even in the concrete of the chapel, with no flowers and no jam, they still knew where she was.

Then, out of the blue, and making her jump, Haydn clapped his hands together. The sound echoed around them, setting the disgruntled pigeons squawking again.

'Got it,' he said. He looked down and trod his foot into the ground.

'Got what?'

'The wasp.'

'You *got* the wasp?'

He bent down. When he stood, she saw he held the curled-up corpse of the wasp by its wing.

'You killed it with your hands?'

'You have to do it quick.'

'With your bare hands?' Lizzie looked in wonder at Haydn. He didn't seem the tiniest bit flustered or pleased with himself. 'It didn't sting me.'

'That's the most incredible thing I've ever seen!' And in the clap of hands, Superdad was no more.

'You shouldn't get so freaked out by them,' he said.

'I know, but,' she paused, 'I'm sort of allergic.'

'Oh. I didn't know.' He paused. 'Badly?'

'They can kill me.' She lifted her bag. 'It's why I carry this. It's got adrenalin in it.'

'You should have told me.'

She shrugged. 'I'm not that good at talking when they're near me.'

Haydn chucked the wasp on to the floor. 'How about we get some food?'

Lizzie nervously eyed the wasp in case of resurrection. 'That sounds good. I'm really hungry.'

'What do you want?'

'I thought you were in charge of today.'

He smiled. 'I'm being polite. What do you fancy?'

'Burger?'

He shook his head. 'No beef.'

'You're vegetarian?'

'Nope. I eat lamb, chicken, and fish fingers and that. Just not beef.'

'How come?'

'It's the farting.'

Lizzie's explosion of laughter blew the memory of the wasp stratospheric.

'It's not a laughing matter. Their farts are melting Antarctica, man. Cows are drowning the world.'

'You mean the methane build-up?'

He nodded, his face deadly serious. 'If we didn't eat beef, you know, we'd save the polar bears.'

Lizzie giggled. 'I'm sure if you boycotted long-haul flights and Kenyan runner beans you'd be able to have a burger every now and then.'

'No,' he said. 'It's the farting cows. Dodo time. They gotta go.'

Then he pulled Lizzie towards him and draped an arm over her shoulder, and kissed her nose. 'Let's get pizza.'

It was all she could do to stop herself scaling the rafters and singing out from the rooftop.

What Rebecca Saw

Kate's heart leapt into her mouth when she answered the door.

'You can't be here.'

Rebecca looked at the floor and shuffled her feet. 'I need to talk to you,' she mumbled.

Kate checked over her shoulder, then up and down the street, and rubbed a hand across her mouth. 'You can't,' she said. 'Look, Rebecca, you have to go home. Call your mum and get her to pick you up. I'm not allowed to see you.'

'I thought you wanted to talk to me.'

'I do. I did . . . but, no, Rebecca, you have to go.'

Kate was panicking. The policeman who'd interviewed her made it clear. She was to keep away from Rebecca. If she didn't, if she tried to make contact, or was seen to be influencing the girl in any way, her situation could get an awful lot worse. She shuddered as she recalled his lack of surprise when he'd interviewed her. She'd expected him to look shocked, or even disappointed, but he'd obviously seen it all: friends shooting friends, ten-year-olds robbing booze shops, dads raping babies, middle-class mothers beating up other people's children at memorial services. There were no surprises left.

Rebecca pressed her chin into her chest and kicked at nothing on the doorstep. She looked scared and ill, like she hadn't slept for days. Part of Kate wanted to wrap her up in a hug, usher her inside and make her a hot drink. She wanted to tell her how sorry she was, hold her tightly until they both forgot what she'd done, then calmly listen to what she wanted to say. But then she heard the policeman's caution again. She was in serious trouble. She had to watch her step. This wasn't a joke.

'Rebecca, did you hear me?' Kate took a step backwards. 'I'm going to shut the door now.' Kate watched Rebecca, waiting, wondering, if she was going to speak before she closed the door. There was nothing. 'Rebecca. I'm going inside. You need to go home.'

Then Rebecca jolted into life. She lunged for the door and pushed against it. They stared at each other. Kate knew she should push her away, but whatever it was that Rebecca knew was right there, hovering beneath the surface of her eyes, goading Kate to shun common sense. Kate fought herself. She conjured Jon and Lizzie in her mind, hoping they would make her see sense.

'No,' she struggled. 'You have to go.'

But Rebecca grabbed hold of Kate's jumper and pulled her close. She leant her face against Kate's ear. 'You were right. I do know something. I know something about Anna,' she whispered.

Rebecca's hissed words were like an electric shock. There was a malevolence in her that suddenly scared Kate and she pulled back as if she'd been hurt, but Rebecca held on. Her eyes stared right into Kate's as if she were trying to burn holes in her. Then her face tore into a smirk. 'It's about her and Dr Howe.' She kept her gaze bolted to Kate and leant close, her eyes now round and wide. 'You want to hear, don't you? Well, I hope you're ready.' She paused. 'Anna and Dr Howe were *fucking*!'

'What did you say?'

'They were fucking. Like nasty, dirty rabbits,' she leered. Rebecca moved away a little, then raised her eyebrows and smiled like she'd handed Kate the largest present from beneath the tree.

'Get away from me.'

Rebecca fixed her eyes on Kate. Was that glee Kate saw?

'I said get away from me.'

'It was her idea, you know. She loved it!'

Kate was paralysed, as if she weren't inside her body any more, but floating somewhere nearby, impotent and numb.

She closed her eyes to block Rebecca out. She tried to steady herself. *Keep calm*, she told herself, *just get rid of her, then get to your studio.* She tried to think of how she would paint Anna. As a child, definitely. Eighteen months old, maybe? Yes, eighteen months old and riding the little yellow tractor that Jon's mother had retrieved from the loft. The tractor had been Jon's. Even after two and a half decades it was in immaculate condition. It was sunny and Anna giggled as she scooted round Kate's mind, her legs chubby and pink, tiny feet madly pushing herself along, her chestnut hair on fire in the brilliant light.

Kate opened her eyes.

'You're lying,' she said, calm and steady. 'And I want you to leave.'

The creepy smile fell off Rebecca's face. 'I'm not lying. He wasn't her first. You don't know. She thought it was hilarious you thought she was such a good girl. Such an angel. She laughed about it.'

Kate felt sick. She tried to bring baby Anna and the little yellow tractor back, but both had vanished. 'Go away.'

'Not until you say you believe me, that Anna was doing it with him.'

'Why do you keep saying that? I thought you were her friend.'

At this Rebecca's eyes filmed with tears and she looked away.

A laughing couple, arm in arm, walked down the pavement. They looked across at Kate as they passed and gave a convivial nod in unison.

'Don't move,' Kate growled.

She turned and went back into the house, moving mechanically, her head a jumble. She needed to hear Rebecca admit she was making it up, then Kate could tell her to go home and keep the hell away from her and her family.

Jon and Lizzie were chatting as they made supper in the kitchen. Kate grabbed the car keys from the bowl on the side.

'Going out?' Jon called after her.

'Yes,' she said, without turning back.

She knew she should tell Jon. Even take him with her. She could hear the voice in her head telling her she should pass this over. If talking to Rebecca on the doorstep was inadvisable, being alone in a car with her was plain moronic. Jon would be beyond angry. But there was nothing else she could do. She didn't want any other person, especially not Jon or Lizzie, to hear Rebecca's filthy lies. It would be like giving them poison. She wouldn't do it. They didn't need to have that image in their heads. She walked back down the hall, her heart racing so fast she could barely draw breath.

'I'm going to get ice-cream.'

'Great,' she heard Lizzie call. 'Cookies and cream, please!'

Kate closed the front door behind her and walked straight past Rebecca, who was hunched at the side of the path. 'Get in the car.'

Kate drove to the end of the road, turned the corner, then parked opposite the block of high-rise council flats, next to the wheelie bins and cardboard boxes that were forever piled up. She cut the engine. All she could hear was Rebecca's uneven breathing. She hated her right then. She thought of the history they shared. She and Rachel keeping each other sane in the mundane world of newborn babies, then the girls starting at the same nursery, then school. Listening to Anna nattering away to Rebecca behind the closed door of her room, wondering what on earth the two of them could possibly talk about for so many hours on end. Then all those times she'd driven the girl around, dropped her at the cinema, taken her shopping, welcomed her into her home, Christmas presents, birthday presents, hugs and kisses. Ignored her own prodding jealousy at how close Anna was to this monosyllabic girl.

Kate turned in her seat to face her.

'Right. Listen to me. I'm not interested in why you told me those awful lies about Anna. I don't know why you would want to hurt her. But if you ever talk about her like that again, or mention anything to her dad or sister, God help me for what I might do.' Kate hoped she sounded convincing.

'I'm not lying.' Rebecca spoke so quietly Kate could hardly hear her.

'Of course you're bloody lying,' Kate said, desperately fighting to keep her voice level.

Rebecca shook her head. Kate noticed she had begun to cry. 'I saw them,' she whispered. 'I saw them.'

'For goodness' sake! It's all in your head. You're making it up, to get back at Anna because you're jealous or something, because she had other friends and you didn't. Or maybe because of what I did to you. I don't know, whatever it is, you're making it up!'

Rebecca's crying turned to racking sobs that heaved her shoulders up and down. Kate stared at her. The anger, frustration and loathing raged inside her. She had flashes of the memorial, of Rebecca's eyes as she hit her, the acceptance in them, the admission that she deserved it. Kate gripped the leather seat and dug her fingers into it. She had to keep calm. She had to. She closed her eyes and breathed, the type of breathing she'd practised in her antenatal classes. In through her nose and out through her mouth, in through her nose and out through her mouth. Then, when she felt her vehemence fade, and though it was totally repulsive, she reached out and laid a hand on Rebecca's shoulder.

'I can see how upset you are. But these stories, about Anna, they won't help you.'

'She . . . made me . . .' she said between sobs. 'They were doing it and making so . . . much noise . . . I didn't want to . . . I didn't . . .'

Everything flared, pushing past Kate's flimsy barricades. 'Shut up!' she shouted. Rebecca recoiled against the passenger door. 'You bloody little cow! Get out of my car. Just get out of my car.' She leant over Rebecca, pulled on the door handle and shoved it open. 'Don't come anywhere near me again. You hear?'

Rebecca didn't move. They both sat still, both breathed heavily. Kate fixed her eyes on the windscreen and concentrated on deciphering the noises from the street. Rebecca pulled her bag on to her lap, but still didn't make a move to get out of the car. Kate saw her out of the corner of her eye; she was looking right at her. Kate turned her head and stared out of the side window. She heard rummaging. Rebecca was looking for something in her bag.

At last Rebecca unbuckled her seatbelt and got out of the car. Kate waited for the door to close, but it didn't.

'So you know,' Rebecca said. 'I'm not pressing charges. The man at the police station said that's what I needed to do to make sure you didn't get into trouble. I don't want you in trouble; my lip only hurt for a few hours anyway.' Then she threw something back into the car. 'And I'm not lying. There's videos.'

Kate watched Rebecca moving away down the street, clutching her bag against her chest, tucked close to the wall, shuffling along with her head bowed and back bent, like a homeless pensioner. Kate waited until she disappeared out of sight, then she glanced across at the passenger seat.

Lying on the grey leather upholstery was a pink mobile phone with cartoon stickers all over it.

The Horrors of Modern Technology

'What flavour did you get?' Jon called when he heard the front door.

Kate walked straight past the kitchen and disappeared upstairs. His heart sank. He turned to Lizzie and tried to smile. 'Maybe she's tired,' he said.

Lizzie nodded. The look on her face made his heart clench. Resignation, compassion, disappointment, covered thinly with a forbearance he recognized from his mother. It had to be almost impossible for Lizzie, what with Kate's emotional dips and plateaux, and his inability to make things any better, all this heaped on top of losing her only sibling. Lizzie's loss was badly overlooked, overshadowed by Kate's and even by his. Anna had brought so much light into their lives, but especially Lizzie's. Always making jokes, laughing, waltzing through life free-spirited, full of verve. In recent years, with Anna, Lizzie seemed to be finding the confidence to come out of herself. Then Anna was snatched away and Lizzie was plunged back into her shy and studious self. She relied on Anna, they all did, and with her gone it was as if their engine room had been destroyed. He could see how alone Lizzie was, and he wished he could make things lovely for her. He remembered the first time he held her, fresh out of Kate's body, wrapped in a scratchy hospital blanket. Anna was in his other arm gently batting her new sister with perfect podgy fingers. He promised them everything that day, a safe and happy world, tinted pink at every turn. But a terrible accident had taken one of those girls and left the other suffocating in the mess left behind. It wasn't the promise he'd whispered.

'I was rather looking forward to pudding,' he said.

'Don't worry,' Lizzie replied. 'There's tinned peaches. We'll have those. And I'll make some Bird's. We haven't had that for ages.'

He walked over to Lizzie and kissed her head.

He was surprised to find Kate in their bedroom. He expected her to be in her studio painting Anna with that frantic desperation that terrified him, convinced as he was that the behaviour was the outward manifestation of some morbid insanity. He had raised his concern once. It was five weeks after the funeral, and Kate had shocked him with her calm and reasoned response. She didn't shout or cry, she just explained in even tones that it helped, that painting had always been a form of self-help for her, ever since she was a child. She described the panic attacks that took her. Told him how painting eased them, and that it was her alternative to medication and, far from being detrimental, it was a positive vent for her grief until she eventually came to terms with Anna's death. But it had been over a year and Jon could see no sign of his wife coming to terms with anything. She was shutting herself away more and more. The painting wasn't working. If anything it was holding her back. She needed something else. Maybe Rachel's insinuations were right; maybe Kate needed a doctor, but he knew if he brought it up again, she wouldn't be reasoned, she'd be angry, defensive, like a wounded tiger. She'd shout, question his love and support, his patience. Then she'd say that painting was the only thing that helped her, and he would feel bleak with inadequacy.

He sat beside her on the edge of the bed and stared out of the window as she did.

'Did you forget the ice-cream?'

She didn't move.

'It doesn't matter. Lizzie's making custard. Would you like some?'

'I lied. I didn't go out for ice-cream. I was with Rebecca.'

Kate's voice was expressionless. Her eyes were fixed. She looked numb, just like she had after she'd lost it in the playground. Panic surged, and he gripped the bedstead.

'Please tell me you didn't do anything. You're not allowed anywhere near her. Kate, what did you do?'

'I didn't *do* anything.'

Jon breathed again.

'She's not pressing charges.'

'What?'

'Rebecca isn't going to press charges.'

'Oh, my God, Kate! That's fantastic news!' He sat next to her on the bed. 'So that's it? Nothing's going to happen to you? No charges, no courts, no nothing?'

Kate shook her head.

'Thank God! Thank God, thank God,' he said. He put his hands on his hips and blew against his fringe. Relief washed through him, flushing out the anxiety that had dogged him since the memorial. 'I've been so worried, Kate. I don't think I even knew how much until just now. Christ, the thought of you going to court, maybe even—'

He stopped short of *prison* and looked at his wife. He noticed, then, how pale her face was, pale with tight lips, body rigid like stone.

'What's wrong?' he asked. 'Aren't you relieved?'

137

Kate didn't look at him. She stretched out her hand and opened her fingers to reveal a phone. It wasn't hers. Jon assumed she meant him to take it, so he did.

'I need you to see if there are any films on it.'

'What?'

'She said there's proof.' Kate nodded at the mobile in his hand as if it smelt of shit. 'On that phone. I need you to look. She told me things about Anna. Lies.' Kate's voice began to drift away. 'I know she's lying . . . I need you to check.'

'What lies?' Jon didn't understand. 'What did Rebecca say? You shouldn't have talked to her . . . you know—'

Kate whipped her head round to look at him. 'Just look at the fucking video!'

Jon shook his head, beaten by Kate's temper. He didn't want a row, not with Lizzie waiting for him downstairs. He sighed and sat back down on the bed, this time on the corner, away from Kate, his back to her. He brought up the menu on the mobile and began to scroll through the videos. A few seconds of girls in school uniform pulling faces. A different girl laughing hysterically, tears rolling down her rounded cheeks. Then boys playing football.

'This is idiotic,' he said, stopping the football film and scrolling to the next. 'It's just films of kids mucking about at school. It's—' And then . . . 'Oh my God,' he breathed.

'What?' Kate was at his feet, on her knees, her face stricken. 'What is it? Please tell me it's not her. Please, Jon. I'm begging you. Please tell me it's not Anna.'

Jon didn't reply. He couldn't. His voice was strangled by what played out on the tiny screen. His throat tightened around his breath and his eyesight faltered. He wanted to throw the phone away, as far as he could, crush it, burn it, but at the same time he couldn't let go of it. There she was. Not dead. Alive. But not how he remembered her. He felt something – a knife? – ram into his stomach. Her skin was flawless and her body like a delicate lily, and there was a man. Could it be him? Swamping her. Thrusting himself into her fragility.

Jon watched in horror, the knife in his stomach twisting, slicing his insides to pieces. His hand uncurled and the mobile fell to the floor. He staggered out of the room towards the bathroom, away from the film and Kate's curdling moans, begging a God she'd never believed in to help her, her shivering, wretched, mother's body rocking.

He was sick, his stomach emptying with the revulsion. When he felt able to stand he splashed his face with cold water and walked back into their room. Kate was on the floor, kneeling, as if praying, staring at the mobile phone in her quivering hands, and her head shook with disbelief as the sounds of Stephen Howe having sex with their child dirtied the air around them.

A Borrowed Scarf

Lizzie's heart raced as she leapt up the stairs two at a time. Since she'd last seen him, the seconds had passed like hours. She hadn't been able to sleep the night before. It was worse than Christmas Eve. She still couldn't believe he'd killed a wasp with his bare hands! He was amazing!

She flung open her wardrobe and stared at the neatly hanging clothes inside. After a few minutes' staring she wondered why she hadn't noticed how dreadful her clothes were until this very minute. Not one thing screamed *wear me*; it all just hung there looking sheepish.

Twenty fraught minutes later her room lay scattered with every item she owned, discarded victims of a desperate frenzy. She stood amidst the aftermath in her bra and pants, despairing and chewing the corner of her thumbnail. What would Anna have worn? Again she searched the floor for signs of life. But there was nothing. She pictured Anna – she always looked great, easily chic, her clothes a stylish mix of fashion and individuality. Then she thought of those very clothes hanging unworn in the cupboard next door.

You can't, she told herself firmly. *You just can't.*

The other side of Lizzie tried to work out whether Anna would actually mind. She closed her eyes and conjured her there, sat her on the corner of the desk, and tried to imagine what she would say if she asked to borrow something for her special date.

Of course, thought this other side of Lizzie. *She would have grinned!*

She could see her, right there on the corner of her desk, grinning like the happiest Cheshire cat.

'Go for it,' she said. 'Raid away. It's not like I can wear them any more.'

Lizzie smiled at her. Then she glanced at her clock. Fifteen minutes until she was supposed to leave, and she still hadn't tamed her hair or put any make-up on.

She hesitated outside Anna's room, her hand hovering over the door handle. 'It's just clothes,' she whispered.

Anna's room was museum-quiet and as clean as a pin. Her mum went in there every other day to dust and polish. The alarm clock was kept to the right time, the spider plant on the window sill was watered and trimmed, she even opened and shut the curtains every morning and every night. Lizzie knew a psychiatrist would probably think it was wrong, but she liked that her mum did it. She wasn't sure she'd want Anna's things to be packed into boxes for Oxfam, her bed collapsed and the sheets folded in the airing cupboard. It seemed right to keep the room as Anna had it. It would feel like they had rubbed her out of their lives if they didn't. And anyway, Lizzie loved Anna's room; it was a peaceful, contemplative place, and if she ever felt that the little things were getting on top of her, like some of the nastier girls at school or exams, a few minutes sitting quietly on the floor in her sister's room absorbing the vibes always helped. In her room, nothing else mattered. How could anything matter as much as losing your sister? It helped with perspective. There were even times, when Lizzie was feeling especially lonely, that she climbed into Anna's bed and pulled the duvet right up to her chin and lay there until the pain in her stomach eased. But standing in front of the ward-robe about to steal, she didn't feel comforted. She felt treacherous. She chewed on the corner of her thumb. But then again, all those clothes, attracting moths, gathering dust, becoming musty . . .

Lizzie took a deep breath and opened the cupboard door. She stared at the clothes. Each item brought a violent flash of Anna wearing it like a slide show; each sweater, shirt, skirt, pair of trou-sers, threw up Anna at her in the garden, on the beach, on the sofa watching TV, shopping in Hammersmith on Christmas Eve.

Her eyes settled on the red and orange scarf. It was Anna's favourite and she wore it all the time. Lizzie remembered so clearly the small stab of envy at the casual swathe around her neck, the perfect length of scarf that hung each side, the loop exactly the right distance below her chin, just a simple striped Topshop scarf that belonged on the catwalk. Lizzie shook the memory away. 'Just choose something quickly,' she whispered out loud. Then she grabbed herself an outfit – a pair of combat-style black trousers, a grey T-shirt with a pop-arty picture of Elvis Presley and the striped scarf. She gazed at the neat row of shoes and boots. It seemed such a shame to be stuck with her grubby old trainers, but what else could she do? Her feet were still two sizes smaller than Anna's had been.

With the clothes clutched to her chest she shut the cupboard door, made sure the room was as she found it, then ducked back to her own bedroom and closed the door behind her. She changed, then checked her reflection.

As she did her stomach pitched.

She lifted her hand to block her face out of the reflection and there was Anna again, but this time standing right in front of her, her hand held up to mask her face.

Lizzie sat down on her bed, and pulled her knees tight into her chest. She was paralysed by guilt, a sudden all-consuming guilt about taking her clothes to meet Haydn. Anna's boyfriend. As she allowed the guilt to settle, it began to build in layers, guilt on top of guilt. Not just the clothes and Haydn, but guilt that she was alive, still able to dress up and have fun, the one who could kiss and laugh, who wasn't buried in a tacky brass urn in the unfriendly, characterless graveyard two and a half miles away.

When she finally felt able to move, she slowly turned her head and looked at the clock. She was late, but even so, she couldn't get up. She stared at the clock waiting for her strength to return. Eventually, she pushed herself upright and swung her legs on to the floor. She took a few full breaths, then stood, allowing her head to settle. She took her long winter coat out of her cupboard and started to button it up. Two buttons done, she hesitated. Would her mother think it strange she was wearing a heavy coat in this weather? Would she make her take it off? Then see her wearing Anna's clothes? Lizzie shuddered at the thought. She buttoned it all the way to her chin; she'd blag it, blame it on a slight chill or something.

When Lizzie poked her head around the kitchen door, her mum was staring out of the window. She held a carrot and a potato peeler loosely in her hands.

'I'm going to the library,' Lizzie said. 'I'll be back after lunch.'

Her mum turned and Lizzie saw she was crying again; she didn't need to worry about her noticing the coat, at least.

'You can't.' Flat, uncompromising, a voice that offered no option.

'What?' Lizzie's tummy started to fizz. 'I've got a project to hand in, and the information I need is in the library.'

'But you've finished your exams.'

'Well,' she said, faltering. 'We still have homework, and . . . I've got GCSEs next year. Remember?'

'You can do it tomorrow.'

'It's Sunday tomorrow.'

Her mum looked at the carrot in her hand as if she were surprised to find it there, then drew the peeler unenthusiastically down its length, allowing the ribbon of skin to fall to the floor unnoticed.

'The library will be shut,' Lizzie persisted.

'Not in the morning.'

Lizzie nodded vigorously. 'It's shut. I promise.'

'No, they extended the hours. It's open till noon on Sundays.'

'But I need to go now.' Lizzie was panicking. She had to see Haydn. If she didn't, she'd die.

'Uncle Daniel's coming in from New York.'

'But I have plans. I—'

Her mum then seemed to find some life from somewhere. Her eyes fixed on Lizzie. 'You can work tomorrow. Uncle Daniel will be upset if you're not here.'

Lizzie knew Uncle Daniel wouldn't give two hoots whether she was there or not. She spoke to him on the telephone once a year on Christmas Day for approximately a minute and a half, to say thank you for the present her dad had bought her from him. The last birthday he'd remembered was her eighth. He came over for Anna's funeral, but left the next morning, and if he had spoken to Lizzie then she certainly couldn't recall it. 'What if I go for a couple of hours—' *Enough time for some kissing and a coffee*, she thought '—and get back to see him after?'

'Lizzie, I'm not talking about this any more. Get upstairs. Get that coat off. Then come back down and help me with lunch.'

Her mum was getting cross. Lizzie looked at the floor. She was wary of upsetting her, especially given how upset she was already, but not seeing Haydn? It was too unbearable for words.

'No,' she said. 'I have plans.' The strength of her voice surprised her and she could tell by the look on her mum's face that it surprised her too.

'Excuse me?' Her mum crossed her arms, and for a moment or two Lizzie considered apologizing. She remembered the fights her mum used to have with Anna. Blazing rows, screaming, things thrown, doors slammed, her mum muttering under her breath as she paced around shaking her head, referring to Anna as *your daughter* when she later filled her dad in on the row. Lizzie loathed listening to them. Confrontation of any sort terrified her. But this wasn't fair. She wanted to be kissing Haydn, not staying in to play perfect niece to some uncle who couldn't pick her out in a line-up. Lizzie was starting to fume. She knew *exactly* what seeing him would be like: a pathetic state-the-obvious comment on how much she'd grown, followed by a handful of uncomfortable pauses when Anna was inadvertently alluded to, then pointless questions about school, which GCSEs she was taking, do-you-know-what-you-want-to-do-afterwards, then lastly silence, and she would end up sitting in the living room trying not to look at the spot on the mantelpiece where Anna's urn had sat, listening to boring adult rubbish. She was nearly sixteen. That was nearly old enough to get married and live in a completely different house. She should be allowed to go to the library whenever she wanted.

'You know, you can't tell me what to do all the time. I'm nearly sixteen.' Lizzie felt a slight buzz as a shot of adrenalin hit her system.

'No, Lizzie, you're only just fifteen,' said her mum, as if she were talking to a three-year-old. 'You were fifteen in April and it's only June. But sixteen, four, twenty-seven, it doesn't change the fact that your dad's brother is arriving from America and he's coming here before he goes to your grandparents and you should be here to see him.' She turned her back on Lizzie and began to peel carrots as if her life depended on it.

'Well, he'll have to see me some other time. I've. Got. *Plans*!'

Her mum whipped around and pointed the peeler at Lizzie. 'Don't you dare raise your voice to me!' she shouted. 'I don't get you. It's the library! You can go tomorrow. You're usually so reasonable. Why on earth are you choosing today to be like this? Honestly, Lizzie, I thought you were above all this childish nonsense.'

'But, you don't—'

'Lizzie!' she shrieked as loud as a gunshot. 'I can't talk about this anymore!'

Then she seemed to collapse from the stomach as if she'd been popped. The back of her hand went up to her mouth, and she dropped her head forward. 'Please, Lizzie,' she whispered. 'Please don't do this.' Her eyes welled with a fresh batch of tears and Lizzie knew she wasn't going to see Haydn that day.

Her mum turned and went back to the carrots, the noise of her peeling too faint to crack the angry sadness around them. As Lizzie made to leave the kitchen they heard the sound of the car pulling up outside, then a misplaced cheery hoot of the horn. Lizzie looked back at her mother, who silently swore under her breath, then dragged her sleeve across her eyes and smoothed the front of her shirt. Lizzie ran upstairs before her dad and Uncle Daniel came in. She shut her door and fell on to her bed. What on earth would she say to Haydn: I'm staying in because my mum told me I had to? How pathetic. She felt sick. She sent a text so she wouldn't have to hear the scorn in his voice.

mums freaking out :s i cant see you sorry xx :((

Then she stared at the phone in her hand and waited. It bleeped back.

:L all parents are twats . . . talk to you later bye sexxy

146

She couldn't help her smile.

bye sexxy

He thought she was sexy!

All the frustration pooled from the argument with her mum evaporated. She collapsed back on her pillow, clutching her phone to her chest and imagined kissing him. Then she lifted the phone and reread the text. Could she brave a call? She chewed on her lower lip as she considered it. Then she dialled, her fingers hesitant, her tummy turning over and over.

'Hey,' he drawled.

'I'm sorry about today.'

'Your mum wouldn't let you out?'

'No, I can't believe it.'

'What a total bitch.'

Lizzie flinched with the shock of hearing him call her mum a bitch, and in an instant went from hating her to being fiercely protective of her. 'My uncle's arrived from abroad, so, actually, it's right that I stay in.'

'You're going to be bored shitless.'

'He's OK. In fact, he's quite cool.'

'Oh yeah?' Haydn sounded like he didn't believe her.

'Yeah, he's, like, this famous artist. He went to art school with my mum and he lives in New York, and he's really different, with this American accent on some words, and he swears and smokes and stuff. And he wears clothes like leather jackets and beaten-up baseball caps.'

'He sounds like a prick.'

Lizzie didn't want to talk to Haydn any more. 'Well, he's not.'

'Hey,' said Haydn. 'No need to get pissed off at me. I'm on your side, remember? It was you who was grounded and can't come out with me, not the other way round.'

147

'I know. Sorry.' Lizzie looked at the ceiling and sighed. 'Can I see you in the morning?'

'Sure. Come by my house when you can get out.'

She hung up and lay back on her pillow. She pushed Haydn calling her mum a bitch out of her mind and concentrated on the *bye sexxy*.

The following morning she jumped out of bed as soon as she woke and got dressed into Anna's clothes and her long coat. Haydn annoying her was forgotten; all she could think about was touching and kissing him. She crept down to the silent kitchen and made toast and tea, enough for three, ate and drank hers while she set a tray for her parents. Then she carefully carried the tray upstairs. Her dad wasn't in bed and her mum was fast asleep. Lizzie stared at her. She thought she looked like an angel. Her face was soft and untroubled; there was even the shadow of a smile across her mouth. Lizzie could see she was dreaming beautiful, happy things and decided to leave her sleeping, but left the tray of tea and toast by the bed so that when she woke up, even though it would be cold, she'd know she'd thought of her.

She went back downstairs and met her father coming in through the front door.

'Hey Dad,' she said. He looked dreadful. His hair was scruffed, his clothes crumpled, and his skin grey and puffy with his eyes rimmed red. He was holding a blanket and a pillow.

'I made you tea,' she said. 'It's upstairs on a tray next to Mum.'

He smiled, but then the smile turned into the saddest face she'd ever seen. 'Dad?' She walked over to him and gently touched the top of his arm. 'Are you OK?'

He didn't say anything.

'Where have you been?'

He hesitated and looked at the floor. 'The car,' he said finally.

'You slept in the car? Why?'

'It doesn't matter,' he said. 'Thanks for the tea.'

Lizzie told Haydn about her dad sleeping in the car.

'I mean,' she said, 'what's the point of getting married if you can't talk your problems through and one of you ends up spending the night in a car?' She leaned back against his wall and picked at the corner of a Dennis the Menace sticker on the headboard. 'Like, I could understand if it was a camper van with a bed in it and stuff, but a Ford Focus? How rubbish is that?'

'My parents never talk to each other,' Haydn said.

'Really?' Lizzie was surprised. 'But I've seen how your mum looks at your dad when he's doing assembly. She's always smiling, as if she's the proudest wife on earth.'

'It's an act. He's a twat. Mum hates him.'

'He seems OK.'

Haydn shook his head. 'He's a total loser. I wish she'd left him when I was a kid; that way I'd never have known him.'

Lizzie couldn't believe what Haydn was saying. It was awful to hear him talk like this about his dad. Lizzie couldn't imagine hating her dad. She couldn't even imagine hating Dr Howe. Mrs Howe, maybe – she could be scary, especially if she caught some-one running in the corridors or copying homework.

'Anyway,' he said, 'all parents hate each other. That's just what happens. Too much stuff gets said and done, stuff you can't take back and you can't make better. It's shit.'

Lizzie wanted to tell him her parents were different. That

before Anna they were always laughing and hugging and exchanging whispered words. It was only when one of their daughters died that things went pear-shaped. But Haydn didn't seem too interested in the conversation any more. He was standing at his desk shovelling tobacco, papers and lighter, some small change and his travel card into his pockets.

'Let's get out of here,' he said.

Haydn's mum was standing at the bottom of the stairs with her arms crossed. She stared up at them. 'Are you going out?' she asked.

Haydn didn't say anything. When Mrs Howe turned to Lizzie, Lizzie in turn looked at Haydn. But his eyes were on the floor. He looked nervous and about five years old.

'Haydn? I asked you a question.'

Haydn managed to nod, but still he didn't speak.

'We thought we'd go for a walk,' Lizzie said, quietly.

Mrs Howe's eyes narrowed and Lizzie wondered if she was going to tell them off for something. 'I thought you had some work to do for college.'

'I finished it,' he mumbled.

'You said you'd wash the car.'

'I will.'

Lizzie suddenly got the horrible feeling that they were going to be kept apart for a second time. 'It's just a quick walk,' she blurted. Mrs Howe glared at her. Lizzie felt herself flush. 'If that's OK.'

'I'll be back in an hour,' Haydn said. 'I'll do the car then, inside too.'

Then he turned and walked past her towards the front door, his eyes fixed on his feet.

'You know, I'm just not sure you two should be spending time together, Haydn.'

Mrs Howe stared at him, direct and penetrating, like she was trying to talk to him telepathically. Lizzie felt uneasy. The atmosphere between them was charged with something peculiar, like they'd had some awful row before she arrived.

'We're just walking, Mrs Howe.' Lizzie couldn't believe she'd just spoken so forcefully; it was as if the words had jumped out by accident. Mrs Howe flipped round to look at her. They held each other's gaze for a few seconds. Then Mrs Howe nodded.

'Fine,' she said. 'But not long, Haydn. There's something we need to talk about. Go for your walk and come straight home.' She waited for a response from Haydn, but he didn't say anything. 'Did you hear me?'

At last he nodded, but still didn't look up. Lizzie willed him to get out of the house. Finally he opened the door and went out. Lizzie moved to follow him.

'So, a walk?' Mrs Howe said.

Lizzie stopped and nodded.

'Are you sure, Elizabeth?'

'Sorry?'

Mrs Howe forced a smile. 'Going for a walk. With Haydn.' She paused. 'Given his and your sister's relationship.'

Lizzie's heart stopped.

'Please don't look like that; I'm not trying to upset you. It just seems odd, that's all. I mean, you're a bright girl; I would have thought you might consider the ramifications of what you're doing a little more thoroughly. Personally speaking, I don't think it's healthy.' The smile slipped off her face. Lizzie dropped her head and walked past Mrs Howe towards the door.

'It's just a walk,' she mumbled.

'Fine,' said Mrs Howe. 'Oh, and Elizabeth?'

Lizzie stopped and turned to face her.

'Anna's scarf suits you, by the way.'

Stress, Lies and Videophone

'I think we're making a mistake,' said Jon.

They stood on the front doorstep. Kate shivered as if it were February, her stomach churning.

'We have to,' she said. 'I can't sleep. Or eat. I can't think. You and I are fighting. I have to talk to him.'

'What on earth are you going to say?'

Kate had no idea. She lifted her hand to ring the bell.

'Please, Kate,' he whispered. 'Let's go. We haven't thought this through. We need to be absolutely straight—'

'Kate, Jon, are you all right?' asked Angela, interrupting Jon as she opened the door. 'You sounded so upset on the phone.'

Kate couldn't look her in the eyes. Every muscle had frozen solid and, standing on the doorstep of the man she hated more than any other in the world, under the searching eyes of his wife, she suddenly worried that Jon was right. That this was totally the wrong thing to do, that the right thing to do, the only thing to do, was to leave the putrid business buried. The night before, when they'd fought so fiercely, she'd been certain, but now she was anxious and terrified, unsure of what to say, and wondering if she'd dug her heels in too quickly. She'd got so blind angry. That was the problem, like always. Her anger erupted too fast to let reason get a look-in and the things he'd said last night made her so furious she'd have argued the weight of a kilo. He called the sewage on the phone an affair, for God's sake!

'It's not an *affair*! An *affair* is what people have when they fall in love! When they're both adults. Anna was a child! It was fucking abuse, Jon. He fucking abused your daughter.'

'You saw the film. It wasn't rape. She looked like she was—'

'Don't!' Kate had screamed, blocking her ears with her hands like a child.

'For crying out loud, what do you want him to say to us? There's nothing he can say that will make any of it any easier. It will only make things worse, Kate. Please don't do this to us. Don't do this to Anna, don't drag her name through the dirt like this.'

'So what do *you* want to do?' she retorted. 'Stick your head in the sand like a bloody ostrich? Cross your fucking fingers and hope it goes away? It's not going away! This vileness will be with us for ever. That man needs to be brought to justice. He needs to be held accountable. He's a headmaster and he had sex with a pupil. An underage one. *Our* daughter. They should lock him up and throw away the key. He shouldn't be allowed near children again.'

'But that's just it. They won't throw away the key. Do you know how long these men get? Even if he does get sent to prison, which isn't certain anyway, he'll get, what, a year? Maybe eighteen months. How is that justice? We'll end up feeling cheated.' He paused. 'And what about Lizzie?'

Kate screamed at him then. How dare he use Lizzie as an excuse? She questioned his love for Anna, called him names, insinuated he was too scared to face the truth. She had needed a fight, a diversion from everything she was feeling, so she'd pushed and pushed; the things she said to him got meaner and meaner. But rather than shout back, rather than give her what she wanted, he turned away from her. He took his pillow and the throw from the foot of the bed and walked out of their room, and she was left alone with nothing but her own vindictiveness, a suffocating miasma around her.

In the morning they'd tried to talk again, but it was clear he was never going to see her point of view.

'I don't care any more,' she said. 'I'm going to see him. I need him to know I know. I can't explain why. I just do. If you can't face it I'll go alone.'

Jon stared at her and she held his gaze, set her mouth, crossed her arms. She could tell he was beaten. It was in his eyes – he was emotionally spent – and sure enough, a moment later he gave a weary nod. 'OK. We'll go.'

'Are you both all right?' Angela asked again.

Kate's legs felt like jelly.

'Is this something to do with Elizabeth and Haydn?'

It took a moment for Kate to register Angela's question. 'Lizzie and Haydn?' She shook her head. 'I don't know what you mean.'

'About them seeing each other?'

'Seeing each other?' Confused and wrong footed, Kate searched Angela's face for explanation.

'Oh, didn't you know?' Saccharine sweet. 'Clearly, young Elizabeth's been keeping secrets from you. Teenagers!' She shook her head indulgently. 'She came here about an hour ago. They've gone for a walk together. They've been spending quite a bit of time in each other's company since,' she paused, 'the memorial. He's helping her a great deal.' Her face fell serious. 'I have to say, though, I would prefer them *not* to see each other. Haydn was devastated when Anna died. It's taken him ever such a long time to recover.' She paused. 'It doesn't seem right, the two of them together. I assumed you were also unhappy about it and wanted to discuss how we dissuade the friendship. I had no idea you were so in the dark.'

Kate tried to process what she was hearing. She had come to talk about Anna and Stephen. This talk of Lizzie was muddling her.

'I don't understand Elizabeth's motivations at all. It seems a peculiar thing to do, to court your dead sister's boyfriend.' She looked at Kate as if she were a naughty pupil sent for disciplining.

Kate didn't know how to respond. How could Lizzie be seeing Haydn? How could she be with him right now? Lizzie wasn't even interested in boys. And if she was, it certainly wouldn't be with Haydn Howe of all people, the boy who tempted Anna out of the safety of her bed, who plied her with drink, who sat back and watched as she danced the tightrope on the edge of that roof. No, it wasn't possible. Not Haydn. Not with Lizzie.

Jon cleared his throat. He took Kate's hand and stepped in front of her. 'We need to talk to Stephen.'

'He's not here.'

'We'll wait,' Jon said, and pulling Kate behind him, he walked past Angela Howe, who tried and failed to block their entry.

Stephen Howe was standing just inside the living-room door, his large frame filling their immaculate living-room with its dusky pink carpet and mawkish floral curtains.

'I think you should sit down,' Jon said to him.

'I want to know why you are here,' said Angela. Kate saw that she had paled a fraction, her fists had clenched at her sides and her eyes flicked nervously to and fro.

Oh my God, thought Kate. *You know, don't you?*

'We want to talk to him,' said Jon.

'If it's something to do with Elizabeth and school, then the time to discuss it would be during school hours, not on a Sunday, an hour before lunch.'

'It's not about Lizzie. And it needs to be discussed today. Now. With Stephen. And I'm not sure you should be here to hear what we have to say to him.'

Angela's fists flexed and reclenched. 'Whatever you have to say to my husband can most certainly be said in front of me. You really have no right to barge into our home like this. You—'

'Oh, I have every right,' said Jon through gritted teeth.

Kate saw him lean close to Stephen's face. There was a threatening strength to his shoulders, a set of his mouth, an aggression about him that didn't sit right. Jon loathed violence. He thought it impractical and childish, and Kate remembered suddenly how much she loved that about him, the way he'd tut with disdain when tragic news from Iraq or Afghanistan was beamed into their living room. *Bloody waste*, he'd mutter. *Those boys losing their lives for another man's politics and pocket.* Kate often wondered what her father might say about him. Though he'd left her and her mum when she was small, she could still remember the fights he got into.

'Any fella so much as look at y'pa the wrong way,' she'd tell Kate with undisguised pride as she patched an eye or a lip with peas from the over-frosted freezer drawer, 'most likely end up with teeth on the floor.'

It was unforgivable that she'd called Jon weak the night before, that she'd goaded and bullied him into this situation, and she felt an agonizing stab of guilt.

'I have more right,' Jon continued, 'than anyone to talk to this man, don't I, Dr Howe?'

Stephen's face fell to the floor and Kate winced.

It's true then, she thought.

Though she'd seen the film and heard with her own ears those contemptible moans, she had so desperately hoped it wasn't real. Lying awake the previous night, as the hours loped on in a sleepless, anxiety-ridden marathon, she had willed Stephen to look stunned and then furious, to angrily demand who'd spread such evil rumours. She imagined him reassuring them he could never do such a thing. She saw him insist on questioning Rebecca, who'd then break down, admit her lie, explain how she'd contrived her monstrous film. But the guilt, his admission, was loud and clear in those lowered eyes.

'Stephen,' said Angela, firmly. 'You need to tell these people to leave. If they need to speak to you they can make an appointment like any other parent.'

'We're not leaving,' Jon said.

Kate allowed her eyes to drift to the picture on the wall above the Howes' gas fire. It was too small for the chimney breast and looked out of place, as if it were only temporarily hanging there, waiting for them to find something more suitable. It showed a horse and farmer ploughing. The sun was low in the sky, bathing the earthy field in a sticky sweet glow. She loathed paintings like this, mean and chocolate-boxy, romanticizing scenes of hardship from a bygone era, rewriting historical fact, like showing poverty-stricken Victorian kids with clean plump cheeks playing marbles in spotless gutters. It wasn't real. Where were the blisters on the farmer's hands, or the ribs of the overworked horse? Where were the rocks in the soil that broke the cartwheels? Why was he so contented-looking when his children were hungry and cold and his wife had calluses from scrubbing? And what on earth gave little-talented artists the right to bathe these people and their breadline existence in pink sunshine?

'Not until we've talked to him,' Jon said.

'For God's sake,' Angela said.

'We know what you—' Jon's voice cracked. Kate's stomach clamped and she tore her eyes off the ploughing horse. Jon's eyes were closed and his face showed every bit of pain he was feeling. 'We know what you did to Anna.'

Stephen glanced nervously at Angela. Kate did too, and saw her face twitching, as the cogs in her brain whirred and whirred. 'Did what to Anna?' she said then.

'Had sex with her,' Jon said.

Angela Howe didn't flinch. Not a flicker of anything. 'That's ridiculous,' she said. 'Where did you come up with such utter nonsense?'

'Rebecca Finch told me!' Kate suddenly blurted, her tongue freed by Angela's calm refute. 'She told me all about it, how your husband had sex with my daughter.' Kate turned on Stephen. Just looking at him made her nauseous. 'She was just a child! How could you? How could you look me in the eye?' She stared at him, her eyes flicking over him, willing him to do something, to drop to his knees and beg her forgiveness, or to cry, or to say sorry. But he did nothing. 'You filthy bastard,' she breathed.

'How dare you speak to my husband like that! This is defamatory garbage. I am horrified you would think this appropriate. I insist you both leave our house now!'

Nobody moved.

'I don't care how upset you are about Anna's death; to have the audacity, the *front*, to barge your way into our home and start throwing around disgusting accusations that are, quite frankly, not only offensive, but complete fabrication. You have no grounds for what you're saying. The word of one child? A child who is in and out of the headmaster's office like a yo-yo, who's been suspended, and who has every misguided reason to make a malicious allegation against Dr Howe for personal reprisal. Do you know how many teachers are falsely accused by grudge-bearing pupils each year, Mr and Mrs Thorne? And let us not forget this was a child whom *you* assaulted in front of five hundred witnesses. A child you repeatedly hit.'

Kate felt her skin redden. 'Rebecca wasn't lying,' she managed. 'Stephen had sex with Anna. You did and you know it,' she said, turning on Stephen. 'You're an evil piece of shit!'

Stephen didn't move a muscle. The way he hung his head, his shoulders rigid, arms straight, reminded Kate of how a child might stand when getting a telling-off, trying to be as unobtrusive as possible in the hope that it might reduce the punishment.

'You think this is going to help you, Mrs Thorne?' Angela Howe continued. 'You think judges take kindly to women who attack children, then attempt to denigrate upstanding members of the community without due evidence?'

'So why's he not denying it?' Kate narrowed her eyes and lowered her voice, now switching her glare back to Angela. 'You tell me that. Why's he stood there like a mute idiot? If I was him and I was innocent, I'd be yelling it by now. He knows what he did. Your husband sexually abused my daughter. Did you know about it? Did you know what a vile paedophile he is?'

Then Angela's eyes filled with tears. Two spilled over, tumbling down her ruddy cheeks. She shook her head, lifted her chin and waited, breathing deeply until the tears had gone. When she looked back at Kate her face was once again hard and glassy.

'Stephen is as shocked as I am. He has done no such thing. You have no proof and you must be stupid to believe such lies. To walk in here and accuse my husband of such a serious and foul crime on the say-so of a child as troubled as Rebecca Finch, as prone to lies and exaggeration, is ludicrous. I am asking you to leave my house now. If you don't, I'll call the police.'

'We do have proof.'

Kate had promised herself she wouldn't show the film. Being in the same room as Stephen with the film playing would be unbearable, she knew that, and as her fingers fumbled with the keypad, unable to do what her brain asked them to do, she began to feel weak with sickness. Then she felt Jon's hand on hers. He stilled her fingers, brushed his thumb against her and took the phone. She heard snippets of the other films, of the laughing children, those playing football, teasing, then Jon threw the phone into Stephen's lap. He reached for Kate's hand. She held him tightly, longing to get out of there so she could tell him how sorry she was that she'd forced them into this.

Stephen Howe picked up the phone and stared at the screen. Kate sang a song in her head so she wouldn't have to listen to the sounds of the film. She saw his eyes widen as he watched, saw him shake his head like a drunk man trying to fight double vision. He looked at Angela with disbelief and bewilderment. She ran to her husband and snatched the phone. She stared at it, motionless, her eyes wide.

'But—'

'Be quiet, Stephen.'

'But—'

'I said be quiet!'

Angela Howe swallowed. Her face was stricken, not with anger or shame, but with what looked to Kate like abject fear. She was frantically chewing on the inside of her cheek. Her hands had started to quiver as if there were an electric charge running through her. Then as Kate watched, her breath bated, waiting for one of them to speak, Angela's body relaxed and a fine veil of composure settled over her. She held the phone out towards Jon and a curious sneer cast a shadow across her face.

'Well, Mr and Mrs Thorne,' she said, crossing her arms as her sneer darkened. 'That is certainly your daughter in all her glory, but the man in that film isn't my husband.'

'What?' said Kate. She looked from Angela to Stephen, whose eyes were locked on his feet.

'The man your daughter is so *enjoying* isn't my husband.'

Kate grabbed the phone from Jon. 'Of course it is.'

She pressed play.

'That's him,' Kate spat. She faced the phone towards Stephen. 'That's you, isn't it? You sick bastard.'

Angela took hold of Kate's hand and turned the phone towards her face, pushing it close, about an inch or so away from her nose. 'Look very carefully, Mrs Thorne. That's no more my husband than it is yours.'

Kate stared at the phone, the picture blurred in its proximity. 'It's him,' she whispered. 'I can see it is.'

'You can't see anything. The picture's far too grainy. Far too dark. I could find you a thousand men it could be. It could be anyone.'

'What are you talking about?' Kate moved her head back until the film came into focus. Yes, the picture was dark, and there were certainly shadows over the man whose head was obscured behind hunched shoulders and the lithe limbs of her daughter, whose perfect white skin glowed spectral in the gloom. It was also grainy, but she could still see it was Stephen. It was definitely him.

Surely, she thought, *surely I haven't got this wrong.*

'This wouldn't stand up in any court in the country. A lawyer with a degree from eBay could rubbish this. You'll be laughed out of the room.' Her voice suddenly lost its cruel edge, and she adopted the firm unwavering persuasion of her deputy-head alter ego. 'You have clearly been the victims of a cruel and childish prank.'

'No,' said Kate, shaking her head, desperate to keep her thoughts straight. She'd seen Rebecca's face. She wasn't lying. Kate wanted

161

her to be lying more than anything else. But she knew it wasn't lies. She could see the truth in Stephen.

'No,' she said. 'It's you.'

'It's lies, Mrs Thorne, the girl made it up. She . . .'

Kate was suddenly overcome with dizziness as her vision faltered and the floor began to shift beneath her weight. She blinked hard, forced herself to concentrate on what Angela was saying.

'. . . your unprovoked and vicious attack. And it's worked. She's got into your heads, got you believing things that aren't just false, but are farcical. She's playing you for idiots and taking advantage of your vulnerability. She's probably laughing at you right now for being so easy to manipulate. Go home. Throw the phone away and get on with your lives. My husband would never do such a thing. He would never jeopardize his career; he's worked too hard. We've both worked too hard. What possible reason could he have for ruining his life like this?' Then Angela turned to Stephen. 'Tell them, Stephen. Tell Mr and Mrs Thorne you've done nothing wrong.'

The room was silent for a moment or two. Kate held her breath, head still spinning, her palms sweating. Then Stephen lifted his chin and squared himself as if he were a bloodied general preparing to fight on.

'It's not me in the film.' Stephen spoke in a monotone. 'Rebecca Finch is making it up. I didn't do what she said. It is not me. I have no idea why she would say such a thing. I haven't done anything wrong.'

Angela breathed out a sigh, then went to his side and stood facing them, shoulder to shoulder, like the brave wife and miscreant politician in front of a news crew. And for a second or two Kate was taken in by their show of togetherness. But as she stared at them, Angela's relief hardened into a look of smug defiance.

No, thought Kate, *this isn't some sludgy infidelity that can be washed clean by flimsy denial; this is child abuse. Abuse of my child.*

And then everything around her felt suddenly unclean: the air, the vacuumed carpet, the polished furniture – it was all polluted. She needed to get out. Her knees began to buckle and she had the horrible feeling she was going to collapse in a suffocated heap on their septic floor.

Jon put his arms around her. 'It's OK, sweetheart. We're going home. I'm going to take you home.'

'He's lying, Jon. It's him in that film. He's not telling us the truth.'

Jon gently hushed her.

'You have thirty seconds to leave.'

Jon ignored Angela and, keeping Kate clutched to his chest, he turned towards Stephen. 'Whether or not that film is admissible in a court of law is beside the point. You and I both know it's you with our daughter, and for this I hope you never sleep soundly again.'

The First Forbid

'I don't understand why you won't cancel.'

'How can I? It's his birthday for goodness' sake.'

'No, his birthday's on Wednesday.'

Jon didn't reply.

'How can you even think about smiling politely over the parsnips, then singing Happy bloody Birthday after this morning?'

'I can't! In fact, I can't think of anything worse, but I'm not going to cancel, because my mother has cooked a Sunday lunch to celebrate my father's birthday and I don't want to let her down. I knew it would be impossible to do anything after seeing Stephen, which is precisely why I spent the whole of last night trying to persuade you not to go. But we did go. I went. For you. Now I'm asking you, if only in return, to come with me.'

He could see Kate remained unconvinced, but thankfully she finally nodded and Jon breathed a whispered thank you.

'I have to talk to Lizzie first,' she said.

His heart sank. 'About what?'

She looked at him like he was an imbecile. 'Haydn Howe?'

'For God's sake, not now.'

Kate raised her eyebrows. 'If Lizzie's seeing that boy I want it over with. Christ, he looks like he takes cocaine for breakfast. Just the thought of him even looking at her turns my stomach. I mean, what if he takes her home and Stephen's there?'

She was quiet for a bit and he knew she was waiting for him to reply but he didn't; he was too exhausted. Too much arguing, not enough sleep. There was no chance of it; every time he closed his eyes he saw them. He heard them too, even when he hid his head beneath the pillow and clutched it tight around his ears.

'Jon? Is that what you want? Haydn with Lizzie? That man's son touching your daughter? We need to talk to her. What if he gives her alcohol, like he did Anna? You'd be happy with that?'

Jon took a long slow breath, reminding himself to keep calm. Kate did this. She said things to provoke him. It was her way of coping with stress, and at this moment she was battling the bleakest pinnacle on a mountain of stress. They had argued again on the way home from the Howes'. It wasn't a long or vicious argument – they were both too shell-shocked to have a serious fight – but once again they disagreed on what to do next, their closeness in Stephen's house all too quickly forgotten. She wanted to go to the police. He didn't. And now they had to go to his parents' house for a birthday lunch for a father who didn't recognize him, and he couldn't think of anything worse.

'We'll talk to her as soon as we get back.'

Kate nodded, and then pinched the bridge of her nose to stop herself crying.

'Look,' he said then. 'If you'd really rather stay behind, then do,' he said. 'I can tell Mother you're not feeling well.'

Kate seemed to shake herself from the inside out; she stood tall and gave an almost imperceptible nod. 'No, you're right. She's asked Dan to come back, she's arranged lunch, we should go.'

She went to the bottom of the stairs. 'Lizzie!' she called up. 'We need to leave!'

'What?' came the call back. Her head appeared upside down at the banisters. 'Where are we going?'

'To your grandparents'.'

She shook her head. 'But I'm going to the cinema with Sammy. It's her birthday, remember?' Lizzie pushed off the banister and ran down the stairs two at a time.

'No, I don't remember.' Kate glanced at Jon and raised her eyebrows.

'It's Grandpa's birthday. Your grandmother's cooking a special lunch for us all,' Jon said.

'But I told you last week,' Lizzie said with cartoonish petulance. 'We're meeting at half one and seeing a film and then going for pizza. And it's not Grandpa's birthday today. It's on Wednesday.'

'Lizzie, it's important you come—'

'You did this yesterday, Mum. It's not *fair*.' She was struggling not to cry. 'I stayed in to see Uncle Daniel like you wanted.'

'You've already been out this morning.'

'I went to the library. Remember? You told me to go today instead of yesterday!'

Kate looked at Jon and raised her eyebrows again.

'You can't make me miss this,' Lizzie went on. 'Sammy will be gutted. She's had it arranged for ages. I did tell you. I promise.'

'You didn't tell me. If you had, I'd remember.'

'You were on your way up to the studio so maybe you didn't hear me.' Lizzie paused. 'Anyway, Grandpa doesn't even know who I am. He's not even going to know if I'm at the table or not.'

'Lizzie!'

Lizzie grimaced and glanced at Jon. 'Sorry, I didn't mean that like it sounded. I was just trying . . . Look, I'll go and see him after school on Wednesday. On his actual birthday.'

'No, you'll come with us now.'

166

Jon could see his daughter beginning to panic. 'If I go on Wednesday,' she said, 'and you go today, then he gets more people to see him.'

Jon stepped closer to Kate and took hold of her elbow. 'You know, I think that's a good idea. It sounds like there's been wires crossed. She should go to the cinema—'

'But—'

'It's OK, Kate. My mother will understand. To be honest, none of us are in the mood and I'm not sure anyone will mind Lizzie seeing her friends.' To appease Kate he said to Lizzie, 'You can go, but you need to come home after the film has finished.' He looked at his watch. 'Four thirty. We'll be home by then. That's three hours.'

'But we're going for pizza.'

'Not today. We'd like you to come home.'

Lizzie's eyes welled and then rose to heaven in exasperation. 'Fine,' she said. 'But Sammy is going to be *really* unhappy, and it's *all your fault*!' She spun on her heel and thumped back up the stairs.

'You know,' called Kate after her, 'I've never heard you mention a Sammy.'

Jon pulled on her arm. 'Come on,' he whispered. 'Not now.'

Lizzie stopped and turned. 'Yes, you have. I talk about her all the time.'

'Nope.' Kate crossed her arms. 'Never heard her name before.'

'What are you trying to say?'

'She's not trying to say anything,' said Jon. 'We're late, Kate.'

'It means you say you're seeing Sammy, but I don't think you are.'

'Well,' she hesitated. 'I am.'

'What film are you seeing?'

'We haven't decided yet. Whatever's on and looks good.'

'Whatever's on and looks good?'

'Yes!'

'Because I'd hate it if you were lying to us.'

Then Lizzie walked back down the stairs with a defiance about her that Jon hadn't seen before; her resemblance at that moment to her sister snatched his breath, and he felt Kate tense.

'When have I ever lied to you?' Lizzie said with pointed control. 'When have I ever been anything but the well-behaved daughter? Have I ever given you *any* reason to worry? And why *are* you so worried, anyway? I'm old enough to go out for a few hours on my own.'

Kate seemed unfazed by Lizzie's sudden fortitude. 'I'd just like to know where you are,' she said.

'At all times?'

'Yes, Lizzie. At all times. If that's not too inconvenient.'

Lizzie and Kate locked eyes.

'Fine,' said Lizzie. 'Until four thirty I will be at the cinema with *Sammy*.'

'Just so long as you're not with Haydn Howe.'

Jon could have screamed. She just couldn't resist it, and it dumbfounded him. He looked at Lizzie and saw her turn a guilty red, and his stomach knotted.

Lizzie looked from Kate to him then back at Kate. 'Who?'

'Haydn Howe.'

'Haydn? Why on earth would I be seeing him? No. No, of course not. Why do you say that?'

'We were told you were seeing each other.'

'Well, whoever told you that got it wrong.'

Jon checked his watch; they should have left. His mother would be tutting.

'Even if I was,' Lizzie went on, 'I don't know what you've got against him.'

Kate didn't say anything, but Jon could feel her bristling beside him.

'What? You really think it was his fault Anna fell?'

Again Kate didn't speak.

'It wasn't his fault. He loved her.'

The silence that followed was loaded with unspoken words.

'I'm not seeing Haydn!' Lizzie shouted suddenly.

'Kate, this isn't the time. We need to leave,' Jon said.

'You are not allowed anywhere near him!'

'Enough, Kate. We'll see you back here at four thirty,' Jon said to his daughter.

Lizzie nodded, sending tears spilling down her cheeks. She turned and ran back up the stairs. Kate and Jon heard her bedroom door slam.

'She's not telling the truth.'

'Fine, I agree, but you made your point. You told her you don't want them to see each other. Anyway, it didn't seem like a romantic relationship; she mentioned him loving Anna, for starters. Come on. Please. I'd like to get to lunch. The sooner we get there, the sooner we can get back. We'll talk to her later. Calmly. OK?' He waited for an answer. 'OK?' he said again.

Kate nodded reluctantly, and finally stepped in the direction of his pull.

They arrived at his parents' house and his mother showed them through to the living room. As they walked, Jon explained about Lizzie, but his mother seemed unbothered.

'She said she'd pop in on Wednesday.'

'If she has time that would be lovely.'

Dan was sitting in his father's chair, rolling a glass of red wine around in his hand. Jon had no idea how his brother got away with wearing what he did. That day it was a brown suede trilby, a grey and black striped silk shirt beneath a corduroy jacket, and what looked like a maroon pashmina draped around his neck. He wore stonewashed jeans and pointed blue snakeskin shoes, and he'd grown some tufts of facial hair, which would have looked ridiculous on a man even half his age. It was completely galling how bloody handsome he still looked. Jon shifted uncomfortably in his collared shirt and v-neck sweater.

'Would you like a drink, Jon?'

His mother looked at him and he nodded. 'A glass of wine would be lovely.'

'And for Kate?' she said to Jon.

Jon looked at Kate, who rolled her eyes to the ceiling. 'Yes, please,' he said.

Kate poked her tongue out at his mother's back, and Dan smothered a laugh.

'For goodness' sake,' Jon whispered.

He turned to Dan and held out his hand for a formal hello. 'So, how are you?'

'Good, thanks.' Dan stood and shook his hand, then strolled over to Kate. 'And the divine Kiki. Thank you for a delicious meal yesterday. You know, I dream of your cooking in NYC.'

'That was the first time I've cooked in months and months,' she said.

'What an honour. Thank you even more.'

Dan kissed her three times, then stepped back and made a big show of peering into her face. 'Are you OK? You don't look so happy. What's happened?'

Jon saw Kate give a second thought to telling him. 'She's fine,' he said quickly. 'We're both tired.'

Dan tweaked Kate's cheek. 'One day we'll get that car-crash smile of yours back.'

Jon clenched his teeth. Kate sat down and Dan followed suit, picking his wine glass off the floor.

'So, you think she's got it right?' Dan said, as he sat back and made himself comfortable. 'You think this is the old boy's last hurrah?'

'What kind of question is that?' Jon said.

'Just wondering aloud. You never know, there might be a bit of cash coming our way.'

'Jesus, Daniel.'

'It was a *joke*, brother dear.' Dan smiled and drained his glass.

'As if you need money anyway. You must be the only artist in history that gets rich while they're still alive to enjoy it.'

'There's that Hirst chap.'

Jon didn't reply.

'And that dreadful woman with her spunked-on sheets.'

Kate smiled, just briefly, but enough for both Jon and Dan to catch it, and Jon's gut twisted.

'Did I see a smile, Kiki?'

'Stop calling her that,' Jon snapped. 'You're not bloody twenty any more.'

'For fuck's sake, *Jon*. Stop being so fucking serious all the fucking time.'

'Do you have to use language like that?'

'Mother's too deaf to hear from the kitchen and dad's bonkers. So who gives a *fucking shit*?'

'Do you try to be offensive or is it something that just comes naturally?'

'An artist who doesn't offend is as pointless as—' He stopped himself and looked at Jon mock quizzically. 'What is it you do again?'

Jon's mother came back into the room, which allowed Jon to

stop his dulled brain searching for a suitable retort to Dan's dig. She handed him two glasses of red wine, one of which he passed on to Kate.

'I think we'll sit down to lunch right away; the meat's been in the oven far too long already. I'll go and get your father.'

'Do you need some help?'

'No, Jon, I'm fine. If you want a job you can take Lizzie's place off the table.'

When they moved through to the kitchen Jon was surprised to see how chaotic the place looked. There seemed to be even more piles of books and papers than normal, the kitchen worktops held dirty crockery and pans and there was a basket of laundry in front of the washing machine that spilled clothes on to the floor. He hadn't noticed dust in the house before, yet he could clearly see its dull sheen across the surfaces and sparkling swathes of it drifted in the shafts of light that came through the windows.

'You could have given her a hand with the house this morning,' he said to his brother.

Dan chose not to acknowledge him.

Then his mother and father appeared at the door. His father, as always, frail and pallid, was dressed in perfectly ironed red trousers, a white shirt and a dark green sweater. His brown leather shoes were well polished and as always his hair had been carefully brushed and set. Jon stood and was about to wish his father a happy birthday, but his mother spoke first.

'These are the people I was telling you about, Peter. They've just dropped in for a spot of lunch. Would you like to join us all? It would be nice, especially given how smart you look today.' She glanced at Jon.

His father suddenly looked frightened.

'Come on, darling,' she said. 'There's roast beef.'

But his father looked at them all with apprehension and began to shake his head. 'No, no. I'd like to go back to bed. I think I'd like to go to bed.' He tried to turn around but Barbara held on to him, stroking and patting his arm and giving gentling shushes to try to get him to walk with her.

'You know it's your birthday today,' she said.

'Birthday?' He looked confused, but then gave a smile.

'Yes.'

'How old am I?'

'You're seventy-eight.'

'Seventy-eight?'

She nodded and smiled. His father's smile grew broader, but rather than easing Jon's feelings of disquiet, the smile, which bordered on the maniacal, worsened them. His father stared around the room, taking in each of his sons, then Kate. But as quickly as it had appeared, the smile vanished and thick panic returned.

'No,' he said, trying to turn again. 'No. I . . . I want to go back up the stairs . . .' He was getting more and more agitated, but again Jon's mother tried to lead him towards the table. 'No!' he shouted suddenly, yanking his hand out of her grip. 'NO!'

'Please, Peter,' his mother said. 'Please will you eat with us?' The desperate plea was heartbreaking.

But his father shook his head over and over and stepped backwards towards the door. He was terrified. Jon's mother breathed in and stood tall, then turned and went to her husband. She reached out for him but he flinched, and then backed out of the room, shuffling towards the staircase.

'I'll take him back to his bed,' she said to nobody in particular. 'I was stupid to think he'd be up to this.'

'Let me take him,' said Jon, without moving.

'I'm fine.' His mother started after her husband, issuing terse instructions as she went. 'The plates are in the oven. One of you boys carve. The other can do the vegetables. I'll be down in a few minutes.'

Jon hated how relieved he felt as he watched his father disappear up the stairs, one step at a time with a pause between each.

Dan began to carve the meat, and Kate and Jon got out the plates and bowls of vegetables from the warm oven. They silently passed grey parsnips and potatoes, mushy runner beans and unrisen Yorkshire puddings between them, distributing a small amount of each on four hot plates. His mother possessed an extreme culinary impediment quite in contrast to Kate, who was a tremendous cook, but even so Jon found the anticipation of a plate of the bland food of his youth strangely comforting.

His mother came back into the room without a word and sat down. She stared at her plate, gathering her thoughts, then put her hands palm down on the table and lifted her head to look at them.

'He's settled now. I've put him to bed.'

'He seems to be going downhill.'

Jon's mother shot him a hard stare. 'There is no need to comment on his medical condition, thank you very much. He's fine. He has good days and bad days, as well you know.'

They were all quiet. His mother reached for the jug of water and poured herself a glass.

'You all have to remember it's the disease we're seeing. Not your father. It's this repugnant disease that has hold of him.'

'Yes, but—'

'There is no *but*, Jon. Now eat your food before it gets even colder than it already is.'

Jon looked across at Kate, who stared at her food blankly. He felt a pang of sadness for times past, when she would have cast him a sideways glance and mouthed *good luck* before diving in for a whole grey potato.

The food was far less comforting than he'd imagined it would be; the beans disintegrated in his mouth, the parsnips weren't cooked in the centre and the meat was too tough to chew.

'You need help with him,' Jon said, breaking the silence. He watched her carefully push a piece of beef to the side of her plate with her knife. 'I think you need a full-time carer for him.'

She didn't respond; it was as if he hadn't spoken.

'There are trained, experienced people,' he continued. 'They will come and live with you both. They can help with him, do some housework.' Still nothing from her. 'Maybe cook a meal for you.'

Then she turned her head and fixed on Jon. 'I have absolutely no need for a *carer* to look after Peter. *I* am his *carer*. I couldn't think of anything less pleasant than having some imbecile sharing the house with us. I mean, exactly how would it work? She puts my husband in the bath, on the loo, into bed, and then she and I sit down in front of the news with bowls of soup on our laps and chat about the weather?' She paused. 'And do you have any idea how expensive these people are?'

'That's a consideration, Jonny. I mean, you shouldn't go spending the old inheritance willy-nilly.'

Jon would have kicked him if they'd been sitting closer. 'What the hell is wrong with you, Dan?'

Dan groaned. 'Oh for goodness' sake, Jon. It's not what the hell is wrong with me, it's what the hell is wrong with *you*. It was a bloody *joke*. It's way too heavy in here, and it's supposed to be a birthday party.'

'Christ, Dan! This isn't a bloody party!'

'You should get over yourself, you know. So Dad's got

Alzheimer's. It happens. Mother's dealing with it bloody well. She wants to deal with it. Why don't you just relax and let's all try and enjoy our lunch? When Mother wants some help with Dad, then all she has to do is ask. She knows that. Don't you, Mother? Just leave her alone. You've been trying to help since you got here and you've actually done nothing to help at all.'

'Well, that makes two of us then.'

'Boys, that's enough nonsense,' their mother said. 'Be quiet and eat your food. I know you're worried, Jonathan, but you don't have to be. I am perfectly all right and I have no issues in looking after your father.'

They ate the rest of their lunch with only the harsh scraping of knives and forks on their plates to break the silence. When they'd finished, Jon cleared the plates. He ran a sink of water, added some washing-up liquid and then splashed the water to make bubbles. The growing bubbles reminded him of the hot bubbly baths he used to run the girls when they were small and overexcitable. There was a call from his father upstairs. His mother stood up and he bit his tongue to stop himself making yet another offer of help. She left the room without speaking and Jon walked back to the table to collect the wine glasses. Dan put his hand on his to stop him taking it.

'I'm not finished,' he said.

'The bottle's empty.'

'So I'll open another one.' Dan stood and went to the cupboard where his parents stacked their wine. There were only a couple of bottles left. Dan picked them both out, studied the labels and chose one.

'Right,' said Dan. 'I'm taking this bottle outside for a cigarette. Fancy one, Kiki?'

'Actually, I do,' she said, with no hesitation.

'You don't smoke,' said Jon.

'Leave it, Jon.'

They went out of the back door into the garden, and Jon stood alone at the sink. He thought of his father upstairs, of how he had looked vacantly through him, his own sons no more familiar than strangers in a crowd. It amazed Jon how much his mother still loved him. He wondered then if it was love. Perhaps, instead, it was just her overwhelming sense of responsibility. In a way he found this easier to understand. He could see how she put up with everything because she had to rather than chose to. But then he remembered how she'd cradled his foot to put on his slipper, and how gentle her voice had been when she told him how old he was and the look in her eye when she told them to remember it was the disease and not him they were seeing. *No*, he thought, *not because of a sense of duty; definitely because of love.*

He washed up the plates, then wrung out the J-cloth and wiped the table. When the kitchen was clean, he walked through the kitchen door to the patio. It was a beautiful afternoon, with the sun high in a cloudless sky and birds singing for the hell of it. The smell of barbecues was strong, and the sounds of children playing and happy friends and families clinking beers and laughing came from all directions.

The garden was in need of some attention, and his heart went out to his mother again. The grind of her nursing reflected in the neglect, in the weeds that pushed their way through the York pavers, in the overgrown square of lawn, the bushes that reached their tangled branches out to find whatever sunlight they could. She loved this garden. Whilst his father had his books and writings and positions on councils, committees and think tanks, she had the garden, and could happily spend hours at a time deadheading roses, clearing beds of the tiniest weeds and fallen leaves, mowing grass, tying climbers or pruning the ancient apple tree that grew in the far corner. She had a special straw gardening hat and basket that she carried worn, wood-handled tools in. The garden like this was evidence of how unfair life could be; there would be no long summer evenings sharing wine with her husband in the garden she'd spent years attending to. Their comfortable twilight had been snatched away, replaced with incontinence, paranoia and exhaustion.

Kate and Dan were smoking at the wrought-iron table on the terrace. Kate hadn't smoked in years; the sight of her holding a cigarette was odd and he felt even further distanced from her. When they saw him they stopped their conversation.

'What are you talking about?' he asked.

'Kiki was telling me about the headmaster.'

Kate avoided Jon's eyes.

'What he did to Anna.'

'She shouldn't have.'

'Dan agrees with me,' said Kate. 'He thinks Stephen shouldn't be allowed to get away with it.'

Jon felt like punching his brother. A raucous burst of laughter came from next-door's garden. 'Will you keep your voices down?' he said to Kate and Dan. 'You've no idea who can hear you talking.'

'Of course he shouldn't get away with it,' Dan said, pushing back in his chair.

Dan took a cigarette from the pack and lit it from the one he was smoking. He pushed the spent one into an ashtray overflowing with butts on the table.

'I mean, if it was my daughter that some dirty git had slept with? Well, Christ, I don't know how you haven't killed the fucker.'

'Jesus, Dan, what century does your drug-shrivelled brain

178

inhabit? You're like some Neanderthal teenager. How exactly do you think me going to prison for the rest of my life is going to help?'

'I didn't mean you should actually kill him, you tosser. Purely turn of phrase. But you should turn him over to the cops for sure.'

'It's the police, Dan. In England we call them the police. Cops only exist in American crime-show drivel.' Jon stepped down the two steps on to the unkempt lawn. He shouldn't let Dan get to him. His brother didn't live in the real world. He never had. 'Kate and I can discuss this later,' he said.

'You know, you should listen to Kiki. She's got a right to her opinion.'

'Jon does listen to me, Dan. It's not that cut and dried. When we went to his house it was horrible. But,' and now she addressed Jon, 'I just don't see why it's you and me in such a mess while he carries on as normal. He can continue his life, uninterrupted, back at school, everybody in this bloody borough thinking he's the bee's bloody knees, and all the while he's a perverted criminal who isn't safe to be around kids.'

'You see,' interjected Dan. 'Kiki's got a point.'

'Would you stop bloody calling her that!' Jon shut his eyes against the anger that heaved inside him. He breathed deeply. 'Let's go home, Kate. We need to talk about this in private.'

Kate didn't say anything.

'Don't go. Look, I'm sorry. It's your business. I should keep my nose out of it. Stay. Have another drink. Something strong.'

'I'd love a drink,' said Kate.

Jon caught Dan's smile.

'Come home with me, Kate.'

He willed her to stand up and go with him. When she did, he was more relieved than he could ever have thought possible. They didn't say goodbye to his mother. She was still upstairs with his father. Jon wrote a quick note saying thank you for lunch and left it on the worktop beside the hob with the present he'd bought for his father. He was relieved they weren't going to have to watch him open it. It was a CD. The London Symphony Orchestra playing Mendelssohn. Uninspired.

When they arrived home he turned the ignition off. Rather than get out of the car they both sat quietly; the still of the silenced engine was restful. After a while Kate patted his knee. 'Try not to worry about your mum,' she said. 'You can't force her to have help.'

'One day she'll have to have help. She can't carry on for ever, and it's not going to be that long until she needs help herself.'

Kate was quiet.

'What do we do then?'

'I don't know,' she said. 'I can't think that far ahead.'

'It might not be so very far ahead.'

'To be honest, Jon, I can't even think past now.'

They were quiet again.

'Thank you for coming to lunch,' he said.

'No problem.' She opened the car door. 'I'm sorry I smoked.'

Musical Interlude: Number 2

'I need to be back by four-thirty,' said Lizzie, as soon as Haydn appeared on the corner of the road. 'I told Mum and Dad I was going to the cinema with a friend and they said be back by then.'

'Why do you need to tell them anything?'

She shrugged.

'Just tell them you were seeing me, and they can deal.'

'Mum seemed to know already.' Lizzie paused. 'She didn't seem too happy about it.'

'So?'

'So . . .' Lizzie recalled the disappointment and worry in her mum's voice, but couldn't think of anything to say to Haydn.

'Forget it.' Haydn reached into his jacket pocket for his cigarette-rolling gear. Lizzie waited while he carefully tipped the last dregs of spidery brown tobacco into the flimsy paper. She felt a flash of desire as he ran the tip of his tongue along the edge to seal it. 'OK,' he said, holding the cigarette in the corner of his mouth and lighting it. He squinted against the smoke, inhaled and took it from his mouth. 'Our second date of the day. What shall we do?'

'What do you feel like?'

'It's your turn, remember? I did the cemetery.'

'OK,' she said, dragging the word out as she thought. 'Right, let's start with another walk, and then, well, I've got something pretty special.' She tried to sound as mysterious as possible, hoping a fabulous idea would come to her soon.

Haydn smiled. 'Cool.'

They walked hand in hand. Talk was easy now, flowing from both of them like melt-water, bubbling over with sparkle and energy. Anna popped in and out of the conversation with ease, and Lizzie loved being able to share memories of her sister. It was liberating to laugh about her, hear stories she didn't know, and to refer to her in passing without a wounded silence or gut-drenching guilt.

They stopped at a corner shop for him to buy more tobacco, and while she waited Lizzie absent-mindedly brushed her fingers over the packets of chewing gum displayed by the till. When she felt someone watching her she glanced up to see it was the shop-keeper, who looked incredibly suspicious. She dropped her hand away from the rack of sweets and then spoke without thinking.

'What happened the night she fell?'

The question tumbled out of her by mistake and she hoped for a moment that maybe he hadn't heard. Though it was a question she asked him in her mind all the time, it was something she'd been determined not to *actually* ask him. After all, he'd told the police what he knew; it was all there in their report. She practic-ally knew it off by heart. Anna had called him and told him to take his dad's keys and meet her at school with a bottle of vodka. They went up to the roof, and over the course of a few hours they finished the bottle between them. They were both very drunk. He was so drunk he felt ill. He had asked her to go home but she said no. She climbed up on the roof ledge. She laughed when he asked her to get down. She started dancing on the ledge. He was terrified, but she kept refusing to get off the wall. He didn't know what else to do so he went back to the cushions where they'd been drinking and used her phone to call his parents, who said they'd come and pick them up. As he was going back towards her, he saw her stumble and that was it. He had been too far away to help her. The rest of the report came from Dr Howe. He and his wife had arrived at the school and found their son on the roof in a state. Haydn managed to explain that there had been an accident and while Mrs Howe stayed with him on the roof, he went down and found Anna in the playground. He checked her pulse. She was dead. Dr Howe went to his office and called the emergency services and then her parents, who came immediately. The death was estimated at sometime between Haydn's phone call at three minutes to midnight and twenty-four minutes past midnight. These facts Lizzie knew. It was the incidental detail she was interested in. She wanted to know what they talked about, what song she was singing when she danced around the roof in the humid warmth of that fated night, whether Anna was happy or suicidally sad.

But looking at Haydn's face she knew she should have kept her mouth closed. It was just too painful, and she could have kicked herself. He walked out of the shop in a thundery silence and she followed like a beaten puppy.

'I'm so sorry. Haydn? Don't be cross. I shouldn't have brought it up. The man was staring at me; he thought I was stealing gum . . . I . . . wasn't thinking. It just popped out.'

She glanced up at him, and her heart sank to see him closed off from her. He was having bad thoughts. She could see them wavering behind his beautiful eyes. She wished she could rub the dumb question out of his mind so he'd never even heard it.

'I told it all to the police,' he said.

'I know . . . I know. It was a stupid question.'

Haydn didn't say anything. He opened his new packet of

tobacco and began to roll a cigarette, making a conscious effort not to look at her. Lizzie looked away from him, tears spiking her eyes. She watched a group of kids across the road who were kicking a football up and down the pavement to each other. They celebrated imaginary goals, lifting their T-shirts over their heads and punching the air victoriously. Then a man in a suit on a bike with shiny brown brogues and a fluorescent safety sash was cycling on the pavement towards the boys. He tutted and shook his head when they didn't move out of his way. Lizzie wondered if he knew he shouldn't cycle on the pavement. He swerved around them, narrowly missing a post box. The boys laughed as he wobbled onwards and then went back to their game.

'She and I were never together, you know,' Haydn said.

'Sorry?' She stopped looking at the boys and turned back to him.

'When you talk about her, you talk as if we were, you know, together.'

'She told me you were.'

He shook his head and lit his cigarette.

'But I remember helping her pick clothes to wear when she was going to meet you. She used to tell me stuff . . . about what you did.'

Lizzie felt her cheeks redden as she remembered those chats with Anna, lying next to her on her bed, giggling, desperate for her to tell her more, trying to disguise both her curiosity and envy.

'I kissed her once. But after that she didn't want anything to do with me. Not like that, anyway. She said I was too good a mate to be a boyfriend. Her BBM. Best boy mate.' He laughed and shook his head. 'That was my problem; I was too nice, she said, like a brother or something. She was weird. She used to come round our house a lot. You know, watch TV, hang out and stuff, like we really were best mates or whatever. Then other times she'd totally blank me, walk right past me in the corridor at school like she didn't even see me. It made me crazy.' He glanced at Lizzie and gave her an embarrassed smile. 'Because, well, I was in love with her.'

Lizzie's stomach knotted with sudden jealousy and Haydn closed his eyes, his face scrunched up, and then he covered his pained expression with the flats of both his hands, his cigarette burning between two yellow-tinged fingers. Lizzie felt as if she were spying on him and dropped her eyes for a moment, as if to give him a moment of privacy to deal with whatever thought had jabbed him.

'She let me watch her undress once,' he said then.

'What?'

'All the way, no underwear or anything.'

'You have to be joking!' said Lizzie, stifling a nervous burst of laughter.

'On my life,' he said, and held a hand against his heart.

'And you weren't boyfriend and girlfriend?'

He shook his head. 'I know. Insane.'

'Blimey,' breathed Lizzie. 'I can't imagine *ever* doing something like that.'

'And Mum and Dad were downstairs.'

'No way!'

He nodded. 'She left the door open, like she got a kick out of them coming up and catching us.' He paused and glanced at her, then drew on his cigarette. 'She also made me, you know, touch myself in front of her.' He paused, waiting perhaps for her to say something. She didn't, though, so he went on. 'She said she wanted to make sure she could do it properly, you know, see exactly what happened and stuff. So she sat on the bed next to me, got me to unzip my trousers, then told me to get on with it while she watched. She was asking me what it felt like, how hard I did it and that. Then when it was over she just got up as if nothing had happened.'

Lizzie kept her eyes fixed on the pavement in front of her, making sure she stepped over the cracks between the slabs. She felt terribly uncomfortable. It was one thing to enjoy talking openly about her sister, but it was a whole different game listening to graphic stories about her doing things that made her shiver with revulsion. The way he spoke about it made it sound as if it were quite normal to ask a boy to masturbate in front of you, perhaps a bit out there but not totally bonkers, no more shocking than dissecting a rat in biology.

'Don't tell me anything more like that,' she said. 'I don't want to know that about her.'

'Sorry.'

She shrugged.

'You know, we used to go up on that roof all the time.' He put his hands into his jeans pockets and hunched his shoulders. 'There were all those old cushions and rugs up there, and I'd take my iPod and we'd listen to music. It was our place. Even though other people went up there, it was us that discovered it, so we always said it was ours.' His voice cracked and Lizzie saw him swallowing hard. He shook his head as if the memories playing were so sharp they were making cuts in his brain. 'I go over what happened, putting the key I copied in my pocket, buying the vodka with my fake ID, unlocking the school, walking up the stairs. How dark it was, my heart thumping mental, Anna giggling in front of me, her shoes tapping on the concrete, echoing like we were in a cave or something.' His head was low to his chest. 'If I'd said no, if I'd made her meet me in the park or in my room, she'd still be alive. And why didn't I pull her off that wall when I had the chance? Hold on to her so hard she couldn't have fallen, no matter what happened.'

'You can't think like that,' said Lizzie. She lifted his chin to look at her. He moved without resistance, but when he met her eyes he suddenly turned away from her. 'Haydn,' she said. 'It doesn't help. We can all say what if. There are a million things that we all could have done differently that might mean she was still here.'

Lizzie lifted her hand to touch his elbow, but he jumped backwards as if she'd given him an electric shock. Then he turned and ran at a garden wall that flanked the pavement, kicked it twice with his boot. He kicked it a third time and as he did he spun and collapsed with his back against the wall, arms crossed across his bent knees, head buried in the crooks of his elbows. He began to cry like a badly hurt child, his body raked with fierce sobs. She knelt next to him and put her arm around his shoulders. She rubbed his knee with her other hand, tried to shush him, but he only cried more, and she began to feel scared. She wanted to help him but had no idea what she should do. She looked up at the people walking past, hoping to catch a kindly eye, but nobody allowed a kindly eye to wander. Instead they passed on by, pretended the crying boy and the fretful girl didn't exist, turned their heads in the opposite direction, pointedly checked their watches for the time and crossed the road.

'Haydn,' she said. 'Haydn. It's OK. Please. It's OK.' She put her other arm around him and held him tightly to her.

He lifted his head. Snot and tears streaked his face. His eyes were bloodshot and puffed and searched her face backwards and forwards. 'She was dead.' He began to scratch at his forearms, raking his fingers up and down through his T-shirt. 'I'd saw her lying on the ground. This weird, still shape on the ground. How could she be dead?'

Lizzie pulled one of her sleeves over the heel of her hand and gently dabbed his face dry like a nurse cleaning the wounds of a soldier. They stared at each other. Her pupils fixed to his and she marvelled how deep and black they were, how she felt like diving into them just to find out how far they reached. A stab of hot desire shot through her. She would have kissed him, but he opened his mouth as if to speak, then shook his head, let out a frustrated sigh.

'What?' whispered Lizzie. He hesitated; there was definitely something there, something he wanted to say. 'What?' she asked again.

But he closed his mouth and shook his head.

She stood and held out her hand for his. He took it and hauled himself up, and as he did, her body, her fingers and toes, her insides, everything, began to tingle madly. She stood on her tiptoes to kiss him. She tasted the tears on his lips and was hit with a sudden lust, so intense she imagined her body might burst into flame. She pulled his T-shirt free of his jeans and ran her hands up underneath it. The feel of his skin was warm and smooth. His sandpaper hands were on her cheeks and neck. She lost herself to him. Pushed him backwards against a parked car. Brought his hands to her chest. She wanted him to touch between her legs. She ached all over, possessed by white-hot desire. Anna hadn't had him like this.

He was all hers.

In the void outside her lust she heard a group of people laughing as they walked past. *Get a fucking room*, a voice said. Then more laughing. She drew back from him. His cheeks were red, her need mirrored in his glazed eyes.

'Let's go somewhere,' she rasped. Her heart thumped; all she wanted was him, but the exhilaration, the nerves and the fear of what she was feeling, of what was about to come, threatened to overwhelm her.

'Your house?'

Lizzie imagined her mum finding Haydn in her room. Just the thought of Lizzie laying eyes on Haydn had been enough to make her angry. If she walked in on them kissing and more she'd go nuts.

She shook her head. 'I know where, though.'

'Where?'

'Wait and see.'

They burst into excited giggles, the trauma of earlier forgotten as easily as a bad novel. They broke into a run, hand in hand, weaving in and out of people, dogs, kids on scooters, whole families Sunday-strolling to the park or river. Not running to have sex!

They stopped outside the small gate that led to her grandparents' garden, out of breath, their desire still raging. There was a code pad. She tapped the numbers in, barely able to think, panting and giggling nervously, gripping his hand as if letting go would mean death. The gate creaked open and she grinned at him. Then their faces fell serious with the realization of what they were about to do. Haydn tucked some hair behind her ear and she leant against his hand, turning her face to softly kiss his palm.

They crept in, and Lizzie pulled the gate shut behind them. They heard voices further away in the garden and both of them froze.

'My parents are having lunch here,' she whispered. 'But the shed behind this bush is mine and Anna's; my grandparents gave it to us. They never use it because they're both too old. Nobody ever comes up here now. Only me.' She bent down and crept forward a couple of steps to peer through the leaves that shielded them from the terrace. Her heart was pounding. She could see her mum and dad talking with Uncle Daniel, though she wasn't close enough to hear what they were saying. Her dad was standing on the grass, and her mum and uncle were sitting at the table.

'What is it?' Haydn whispered.

Lizzie flapped a hand to quieten him. He put his hand on her bottom and she stifled a giggle.

'They definitely won't come up here,' she whispered, watching her parents go into the house. She waited. Her uncle got up and followed them in. 'They've gone inside. Come on,' she said to Haydn over her shoulder. 'I'll show you.'

'What if they get home and you're not there? You'll get grief, won't you?'

'Ohmigod,' she said. '*So* don't care!' She grinned and pushed open the door. It was such a familiar place, with the upturned crate, its stub of candle glued to it with old wax, the ancient tins of soup, the box of toys, the postcards nailed to the walls like paintings, but it had a different feel right then, a frisson, the air molecules within it fizzing with a startling energy.

'This place is mad!' laughed Haydn.

Lizzie pushed the crate and box of toys to the side and tried to ignore the vivid memories of playing happily with Anna. She sat on the dusty floor with her arms linked around her knees and smiled up at him. He dropped down beside her, then took her face in his hands and kissed her. Her heart thumped and her stomach pitched with nerves. She lifted her shirt over her head and lay back, suddenly painfully aware of how small her breasts were, how unsexy her plain white bra was, of how many dark moles and freckles splattered her pale skinny body.

Haydn drew in a breath. He stretched out his hand and trailed his fingers from her neck to her tummy button. Then he pulled his own shirt over his head. There wasn't an ounce of fat on his body and she could see every one of his muscles, defined and toned, not big like a body-builder, more like a long-distance runner, or maybe a tennis player. His skin was clear, but then she noticed his arms. She'd never seen them before, covered as they were with long sleeves, and she gasped in alarm. The skin between his wrists and elbows was laced with scars that criss-crossed like cobweb. Some were raised and white, while others were fresher with rough scabs of brown. Some had been opened up with fresh blood seeping from the edges, no doubt from before in the street when he'd scratched against them, so upset by thoughts of Anna's death that he obviously hadn't felt it. There were some really thick ones, but then others that were no more than scratches, the kind you might get from an overly playful kitten. She lifted her hand and ran her fingers over them.

'What are they?'

'They're nothing,' he said. 'I don't want to talk about anything. I just want to kiss you.' His lust-filled eyes burrowed into her and the cuts and scarring were forgotten. She let her hand drop from his arm to rest on the waistband of his jeans.

'You know,' she said, 'we'll probably get splinters.'

'I don't care.'

Then they kissed again and the passion from the street relit in moments, his hands on her, hers on him, their lips together. Her hands fumbled for the zipper on his jeans. His tore at the catch on her bra. Shiver after shiver of lust. Then he lifted his face from hers.

'Are you sure?' he said. His voice was throaty and gruff. His eyes were glazed again. The skin around his lips was red from kissing.

She nodded.

'Hang on then,' he said, and reached for his jacket. He rummaged in the pockets.

Lizzie's stomach churned with nerves. This was it. Losing her virginity; she was suddenly terrified. Was this how she imagined it?

Certainly she'd imagined it with Haydn, almost from the memorial onwards, but in all those imagined times it was never in years of dirt on the hard floor of the shed in her grandparents' garden, toys and memories surrounding them on every side. *No*, she told herself firmly. *This is what you want. This is your new beginning.* She took a deep breath and tried to relax.

Haydn threw his jacket back on the floor and she saw he held a condom in one hand and his iPod in the other. He put the condom on the floor beside them and then he put one headphone into her ear and one into his.

'I made us a playlist.'

He pressed play, and she recognized the first song immediately. It was the Chris Isaak song that Anna loved. The one they'd talked about in the cemetery. Lizzie remembered Anna singing it in her room at the top of her voice, Lizzie sitting and watching her sister dancing around in her underwear, her womanly hips pushing through white lace knickers, her arms moving gracefully above her head, twisting and twirling, full of music, full of life.

Lizzie smiled, then closed her eyes and waited for him to kiss her.

The song and Haydn engulfed her. Were those really psychedelic lights when he kissed her? Electricity when he touched her? He kissed her breasts, sending blissful quivers through her so that she arched herself up to him, desperate for more.

'I love you,' he said. The words floated over the song and settled on Lizzie like three strands of drifting gossamer.

'I love you, too,' she whispered.

'Say it again.'

Lizzie almost burst. 'Oh Haydn, I love you so much. To the moon and back. I will love you for ever.'

Then he was inside her with a flash of pain.

Afterwards they lay in each other's arms, their hair full of leaf bits and dirt, her body tingling up and down.

'Do you think she could see us?' Lizzie asked him quietly.

'Yes.'

'Do you think she was happy for us?'

'Yes.'

'I miss her, Haydn.'

He leant up on one elbow and picked a piece of something out of her hair. 'I meant it when I said I loved you.'

'Really?'

'We share something.'

'Maybe it's Anna.'

'No.' He lay back down with his hands behind his head and closed his eyes. 'We were meant for each other. She brought us together. This is what was meant to happen. Life is one great plan, one way through it, and sometimes things you can't explain, get explained.' He turned his head and smiled at her. 'Tell me you love me again.'

'I love you.' Lizzie lay her head on him and stroked the flat of her hand across his hairless chest. 'I love you so much I can't breathe.'

The Witching Hour

Kate's eyes stung as she stared at the computer screen. The light from the monitor lit the room with an electric white-blue glow and the computer hummed loud against the night-time still of the house. It was very late, into the small hours, when the only thing that moved in silence was the minute hand on the kitchen clock. She'd seen this time of night a lot since Anna died. Sleep was one of those luxuries that had become elusive. Sleep and sex and laughing, luxuries she'd previously taken for granted. If she could sit her young self down and have a chat, she'd tell her to treasure every moment of laughing and making love and sleeping as if they were one-carat diamonds; life without them was arduous.

Kate double-clicked the mouse and the printer whirred into action. She waited for it to spit out the printed page and then bent to pick up the warm piece of paper and added it to her pile.

'I made you some milk.'

Kate turned to see Jon in his dressing gown, his hair sticking up. He held out a mug.

'That's kind of you,' she said. She turned back to the computer. 'Did I wake you?'

'No.'

'I'm sorry if I did.'

'You didn't.' He pulled up a chair and sat next to her, placing the mug beside the keyboard. 'I thought you were painting.'

'No.' She bit her lip and stared at the screen.

They were silent. When the screensaver flicked on, the room was plunged into darkness. She stared at the Microsoft logo twisting randomly around the black screen.

'Will you come to bed? It's past four.'

'We need to go to the police.'

Jon's head sank forward and he sighed, then rubbed his eyes.

'You saw his face, Jon. He did it. It was him.'

'He'll deny it,' said Jon, after a weary pause.

'So? We'll prove it.'

'How? You heard them. He said it wasn't him. It's his word against Rebecca's.'

'And the film.'

Jon was quiet.

'He can't get away with it. He just can't.' Her voice was strained and desperate.

Jon took her hand and stroked it. 'I know he's guilty too,' he said. 'But I can't see what good it will do anyone to fight a nasty battle. What good will it do us? Or Anna? Her memory. Everyone will be talking about her. My parents, people at school, strangers. It'll be in the newspapers. We'll have journalists hanging around.' He paused. 'And even if we put ourselves through all of that and he's found guilty, he'll only get a year, maybe six months.'

'No,' she said, grabbing at her pile of printed papers and thrusting them under Jon's nose. 'It's all here, in the Sexual Offences Act. Here . . .' She frantically leafed through the paper and snatched at a piece. Then she grabbed the mouse and shook it against the table to get rid of the screensaver and turn the monitor light on.

She leant close to the screen to read. 'Abuse of Position of Trust. If a person in a position of trust – that's a teacher – over eighteen touches a person *under* eighteen, and that touch is sexual, and that person knows the other is under eighteen, it's an offence. She was *fifteen*, and he knew that, Jon. At age fifteen, there's no question . . .' She rifled for another page. 'See . . . here. Penetration of a child of fifteen carries a prison sentence of up to fourteen years. Jesus, he'd get ten years just for having Rebecca watch. This isn't games, Jon. It's not some minor indiscretion; it's deadly, deadly serious. You should read this stuff. You should. Even if he wasn't a headmaster and she wasn't one of his pupils, having sex with a fifteen-year-old isn't something wishy-washy. He's committed an offence and it needs to be handed over to the police.' She paused. 'What if this isn't the first time? What if he does it again? To an eleven-year-old? How would we live with ourselves?'

Jon nodded faintly and took the printouts. He cast an eye over them for a moment or two while Kate sat quietly and watched for his reaction.

'The look on his face made me sick,' he whispered, his eyes still reading. 'The way he denied it. I wanted to kill him.'

Kate leant forward and laid her head on Jon's shoulder. 'Why is this happening to us?'

He wrapped his arms around her and rested his cheek against her head. 'I don't know. But gunning for Stephen, striking up a lengthy court battle, it's not going to make it any easier.'

She sat back from him and turned her head to the screen. 'I must be a very bad person.'

'You're not.'

She knew differently, though. She had none of Jon's control, none of his Herculean ability to turn the other cheek; she wanted Stephen to suffer. Like she was suffering.

'Jon?' she whispered.

'Yes?'

'What if he killed her?'

Jon tensed.

'What if she didn't fall by accident?' She drew back from him, waiting for an answer, but he said nothing. 'What if she wasn't dead when he got to the school?'

Kate didn't go to bed that night. Jon left her at the computer. Eventually, she moved to the sofa and pulled the throw around her shoulders and laid her head down, stared into the dark, her mind racing helter-skelter over everything that had happened that day.

She was woken by Jon speaking on the telephone.

'I'll try to get in by lunchtime. I'll ring if I'm not going to make it . . . No, no, all well . . . just a minor domestic situation I have to deal with . . . that's kind of you, no, we'll be fine . . . if you could just let David know . . . yes, check my dairy, but off the top of my head I think Tuesday should work . . . OK, sure . . . Thank you, Laura.'

Kate stood and stretched her back, which ached horribly. She folded the throw and laid it over the arm of the sofa, then went into the kitchen. Lizzie was sitting at the table eating her breakfast.

'Morning, Mum,' she said, without looking up. 'I can't find my hockey kit. Do you know where it is?'

'Your hockey kit?'

Lizzie nodded.

Kate tried to think, but her mind was blank, numb from her sleepless night. 'I haven't seen it.'

'I brought it home to wash,' Lizzie said through a mouthful of cereal.

Kate's head was beginning to ache. 'I can have a look, but I don't remember seeing it.'

Lizzie checked her watch and then quickly shovelled the last spoonfuls of cereal into her mouth, milk dripping from her spoon as she did.

'I'm late; I'll check at school,' she said.

She grabbed her school bag from the table and kissed both Kate and Jon on the cheek. Then she rushed out of the kitchen and slammed the front door behind her.

Jon handed her a cup of tea. She checked the clock; it was eight thirty. If she ever missed her seven o'clock tea, she would always make herself wait until her nine-thirty cup. She looked at the tea and then at Jon.

'It won't hurt you,' he said.

She was about to explain to him for the hundredth time how her routine, however insane it seemed to him, was the backbone of her day, but decided not to. She reached for the tea and thanked him. She took a sip. It was just what she needed. She gave him a small smile and took another sip.

'When you've finished that, you'd better go up and get some clothes on,' said Jon. 'I'm not going to work. We're going to the police.'

A Floating Kiss

Jon stood alone in the kitchen. Kate had gone straight upstairs to paint. It had been hard at the police station. Harder than he imagined. The policeman they'd spoken to, an older man with grey hair and deep craggy lines, had been gentle but unemotional when they told him about Anna and her headmaster. He asked them to sit in the waiting room and left them for nearly forty minutes. Kate picked up a magazine and turned the pages too quickly to be reading. When the policeman came back he asked them to come with him and led them to a small interview room with no windows and an empty desk, three chairs and a water cooler, and took their statement. Jon had given it. He expected Kate to interrupt with incidental detail he might have forgotten, but she stayed quiet, running her finger up and down a gouge in the wooden desk. Jon played him the film. The policeman watched it without registering anything on his face, then nodded twice before turning the phone off and pushing it very deliberately to the middle of the desk so it sat like an unexploded bomb between them.

'What happens now?' Jon asked.

'We are obligated to follow up your allegations with an investigation.'

'Will he be suspended?'

'I can't tell you whether he will or not. However, in my experience, it is usual for any teacher to be suspended following an accusation of this nature.'

'Will he go to prison?' said Kate. She didn't look up from the gouge in the desk.

'That will be for the court to decide.'

'He'll deny it,' said Jon.

'They always do,' said the officer.

Jon flicked the kettle on and stared at nothing while he waited for it to boil. When its click jolted him out of his staring, he put a tea bag into a mug and went to the fridge for the milk. The milk carton was empty. He couldn't remember putting an empty one back that morning. He must have been in a daze; that sort of thing was very unlike him. Must have been Kate or Lizzie. He fished the tea bag out of the tea and put it in the bin, then he picked up his keys and walked out of the front door, thrusting his hands deep into his pockets as he kicked along the street.

As he turned into the corner shop, someone said hello to him. He looked up. It was Rachel. She was standing at the counter wearing a lemon-yellow sundress and brown leather flip-flops. Her hair, which shone like a shampoo advert, was held out of her eyes by sunglasses perched on her head.

'Hi Jon,' she said. 'How are you?'

'Fine, thanks.' He grabbed a pint of milk from the chiller. 'No milk, though.'

She pointed at the loaf of bread she'd just paid for. 'I'm no bread. I had an almost pregnant craving for a tuna mayo sandwich for lunch; no good without bread.'

'I've a cup of black tea waiting at home for me.'

She smiled, then: 'You look tired.'

Jon nodded.

'Do you want to talk about it?'

He didn't want to talk about it. He smiled at her and shook his head as he handed the milk to the boy behind the counter.

'Fifty-two, please.'

Jon patted his empty jacket pocket, then closed his eyes and swore silently.

'Don't worry,' Rachel said. She opened her purse and counted some change on to the counter.

'Thank you,' he said.

'No problem.'

'I'll drop the money round later.'

'Consider it a present.'

They walked out of the shop and Rachel turned in the direction of her home. Jon was about to say goodbye, but had a sudden dread of being alone. 'Rach, do you mind if I walk you home?' he asked. 'Five minutes' company would be a good thing for me, I think.'

'Of course. That would be nice.'

Though they were quiet, the quiet was a cosying one. The quiets that he and Kate now shared were laden with sadness or anger and were gruelling in their weight. It was nice to be with Rachel – it felt comfortable; she was a link to good times past.

'You know,' he said at last, 'she still changes Anna's sheets. Every Monday morning.'

'I can see why,' Rachel said. 'It must be hard to stop doing that sort of thing.'

'When I was a child, our dog died. I found him. He'd been run over outside the house. The person who hit him drove off and left him at the side of the road. His leg was broken, and there were all these splinters of bone and gunk, and his mouth was open with his tongue hanging out. He'd been dead long enough to look dead, if that makes sense – his fur was all matted and his eyes had lost their shine, and when I poked him he was stiff like he was made out of stone. I remember being scared to pick him up in case he moved suddenly.' He paused. 'It was my fault he died because I left the front door open. My mother said that. She said, "I've told you so many times, Jonathan, if you leave the door open the dog will run out and he'll get hit by a car. You know that. We live in London. There are too many cars." I didn't leave the door open on purpose. I'd run in for the loo because I was desperate. I was ten.'

They reached the bus stop opposite Rachel's house. Jon sat on one of the red plastic seats under the canopy. There was a pile of broken squares of glass on the floor where one of the panels had been smashed. He kicked the bits of greeny glass as Rachel sat herself next to him.

'Losing a pet is hard when you're a child,' she said. 'But anyone could have left the door open. Anyone could have made that mistake. It only takes a second for something to go wrong and an accident to happen.'

'I know that now, but that pain stayed with me for years and years – crying on to my dead dog, saying sorry over and over, wanting him back more than anything.' He kicked at the ground, sending squares of glass skittering across the road. 'And then I see my daughter dead. My Anna lying on an ambulance stretcher, her face broken, blood knotting up her hair, her eyes staring straight ahead with nothing behind them, as if they were made of glass, and I think if I could lose that stupid dog a million times it would taste like honey compared to this.'

Rachel reached for Jon's hand.

'When is this ever going to leave us?'

'It's not,' she said. 'This is something that will be with you

202

every day until the end. There's no other way. You and Kate are Anna's parents. You will never forget her. You will never stop wondering what might have been, and you will never get over her. But you will eventually learn to live with it. You'll learn to go through life, step by step, and not be floored at every turn by reminders. You'll get used to the pain, and when you get used to it you'll be able to live more normally.'

'I can't imagine that. So much of the time Kate can't even look at me. She finds it easier to shut me out. We have a moment of closeness and then it's gone and she's alone again. I feel like I'm losing her.'

'You're not losing her. You both need time, that's all.'

'And then to top it all,' he said, 'my father's ill.' Jon laughed bitterly.

'I'm sorry.'

'Alzheimer's. I can't bear to be in the same room as him; just looking at him scares me.'

'That's natural. It's a horrible illness.'

'You're being kind. It's the least natural thing I've ever felt, and I hate myself for it.'

'You seem to hate yourself for a lot of things.'

He was silent.

'You mustn't hate yourself. You're a lovely person. I thought so the minute I met you. You remember? That dreadful bring-a-dish Sarah Roberts did for Valentine's Day for the NCT crowd so we could all meet the husbands.'

Jon nodded. He did remember; Kate had shone that evening. He'd got stuck with two dull men with baby boys who'd asked him what his son was called. When he replied he had a daughter called Anna, they looked at him pityingly then ignored him, talked non-stop about which rugby club their boys would join and the optimum age they should start if they wanted a shot at the national squad. Then Kate floated up behind them. She was a vision that night in a fitted black above-the-knee dress, her milk-full breasts spilling over just enough, her stomach almost flat. Pregnancy and birth had given her a glow and motherhood suited her. Unfair as it was, next to the other exhausted, bloated mums she was a goddess, and when she pressed her lips against Jon's cheek both men were silenced.

She leant close to his ear and whispered: 'Your challenge, lovely boy, is to get as many different fruits into conversation as possible.' Then she kissed him again and winked at the other two, before coming back to his ear. 'I'm doing veg.'

He snorted a burst of laughter that fired a spray of mustard-glazed cocktail sausage. Kate flashed the men her brightest smile. 'Goodness, what turnip wouldn't I shag to get a slice of roasted aubergine right now!' Then she sashayed through the crowd and away from him.

'Your wife?' one of the men asked, his eyes crawling after Kate.

'Sure is,' Jon said, popping an olive into his mouth. 'The apple of my eye. A real peach.'

Jon looked at Rachel. 'I remember.'

'You were the most desirable man in the room,' Rachel said.

Jon wrinkled his brow in disagreement. 'That's a sweet thing to say. Untrue, of course.'

'We all said so. We were hormonal, remember, and most of us were stuck with pretty rubbish husbands. We were jealous of Kate from the off.' She smiled and patted his hand. 'You've got to be kinder to yourself.'

He looked at her and was suddenly knocked sideways by the suggestion of a kiss that leapt out from nowhere to hang in the air between them. Rachel cleared her throat with a quiet cough, then fixed her eyes on something over his shoulder. He rubbed a hand around his face, pressing his forefinger and thumb hard into the bridge of his nose and then he stood.

'I should get back.'

'Yes,' she said. 'Me too. I've a bowl of tuna mayo waiting for some bread.'

'You'll be all right getting home?'

'I should be OK,' she laughed. 'I'm not sure I'm in too much danger in Brook Green at midday as long as I stop, look and listen, of course.' She nodded in the direction of her house, directly across the road from them.

Jon looked over and his eyes immediately settled on her front door. The kiss in the air was forgotten as he stared at the door through which his daughter had escaped. He saw her then, so clearly, watched her step out of the house, close the door quietly. She stood motionless, holding her breath and listening hard, making sure she hadn't been heard. Then he saw her creeping through the shadows, turning on to the pavement, and once she was clear of the house, he saw her break into a jog in the direction of the school.

Rachel stepped up to the curb. 'Enjoy your tea,' she said.

She crossed the road and walked the short distance to her house. Her lemon-yellow sundress shone as if it were the only splash of colour left. Like that film, Jon thought as he watched her, the one with the child in the red coat who wanders through the greyscale decimation.

Scars

Lizzie felt like a prison inmate in a bid for freedom, terrified that any minute there'd be a shout, the click of aimed rifles, the wail of an urgent siren.

She kept her head down and walked with purpose, counting her steps to the front gates to ease her thumping heart. The unfamiliar kick of being naughty jumbled with the thrill of seeing Haydn, knowing that in a matter of minutes she'd feel his skin against hers and smell his sweet tobacco-tainted breath, and sent adrenalin pumping into her blood by the litre.

As she got closer to the school gate and the promise of beyond, a sweat began to crawl over the palms of her hands and down the hollow of her back. *Surely it couldn't be this easy*, she thought. But then she was out, through the gates. She laughed out loud as she pulled her tie loose and stuffed it into her bag. She'd been sure someone would stop her. She'd been worrying about it all morning, so engrossed with watching the clock on her classroom wall that she'd not heard a word from anyone. But there she was, out of school, sunshine on her face, about to meet her boyfriend. Her boyfriend! She still couldn't believe it.

When she turned the next corner he was there, leaning against the wall and smoking, his iPod plugged in, hair covering his face, and jeans so tight she could see every line of his leg. She smiled and broke into a jog. When he caught sight of her he pulled the earpieces out of his ears and wrapped them around the iPod, which he slipped into his jacket pocket. Then he smiled back and she ran faster, jumping into his arms as soon as she could. He twirled her twice around and nuzzled his face into her neck.

'I can't get you out of my mind,' he whispered into her ear. 'I've been thinking about you every minute.'

'And me you,' she said. She kissed him.

'Let's go back to my place,' he said.

'Are you sure?' She wasn't. She would have been much happier to go to her shed. She felt safe there. But he nodded and grabbed her hand and her worries were swept away.

They didn't talk as he unlocked his front door. She put her arms around him from behind and rested her cheek against the rough denim of his jacket. This was bliss. Three weeks before, she could never have imagined she would be this happy. She wouldn't even have thought she was *capable* of feeling this happy. She'd imagined it, of course, but she assumed it was just fantasy and would remain so, captive like she was in the misery of her family tragedy. But she had emerged, the butterfly she always hoped she was. Haydn was her brave new world.

They ran up the stairs to his room and closed the door. Within seconds they were kissing, tearing at each other's clothes, tumbling towards the bed and collapsing on to it in a lustful giggling heap.

'This is *definitely* better than hockey,' she said.

'I can't believe you bunked off. I thought you were, like, the world's best-behaved pupil.'

'That was the *old* Lizzie. The *new* Lizzie does all sorts of bad, bad things.' She took his hand and put it between her legs.

'So she does,' he said, his voice a rasp, which made Lizzie smile. 'I like her.'

'Me too,' she said.

'You're so fucking gorgeous.'

'You are too.'

'I'm not.'

'Oh my God! You completely are. You're the best-looking person I've ever met.'

'Not like my dad, though,' he said.

'Your dad?'

'All the girls at school were always going on about how handsome he is and that. I used to hear it all the time; it got so fucking boring. I'm glad I don't go to that school any more so I don't have to keep hearing that shit.'

'Well, they're all freaks. You are *so* much better-looking than he is. Like a million times more.'

And then he kissed her. Hard. As if he was never going to stop.

They kissed and groped and fumbled, submerged in this new and exciting place, where the body ruled and the mind followed like an acquiescent slave. Lizzie was totally absorbed until she heard a noise somewhere outside Haydn's room; her heart almost stopped with the shock.

'What was that?' she said, pulling away from him and sitting up, clutching the sheet over her chest.

'What was what?' He tried to pull her back down.

'No,' she said, and shushed him with a hand against his mouth. 'I heard something.'

'It wasn't anything.'

'Your parents?'

'Don't worry about it. They're both at school. They never leave that place. Come on; you can't stop.'

She hesitated.

'Look, it was probably the cat,' he said. 'The stupid fleabag is always knocking shit down.'

She laid her head on his chest and stroked his shoulder down to his hand, feeling the bumps of those scars on his arms. She put the tips of her fingers to one of the thickest, risen as if it were embossed, and traced its length.

'How did you get them?'

Haydn shrugged.

'There's so many.'

He stayed quiet.

'This one must have been nasty.'

Still he didn't speak.

'What happened?'

'Stanley knife.'

'What?'

'I did it with a Stanley knife,' he said, with grim admission.

'But why would you do that?' She sat up, unable to hide her alarm. 'Did you do them all?'

He nodded.

'But why?' She felt sick that he could hurt himself.

'It helps.'

'With what?'

'With lots of shit.'

There was silence as she eyed the now seemingly hundreds of scars that struck his body with random malice.

'How does it help?' she asked, steadier now as her initial horror ebbed. She laid her head back on his chest.

'It's hard to explain,' he said. 'But if something is hurting inside me, you know, from what I'm feeling or thinking, then I cut, which is properly painful, and it sort of takes my mind off the other shit for a while.'

She tried to imagine cutting into her own skin. She bent down and touched her lips to the scar nearest the crook of his elbow and then she moved down his arm, planting the lightest of kisses on every one. With each kiss she became more and more upset until she found she was crying.

'Hey,' he soothed. 'What's wrong?'

'I can't bear the thought of you doing that to yourself.'

'Don't be dumb. Now I've got you I'll never do it again. Ever.' She shifted her head to look up at him. He smiled at her then pulled her up to him. 'You've made me OK again.'

He kissed her then, hard and passionate, different from before, more demanding. He moved her around, using his hands to guide her on to him. He was almost rough, as if he'd lost control of himself, and though at first she felt unnerved, she soon began to enjoy it as the force of his desire excited her. As he climaxed he shouted out her name.

Afterwards, Lizzie lay curled into him, her stomach clenching with the aftershocks of sex. 'I wish we could live in your room for ever,' she said.

He laughed and reached over her for the cigarettes on his desk.

'No, seriously. I mean obviously we'd have to get food and have somewhere to, well, you know, pee and stuff, but otherwise, I wish we could lock that door and never leave.'

'I'm going to sit outside your bedroom window tonight,' he said.

It was her turn to laugh. 'You're what?'

'Tell me which window is yours. I'm going to sit outside it. So I'm close to you while you sleep.'

'No, you're not.' She laughed again and kissed his chest.

'Which window?'

'Don't be dumb.'

'Tell me.'

'It faces the road, upstairs, far right.'

'I'll be there.'

'Freak.' She smiled at him. 'Now, how about you kiss me again? We might as well make bunking off worthwhile.'

Paint

'Your teacher called.'

Kate watched as guilt rouged her daughter's face from the neck up. Lizzie took her school bag slowly off her shoulder and hung it on a chair. She moved deliberately, her eyes lowered.

'Really?'

'She said you missed hockey and afternoon registration.'

Lizzie looked at her mum and Kate saw her take a deep breath. 'I couldn't find my kit this morning. I asked you, remember? When you came into the kitchen. You didn't know, so I thought it was at school, but I couldn't find it there. It must be here somewhere.'

'You were seen leaving the school.'

Kate was fuming. Following her dreadful night, talking to the police and her blinding headache, the last thing she expected having to deal with was a phone call telling her that Lizzie had bunked off school.

'I can't believe you did that.'

'It's only hockey.' Lizzie adopted a surly teenage slouch that a year ago would have made Kate smile.

'You left school premises. Anything could have happened to you. If you're supposed to be at school but instead you're gallivanting about the place, how can I know you're safe?'

'I'm nearly sixteen; I can cross a road.'

'*Don't* take that tone with me. You are not nearly sixteen and you do *not* bunk off school.' Kate tried not to think of the number of times she'd played truant; at Lizzie's age she was out of school more than she was in it. 'Where did you go, anyway?'

Lizzie folded her arms 'Nowhere.'

'Don't.' Kate tightened her voice and raised her eyebrows.

'For a coffee.'

'On your own?'

Her daughter's eyes dropped to the floor. 'Uh-huh.' Then she looked up, and the two of them stared at each other. Kate saw for the first time how much Lizzie had grown up. She was staring at a young woman, taller, more beautiful; her slimness had become graceful rather than stringy, and she wondered how she'd not noticed these changes until now. Kate tempered her face.

'Look, Lizzie, I don't mind you missing hockey; I hated sport. But you can't leave the school. Promise me you won't do it again. I need to know you're safe. I can't be worrying about you all day, every day. Do you understand?'

Lizzie didn't move for a moment or two, then reluctantly nodded.

'She said you'd be given detention.'

Lizzie looked away from her and flushed again. 'Who saw me leave?'

'Mrs Howe.' Kate clenched her fists at her sides. Of course it had to be that woman who'd seen Lizzie leave. The fact that her daughter had skipped school for a few hours was neither here nor there; it was being spotted by Angela Howe that boiled Kate's blood. She was just thankful it was Lizzie's form tutor who called instead of her.

213

Lizzie seemed to turn a few shades paler. 'I'm going to my room; I've got some reading to do.'

Kate made her way up to the studio. She wondered how many times Anna had bunked off. She'd like to think never; it unsettled her to think of her daughters doing things behind her back that she had absolutely no notion of. Kate was suddenly hit with another graphic image of Anna with Stephen Howe, and squeezed her eyes shut to concentrate on driving the filth out of her head. Repelling these flashes drained her; she loathed the way they snuck up on her at any time, haunting her with their vileness, playing with her mind like water torture.

She picked up her paintbrush and dabbed it into the smudge of brown oil on her palette. Then she lifted it to her canvas. She closed her eyes and waited for the familiar calmness to settle over her. When it did there came a perfect conception of Anna as a baby, gurgling, holding her feet, her chubby legs dimpled at the knee and creased at the thigh. Her shock of chestnut hair, innocent and untouched, was a thousand miles from the alien Anna in the gritty films that plagued Kate's devastated world.

It was late when she finally put her brush down. Anna was on the canvas grinning a gummy smile at her. Though the twinkle in her eye was a masterpiece of Kate's recollection, there was something about her mouth that didn't work, but she was done. She was tired.

Jon and Lizzie were already in bed. The kitchen was dark and quiet, save for the restful whirr of the dishwasher. She opened the fridge, squinting against the light inside, and looked for something to eat. She wasn't hungry; it was habit. She was never sleepy after she'd painted and often made herself a late-night snack to fill the wakefulness. Nothing grabbed her, though, so she closed the fridge door and the kitchen fell back into darkness. Moments later the phone tore into the stillness. Kate jumped and made a lunge for the receiver.

'Hello?' she said quietly, glancing at the clock on the oven. It was past eleven.

'Kiki, it's Dan.'

'Why the hell are you calling at this time?'

'Were you sleeping?'

'No.'

'That's OK then.'

'Jon and Lizzie are.'

'I wondered if you wanted that drink.'

'At this time?'

'If you'd like.'

She thought for a moment. She was wide awake, hyped up; if she went to bed now it would only be with yet more thoughts of Stephen Howe and Anna.

'Yes,' she said with a sigh. 'OK.'

'Only if you want to.'

'I might as well. I've had a day and a half. I won't be able to sleep anyway.'

'Thinking about that cock?'

'I can't think of anything else.' She paused. 'We went to the police today.'

'And?'

'God, Dan, this whole thing's so hideous—' Kate pinched the bridge of her nose and breathed for a second or two to stem her tears. 'I'm sorry. It's been a hard day. A drink would be great.'

'I'll be with you in ten.'

She filled herself a glass of water, and as she drank she heard Jon's voice calling her from the landing.

She went to the door and peered up at him. 'Sorry?'

'On the telephone?' he asked, his voice croaky with sleep.

'It was a wrong number,' she lied. 'Kids mucking around.'

He nodded and then turned and trudged back to bed. Kate felt guilty for lying and she considered calling Dan back and telling him she didn't feel like a drink any more. But in truth she'd never felt more like a drink. She opened the coat cupboard and found a jacket, and then slipped out of the house to wait for Dan on the street.

It was a warm night with a clear sky, no clouds and lots of stars. Someone coughed from the other side of the road. She looked over to where the noise had come from, but couldn't see anyone.

It wasn't long before there was a screech of grating gears at the top of the street and she allowed herself a brief smile; Dan was an appalling driver. She walked up to the pavement and waited for him to pull over.

Dan wound down the window. 'Good evening, my dear. Fancy picking someone of the likes of you up on a street corner.'

'It's not a corner.'

He waved her away. 'Devil in the detail.' He got out of the car and walked around to her. He was grinning, that ridiculous trilby set far back on his head. He held out a bottle of whisky.

'Your drink, m'dear.'

She eyed the bottle. 'Whisky?'

'Well, if you need a drink, you should have a drink.' He paused. 'Not that I want to be a bad influence, or anything.'

'Liar.'

He grinned again and reset his trilby.

She hesitated, then grabbed the bottle. What the hell, she thought, and tipped it to her lips. The liquid burned her throat and she whistled.

'Right,' he said, taking back the bottle. 'Hop in. We're going for a drive. It'll be like the olden days. You, me, a set of wheels and some booze.'

She looked over his shoulder. 'I seem to remember you were driving your parents' car back then, too.'

'Ahh, but it's a Mercedes now. The days of squeezing you into a Morris are gone.'

Against her better judgement she smiled. She was fond of Dan. They'd shared good times, been part of a wild group at art school. She couldn't remember much of that first year. She remembered having fun, though; anarchic, irresponsible fun. It seemed like centuries ago.

'Was that a smile?'

'It's good to have a break, that's all.'

'Come on,' he said. He turned and opened the door, then removed his hat and waved it extravagantly to usher her in. Again she hesitated, but only for a moment, then she climbed in. The car smelt of paint.

'More whisky?' He nudged her hand with the bottle.

'I'm not sure Jon would think this was a good idea.'

'Being with me?'

'No,' she said. 'Proof alcohol as the solution to trauma.'

'Ahh, well, what does he know?' Dan took the bottle and swigged. 'Millions of alcoholics can't be wrong.'

She closed her eyes and concentrated on the warm feeling of the whisky in her tummy. She breathed in, aware again of the unmistakable smell of paint. She turned in her seat, the leather squeaking under her as she did. On the back seat of the car were tins and tins of house paint piled up on an old rug.

'What's that?' she asked.

'And I thought you were an artist.'

She held up her paint-smudged hands by way of an answer.

He laughed. 'Good to see you've not stopped.'

'I'm not sure Jon would say the same.'

'Are you guys having a tough time?'

'Of course,' she said. 'It's hard.' She sighed. 'You know, we try, especially him, but then something gets in the way. I know it's me. I put up these walls and he doesn't know how to handle it. He hates it and I hate myself for doing it, but I feel I haven't got anything left for him. To be honest, it's a struggle just getting myself dressed in the morning.' She paused. 'But I still love him. Very much.'

It was true; she loved him deeply. Jon was the constant in her life. Intelligent, loyal, kind and steady, passionate in a restrained and old-school English way. She loved the way he used to smile at her when she talked too much at parties, how he gazed at her when she danced. He used to say he wouldn't change a hair on her head. He used to make her feel like she was the centre of the universe. Used to. Before Anna died. Everything was so different before then.

'I feel sorry for him. I'm not myself any more. The woman he loves has vanished.'

'The woman we all love is very much still here.'

She opened her eyes and turned her head again. She smiled. 'You never loved me, you lunatic.'

He drank from the bottle. 'We were great together.'

'No, we weren't.'

'We were; you know it. We'd still be great together.'

'You're making it up,' she said and took the bottle back. 'We'd have ruined each other – emotionally and physically – in a matter of months.'

'I should never have let you go.'

'You didn't let me go. I left you. For Jon.'

'He's a lucky man.'

'No, Jon is the least lucky man I know.'

'You'll be OK, you know,' said Dan. His voice and face had fallen serious, the bravado gone, in its place the concern of an old friend. 'You and Jon will be fine.'

'Thank you, Dan. But it will never really be OK. It's whether he and I can find a way to live with that.' She drank some more whisky. 'Can we talk about something else?'

Dan nodded, then hit his thighs gently with his hands. 'So, no more chat . . . how about we misbehave a bit?'

'What kind of misbehave?'

He handed her the whisky, she took it and as she did he lifted himself up in his seat and reached into his back pocket. Then he faced away from her so she couldn't see what he was doing. When he turned back he proffered a closed fist and lifted his eyebrows.

'What?'

He uncurled his fingers to reveal two pills, white and round, sitting in his palm like a pair of freshly laid eggs.

'I take it that's not Nurofen.'

'Correctamundo.'

She laughed under her breath. 'Fuck, Dan, those days are over. I haven't touched anything like that since I got pregnant with Anna.'

'And so I am here to make sure your mind and body are never denied that way again.' He picked up a pill between finger and thumb and held it up between them. 'Think of this as a celebration of our youth. Remember the water balloons?'

She knew exactly the night he was talking about, though admittedly most of it only vaguely. 'Milton Keynes.'

He nodded. 'Us against the establishment!'

'Those poor men,' she smiled, remembering the dreadful cocktail of drink and drugs they'd taken before crouching below a window in a friend's squat throwing condoms filled with water at tipsy suited men as they left their offices after a party. Dan joked that it was some poor wanker retiring after half a century chained to a desk, his skin the same grey as his hair, soul shrivelled like a walnut.

Kate was suddenly hit by an explosive burst of laughter. She recalled the looks on their poor faces as they searched the street for their ambushers. Tears started to roll down her cheeks and her tummy muscles began to spasm. As she laughed she felt released, and so she laughed more. She hadn't laughed, not properly, in a year, and though she knew it wouldn't last she allowed herself to enjoy it.

'They'd no . . . idea . . .' It was hard to get the words out amid her hysterics. 'Where . . . these bloody condoms were . . . coming from . . . and then one of them put his brolly up . . !' She exploded again.

Dan was laughing too. Slapping his legs, eyes creased up, one hand over his mouth. 'And you . . . you . . . chucked one and it bounced off the umbrella and hit the man next to him . . .'

'. . . God, those poor people . . .'

'And . . . then . . . you made me promise we'd never be like them!'

His words smothered her laughter like a cloche. She dried the tears from the corners of her eyes and then eyed the pill, as gentle snorts of recovery followed in the wake of her laughing. 'So,' she said. 'What is it?'

'Nothing too much. It'll soften the edges, that's all.'

She hesitated.

'Honestly, it's nothing. You can probably buy it over the counter. It'll just make you feel,' he paused, 'less bogged down.'

Then she felt something rebellious stir inside her, something that had been dormant a very long time, something she'd quashed when she'd married her lovely husband and moved into a lovely house near a lovely school with a lovely headmaster. What had she been thinking? She should have stayed in Milton Keynes, throwing condoms at the suits.

Without another thought she filled her mouth with whisky, snatched the pill and swallowed it down. Nerves fluttered inside her and she felt a shiver of anxiety. *There's nothing you can do about it now*, she told herself; *just ride it out*. She closed her eyes and lay back against the headrest.

'You know,' she murmured after a while. 'I should get back indoors; Jon will be worried.'

'Jon was born worried.'

She felt the drug creep into her blood and flow through her veins, and began to feel nauseous, as if she were seasick. She imagined herself on a ship, rising up and down with the waves, her stomach pitching and listing. She was standing right on the edge, holding on to the railings, with the wind and sea spray hitting her face. There were gulls wheeling and calling above her. She looked down into the green-grey water, the ocean floor hundreds of metres below, peaceful and sandy and very quiet. She wondered what it might feel like to dive into the water and keep on swimming until she couldn't hold her breath any longer, then in one easy movement, she would open her mouth and breathe the salty water into her lungs. Then she saw Anna next to her. Her chestnut hair floating around her head like a mermaid, her mouth opened, eyes vacant and staring, dead eyes. Kate reached a hand out to her, hoping she would grab hold. But as she did Stephen's face appeared behind her. His fingers crept over her daughter's shoulders and she saw them dig in. He grinned, his mouth twisted into an evil grimace. Then he pulled Anna away from her. Kate tried to swim after them, but she just couldn't move fast enough and they faded into the watery shadows.

'Kate? Are you OK,' said Dan's voice from somewhere outside her head.

She opened her eyes and looked at him.

'I hate that man more than I've ever hated anyone.'

Dan nodded. 'I can imagine.'

She sighed deeply and turned away from him. 'Christ, I've got to get to bed,' she said, rubbing her face with her hands in an attempt to sober herself.

'He shouldn't get away with it.' Dan didn't move. He took another swig from the bottle.

'Well, he will,' she snapped. 'We've been to the police. They said they'd look into it. When they talk to him, he'll deny it. There'll be nothing they can do. So he will get away with it. We're *fucked*, Dan. He gets to sail through the rest of his life and me and Jon are fucked!' She gave a frustrated growl.

Dan picked up the bottle of whisky and saw it was empty. He threw it into the back of the car and then reached across her and opened the glove box. He rummaged around, throwing papers and maps in the foot well, and came out with a battered hip flask, then unscrewed the lid with his teeth and spat it on the floor. He put the flask to his mouth, then handed it to Kate. She shook her head.

'The police are a load of crap.' He paused. 'I think we should do something a bit more old-fashioned.'

She put her elbow against the car window and leant on her hand. Her head swam, and for a second or two she thought she might throw up.

He reached over the back seat and with a grunt pulled up one of the five-litre paint tins. He held it up. 'Paint.'

She looked at him blankly.

'Come on, Kiki, I thought you were an artist. Where's your imagination?'

Coco Mademoiselle

Jon watched the car the entire time it was parked outside the house. His eyes didn't move from it; his nose was so close to the window that a circle of mist grew and shrank as he breathed.

He had been halfway to sleep when the telephone had rung. He loathed phone calls in the night. Just as Kate did. They discussed it once, and unearthed equal feelings of dread at even the thought of a phone call after ten o'clock. So when it rang, he jumped out of bed and ran straight to Lizzie's room, his heart thumping, but she was there, safe and awake, reading in bed.

'Are you OK?' she asked, sitting up on one elbow.

He nodded. 'Sorry to disturb you.'

'You didn't,' she said. 'I'm reading. Who was that on the phone?'

'I don't know.'

'Maybe Granny?'

'Could be.' He hoped it wasn't. If it was, it could only be fateful. 'Don't read too long,' he said. 'It's late.'

'Just finishing the chapter.'

'Sleep well, darling,' he said, and closed her door.

He leant over the banister and listened. He couldn't hear her on the telephone, only the sound of a running tap.

'Who was that?' he called.

She appeared at the kitchen door. 'Sorry?'

'On the telephone?'

'It was a wrong number,' she said. 'Kids mucking around.'

He could always tell when she was lying. He went back to bed and lay still, holding the duvet up to his chin, waiting for her to come to bed.

But then there was the noise of a car pulling up outside their house. So he went to the window and saw his parents' vintage red Mercedes, the dent in its front wing reflecting the moonlight, and standing in front of the car, at the end of their path was Kate. His stomach seized.

The window of the car wound down and in the orange hue of the streetlamps he clearly saw Dan. His brother got out of the car and stood grinning at her with that absurd trilby skating off the back of his head and a bottle in his hand. He thrust the bottle towards her. Jon knew he should bang on the window to let them know he could see them, so they'd stop, so Dan would get back in the car and Kate would come back inside. But he didn't. He just watched, bound and shackled by invisible chains, an impotent spectator. He watched his brother open the car door for her. He watched her shake her head indulgently as he flourished a bow to guide her into his lair. A wolf and a lamb. He saw her smile.

And then he watched her walk away from him into the arms of his brother.

Was he surprised? Of course not. As he watched, a feeling of inevitability took hold, an admission that what was happening was predetermined. Even on their wedding day, as he slid the thin gold band on to her finger, he'd half expected her to stop the ceremony and skip over to Dan and take his hand instead. Perhaps it was this expectation that stopped him haring down the stairs and pulling her back to him.

She and Dan had sat in the parked car for what seemed like hours. He couldn't see through the windows; it was as if they'd drawn curtains. Jon's head turned upside down as he imagined them kissing and laughing, tearing at each other's clothes like lusty teenagers, struggling desperately for sex, banging their heads on the car, teeth and noses colliding, laughing more as they tried to get comfortable. He tried to stop his mind playing games. He tried to tell himself they were just talking, that it was totally innocent, that Kate and Dan were old friends and nothing more.

He grew numb, cold outside and in; his bones ached. How long had he been standing at the window? One hour or two? Maybe more. When the car engine fired he startled. He rested his forehead against the glass and waited for her to emerge. But she didn't. The car sped off, no headlights, gears grinding, Kate inside. He watched the empty street for a few minutes, and then turned away from the window and pushed the pile of his neatly folded clothes off the chair and sat. He dropped his head into his hands.

'For God's sake pull yourself together,' he said out loud. 'It's no bloody wonder she went to him.'

He made himself stand and walk to the bathroom, where he doused his face with water from the tap. Then he went back and picked his clothes off the floor and dressed. He needed some air. His head was thick.

Outside was warm and still; it was a beautiful night. The street was empty, apart from a boy across the road smoking a cigarette and next-door's cat, which sat on their wall licking its paw. Jon turned left, the opposite direction to that which Dan had driven. He didn't want to find them. He breathed deeply, enjoying the fresh air as it displaced the stale stuff from their bedroom, and as he walked he felt better, less passive. He'd walked the night Anna was born for similar reasons, to feel less useless, to gather himself. It was unbearably stressful watching Kate in labour. She appeared to be in so much pain, struggling with every relentless contraction. After a while she slipped into a trance-like state with beads of sweat sitting on her brow like tiny see-through pearls. Their midwife was a rotund Irish woman with blonde hair tied back in a scruffy ponytail and laughter lines dug deep into her face. He'd taken her aside and asked how long the baby would be.

'Only the Lord God himself knows the answer to that one,' she said in her thick Gaelic drawl.

'Do I have time for a breath of air?'

'She's only four centimetres. We've a while yet.'

He went back to Kate and kissed her damp cheek. 'I need the loo; I'll be two minutes,' he said. 'You're doing so well.'

She smiled weakly and closed her eyes.

He had walked down to the corner of the street and back, reminding himself that women all over the world did this every second of every day, and most in considerably less safe environments than Queen Charlotte's in west London. But it was only a few hours later, when Anna slid on to the table, her piercing healthy cry prompting Kate to call out with joy and relief, that his nagging fear left him alone.

Jon stopped walking and tipped his head back to look at the stars. He wondered which one was Anna. He saw a tiny bright one low in the sky to his left, and imagined her sitting on its edge waving at him. Her hair was loose and she was wearing a pair of clean white pyjamas and some pink fluffy slippers. He looked away from the star and saw how close he was to the bus stop with broken glass that he and Rachel had sat at after she bought him the milk. He owed her fifty-two pence; he mustn't forget to give it to her. He

226

thought of her then, asleep, close by, with her kind words and soft smile, and a warmth passed through him. He looked up the road towards her house and, as if dragged by a siren, he began to walk.

When he reached the front door he rested his palms flat against it, and wished, like Kate, that Rachel had locked it and hidden the key that night, perhaps just enough of an obstacle to keep Anna alive. He thought about knocking, about waking Rachel; maybe they could chat and drink hot milk. Then he thought of the kiss in the air. Had he made that up? Did he want to kiss her? He closed his eyes and thought about kissing her, and thinking about it made him want to be at home because he didn't want to kiss Rachel; he wanted to kiss his wife. He turned away from the door and walked home in a daze, not seeing anything, not hearing anything, not even thinking any more.

He slipped into the house as quietly as possible. When he got up to their room he saw Kate asleep in their bed. His knees gave way and he grabbed at the doorframe. He walked to the bed and knelt beside her. She was sleeping heavily with gentle snores, and a pungent veil of alcohol clung to the air around her. Her head was half on, half off the pillow, an arm hung over the edge of the bed and her legs were sprawled beneath the duvet that was tied around her like an unravelled shroud. She looked so peaceful it tore Jon's heart in two. He reached out and stroked the hair out of her eyes. She didn't move a muscle. He breathed the air she breathed out, sweet and sickly with Dan's whisky. He stared at her mouth, which was open a fraction. The thought of his brother kissing it cut him up. He leant forward and touched his lips to hers. She murmured something. Her head moved restlessly on the pillow then she turned away from him. He stood, pausing for a moment, wondering if he should wake her, wondering if they could talk things better. But maybe it had passed that point now.

He walked out of their room and down the corridor. He stopped at Lizzie's door and opened it quietly. She was fast asleep. He heard her grinding her teeth. She'd never been a quiet sleeper. Anna had slept in their room for her first eight months, first in a Moses basket and then in an antique cradle his mother had given them. Kate would reach through the bars in the middle of the night and stroke her open palm as she lay, quiet as a mouse, sleeping as babies do with their hands thrown up in surrender. A year or so later they had tried the same with Lizzie, but the constant sniffles and snuffles, grunts and moans had meant she was banished after only a few weeks by a teary, exhausted Kate.

Jon stepped back and closed Lizzie's door as quietly as possible. Then he moved on to Anna's room. He reached for the handle and opened the door. He stood on the threshold like a nervous child and looked into the room. It was so peaceful. Kate had drawn the curtains for the night and Anna's cuddly toys waited patiently for her at the foot of the bed. Gertie the porcelain doll was perched as always on the bookshelf next to a selection of Anna's favourite books – *Little Women*, *Black Beauty* and a handful of trashy teenage novels with too much sex and weak moral messages about bullying and fitting in. He took a breath and stepped on to her carpet and then he walked over to the dressing table. He remembered her asking him for it.

'Please dad,' she begged in that cutesy whine she saved just for him. 'I *really* want one, an old-fashioned one with an oval mirror that I can hang necklaces and scarves and stuff on. And it needs a stool with pretty material on it. Like pink velvet, but dark pink not baby pink.'

He turned on the chain of fairy lights that hugged the rim of the mirror and trailed his fingers over the smooth glass top of the dressing table. Not a speck of dust. Just as if she were still alive.

228

He lifted the lid of her jewellery box. The tinny music broke into the silence and he gazed at the plastic ballerina twirling her repetitive dance. Then he closed the lid and sat down on the stool. The scarves and necklaces hung as she'd promised, and the dressing table held open boxes of make-up and other bits and pieces. He picked up a pot of nail varnish then carefully placed it down. He saw her bottle of perfume. Kate had chosen it for her. It was Chanel. Coco Mademoiselle. Anna loved it. She unwrapped it the Christmas before she died, jumped up and bounded over to them, smiles and sparkles and too many *thank you, thank you, thank yous*. She kissed them both then ripped open the packaging, casting bits of cellophane and torn cardboard like confetti. She pulled out the bottle and grinned at them as she sprayed too much of the scent on her wrists and neck. Then she skipped back to her father and gave him her neck, tipping her head to allow him to smell.

'Beautiful, my darling. You smell beautiful.'

She grinned and kissed him again.

Now Jon reached for the bottle. Half empty. He pulled the lid off. Lifted the perfume to his nose and breathed in. It smelt exactly of Anna. Then he held out his wrist and sprayed. One spray on one wrist, then he swapped hands and sprayed the other. He put the bottle back on the table, lifted his hands and held both wrists together beneath his nose then closed his eyes and breathed her in. He saw her skipping over to him. Tilting her head to let him smell her. Her eyes gleamed, the coloured lights of the Christmas tree reflected in their shining brown.

Jon opened his eyes and stared at his face in the mirror. He didn't recognize the man who stared back. Even in the dim fairy-light glow he could see the dark rings that surrounded the eyes. The man's hair stood up all over and his clothes were ruffled and creased. He was unshaven, and appeared not to have had a shower in days.

Jon broke the stare-off with the man in the mirror and reached for the purple make-up bag that sat next to the music box. He unzipped it. Rooted through. He found a lipstick. He opened it and lifted it to smell its oily waxiness. He looked back at the man in the mirror and put the lipstick to his mouth. Then slowly, ever so slowly, he pushed it on to his lips. The lipstick that had last touched Anna's lips. He stared at himself again, and watched his newly scarlet mouth twist into an angry snarl. His eyes narrowed with hatred. Then he reached out and scrubbed the lipstick into the mirror, scribbling over the reflection of the pathetic man until the lipstick was used to the nub.

Jon pushed away from the dressing table and went over to her bed. He pulled off the freshly laundered duvet and grabbed her pillow, and then he lay down on the floor and wrapped himself up in a tight cocoon to hide himself from the shit that stank up the world outside her room.

Graffiti

i bet you're not here :p xxx

*   *bet i am . . . xx*
*   *you're mad!! :O xxx*

She peered out from behind the edge of a curtain and there he was, leaning against the wall on the opposite side of the road, just outside the circle of light from the streetlamp. He looked up and she jumped away from the curtain and leapt back into bed, her heat racing.

Oh my God, she thought. *He's outside my room! He's actually there!*

She wanted to go down to him but she could hear her mum was up and about. So she decided to text him instead. Then the phone rang and for a dreadful moment she imagined he'd lost all sense and called the house. Her heart beat almost out of her chest. And then her dad had come into her room. She'd only just managed to grab a book in time. He had looked so upset she thought for another dreadful moment it was Haydn on the phone. She braved asking him who it was, but he didn't know.

are you still there? did you just call our home phone!? she typed when her dad left. She pressed send and waited, her stomach thundering with nerves.

yes still here and no didn't call . . . xx

231

He was still there!

She jumped out of bed again and looked out of the window. He was standing on the wall, his arms thrown out wide. She laughed and waved at him. He blew her a kiss and then another. Lizzie put her hands against the window and kissed the glass.

I love you, she mouthed, but she knew he couldn't read her lips from where he was.

i love you :)! xxx. She pressed send and stared at him. She giggled when he reached into his pocket and pulled out his phone. She saw him typing and her tummy fizzed. It was like every Christmas, birthday and New Year rolled into one spectacular moment.

i love you too more than youll know . . . you are my world xx

She kissed the window again, closing her eyes and letting the smooth, cold glass be Haydn's lips. Then she heard a noise downstairs and sprang away from the window and jumped into bed, pulling the covers over her head, her heart smacking against her chest. Nobody came into her room. She lay in the warm, dark den and thought about Haydn kissing all over her body. It was just too heavenly to imagine! Then her phone beeped a text.

your mums just come out xx

can she see you?! xxx

i dont know :L xx

dont let her!! xxx

shes looking this way :s xx

OMG!! :s :O xxx

ah its ok shes got in a car :) xx

wheres she going?? xxx

how the fuck shd i know?? i wish you were here with me . . . x

me too :(. . . are you leaving?? xxx

no i want to be here while you sleep xx

i really love you . . . xx

232

Lizzie checked he was there twice more that night. She didn't let him know though. It felt special to know he cared, that he was just there because he wanted to be near her, outside her house, as close to her as he could get. When she checked at two he was sitting on the pavement with his back against the wall, a dark shadowed figure, the orange glow of his cigarette flaring as he inhaled. She climbed into bed and pulled her knees up to her chest and hugged them to her. This was amazing. She wondered how many other people in the world were as lucky as she and Haydn. Not many. She actually felt sorry for everyone else; to live and not experience what she was experiencing was a tragedy.

She was woken by her phone bleeping a text. She fumbled in her sleepy haze and grabbed at the phone on her desk. She squeezed her eyes shut and open to try to get them to focus on her phone.

i need to see you

when?? xx

asap fucking shit here :L i shd have stayed outside your house . . .

leaving now whats happened?? xxx

wait and see

i'll be 10 mins xxx

As Lizzie turned into his street she was met by chaos. People were standing around the Howes' house. There was a police car. A man was taking photos on his phone. Some kids were laughing. Women and men looked shocked, their hands covering their mouths, shaking their heads, whispering. A mother held her child on her hip, a protective hand placed against his cheek. Her face was ashen.

When Lizzie saw what was causing the commotion, she stopped in shock and amazement and stood bolted to the pavement beneath her.

Graffiti.

Black, red, navy blue. Across the front door and the up-and-over garage. Splashes of paint slashed the front lawn and over the brickwork of the house.

Paedophile. Child abuser. Bastard pervert.

Lizzie didn't want to go any nearer. The scene scared her. She hung on the corner of the road and texted Haydn to tell him she was there. She waited, but there was no reply and no sign of him. She shifted uncomfortably, unsure whether to go or to stay. Then there was a hand on her shoulder.

Haydn stood beside her. He wore a hooded top with the hood pulled over his head. His shoulders were hunched and his hands were thrust deep into the pockets of his jeans.

'I snuck out the back and jumped over the wall. Let's get the fuck out of here.'

With their heads low and feet moving quickly in time, they walked hand in hand without talking. When they were clear of the road they broke into a run in the direction of her grandparents' house. They didn't stop until they got there so that her lungs burned as she tapped in the entry code and tried to catch her breath.

As soon as the shed door was closed behind them, she curled her arms around Haydn and held him until he stopped crying.

Shepherd's Pie

'Hello?'

As soon as Kate answered the phone she wished she hadn't. Her head pounded and she felt as if she might throw up at any moment.

'Kate, it's Marlena.'

Marlena Sanders was the mother of a child in Anna's class at school. Her daughter, Emmie, had joined primary school with Anna and the two girls had not been friends ever since. Marlena used to run the PTA, but quit because she fell out with three of the governors. She baked a cake every Thursday, and passionately loathed dogs, travellers, modern art, *Big Brother* and the homeless 'who will insist on lingering around looking dirty'. She was, to all intents and purposes, a pain in the arse. The last time Kate had heard from her was a trite sorry-for-your-loss card that gave the impression Kate and Jon were burying a gerbil in a shoebox rather than their eldest child.

Kate considered putting the telephone down.

'Hello, Marlena,' she said instead. 'How are you?'

'I'm, well . . . I'm obviously a little concerned . . .'

'Oh?' Kate tried to sound interested.

'Haven't you heard?'

'Heard what?'

'Oh my goodness. I can't believe you haven't heard!'

Kate didn't reply.

'Dr Howe's house has been vandalized.'

Kate's stomach hit the floor and she reached to steady herself on a kitchen chair.

'Graffiti. All over it.'

Kate's head swam as she struggled to breathe. 'When?'

'Last night.'

She looked at the ceiling and quietly swore.

'Kate?' asked Marlena.

She held the phone away from her and took two deep breaths. 'I'm sorry, Marlena, I'm not feeling too good today. Do they know who did it? Kids, I suppose.'

Kate imagined policemen sitting in a darkened surveillance room at that very moment, poring over flickery images of her and Dan daubing the house.

'You know, I don't think it is youths.' She paused. 'Or even *hoodies*.'

Kate held on to the kitchen worktop for dear life as she tried to keep her thumping head straight. This was it, she was the most depraved criminal there was; she'd attacked a child, she'd taken drugs, she'd vandalized a house.

'It's the things written that are most disturbing. Awful things about Dr Howe,' said Marlena. She lowered her voice to a stage whisper. 'That he's a *paedophile*.'

Kate wanted to die.

'It's scrawled all over the house, roof to foundations, and this wasn't thugs, no, this was someone who *knows* something. Thugs use spray paint. This was gloss and matt emulsion.'

'I'm sure it's kids,' said Kate, weakly.

'No, this was a warning. The brother or father of some desperate child begging us to find out the truth. I've never liked that man, and I'm a jolly good judge of character. These men, these *kiddyfiddlers,* need to go to prison and have their wotsits cut off by hairy burglars.'

Kate's aching head was cloudy, mussed up, as if someone had shaken it. Vague memories of her scrawling the word *paedophile* on to Stephen's home flashed up. Christ, what had she done? 'It's just words on a house,' she said quietly.

'That may be, but we all know that where smoke billows fire rages—'

Kate put the phone down on Marlena and pinched the bridge of her nose. She took a deep breath, counted to five, then let it slowly out. Her head was so sore. She was losing it. She was going to end up in prison. She thought back to the night before, about how she'd walked out of the house without even a thought to Jon and Lizzie. What kind of mother was she to leave her daughter and vandalize a house?

She was hit with a sudden, overpowering urge to see Lizzie, to hold her, hug her tightly and tell her just how very much she loved her. She looked at the clock. It was nearly three. If she left immediately she'd meet her at school and they could walk home together, or maybe even go for a coffee and a slice of cake like they used to.

Kate hung across the road from the school gates and scoured the children as they poured out of school like a burst dam. She chewed the corner of her nail, worried that she wouldn't be able to see her in the crowd. But then there she was, piling out in a group of girls. Kate lifted her hand to wave and was about to call to her, when something stopped her. Perhaps it was the group of girls she was with; she didn't recognize any of them. One might be Sammy, and Kate wondered if she'd been unfair to disbelieve Lizzie and assume she was making up mythical friends with mythical birthdays so she could spend time with Haydn Howe.

Kate watched the girls as they walked and chatted, holding their books to their chests, laughing and pushing each other playfully. Lizzie threw her head back and squealed, flicked her hair, then readjusted her bag on her shoulder, secure, confident, outgoing. It wasn't a Lizzie Kate knew. When she thought about Lizzie at school, she pictured a fragile girl devastated by her sister's death. She saw her sitting on her own at lunch, head hung, tears falling into uneaten food, bereft, forlorn. But there she was, normal and seemingly happy, carrying on with her life. Kate was surprised by the rush of pride and joy that came with seeing her like this.

Kate watched as Lizzie waved a cheery goodbye to her friends then disappeared around the corner at the end of the road. She stared after her for a moment or two feeling terribly alone suddenly, as if she were the last survivor clinging to a shipwrecked boat, the one not brave enough to swim for it, preferring to sink with the wreckage rather than risk the unknown. This wasn't her. It wasn't who she was. Something lifted off her then. It was as if a blindfold had been removed and she was blinking into the sunshine of a brand new day. Could it be this easy? She wanted to run after Lizzie and grab her and kiss her all over, and tell her they were going to be OK.

She glanced back at the school gates. The flood of children had faded to dribs and drabs, and amongst them was a face she recognized. It was Rebecca. She was on her own, dragging her feet, drawn into herself like she wished she were invisible. If Kate believed in God she would have sworn blind that He had put Rebecca across the road from her right then, on purpose; her first test.

'Rebecca!' she shouted, waving wildly. 'Rebecca!'

Rebecca glanced in Kate's direction, caught sight of her and then began to walk quickly away.

Kate crossed the road to follow her. 'It's OK,' said Kate, as she caught up with her. 'I just wanted to say hello, that's all.'

Rebecca sped up her walk.

'Look,' said Kate, having to jog to keep up with her, something that didn't suit her hangover well. 'I'm sorry I shouted at you when you came to see me. It's just . . . it was, well, a shock, what you told me. And the memorial—'

'Leave me alone,' Rebecca whispered. 'I'm not allowed to talk to you.'

Kate couldn't believe how ill Rebecca looked, thinner than she'd ever been, with dull grey skin and dirty lank hair. 'I really am sorry,' Kate continued. 'My behaviour . . . it was unforgivable.' Rebecca stopped walking, her eyes bolted to the pavement in front of her. Kate laid a hand on Rebecca's arm, but Rebecca flinched and pulled away.

'I wasn't in my right mind. You know that, don't you? It wasn't anything you did. It was—'

'It's not you, OK? Just leave me alone. I'll get in trouble.' Rebecca looked up at Kate with teary eyes.

'With who?' Kate tried to keep her voice calm.

'I shouldn't have shown you that film.'

'Did he say that to you? Dr Howe?'

Rebecca didn't reply. Her lip trembled as she looked over Kate's shoulder.

'Rebecca? I want to help you.'

'You can't.'

Kate stared at Rebecca, realizing then how scared she was. She wondered if maybe the web was thicker and darker than she imagined.

'The video, Rebecca. Did he make you film them?'

Rebecca didn't answer her.

'Did he?' Kate asked again.

Rebecca shook her head. 'No,' she whispered.

'If it was, you have to say something. It's illegal. Do you understand? He should be in prison for making you do it.'

'It wasn't him.'

'So what, you just decided to film them?'

Rebecca shrugged and her eyes filled with tears. She dragged her sleeve across her eyes. 'I have to go.'

'Rebecca—'

Rebecca began to walk away, but Kate reached for her arm and gently pulled her back. She turned her to face her.

'Did he do something to you too?'

Rebecca looked shocked, but then she shook her head.

'To anyone else? Another child?'

'How the hell would I know?' she snapped.

'I don't know. I just—'

'Look, please, just leave me alone,' Rebecca pleaded. 'I have to get to my piano lesson. I'm late.'

Kate let go of her arm and Rebecca sprang away.

'I want to help you,' Kate said. 'I promise. That's all I want to do.'

Rebecca turned away from her and hurried off, huddled and timid.

Kate wondered if Rachel knew what her daughter was going through, how scared she was, how strained she seemed. Had she confided in her mum? Rachel needed to know. If Kate had known more truth about Anna and what she was experiencing, perhaps she could have intervened, stopped the relationship with Stephen, reined Anna in. Maybe that would have been enough to save her life. Kate stared after Rebecca long after she'd disappeared from view. Even though she was tingling with nerves at the thought of facing Rachel, she had to see her; if something happened to Rebecca, if she got into serious trouble, or tried to hurt herself, and Kate hadn't told her mother, she could never live with herself. It had been such a long time since they'd spoken. And lots had happened in that time. Kate shuddered as she recalled the memorial.

You have to, she said to herself. *You have to make sure Rachel knows what's going on. You owe it to Rebecca.*

As Kate stood outside Rachel's front door her pulse began to race, and when she lifted her hand to ring the doorbell she was shocked to see how much she was shaking. There was no answer for a bit, and she was about to turn away but then Rachel opened the door. She wore a clean white T-shirt and khaki shorts with a pair of gardening gloves tucked into the waistband. Her hair was brushed into a neat ponytail and her face was touched red by the day's sun. Rachel was clearly taken aback to see her, which didn't surprise Kate at all; this was the first time they'd been alone in each other's company since Anna died.

Rachel gestured awkwardly over her shoulder. 'I was in the garden.'

'I need to talk to you.'

Rachel didn't step aside to allow her in, but crossed her arms and looked over Kate's head to the street beyond. 'I really don't think we have anything to say to each other. In fact, I think—' But she stopped herself finishing the sentence. 'You know, it doesn't matter what I think. I've nothing to say to you.'

She stepped back from the door to close it, not allowing her eyes to catch Kate's.

'It's about Rebecca.'

Rachel stopped and shook her head bitterly. 'I can't believe you've got the balls to show your face here, Kate. What you did was indefensible; don't you dare try and excuse it.'

'I'm not going to. I'll regret what I did for the rest of my life and I wouldn't insult you by trying to excuse it.' She paused as Rachel's façade weakened a shade. 'But I've just seen her outside school and that's the reason I'm here. I think you need to talk to her.' She hesitated. 'You need to ask her about Dr Howe.'

'Dr Howe? Why?'

Kate breathed heavily out. 'God, look, this is such a mess.' She looked at the floor for a few seconds to ready herself. 'After the memorial she told me something about Anna and Stephen Howe. It's bad. Really bad, and it seems to me that there's more she knows, more she's keeping quiet about.'

'Kate, this is crazy. Just leave it. She's been through so much already. What happened at the memorial really got to her. She's so upset still.'

Kate nodded. 'She was upset before, as well. During the service she was crying and shouting, before I . . . did what I did. She made such a scene. There was something wrong with her then. I—'

Rachel held up her hand to stop Kate speaking. 'I know. I heard the whole story. Not from her, from others. She's not been right since Anna died. Not in any way.' Rachel sighed heavily and shook her head.

'Rebecca knows things.' Kate hesitated and looked over her shoulder. 'I don't want to talk on the doorstep. Can I come in? Just for a few minutes.'

Rachel checked her watch. 'Rebecca's at her piano lesson. She'll be home in an hour or so. You need to be gone by then.'

Rachel stood to the side to allow Kate to come into the hall, then closed the door.

Stepping into Rachel's living room was like stepping back in time to the glory days, halcyon times of happy simplicity. Perhaps her viewpoint was tinted rose, but Kate could only recall good memories in that room. She looked at the leather sofa that sat along the back wall and remembered the day Rachel and Rob had it delivered. It was from Laura Ashley, in the sale, massively reduced because of a tear that nobody could see.

'Go on,' Rachel urged with a giggle. 'Find the tear. Bet you can't!'

And Jon and Kate had set on it, crawling around searching the leather. Eventually, Rachel couldn't bear it any longer. She pulled one of the back cushions out and there was the mark, a livid slash with yellow foam padding poking mischievously through.

'But it's totally hidden!' exclaimed Kate.

'I know!' cried Rachel. 'Seventy per cent off!'

And then Kate laughed and congratulated her on the spectacular bargain as she collapsed on to the sofa, hands behind her head, feet up.

'It's comfy, too!'

'I know!'

Then Jon had climbed on beside her, moving her over with a hefty shove. Kate smacked his shoulder playfully.

'At least it *was* comfy before some big oaf got on and ruined it. I suggest we make a sign for it, Rach: *girls only*. What do you think?'

And then she pretended to try and push him off before giving up and rolling in for a hug.

Kate followed Rachel through the kitchen and into the garden. It had changed beyond recognition, with a decking area where the old concrete paving had been, and lots of pots of green and purple grasses, a Japanese-style water feature and various mirrored balls on a new patch of lawn that reflected the rainbow of flowers in the borders.

'This looks great,' Kate said. 'What a difference.'

Rachel put her hands on her hips. 'Well, I've a bit more time on my hands now I'm not picking up after a lazy husband and don't have a best friend to waste time with.'

There was an embarrassed silence.

Rachel cleared her throat. 'You said Bec told you something.'

Kate's stomach turned over.

The only way is to say it straight, she thought.

'Yes,' she said after a hesitation. 'She told me Stephen Howe was having sex with Anna.'

Rachel inhaled in shock. 'Oh my God! Surely not?' Kate tried not to cry as she nodded. Rachel's face broke in sympathy and her look of genuine concern twisted Kate's gut. Rachel reached out for her, and instinctively they fell into a hug she could have done with every single day of the last year. She began to cry. She held Rachel tightly. Her body felt so familiar, long lost, and it was such a relief to be close to her again.

'It's been awful without you,' she whispered between sobs. 'I've missed you so much.'

Rachel laid quiet shushes in her hair, and didn't move until her sobbing had calmed.

'So much misplaced anger, it covered it up. Covered up how much I missed you.'

'I don't believe it, about Stephen and Anna,' Rachel said.

'I know, it's been so horrible. The whole thing. Such a fucking mess.'

'And you're sure Bec wasn't mistaken?' she asked gently. 'Maybe even making it up? Though why she would, I can't imagine.'

Kate sniffed and shook her head. 'No, it's definitely true. I didn't believe her at first, and, oh God, I was so awful to her, Rach. I shouted at her and said she was lying. But she had a film of them, Anna and Stephen, having sex. It was on her mobile phone.'

'Oh Jesus,' Rachel murmured.

'She seems so damaged. I'm worried about her. She was scared just now, and I know she has every right to be scared of me, but . . . I don't know, it seemed . . . I don't know . . .'

'Why did Rebecca have a film of them?' Rachel asked quietly.

Kate pulled away from her and shook her head. 'I don't know. She said she just did it because. No reason. But I'm not sure. Maybe you could talk to her?'

Rachel nodded. 'Though she doesn't really speak to me any more. She's blank most of the time. And, honestly, in and out of trouble at school like you wouldn't believe.'

'Maybe to do with this.'

'Maybe.' Rachel paused and looked down, rubbing the fingers of the gardening gloves between her thumb and forefinger. 'Kate, you know . . .' She swallowed and turned her head up to the sky, closing her eyes and screwing up her face. 'You know, I didn't hear her leave. I was watching the news—'

'Don't,' said Kate. 'Please don't. I know—'

'I have to.' Rachel paused. 'I'd had two glasses of wine and the TV must have been too loud, because . . . I didn't . . . hear anything at all. Not even the front door, and—'

Kate reached out her hand and touched the backs of her fingers to Rachel's cheek. 'Please, don't. It doesn't matter—'

Rachel pursed her lips as her eyes filled with tears. 'When . . .' She breathed a deep breath. 'When the news finished I went upstairs and listened at Bec's door. I didn't hear anything. I just assumed they were asleep. Anna told me she wasn't well . . . so . . . I thought she was asleep. I went to bed.' Rachel looked over at the water feature, which gurgled happily. 'I thought she was sleeping.'

'I know, and I don't blame you,' Kate said. 'I mean that.' She paused. 'And for Rebecca . . . I'm sorry. I know you won't forget what I did and I don't want you to try . . . but I am so, so sorry.'

Rachel smiled weakly. 'So many sorries.' She cleared her throat and blew out a heavy sigh. 'I haven't even offered you a cup of tea. Would you like one? Or there's a bottle of white in the fridge?'

'I can't stay,' Kate said. Rachel looked disappointed and Kate reached for her arm. 'Another time, though.'

They put their arms around each other and hugged tightly.

'I'm glad I came,' Kate said as she let go of Rachel.

'Yes,' said Rachel. 'I'm glad you came too.'

Kate sat in the car outside Rachel's house for a while. From nowhere a smile came. She had that feeling again, that need to be with Lizzie, and Jon too. She knew what she wanted to do – she was going to cook for them, a proper meal from scratch, and then they could all sit down for it together. She turned the ignition on and the car sparked into action. She was going to cook Lizzie's favourite. Shepherd's pie. With an extra-thick layer of mashed potatoes. And she was going to put Anna's chair in the garage so they could sit down without distraction. Jon could lay the table and they could sit and eat and chat about this and that and nothing. And she wouldn't go to her studio, even though she could already feel the pull. If she needed to paint, she could paint in the morning, just for an hour or so, but not this evening. This evening was all about her and Jon and Lizzie. She thought of Lizzie then: happy and smiling, striding out, flicking her hair as she laughed with her friends, forging onwards, surviving.

Kate was buoyed by her determination. She went to the greengrocer and took her time, chose the straightest carrots and a heavy head of celery. She smelt the melons and picked out the sweetest for pudding. She tested avocados for ripeness, squeezing them gently between her thumb and forefinger. Took a couple for a salad. She loved to cook and it wasn't until now, wandering around the wooden crates of fruit and vegetables, with the strong smell of earth and herbs and strawberries around her, that she realized how much she'd missed it.

By the time she got home it was well after six. She was still feeling good. Rachel would be able to help Rebecca, and she was so excited about seeing Jon and Lizzie, which was why it was even more of a shock to find Stephen Howe in the kitchen when she pushed through the door with her two bags of shopping.

Love and Kisses

Jon watched Kate's face fall as she saw Stephen standing in their kitchen. He wished he had been able to get rid of him before she got home, but the man had been insistent. Jon was thrown completely off guard when he answered the door. In retrospect he should have punched him then shut the door. Instead, he said a polite *hello* and stepped aside to allow him into his house like a welcomed vampire. He even offered him a cup of tea. Stephen thankfully declined, and then asked if Kate was in. He said he needed to speak to them both. Jon said she wasn't home and that he had no idea where she was or when she would be back. Then Stephen said he would wait. The silence they had fallen into was remarkably easy despite the time ticking by. Jon sat at the kitchen table. Stephen stood. Every now and then he was aware of the man shifting his weight or clearing his throat. He sneezed once, and Jon bit his tongue to stop himself saying *bless you*.

'What's he doing here?' Kate asked Jon as she heaved two large carrier bags on to the table.

'I need to talk to you both,' said Stephen.

'I didn't ask you.'

'I've been suspended,' Stephen said. 'It appears the police are investigating me for child abuse.'

The word 'abuse' eddied around them for a while. Jon was surprised at the almost nonexistent reaction he had to hearing the man had been suspended and that the investigation was under way, that somewhere in the police station there was a file with Anna's name on it, with their statement and the name and address of Dr Howe, his age, his profession, his CV, the date they showed them the film. It all seemed irrelevant. They were at the epicentre of the whole thing and yet he felt completely detached.

'Does the suspension include Anna's name?' Kate asked.

'No. They're apparently following an anonymous allegation.' He paused. 'I assume you went to them with your film.'

'It's not *our* film,' said Kate, her contempt undisguised.

'You obviously heard about my house being targeted.'

'Oh? And now you're here to accuse us of vandalism?'

'I'm not here to—'

'Why the hell *are* you here?' she shrieked.

Jon placed his hands on the table, palms down, and splayed his fingers as wide as they would go. The table felt cool and smooth, like the surface of a mirror.

'I don't want you here, not tonight,' she said, her voice faltering. 'I just . . . I just want to be with my family . . . I don't want you here. Why have you come? None of this is our fault. It's right you've been suspended . . . it's right that the police know what you did. For God's sake why are you here?'

Jon glanced up and saw the panic in her eyes. She put her hand on her forehead and turned away, jittery, anxious. He closed his eyes.

'I came to tell you I'm not a paedophile.' Stephen spoke quietly, steadily, as if he were reading from a book. 'The graffiti . . . it said . . . well, I'm not a paedophile.'

'You had sex with an underage child. That makes you a paedophile.'

'No . . . no.' Stephen was hesitant. 'It wasn't,' he paused, 'like that.'

Then from somewhere outside Jon's tangled head he heard Stephen clear his throat, and say: 'I loved her. I loved Anna more than I've ever loved anyone.'

The words were so soft, so unexpected, they might have been carried in on the wind from a thousand miles away. Jon lifted his head. Stephen was looking at Kate.

'I promise you I did everything I could to avoid it,' Stephen said. His words trickled out like dribble. 'But she kept on and on. She told me how much she loved me. I said no.' Stephen looked at Jon then. His eyes were wet with tears. 'She was so beautiful.'

Jon felt as if he'd been stabbed in the stomach.

'She came to me, day after day, for weeks. I tried to resist her. I couldn't. I was besotted. She would come and sit on my desk. Put her hand on me. Between my legs and stroke me. How could I say no? I was powerless. It was beyond my control. She made it impossible to do anything else. I was bewitched by her.'

Hearing him talk filled Jon with repulsion and desperate sadness. He was battered with unwelcome images of Anna dredged from the sordid memories of this man. Torturous images of an Anna he didn't recognize that made him squirm. He wanted to put his hands over his ears to stop the words reaching him.

'Are you trying to say that what you did was OK?' Kate's voice was so thin it was hardly there.

'No, I'm—'

'Because it's not OK.'

'That's what I'm trying to tell you.' He started to cry then. His body heaved with pathetic sobs. 'It wasn't something I did. We had something. She and I . . . we loved each other.'

'And this means what, exactly? That your actions are justified? Is that what you mean?'

'I . . . I don't know . . . I—'

'You should have left her alone.'

Stephen didn't say anything.

'You should have left her bloody alone,' Kate said again.

'I tried . . . I just couldn't . . . Anna was . . . she was a breath of fresh air. She made me feel good,' he said. 'Angela and I have . . . problems. It was strained . . . and . . . I don't know . . . at the time, I knew it was wrong . . . but, I couldn't stop.' He rubbed his face hard with his hands.

'You know,' whispered Kate, 'I think you killed her.'

Stephen furrowed his brow and shook his head as if he hadn't heard her properly.

'Don't look at me like that. I'm not speaking Chinese. I think you killed my daughter.'

And then his face drained of colour; his eyes grew wide. He looked scared. 'What? Why would I kill her? I just told you how much I loved her.'

'But you were there, weren't you? When she died. It's too much of a coincidence. And why was she with your son if you two were so very much in *love*? Maybe you knew they were up there together, and you got angry, jealous. Maybe you didn't mean to, but—' Kate stopped talking suddenly, interrupted by something in Stephen's manner, something about the way he was staring at her, like a trapped animal trying to think of the best escape.

'My God,' breathed Jon. 'Did you?'

Stephen slowly shook his head. 'No, Anna was dead when I got to the school. You know that. I found her on the playground. After she fell. She was already dead. There was nothing I could do.'

'You're lying,' whispered Kate. 'I can see you're lying.'

Stephen hesitated. 'No, Haydn called. He said she was drunk and climbing on the wall. We came straight away. I—'

251

Jon could see Kate was right; there was something. 'What?' Jon demanded.

'I . . .' he struggled. 'Haydn saw her fall. He saw it happen.' He stopped speaking and looked at his feet. 'But there is something,' he muttered.

'And?' Kate said. 'And what?'

He looked up at them and again there were tears in his eyes. 'Look,' he said, desperately. 'The last time we saw each other, I told her it was over. I told her the relationship couldn't continue. Because of my wife. She was so upset. She told me to leave Angela. I said I wouldn't. And she was crying and shouting, and said I had to leave her; if I didn't then she couldn't carry on living. She'd—'

'Oh my God, no,' groaned Kate. 'Don't you do this. Don't you do this to me.'

Jon watched his wife crumple and felt his own legs give.

'I thought it was just a threat,' whimpered Stephen. 'I told her not to be so silly, that she'd find someone else, her own age. But she wouldn't accept it. She was in such a state when she left me. I didn't think she was serious. I thought she was trying it on, to get her own way. But I couldn't do that to Angela.' He put his hands to his face. 'What choice did I have? I couldn't leave my wife and son for her.'

'Get out of this house!' yelled Jon. There was so much anger inside him it spilled out like poison from an abscess. What more could he take from this man: the relationship with Anna, hearing him talk about her like she was some deranged whore, now insinuations she purposefully took her own life because he broke her heart? 'I won't hear another word! You tell us you were powerless to stop an affair with our *child*, and then you say you had no choice but to risk her life to maintain your family? Get out! Get the hell out of my house!' Jon took hold of Stephen's arm and pulled him out of the kitchen.

'But I—'

'Get the hell out. Stay away from us. And you keep your son away from Lizzie, too. Do you hear me?'

'I didn't—'

'You're *filth*.' Jon pushed the spluttering Stephen out of the front door then slammed it behind him. 'You're filth,' he whispered, collapsing his head against the door.

He walked back into the kitchen. Kate was slumped against the kitchen worktop. She was shaking. He stood beside her and reached out to touch her. He hesitated, his hand hovered over her, and then he allowed his fingers to rest on her shoulder. She knocked his hand away with a backwards flap of her arm and ran out of the kitchen.

He closed his eyes and listened to the familiar sound of her feet on the stairs and then the door to her studio slamming shut.

Magic and Candles

Lizzie hurried along the street towards her grandparents' house. To the shed. Haydn said he would meet her there. She'd expected him to talk about what had happened to their house, but he didn't want to.

'He's a total arsehole,' Haydn said. 'I honestly couldn't give a shit. All I care about is you. You make me forget everything else. All of it. If I think about you I get so hung up I can't breathe properly. You rock my world. You rock it so much I can't see straight.'

Then he told her to meet him at the shed at six o'clock exactly. She asked what he was up to, but he'd been cagey, just told her to be patient, to wait and see. He'd scarcely been able to contain himself, and now nor could she.

Her stomach bubbled and her heart raced as she crept through the garden gate. She reached for the door handle and turned it, but when she tried to push the door open it wouldn't give.

'Just a moment,' came Haydn's voice. 'You're early.'

Lizzie checked her watch and laughed. 'Only a minute!'

There was the sound of rustling, then the door opened a crack and Haydn's face appeared. 'You've got to shut your eyes.'

Lizzie grinned. 'What is this?'

'Shut your eyes and promise not to open them, and do everything I say.'

'I'm not doing everything you say; what if you say something bad?'

'Just say that you'll shut your eyes and not open them and do everything I say.'

Lizzie frowned at him, but then couldn't stop another smile.

'Say it.'

'Fine,' she said. She closed her eyes. 'I'll keep my eyes shut.'

'And do everything I say.'

She opened an eye.

'Trust me.' He reached for her hand.

She let him guide her into the shed, ducking involuntarily to avoid imaginary things she might bump her head on.

'It's OK,' he said. 'You won't hurt yourself.'

There was a whirr of a machine as she stepped in. 'What's that noise?'

'A heater.'

She nearly opened her eyes, but his hand covered them, as if he read her mind.

'Now,' he said. 'You need to take off your clothes.'

'Haydn!'

'It's not for that.'

'I don't want to take my clothes off.'

'You have to or my surprise won't work.'

'What kind of surprise involves me taking my clothes off?'

'Wait and see.' Haydn sounded so excited that she smiled and, completely against her better judgement, began to unbutton her shirt.

'You can keep your knickers on.'

Naked and blind she felt nervous, and very self-conscious. 'There's nobody else in here, is there?' she asked.

'Just us.' He kept his hand over her eyes. 'There's a cushion here on the floor. I want you to kneel on it, then put your hands on your lap.'

'But—'

'Trust me.'

So Lizzie did as she was told. Confused, chilly and more than a little unsure of the whole thing, she couldn't help but feel this was a waste of their precious sex time.

'Hands on your lap.'

She shook her head, not understanding in the slightest bit. It was weird. She felt vulnerable, and worried in case they were discovered. Being found making love to your boyfriend was bad enough, but at least it was reassuringly explicable. Being found naked and posed in some strange contortion doing goodness-only-knows-what-Haydn-had-in-mind gave her the quivers.

She was conscious of him fiddling with something beside her, then she felt his fingers in her hair. There was a slight scrape against her scalp. A hairclip, she guessed. Then his fingers were taking another section of her hair, then again the scrape against her head. He continued, wordless, his breathing and the hum of the fan heater becoming hypnotic, and with her eyes closed she found her other senses heightened. The heater warmed her in waves and she imagined the hairs on her arms swaying like miniature palm trees in a hot breeze. The smells in the shed became clear and distinct. The dust. The ancient oil spill in the corner by the window. The damp of the dolls that lay higgledy-piggledy in the old wooden apple crate, with dirtied skirts and scruffy woollen hair.

Haydn was still playing with her hair, but not scraping her any more. She could feel his fingers, parting her hair and then pushing against her head. Then she felt his hands on her shoulders. Then his lips. A kiss on each bare shoulder. Shivers of pleasure and lust shot through her. She was about to speak, to beg him to kiss her properly, but he interrupted and told her to shush.

She heard him shuffle on his knees. A rustling. Then he was back beside her, his breathing loud and steady.

'Now I want you to lift your arms,' he said.

She did. By now she was submerged in what they were doing. There were no longer any questions. She wondered then what he would have to ask her to do for her to refuse. It was like he had thrown a spell over her, a spell of obedience. He had turned her into his slave. But yet, at the same time, it was her who was being ministered to, like she was a queen and Haydn her servant, kneeling at her feet, preparing her.

He looped some sort of strap over her shoulder. She felt something rest against the centre of her back.

'Put them down now.'

Then he wrapped something around her middle. Material, for sure, but fine and light, barely there. She felt him reach backwards with a small grunt, then a tightening of the material around her waist. He arranged it over her thighs. His fingers touched her skin every now and then, each time a shock, surprise and joy.

'Nearly done,' he whispered. 'You look amazing.'

She smiled.

She felt him loop something over her head. Then something else. Another. He arranged whatever they were on her chest.

'OK, give me a few seconds.'

She could hear him moving around the shed. She heard something like a match strike. The flash of sulphur. So definitely a match. Then silence. Another match. A third. Then she heard more rustling. A click. He dropped something heavy on the floor and the thud made her jump. Her knees were beginning to ache.

'Hold this.' He opened her fingers and gave her some sort of stick. 'And put your other hand here.' He crossed her arms and laid them on her lap.

Then he moved away from her.

'OK,' he said, a few moments later, his voice full of eager excitement. 'Open your eyes!'

The shed was lit by what seemed to her to be a thousand flickering candles. They were everywhere, in jam jars, tea-light holders, glued on to upturned instant-coffee lids, all in a hundred different shapes and sizes. It took a few moments for her eyes to accustom, and when they did she found herself staring into a large oval mirror that Haydn held. What she saw in front of her made her gasp out loud and when she did, Haydn laughed.

'Like it?'

She didn't answer, just stared, then smiled, tilting her head in all directions to see. There was almost too much to absorb. Her hair was twirled and pinned into loose loops with tiny flowers dotting her head like fallen snowflakes. There was a wreath that sat like an Alice band, made of twisted twigs and leaves and ribbons, and pink and white flowers, studded with sparkling jewels that looked like real diamonds but couldn't be. There were more little diamonds stuck around her eyes and on her cheeks that she hadn't even been aware of him sticking on her, and they sparkled like fireflies in the candlelight. Then there were wings. Glorious gossamer wings that lifted up above her shoulders and to the side of her waist, scalloped like a butterfly's, translucent white and rimmed with silver glitter. Around her neck were garlands of flowers and leaves that hung down between her breasts. Her skin looked milky white, softened and smoothed by the flickering glow of candles. Around her waist and lying over her knees was a skirt of shimmering green organza. The wand in her hand was silver, with more ribbons and flowers wound up its length.

'You're the fairy princess.'

She didn't reply; she was still taking it in.

'Like you said you always wanted to be but Anna wouldn't let you; she was always the princess and made you the evil goblin. You remember? You told me in the cemetery.'

She nodded slowly, still not taking her eyes away from the reflection.

'You look beautiful,' he breathed. 'The most beautiful thing I've ever seen in my life.'

She watched the tears in her eyes as they filled and spilled over. She felt beautiful. She had no idea she could ever look like this. She tore her gaze away from the mirror and blotted her eyes on the back of her hand.

Haydn leant the mirror carefully against the wall of the shed, and then pulled a camera out of his rucksack. Then he began to take pictures of her. He told her how to sit, how to hold her head. He reached over and tipped her chin to the side and down, so her head was bent like a shy puppy. Told her to look over her shoulder, then right through the centre of the lens. He moved around her, taking shots from every angle. Then he finally put the camera on the floor and she saw his eyes had that glassy look that now sent shivers running through her. He walked on his knees towards her, took her in his arms and laid her carefully down.

'And now,' he said, 'I think it might be time to kiss you.'

'Thank you,' she whispered. 'I will never forget this.'

The Friends' Meeting House

Marlena called first thing.

'Kate. It's Marlena. Dr Howe's been suspended.' She paused, but not long enough for Kate to reply. 'I know; I know, these flames are climbing higher. Anyway, there's a group of parents demanding his immediate reinstatement. We've called a meeting. We need as many people as possible. Please tell anyone you can think of to come. It's at two p.m. this afternoon at the Friends' Meeting House, on Abbotston Road.' She paused briefly again. 'It's short notice, which is why I'm phoning as many people as possible myself, but it was the only slot the place had and we were lucky to get it. The salsa class was cancelled because the teacher broke her ankle. The hall was grateful for the booking, to be honest. Anyway, I know you most probably don't want to show your face at a school function, you know, after that terrible business with that poor girl, but if you could brave it, you know, bums on seats.'

Marlena put the phone down before Kate had time to tell her where to stick her meeting. She had no intention of going. But then, at a quarter to two, she found herself walking out of the house, pulled in the direction of the hall. She crept through the double doors at ten past, keeping her head low beneath the baseball cap she wore so she wouldn't be recognized, and sat on a chair at the back.

Kate scanned the room for people she knew. There were a few, but they were talking intently to people near them and certainly weren't bothered by her arrival. The meeting hadn't started yet and Kate looked around the grotty room. Historically, it was a place of worship for the Quakers, but nowadays it was used for ballet classes and Pilates and the like. It was a cold, grey room with windows set high in the walls originally to limit the distractions of the outside world, but to Kate it now made the room claustrophobic.

A man Kate didn't recognize stepped up on the stage. He was smallish, rotund, with a balding head and wearing an open-necked shirt with a cashmere sweater over the top. He cleared his throat and started to talk. The hum of voices in the room continued over him and he was forced to give a couple of sharp claps.

Clap, clap. 'Hello? People?' Clap, clap. 'We need to start this, we're running over already and we've only got the hall for an hour.'

Gradually, the gathered crowd began to silence.

'Firstly, let me introduce myself. My name is Paul Yarwood and I've been the Chair of the school's Parent-Teacher Association for just over a year now. Secondly, I must congratulate you on this impressive turnout. It's a shame we can't get you all out for the Christmas Fair meeting. I'm sure there's a perfect Father Christmas lurking somewhere out there!' He tried a laugh, but the audience stayed quiet, and his face fell serious. 'No, perhaps not the right time for humour. So I'll cut to the chase. Today we've heard news of Dr Howe's suspension pending a police investigation. You will all have heard different versions, some inflated, some scant. I know that Dr Howe is preparing a letter to send home with pupils tomorrow, which should explain exactly what has happened, but as this meeting has been requested I will inform you of the facts as known, and at the very least this might stop the gossip mongers in their tracks. Dr Howe has had an allegation made against him that relates to a pupil of the school. We do not know the identity of the child in question, nor do we know whether he or she is a current pupil, nor do we know the exact nature of the accusation. At this stage neither does Dr Howe. However, we do know, and this has been confirmed by the police, that the investigation has nothing whatsoever to do with the vandalizing of Dr Howe's house on Monday night, and is solely concerned with a complaint made by the family of an individual against the headmaster relating to improper conduct.'

Kate sank lower in her chair as a rumble went round the room.

'You mean sexual abuse?' called a voice.

A louder rumble.

'It is impossible for me to tell you not to jump to conclusions. It's in all our natures. But I urge you to remain calm, and to consider the facts. The *facts* being that without Dr Howe this school would still be languishing in the rubble of this country's faltering education system. He has almost single-handedly built it up to be the establishment we are all so proud to send our children to. He has had no charge made against him, and I, and many others in the school, including the entire body of staff, feel the governing body has acted rashly in their decision to suspend him at this early stage.'

There was a murmur of agreement in the room.

'Dr Howe deserves our support, not our vilification, and unless I am mistaken, this country prides itself on innocent until proven guilty.'

'But this is about the safety of our children,' called a woman from the other side of the room.

There was a rumble of *yes*es, and a number of people around Kate agreed with vigorous nods of their heads.

'But who's to say our children aren't safe?' Mr Yarwood went on. 'Like I said, there's been no hard evidence presented, no charges brought, no name even to the alleged victim.'

'You talk about innocent until proven guilty' – Kate recognized Marlena's voice – 'but what about the phrase *where there's smoke there's fire?*'

There was another muddy rumble of agreement and disagreement.

'But that's just the type of thing we need to avoid. If we believed every rumour we heard our society would fall into chaos. We live in a world where, for unknown reasons, respect for teachers is diminishing rapidly, and this is making the number of accusations against them by pupils increase at an incredible rate. Because there are never any direct witnesses to pertinent events, and because our automatic reaction is to protect our children, we fall down on the teacher with tremendous ferocity and little desire to listen.'

Kate thought about Rebecca, so thin and gaunt, herself a victim, the direct witness to the pertinent event to which Mr Yarwood was referring. She wondered how she would cope with a trial, and whether they would allow her to testify in a private room, or if because she was now sixteen she'd be made to face the jury, and Dr Howe, face to face.

'It could be a child who's angry with him. Made it up to get back at him!' called a woman.

'I read in the paper this weekend past there's, like, thousands of these finger-points each year and they're all shown not to be right.'

'That's not true! I read that article too; it was in the *Mail*. It didn't say that!'

'I know a teacher who was accused and lost her job, and even though the child admitted she was lying for a laugh the blot stays on my friend's record. It'll never be taken off. That's criminal!'

'It's the fault of them bloody political correct liberal nonces!'

'We haven't got enough teachers as it is, without suspending them all on hearsay!'

'But we've no proof!'

'What if it's true, though?'

'Yes, Mr Yarwood, what if he *is* a child abuser and *your* child's next?'

The room erupted as people started arguing across each other.

Kate sat with her head low, wanting to stand up and say she did have proof. But then she would also have to say that she had no evidence whatsoever to suggest that he had done this or would do this to any other child but hers. She heard Stephen's plaintive plea that they loved each other. Could that be true? Could it be an extreme case of a May to September love affair? And if this *was* the case, did he deserve to lose his job? But then another voice spoke out in her head. Stephen Howe had sex with a child. Fine, he said he loved her, but what if that love was really the twisted desire of depravity and the next time he fell in *love* it was with a child of twelve?

The room was getting hotter, clearly ill equipped to deal with the rising heat from so many impassioned people, and Kate took off her jacket and fanned her face with her hand.

'What we have to do, Mr Yarwood,' cried Marlena, 'is take a stand for what's right, and *not* feel threatened by the media or the teachers' union. We have a right, no,' she paused, melodramatically. 'We have an *obligation* to protect our children.' A roar of assent went up from most of those in the room. 'We need to safeguard their future.'

'Hear, hear!' shouted a number of voices in unison.

'We need to protect them from paedophiles!'

'It's bloody disgusting. We should hang the lot of them!' cried a woman.

'But he hasn't been arrested. He hasn't even been charged!'

'He should be thrown to the dogs!'

'If that man goes back to school my daughter's moving to Woods End. There's space. I rang this morning.'

'Come on, now. Let's keep this orderly!' shouted Paul Yarwood ineffectually.

And in the middle of the mayhem, the doors opened.

There was a collective intake of breath and then excited muttering. Kate swivelled in her chair and saw Angela and Stephen Howe. Silence gathered around them as they walked towards the stage, voices falling to hushed whispers and then to nothing until all you could hear in the room was their footsteps on the wooden floor.

Angela walked in front of Stephen and they climbed the steps on to the stage. Paul Yarwood offered his hand to Stephen, but Kate noticed that he did so self-consciously, and not with the gusto of a man standing shoulder to shoulder with an accused. He whispered something to Stephen, who nodded.

'Dr Howe would like to speak to us. I urge you to be gracious enough to listen to what he has to say, remind you all of his exemplary standing as our headmaster and reiterate how the success of our school is down to his remarkable leadership skills. And, on a personal note, I would like to add that I offer Dr Howe my unerring support.' He shifted his weight and cast his eyes over the seated parents. Kate dropped her head to avoid him. 'I have every confidence that the police investigation will find these allegations to be false.'

Kate glanced up at Stephen, whose eyes were fixed on something above their heads, perhaps the clock, or maybe the seating in the gallery. When Paul Yarwood stopped speaking, he and Stephen exchanged a brief look and then swapped places.

'I have come here today,' he said, in a calm, even voice, 'with Angela, my beloved wife and loyal colleague, to try and put your minds at ease. You will have heard, in some form or another, that I have been accused of sexual misconduct. I am here to reassure you that this accusation is completely and utterly *unfounded*.'

Kate's stomach lurched.

'This is clearly a worrying time for us, as indeed it is for you. But I want to assure you that not one of your children is at risk, or ever has been, from either myself, or from any member of my dedicated and talented staff. Sadly, the allegation means it is impossible for me to continue to work, and therefore I am in agreement with the governors and have accepted their recommendation for suspension pending the outcome of the police investigation.'

The hall reverberated with hundreds of whispered voices.

'To those of you who support me, thank you; to those others I would like to say I understand your concerns, and hope that when this accusation has been shown to be unfounded you will feel able to rebuild your trust in me so that I may continue to steer this wonderful school. I cannot think—' Stephen's voice cracked and he turned his head away from the audience, lifting his hand to his mouth to compose himself. A moment or two later he nodded and faced them again. 'I cannot think of anything I would rather do than be the headmaster of Park Secondary School.'

He held the audience for a while and then nodded once and looked across at Angela, who gestured for him to step away as she moved herself to the edge of the stage.

'The issue of false allegations,' she said, with the voice of a practised public speaker, 'made against teachers occupies time at every gathering of senior members of the profession. The threat of an accusation of this nature is a dreadful worry that plagues a teacher's nightmares. I am not, for one moment, suggesting that a child's allegation should be dismissed without investigation, but what I am saying is the damage done to a career can be devastating. Even when allegations are found to be groundless, they stay on a teacher's record indefinitely and will almost certainly prejudice future employment opportunities. It is both terrifying and shocking that a man who has dedicated over half his life to the care and education of this country's children, a man who has worked tirelessly for you, a revered and respected man within our profession, who is consulted by other headteachers from all around the country, has become the latest victim of this abomination.'

The room was silent. Kate looked at the people around her as they dropped their eyes, quietened perhaps by a sense of shame at their previous zealous anger. Though she understood Angela's loyalty, however misguided or self-delusory it was, Stephen's barefaced lies had skewered Kate. She couldn't sit there quietly. She had to speak, even though the prospect filled her with a nerve-shredding dread.

She stood up.

'Dr Howe,' she said in a loud clear voice that wavered only slightly.

She sidestepped out of the row of chairs and moved around the back of the audience to the central aisle. She saw Stephen's horrified eyes, Angela mouthing something to him.

'I think everybody here understands what damage lies can do. I think everybody here is also aware of the damage that abuse will cause a child and that child's family. All this talk we've heard today, of support, of vilification, conspiracy, the strength of the school, of paedophiles and abuse and hanging, or malicious children and gullible policing, it's all a smokescreen for the truth.'

Kate, who had continued to walk towards the stage, stopped level with the front row of seats. She locked eyes with Stephen; the strength he'd affected for his speech seemed to have vanished. His face had paled, and there was a fine sheen of sweat across his forehead. 'But the one thing that always happens, no matter what, is that the truth will out. It always does. And if you did do it, Dr Howe, if you *did* have sex with a pupil under the age of eighteen then you are guilty of sexual abuse, of abusing your position of responsibility, your position as headmaster of this school, and your reputation and your career is rightly finished; you deserve to be judged. If you didn't do these things, however, if you're innocent, then I know the parents of this school will find a way to support you.'

Stephen tried to exchange a helpless look with Angela, who glared daggers at Kate.

'Hear, hear,' shouted Marlena suddenly, jumping to her feet and clapping. 'Oh, hear, hear!'

Then the hall re-erupted. Kate's heart pumped and her blood fizzed; everything tingled with a mixture of exhilaration, anger, sadness and release. She turned away from the stage and walked purposefully out of the hall, and as soon as the doors closed behind her she broke into a run. When she reached the end of the road, she rounded the corner and then fell against a lime tree. She covered her face with her shaking hands and breathed the hot, trapped air deeply in and out in an attempt to calm herself.

When she got home she went to her studio. She was buzzing. It felt so good to stand in front of Stephen Howe and say what she had without a stutter or a stumble. It had felt good to crack his façade, to see him squirm as her words smacked into him, and to keep control of her emotions, righteous anger, in such a commanding manner. She felt she had won an important battle, not against Stephen, but against herself.

The painting of Anna was sensational. It flew off the canvas in its luminosity. There was something about the way she'd managed to capture her smile. It shone through her eyes and her mouth and the angle of her head thrown backwards in joy. This was the best ever. She used to find it so much harder, and at the beginning they never seemed to work out. She sometimes found herself so desperate and frustrated that she'd tear them up or scrub them out with frenzied strikes of black paint. But this one had come so easily.

As she stepped back from it, she knew it was the last. She wouldn't be able to top this, and if she couldn't do that then what was the point? She sat on the floor with her legs crossed and stared at it. When her back began to ache she stood up and then, very methodically and with great reverence, she started to pack her paints away. She cleaned her brushes, swilling them around a jar of white spirit and watching the paint cloud the liquid in smoky swirls. Then she wiped the palette knives, threw away painty cloths and stacked the canvasses. She kept on until everything was tidy, and the new painting of Anna was left alone in the middle of the room on the easel. Of course, she would paint again, but she would paint for pleasure, not therapy. This painting was what she'd been searching for. It was Anna. Just as she remembered her. She leant forward and kissed the still-wet paint, tasting the paint on her lips as she did.

She carefully climbed into bed and lay back on the pillow. She knew by the way Jon breathed that he was asleep. She eased up the covers and turned her back to him, balancing almost precariously on the edge of the bed. Usually it took her ages to fall asleep after painting, but that night she slept almost as soon as her head touched the pillow.

She was woken by banging on the front door. The noise dawned gradually, forcing her into a drowsy wakefulness. She glanced at Jon's clock, then got out of bed and grabbed her dressing gown from the hook on the door and went down the stairs whilst tying the belt. What on earth could be so urgent this early in the morning? Jon hadn't even left for work – he was still in the shower – and Lizzie wouldn't be up for at least another hour.

She opened the front door to find Angela Howe standing on the doorstep.

It was raining. The sky was a deep, grim grey and the traffic splashed through enormous puddles, wipers working overtime. Angela was soaked to the skin. She looked like she'd been mugged, or something similar – her hair and clothes were all over the place, her eyes were raw and puffed and mascara scooted down her face with the rain.

'You bitch,' she growled, before Kate had a chance to speak. 'And that bitch daughter of yours.'

Kate froze.

'Flaunting herself, dancing around him like some whore off the street.'

Kate tried to speak, but Angela's tone was so menacing that words failed. Angela took a step forward. Kate knew she should close the door on her, but her muscles wouldn't work, her feet somehow nailed to the floor.

'Do you have any concept of how hard I worked to get where I am?' Angela was standing only inches from Kate. Her breath smelt sour and her livid eyes smouldered with hatred.

'Please leave,' mumbled Kate.

'Oh, you'd like that wouldn't you?'

Kate noticed that one side of Angela's mouth was twitching. She remembered how she had looked at her in the Friends' Meeting House. The same glare. The same loathing. Kate tried to remind herself that it was she who should be angry. How dare this woman batter the door down at six thirty in the morning? How dare she use such vile words against Anna? It was her husband who had acted wrongly, and she who'd tried to cover it up for him.

Kate squared her shoulders and stood taller. 'I don't want to speak to you.'

Angela's eyes narrowed. 'I hate you. I hate you for giving birth to that little slut. She *ruined* my life. That whore took everything.'

Kate looked over her shoulder, hoping to see Jon coming down the stairs. Surely he wouldn't be long? But she could still hear the sound of the shower. She lifted an arm made of jelly, with fingers shaking, and tried to push Angela back off the doorstep.

'I clawed my way out of the gutter,' Angela whispered. 'Worked tirelessly, put up with so much *rubbish*, did everything I could to make something of my life. Now look at me. The pathetic widow of a vile paedophile.'

Kate looked at Angela, wondering if she'd heard her properly.

'That's right,' she spat. 'That shit decided to throw himself off your daughter's roof last night.' Angela laughed bitterly. 'The very same roof. Funny, isn't it? Who'd have thought he would do that? He crept out in the middle of the night and jumped. Just like your whore of a daughter did.'

Kate grabbed at the door frame to hold herself upright. 'Anna didn't jump.'

Angela needled her eyes into Kate as rivers of rain streamed down her cheeks and nose.

'Oh, didn't she?' Her voice had flattened and fallen quiet.

'No. And I don't think she fell either.' Kate's voice trembled. 'I think she was pushed.'

'*Pushed*?' Angela looked genuinely shocked. 'What do you mean? What are you trying to say?'

'I think Anna was pushed off that roof by Stephen.'

Angela stared at her. Then her face broke into a derisive smirk and she gave a snort of bitter laughter. 'You really are pathetic, Kate. You just can't believe it, can you? That she might have jumped because she had secrets she couldn't handle. Stupid little girl. Or that she fell because she was drunk, just another out-of-control teenager, too much vodka, foot slipped, and . . . whoops . . . down she went. You hear about her and my idiot husband and you grab at the first crazy straw you can. Anything to make it easier to believe.' She blinked slowly. 'Well, I don't have that luxury with Stephen. Stephen didn't fall by accident. He wasn't pushed. He took his own life. He went up on the roof of that gymnasium, tied the end of a rope around his neck, the other to a ventilation pipe and then he jumped, feeble coward that he was. Snapped his neck. Gone.' Angela flicked her fingers. 'Poof! No goodbyes. Not even a note.'

Kate's head flipped again and again. She tried to blank her mind. Scrub out the images that Angela's ranting threw up. Anna falling. Stephen hanging with his neck broken.

'And I'm left to deal with the mess. He looks guilty now, doesn't he? A child abuser. A man who has sex with seven-year-olds.' Angela stepped backwards, and at last released Kate from her hammering stare. 'We both know that's not true. We know what that little whore did. That bitch was no more a child than you or I. She left the house looking so respectable, didn't she? Not with her shirt unbuttoned, breasts spilling out, skirt hitched up until it barely covered that pert teenage bottom of hers. You didn't know that's how she pranced around school, did you? Did she have the make-up on at breakfast? Or did she stop on the pavement outside school, get her compact out and slap it on like plaster? A couple of baby wipes before she got home, and there you are, filthy whore gone, innocent child returned.'

Kate was shaking now. Her head pounded. Angela was blurring in her vision. The rain seemed heavier than ever.

'And you? Standing up and telling him and the rest of them that he was as good as muck on your shoe? You knew, didn't you? You knew he loved her. He told you. I know he did. He told me he wanted you to know that he loved her. I told him he was a fool to think it would make any difference, but he said it would. He said that if you knew that he loved her it would change your minds. But he was wrong. He was wrong to think that his stupid, blind love legitimized anything. All it's done is destroy my life. We tried so hard to move on, and now he's killed himself and by doing that he's tattooed the word *paedophile* to his sorry soul. We'll be all over the papers, the television, reviled throughout the country. His name is muck.' Angela took another step backwards. 'You rest assured that Jezebel of yours is sashaying through Hell just waiting for you to join her.' Then she turned and walked away, struggling to keep straight, drunk with devastation.

Kate was still standing at the front door when Jon came down the stairs. She tried to speak but found she couldn't; it was as if her lips had been sewn shut.

'Bloody rain,' he said, peering over her shoulder. 'Traffic will be up the kibosh.'

Kate turned and walked past him without a word. She went to their bedroom, closed the door behind her, sat on the bed and shook uncontrollably.

The Rope Jury

Jon stared at the screen in front of him.

Signs, Symptoms and Stages.

The stages seemed simple enough: early-stage, mid-stage and late-stage. Mild, moderate, severe, each stage progressively and significantly worse than the last. He read on, and as he did, his anxiety grew. He was hoping his concerns would be assuaged. He was hoping there would be a paragraph, highlighted or boxed, that would reassure him. Or maybe make mention of a rare, untested herb that users described as a miracle. But there was nothing remotely reassuring in the article, or indeed in anything else he had read.

Jon allowed himself another wary glance at the last paragraphs, at the late-stage symptoms, at what was to come: the seizures, total bowel incontinence, panic attacks, aggression. The words began to swim on the screen. He stared hard, trying to focus through the blur, trying to make out the individual letters.

The phone rang on his desk and made him jump. He looked at the caller ID. It was home. He grabbed at the receiver.

'Hello?'

'Are you busy?'

He clicked the browser closed. 'No.'

'Oh, Jon . . .'

'What is it? What's wrong?'

She didn't say anything, and he could hear she was breathing heavily. 'Kate, sweetheart, what's happened?'

'He killed himself.'

'What? Who?'

'Stephen. Stephen killed himself.'

Jon cast his eyes around the office: open-plan, contemporary, levelling, so good for team morale, bloody awful for conversations best kept private. 'How do you know?' he said quietly. 'Are you sure?'

'Lizzie was sent home from school.'

'Oh my God,' Jon breathed.

'He jumped off the roof.'

Jon didn't say anything.

'The caretaker found him. Lizzie said the place is in chaos.' Kate began to cry. 'This is all such shit.'

'I'm coming home.'

Jon rested his head against the window of the black cab. The driver was talking to him, but Jon wasn't listening. He was trying to make sense of all the different things he was feeling. There was pity, satisfaction, relief, shock, even regret, and the overall mix gave a peculiar sensation; horrifying, but also sickly exhilarating.

He found Kate sitting on the floor in the kitchen.

Her eyes were puffed and red. The sleeves of her black woollen cardigan – far too hot for the weather – were pulled low over her hands and she clutched a disintegrating piece of loo roll. She looked up and began to cry again and held her arms out towards him. He sat beside her and took her hand.

'This is my fault,' she whispered.

'Of course it isn't.'

Kate bit back tears and nodded. 'It is, Jon. It's my fault.'

'How can it be your fault? *He* killed himself. He clearly felt guilty for what he'd done. It was his own turmoil, nothing you or I did. He couldn't live with his actions. You did nothing.'

'There was a meeting yesterday. About him being suspended. I stood up in front of everyone and spoke.'

Jon stayed quiet.

'I didn't want to go, but I couldn't keep away.' She shook her head. 'It was hearing him try and deny it when he'd just been here and admitted it. So I stood up and told him he was accountable for his actions.'

'Did you mention Anna?' said Jon.

'I didn't say anything that would directly link her to him. I just said the truth would get out and he would have to face it. And then this morning, when you were in the shower, Angela came here and told me about Stephen.'

'Angela?'

Kate nodded and her eyes filled with tears.

'Why didn't you tell me?'

Kate shrugged and pushed her sleeve against her eyes to blot the tears. 'I was in such a state. She said terrible things about Anna.' She rested her forehead on top of her knees.

'What things?' he asked.

Kate was quiet for a bit, then lifted her head and looked at him, trying to smile through her tears. 'It doesn't matter,' she said quietly.

Jon put his arm around her and pulled her in for a hug.

'And there's another thing,' she whispered. 'The graffiti.'

'What about it?'

She hesitated. 'Oh, God,' she whispered.

'What?'

'It was me who graffitied his house.'

John pulled back in surprise. 'But you were with Dan that night.'

'Yes,' she nodded. 'We did it together.'

Jon wrinkled his brow with confusion.

'You and Dan?'

She sighed deeply. 'We were drunk. I took a pill. It seemed like a good idea.' She groaned.

Jon was suddenly bombarded with his own recollections of that night. Watching the clock on its relentless march as he waited for Kate, walking to think through his feelings of loss, convinced of her infidelity, crushed by it. His stomach caved in.

'I thought you were having sex with him.'

Kate looked confused. 'Why would you think that?'

'I saw you go off with him. You were gone for hours.'

'How long do you think it takes to get so drunk you can't think, then graffiti a house without getting caught?'

'I didn't know you were vandalizing a house. I thought you were sleeping with my brother.'

'Jesus, Jon! What a fucking idiotic thing to think. I can't even do it with you. Why the hell would I do it with Dan?'

Jon could think of a thousand reasons why she would sleep with Dan and not him.

'You know what?' She stood up. He could see her anger and frustration boiling over the edges. 'Stephen Howe has just killed himself. I have no idea how I'm feeling about it. All I know is that sitting here listening to your pathetic jealousy of Dan for the umpteenth time is the last thing I need. I mean, come on, Jon? As if our family needs an affair thrown into the mix? How could you even think—' She was cut short by the tears she was trying to fight back. She pinched the bridge of her nose. 'How could you think I would do that?'

'You got into his car.'

'So? That doesn't mean I'm having sex with him.'

'I saw you smile.'

'You saw me *smile*? Have you any idea how ridiculous that sounds? Dan always makes me bloody smile! You think just because I smile at him I'm going to jump into bed with him?' She shook her head with total incredulity.

'I don't know . . . you just seem so distant from me.'

'Well, that has a lot to do with the heap of shit that I've had land on me. Believe me, I've got more than enough on my bloody mind than bloody sex. I would have thought you did, too.'

'Why do you do that?' he asked.

'Why do I do what, for God's sake?'

'Say things like that. Insinuate I don't love Anna like you do, that I'm not suffering like you are. You seem to think that me wanting to be close to you, to make love to you, is wrong. But I need that, Kate. I need your love. I need you there for me. I try to be there for you whatever you do. At the memorial. The funeral. God, I watched you throw my mother to the floor at my daughter's funeral, and what do I do? I make excuses for you. Remind people what you're going through. You think you're the only one in pain? You've no idea. And all this time, through all this bastard sadness, I've been terrified of losing you. But you were already gone, weren't you? The night Anna died, you left us.'

He stopped talking, out of breath with the effort of allowing so much out of him. They never mentioned the funeral. It was like it never happened. It should have been a day to remember Anna, to lay her to rest, to honour the short time they'd had with her, but all he had were livid memories of Kate's crimson rage, a demon that thrust its way through the haze of tranquillizers the doctors had pushed, a demon that continued to thrive, unconcerned with the passage of time that everybody said would weaken it.

The morning of the funeral she hadn't said a word, not to anyone, not even Lizzie. She was glazed over, on autopilot. She brushed her hair, got dressed, pinned the silk flower she'd bought especially to her tailored jacket, her face fixed and grim. She sat on the pew next to him and stared straight at Anna's coffin, at the flowers, the sealed letter written by Lizzie propped between them. The church was full of friends and family and strangers, all of them moved to tears by the tragedy. His mother made her way to the front of the church. She adjusted the height of the microphone. Opened her book. She lifted her head and began to read the words she had chosen. She read beautifully. Her voice was soft and gentle, sad, and sang out joyful; her love for Anna beamed through every word.

And then Kate screamed.

She sat there, next to him, and screamed. At first he had no idea what the dreadful noise was. Then he realized people were staring at Kate. Then he tried to calm her; he put his arms around her, but she scratched his face, pushed him away. Then Jon's mother was at their side. She tried to soothe her. Jon, the vicar, Lizzie, they all tried. His mother took Kate's arm and attempted to lead her out of the church, changing the tone of her voice from gentle to firm, then stern.

'Kate, control yourself. This is a *funeral*. We are in a *church*. The people here have come to pay their respects to Anna. Please get a grip on yourself.'

But Kate continued to scream, tearing at her hair, gouging her skin with her nails and leaving red grazes all over her face.

His mother tried to take hold of her arm. 'Come with me now, Kate.' Then Kate shoved her so hard she stumbled backwards, tripping and falling on to the polished stone floor. Jon shuddered at the recollection.

'You have been there for me on those occasions,' said Kate. Her back was to him, her shoulders hung low. 'But there have been times in the past year where I've never felt so alone; when my grief and missing her devours me and there's nobody able to stop it. But I don't blame you for that. I have behaved terribly, irrationally, lost control of myself and said awful things you don't deserve. I can't explain or excuse these moments, and I blame *nobody* but myself. If Stephen was right, if she took her own life, the only person I will blame is myself. I will be responsible for her death because I wasn't a good enough mother, because I wasn't the mother she needed when life got too much for her. You've been so strong for me and Lizzie, and I know you think you've shelved your own sadness, but you haven't. How could you? Of course, I don't think you love Anna any less or more than I do. Love is completely unquantifiable. All I know is that most of my days and nights I can't see straight, or think straight. I've been a dreadful mother and a dreadful wife. And, oh my God, Jon, if this means I lose you or Lizzie then I'll regret it for the rest of my life, but I can't change it. I reacted the only way I could have. We can only look at ourselves, Jon. You need to stop trying to deal with me and deal with yourself.'

And then she walked out of the kitchen and left him at the table.

The phone rang soon after, and though he tried to ignore it, the thing kept on and on at him. He pulled himself to standing and answered.

'Yes?'

'Hello, it's Marlena Sanders speaking. May I speak to Kate?'

'She's not here.'

'Would you be able to give me her mobile telephone number?'

'She hasn't got it with her. I can see it on the kitchen table,' he lied.

'In that case, could you pass on a message?' said Marlena Sanders.

'Yes,' said Jon. 'I can pass on a message.'

'Could you tell her there's a collection going round at school for flowers for Mrs Howe, and that . . .' Her voice fell into a stage whisper. 'I also wanted to make sure she was feeling *OK* . . . you know, about Dr Howe?'

Jon put his finger on the receiver button to cut the call, and then slammed the phone against the table again and again and again as hard as he could.

Alone in the Dark

Haydn and Lizzie sat on his bed and held hands. Haydn smoked. Lizzie stroked her finger against his thumb. She was staring at the photo of herself as a fairy princess, A4-sized, breasts exposed, hair laced with flowers and ribbon. Haydn had pinned it next to Anna's sketch, the one she'd drawn of the girl in the cage with folded wings and pleading eyes. The longer she stared, the more surreal the photograph became. It was as if she were staring at somebody else. The girl in the photo looked so grown-up and self-assured. She was beautiful, too. It didn't look like her. If someone had showed it to her she would have said it was Anna. She couldn't believe how much she resembled her sister. It was mad. All those years she thought they were chalk and cheese, and really they were quite alike.

Haydn sniffed loudly and jolted Lizzie from the photograph. She squeezed his hand.

'How are you doing?' she asked him.

He shrugged.

'I can't believe he did it,' she said.

Haydn didn't reply; he leant over and flicked the ash from his cigarette on to the floor.

'And I don't believe what they're saying about him. Surely, if he had done something like that the police would arrest him. It must be made up.'

'He killed himself, didn't he?'

'Maybe he was just really sad.'

'I don't care, anyway.'

'I can't imagine being so upset that I'd *ever* kill myself.' She laid her head in Haydn's lap and he ran his fingers through her hair. 'You know,' she whispered, 'it's the one thing that terrifies me about Anna, that she might have killed herself. I mean, can you imagine how desperate she must have been if she did do that?' Lizzie closed her eyes against the pain she suddenly felt. 'Why couldn't she talk to me? I'm her sister.'

'Anna didn't kill herself.'

Lizzie sat up then and wiped away her tears. 'We'll never know, will we? I'll always have that with me, in the back of my mind, that maybe she did.'

Haydn leant forward and stubbed his cigarette out on a textbook on his desk and they watched the thin plastic coating on the cover fizzle and melt. 'I know she didn't kill herself. I was there, remember?' He sat back against the wall and looked up at the ceiling.

'I know, but you were drunk. You weren't near her. What if she just decided to do it? It might have looked like an accident to you, but wasn't. She was on that wall, and then it came to her.'

'Look, Lizzie, I'm not going to keep on saying it. But I *know* she didn't jump.' He turned his head and looked straight into her eyes. 'She didn't kill herself. OK?'

Lizzie felt unnerved by the intensity in his face. She knew she wasn't helping him deal with what he was trying to deal with. How stupid of her to talk about Anna right then. 'I am sorry about your dad,' she said.

Haydn broke his stare from hers. 'Yeah,' he said, kicking at the floor. 'Shit happens. But it's fine; I hated him anyway.'

'Don't say that.'

'It's true. He didn't care about anybody but himself, not me, not mum, just himself.'

Lizzie didn't know what to say. She knew that Haydn and Dr Howe hadn't got on – Haydn had mentioned it enough times – but the venom in Haydn's words was shocking, especially given that Dr Howe had just jumped off a roof with a rope around his neck.

'At least he did it at school and not in the house,' Haydn said.

Lizzie shuddered. 'Can you imagine having to live here if he had?'

'Fine if he hung himself, but what if he'd used a gun and blown his brains out?'

'Oh, Haydn, don't!'

'Fucking blood and brains everywhere. That's fucked up, man. How someone does that.'

'What do you think will happen now?' she asked, keen to move their conversation away from the suicide.

'Dunno,' he said. 'I suppose they'll get a new headmaster.'

'I mean to you.'

He shrugged and reached for his cigarette papers. 'I don't want to talk about it.'

'Sure,' she said. 'So do you want to do anything today?'

Haydn didn't answer immediately. 'No, I'm going to stay here, but we could still go to the cinema tomorrow. I reckon I'll need to get out of the house by then.'

Lizzie rested her chin on top of his knee. 'I really am sorry, you know, and it will get easier. Not for your mum, well, not if she's like mine, but you'll be OK.'

He rested his chin on his other knee so their cheeks were pressed together. 'I love you,' he said.

She smiled. 'I love you too.'

Her phone rang then. It was home. Lizzie didn't answer it.

'I should probably get back. That's Mum. She'll be getting stressed and I can't cope with any hassle today, not after this.'

She kissed him on the forehead. 'Text me later?'

He nodded.

Lizzie closed Haydn's door as quietly as she could and checked up and down the corridor. She didn't want to run into Mrs Howe; she had no idea what she would say to her. She trod the stairs carefully, toe to heel, in case there was a squeaky one. When she got to the bottom of the stairs, she exhaled silently and crept towards the front door.

'Elizabeth?' Mrs Howe's voice came from the living room.

Lizzie froze; she didn't know what to do. She wanted to run for it, maybe pretend she hadn't heard anything, but on the other hand, Mrs Howe's husband had just died and she should really say something to her. Lizzie tried to gather some comforting words together, tried to recall some of the best things people had said to her when Anna died, but she couldn't think of a single sentence.

The living room was dark; the drawn curtains had to be lined with blackout lining or something like it because the only light that came through was a thin strip where they hadn't quite pulled together. Mrs Howe sat in an armchair in the corner of the room with the white chink falling across her chest and over her lap like a chalk line.

'I'm very sorry about Dr Howe,' Lizzie said, her voice quivering a little.

There was silence. Lizzie squinted into the darkness. Mrs Howe sat very still. Her hands gripped the arms of the chair. Her face, painted featureless by the shadows, stared straight towards her. The atmosphere was eerie, a touch sinister, and set Lizzie's heart racing. She wished Haydn was with her. She took a step backwards in the direction of the hallway, hoping perhaps Mrs Howe hadn't noticed her come into the room, but then the woman leant forward and her face came into the light enough for Lizzie to see her. Her eyes blinked slowly as if she hadn't slept for months. She looked drawn. Her skin was awful; even in the dim light Lizzie could see it was patched red with spots that had broken out around her mouth and nose. If Mrs Howe were *her* mother she would run her a bath and offer to make the supper. Lizzie made a mental note to suggest it to Haydn as he might not think of it himself, being a boy, and her dad always said the little things made a big difference, even if it wasn't always acknowledged.

'Why won't you leave him bloody alone? He doesn't love you like he loved her. You know that, don't you?' Mrs Howe's growled words were barely audible, and Lizzie prayed she hadn't heard her correctly.

'Did you hear me?' said Mrs Howe. Her lips twisted into a nasty snarl.

'I think . . . I should get home . . .' Lizzie said. She took a small step backwards.

'Yes, you should run along, back to that bitch mother of yours,' said Mrs Howe. 'You know you're not welcome here, Elizabeth. I want you to know that. I don't want you in my house, and I don't want you anywhere near my son again.'

Lizzie turned and ran for the front door and the freedom that lay beyond it. She fumbled with the lock. She finally managed to open the door and was hit by a flood of sunshine that made her blink with fleeting blindness. She knew death made people act in a peculiar way. She'd seen it with her mum. Her mum had hit

Rebecca, for goodness' sake! Mrs Howe hadn't meant to sound so bloodcurdling; it was the grief and shock oozing out of her body. But even though she knew this, as she walked away from the house, towards the pavement and the safe bustle of the street, her body trembled so much she felt light-headed. It was one thing with her own mother, but something else to be with a relative stranger, her deputy head, no less, who was flipping out like that.

'You know what I think?' shouted Mrs Howe's voice from behind her. Lizzie jumped and turned. Mrs Howe was on the doorstep. 'I think that if he'd fallen for you in the first place, instead of that stupid slut, maybe everything would still be OK.'

Lizzie stared at Mrs Howe, who was smiling like she didn't have a care in the world, in front of her house with the smudgy shadows of the scary graffiti that somebody had unsuccessfully tried to remove.

'I'm really sorry about Dr Howe,' Lizzie said, before spinning on her heel and running down the street as fast as she could.

The Second Forbid

'Where have you been?' Kate asked Lizzie when she came in.

Kate had been desperate with worry. Jon left the house soon after their row. She had heard the front door slam from upstairs. She was in their bedroom, hoping he might come up to talk to her. She wanted to tell him things she hadn't managed to in the kitchen. She wanted to tell him that she'd decided to repair herself, and that she wasn't going to paint Anna any more, that she was going to cook, and smile more, that she'd made up with Rachel, and for the first time in this wretched black void it felt like there might actually be a spot of light to follow. Maybe it was all too late? She could see how unhappy she was making him. She knew how difficult it was for him to feel so helpless. He'd loved looking after her and the kids; he relished it, and he'd been good at it. He always used to say that without his three girls to love and look after, there'd be nothing.

She went back downstairs. The clock in the kitchen read past two. She wasn't due a cup of tea until four thirty.

'No,' she said aloud. 'No more routine.' She flicked the kettle on to boil and opened the cupboard to get a mug. She chose one that Lizzie had painted at the ceramics café in Twickenham. It had splodgy purple flowers all over it, the petals made by her tiny fatless eight-year-old fingers. As she looked at it, it dawned on her that she hadn't seen Lizzie since that morning, when she burst into Kate's bedroom, red-eyed and shocked to the core, having been sent home from school because of Dr Howe. Kate was still reeling from the news herself, so she'd sat blank and empty as Lizzie cried and shook her head and eventually got angry and confused at Kate's apparent lack of empathy.

That was nearly five hours ago. She checked the house, including Anna's room, but there was no sign of her. Then she tried her mobile. It rang, but there was no answer. She tried Jon's, but it was switched off. So she made herself a cup of tea and waited at the kitchen table, not sure where she would look for her.

It was nearing three o'clock when she heard the key in the lock. She jumped up from the table, relief surging through her as Lizzie's face appeared at the door. Lizzie didn't say anything, but walked straight up to her and fell into her arms, hugging her tightly, out of breath and hot from running.

'I phoned you,' Kate said.

Lizzie didn't let go of her.

'You know, we've spoken about this. You've got a mobile so I can get hold of you. I was worried.'

Lizzie nodded and stepped back from her; she was still catching her breath, shaking and sucking on her bottom lip, which was something she'd done if she was worried ever since she was tiny.

'What's the matter?' Kate asked.

'Nothing.'

Kate hesitated. 'Is it because of Dr Howe?'

'Sort of.'

'It's a terrible thing; you must all be very shocked.'

'I love you, Mum.'

'Oh, Lizzie.' Kate pulled her close again, strangled by a sudden, overwhelming love for her daughter, so strong she knew she wouldn't be able to say the words without crying.

I love you too, sweetheart, you have no idea how much.

But she didn't want to cry in front of her any more; Lizzie had seen her cry so much, and it wasn't fair. Kate had to be strong for her. She didn't let go of her daughter until the threat of tears had passed.

'Can I get you anything to eat?' she asked, when her voice was strong enough.

'Why do you think he killed himself?'

'I don't know. Things like that don't have easy answers.'

'Was it anything to do with you or Anna?'

Kate's heart started pounding. 'Why? Why on earth would it be to do with me or your sister?'

Lizzie began to chew her lower lip.

'Has someone said something?' Kate was terrified. 'What have you heard?'

'So there is something?' Lizzie said.

Kate didn't answer.

'Mrs Howe said some stuff,' Lizzie said with caution.

'Mrs Howe? She spoke to you at school?'

Lizzie didn't answer.

'When did she speak to you, Lizzie?'

Lizzie lifted her chin and fixed her eyes on Kate. 'Just now. I was at her house.'

Kate tensed. 'Why were you at her house?'

Lizzie didn't answer.

'Please tell me you're not seeing that boy.'

'Haydn.'

'I don't care what his name is.'

'His name is *Haydn*.'

290

Lizzie crossed her arms and stepped one foot in front of the other. Kate saw Anna then. Right there, in Lizzie. She reached for the worktop as her head began to swim.

'I love him.'

For a moment or two Kate thought she might laugh. But the urge left her quickly, and instead, to stop herself crying, she dug her fingers into the worktop. 'I asked you . . . no, I *told* you never to see him. Didn't you understand me?'

Lizzie didn't answer.

'You can't see Haydn Howe again.'

Lizzie continued to stare, her eyes icy, her fingers grasping handfuls of school skirt. She shook her head. 'No. You can't do that.'

'Excuse me?'

'You can't tell me not to see him.'

'Oh, is that right?' Kate folded her arms, mirroring Lizzie's belligerent pose.

'I'm nearly sixteen.'

'You're *not* nearly sixteen!'

'Well,' she said, 'I'm fifteen and I'll see who I want.'

'Not him.'

'Why the hell not?'

'Don't you dare swear in this house!'

'Why not? You swear all the bloody time!'

'Lizzie!' Kate shouted. Lizzie narrowed her eyes. Kate took a breath and stilled her voice. 'It's been a bad week for me. I don't want to carry on with this conversation. You will not see that boy again.' Kate spoke each word slowly, enunciating every syllable, trying to convey the weight of her request.

'*Yes I will*! I *love* him!'

'Of course you don't love him.'

'I do!'

'You've only just met him. You don't know what love is, for Christ's sake. And come on, Lizzie, he was Anna's boyfriend.'

Her daughter pursed her lips and shook her head. 'No, they weren't together.'

'Yes, they were, Lizzie. It's not right.'

'They weren't! He told me. They were never boyfriend and girlfriend.'

'Sweetheart.' Kate tried to steady her voice. 'He was always here. Always ringing her. He sent her flowers. He was always hanging around outside the house. I even caught him on the pavement once, watching her bedroom window at night.'

Lizzie was fighting tears. Shaking her head. 'No! You're wrong. Why do you want to ruin my life? I love him and he loves me. Just leave us alone!'

'If you carry on like this I'll ground you.'

'Oh really?'

'Yes, really.'

'And how long will you ground me for? A day? A week? That won't stop me seeing him.'

'Then I'll ground you until you leave home.'

'Then I'll leave home now.'

'What on earth has got into you? What are you trying to do here?'

'I'm *trying* to grow up! I'm *trying* to get on with my life. You don't let me do anything. Why don't you trust me? What have I ever done to make you think you can't trust me?'

Lizzie breathed heavily. Kate stared at her, incredulous that Lizzie would choose today to morph into the hideous, irrational teenager Kate thought she'd never see in her. Kate tried to get a grip. This wasn't going to work. She needed to keep calm. She needed to use guile, not force. This wasn't a battle she could lose; she would not have Haydn Howe anywhere near Lizzie. Kate took a few seconds to breathe.

'It's not that I don't trust you, I do. It's just . . . him . . .' Kate saw Angela's hateful eyes boring into her, Stephen's stricken face declaring his love for Anna, then him moaning in that vile film, Anna's pale skin against his. Images of him hanging. Echoes of Angela calling Anna a whore. For a brief moment Kate wondered if she should just come out with it, tell Lizzie about Rebecca's film, about what Haydn's father did to Anna, explain how the thought of Lizzie anywhere near the son of that man made her skin crawl. But she couldn't do that to her. 'I just can't let you see him.'

'It's not up to you!' screamed her daughter.

'You don't understand—'

'No, I don't understand! It's bullshit. I love him. He's clever and funny and intelligent. He plays the guitar. He volunteers with wildlife. I bet you didn't know that? He gives up his own time to help with birds and other stuff, like cleaning graves. And he makes me happy. You don't even *remember* happy. You should be pleased for me. Why are you telling me what to do? You let Anna do what she wanted whenever she wanted!'

'Don't you dare bring Anna into this.'

'Why not?' Lizzie shrieked. 'You have no idea what it's been like for me since she died. You walk around as if the world has ended. You're always bloody crying or painting. You never laugh, you hardly ever smile, you cry *all the time*. You say you've had a bad week? What do you think it's like for me living with you when you're having one of your "bad weeks"? It's awful. I don't know what to say or what to do. You won't talk to me. Do you know what that feels like? You miss her so much and your life is

293

so flipping devastated, I wouldn't be surprised if you're the next one off that stupid, hateful roof!'

Kate stared at her, feeling herself collapse as Lizzie's words began to dissolve her.

'When I told you I loved you just then,' Lizzie went on, 'you didn't tell me you loved me back. You couldn't, could you? And that's because you don't!' Tears streamed down Lizzie's cheeks. 'You keep me safe, you worry about bees, knowing where I am or me catching a cold, but you don't *love* me. We don't talk, you don't get excited for me, or sad with me. You're not involved in my life. All you see is Anna's ghost. You shut yourself away from me, and it makes me wish it was me that died and not her. Then at least I wouldn't have to live with you missing her so much.'

Lizzie fell backwards against the wall and covered her face with her hands.

Kate blinked hard. 'How can you say that?' she breathed. 'How can you even think that?'

'Because it's true,' said Lizzie into her hands. 'Because ever since she died you've been so unhappy and there's nothing I can do, and I don't think you love me any more.'

'But I love you more than life itself. I didn't say I loved you just now because I was trying not to cry; just the thought of how much I love you chokes me so I can't speak.' She reached out to bring Lizzie towards her. But Lizzie shuffled along the wall away from her, then dropped her hands away from her face.

'It's no good just thinking it, though,' she said. 'That's no good to me.' And then she left Kate alone in the kitchen.

History Repeated

Kate was waiting for him at the kitchen table. In front of her was a glass of white wine. On the table was another glass.

'Sit with me?' she asked.

She poured some wine and pushed the glass towards him. His head ached so badly the lights in the kitchen stung.

'Where have you been?' she asked. The question wasn't antagonistic. Kate seemed placid. Calm. She had brushed her hair and wore clean clothes – a pair of faded black jeans and a loose-fitting maroon sweater that slipped a little off one shoulder, showing clear, smooth skin. He wished he could lean forward and kiss it.

'I went for a walk,' he said.

'It's late.'

'I was thinking.'

'About us?'

Jon nodded.

'I'm sorry, Jon. I'm sorry for how I've been. I got caught up in my grief and it sort of possessed me.'

'You're allowed to be sad. It's not that, it's . . .' Jon wished he could explain exactly what he was feeling. Hearing her apologize for being sad because of Anna wasn't what he wanted. But when he tried to form sentences from the mayhem he felt, the words sounded petty and juvenile: loneliness, rejection, sexual frustration, feelings of being unloved, undervalued, unnecessary.

'I had a row with Lizzie,' said Kate. She sipped her wine, and then drew a knee up to her chest.

'About?'

'I told her she wasn't to see Haydn.'

'Has she been seeing him?'

Kate nodded. 'Apparently she loves him. Anyway, she didn't take it too well and we had a fight. She's all grown up and I didn't even notice.' Kate drank again. 'She said awful things.'

'She's a teenager. That's her job.'

'She said she wished it was she who had died, not Anna, so she didn't have to live with me being so upset. She said she didn't know if I loved her, and because of that she was scared I was going to kill myself.'

Jon lifted his glass and tipped it to one side, then back again, and watched the surface of the wine waver until it found a peaceful horizontal again. 'That's because of Stephen's suicide. Things like that make children question everything around them.'

He was trying to comfort Kate, but he understood exactly how Lizzie could think those things. He thought similarly himself a lot of the time. It was easy for him and Lizzie to imagine Kate's life being so devastated that she could never truly love either of them again.

'I don't know what to do. I don't want to lose her. Or you. But I feel like I've let that happen.'

Jon refilled Kate's glass.

'Not too much,' she said. 'That last glass has gone straight to my head.'

'Would you like something to eat?'

'Maybe,' she said. 'I think there's some crisps in the cupboard.'

Jon opened two packets of Hula Hoops and emptied them into a cereal bowl, then he put them on the table between them. Kate took a small handful, but didn't eat them. Instead, she stared at them in her open palm like three gold rings.

'Even these remind me of her,' she said.

Jon saw Anna then, at Lizzie's third birthday. She was threading her fingers with Hula Hoops. Three on each finger. Then she ate them, methodically moving along her line of Hula Hoop towers. Her face was serious, occupied, cheeks puffed up like a hamster's. Kate and Jon had cried silent tears of laughter as they watched Lizzie copying Anna, hooking the crisps on to her fingers, her tongue sticking out of the corner of her mouth with concentration. But rather than eat them herself, she had presented her ten crispy fingers to her sister, who leant forward without missing a beat and started to eat. It was Lizzie who beamed as though she'd won the lottery. It was a story that showed Lizzie's generosity, the way she worshipped her big sister, her selflessness. The story was only interesting because of Lizzie.

'The Hula Hoops remind me of Lizzie,' Jon said.

There was a shade of confusion on Kate's face, and then realization as the fog in her memory cleared so that she re-saw the sketch of her young daughters and the Hula Hoops. She put the handful of crisps back in the bowl.

'What's wrong with me?'

'Nothing.'

'But Lizzie? You should have heard her. What if I've lost her?'

'How could you? She's your daughter. You love her and she loves you. She's a great kid and that's because of you, because of the way you brought her up, the things you taught her and the person you are.'

He put his hand on hers. 'We've all said a lot of things to each other today, but it seems to me like we've taken some sort of step forward. Don't you think?'

She looked up at him and nodded.

'I'll go up and have a chat with her. Maybe we should have a late Chinese?' He smiled.

'That would be nice.'

He left Kate at the table and went upstairs to Lizzie's room. The door was closed. He called her name and gave a brief knock. There was no answer. He knocked again.

Still nothing.

'Lizzie,' he said. 'Can we talk? Mum and you need to patch things up. It's silly you both being upset.' He waited for her reply. 'Lizzie?'

He knocked again.

Nothing.

He opened the door and peeked in. It was quiet. The curtains were open and the dusky summer evening light bathed the room a cloudy blue. She was in bed.

He sat on the edge of the bed and put his hand on her. 'Come on, poppet. Don't be—'

His heart stopped.

He pulled the duvet back, horror filling his every cell. Pillows. Two of them in a line down the centre of the bed, then covered up, plumped in the right places, designed to look like someone sleeping. Designed to fool an adult. To give someone the chance to sneak out of the house.

'Kate!' he yelled.

She was upstairs in a matter of seconds.

'Christ, no! Lizzie!' she screamed.

They ran downstairs. Jon was sweating, fingers shaking, head turning over and over. All he could think of was the school roof. But that was totally illogical. That was Anna. Not Lizzie.

'Call her mobile,' Kate said, from behind him. Her face was set and her arms crossed. Jon grabbed his phone and dialled her number. It went straight to voicemail.

'It's switched off.'

'You'll have to call the Howes. She's with him. That's where she is.'

Jon nodded. 'Number?' he asked, his finger poised above the keypad. She ran to grab her address book from the kitchen.

'No answer,' he said, soon after dialling. He listened to the unanswered ring, imagining it sounding in the Howes' living room, the lights off and the dark settling in as the ghost of Stephen Howe made itself comfortable in the armchair. 'Grab your coat and the car keys. We'll look for her.'

'Do we call the police?'

He thought for a moment or two. 'Not yet. It's not even nine thirty and she's been gone, what, a couple of hours?'

Kate thought and then nodded.

'They won't do anything yet. Let's at least have a look before we call them.' Jon rubbed Kate's shoulder. She looked up at him; her face was pale and scared. 'She'll be OK, Kate.'

They drove around, Jon driving at a snail's pace, both of them craning their necks through the half-light up and down the streets, desperate for a glimpse of her. They checked the playground, the park, they knocked on the door of Rachel and Rebecca's house, but there was nobody home. Jon looked in every pub they passed. Kate stayed in the car when Jon tried the Howes' front door. He waited but there was no answer; the house was dark and lifeless. He walked slowly back to the car and climbed into the driver's seat. They sat in silence. He knew they were thinking the same thing. He knew they were both thinking about the school. It was Kate who spoke first.

'I don't think I would survive if—'

'Don't say it,' Jon interrupted. 'Don't even think it. Lizzie wouldn't do anything like that. Why would she?'

'We fought horribly.'

'It was an argument. She's growing up; horrible arguments are a part of that. She wouldn't do it, Kate.'

'What if he took her up there to drink? What if it's happened again? What if she's gone up on that roof with Haydn and—' She began to shake violently. 'Shit, Jon. Shit! What if she's fallen? What if we go there and find her—'

'She hasn't fallen!' Jon shouted.

'I don't want to go! I don't want to know. If she has I don't want to *ever* find out!'

'She hasn't fallen!' shouted Jon again. 'Stop it, Kate!'

He drove towards the school, shivering a cold sweat, flashbacks of the night they drove this journey to find Anna on the concrete. Her face broken, her eyes staring wide with blood in their corners like black tears. The bedlam that met them. Blue lights in the darkness. Cordons. Policemen waving them through. The crackle of walkie-talkies. The uneasy faces of those who took them to her.

The school was wrapped up in the growing darkness. No stars or moon yet, just thick cloud. They parked outside the gates and sat in silence.

Jon swallowed. 'She's not here,' he breathed. 'I know she's not here.' Then he turned to Kate. 'Do you want me to go alone?'

She didn't speak, but nodded, just once.

He nodded back, closed his eyes, then nodded again in the hope it would give him some strength. He opened the car door and climbed out, and then stood for a moment or two, listening. He began to walk. His footsteps echoed around the deserted car park.

'Wait!' called Kate from behind him. He stopped and turned. She was running towards him. 'I'm coming with you. I need to be with you.'

They walked all around the school in silence. The only sounds were their footsteps and the traffic from the street behind the school. They tried any door they came across, but they were all locked. There was no sign of her. Every now and then they stopped and held their breath and listened for her. When they'd walked the perimeter of the building, they had no choice left but to check the playground. Jon could hear Kate muttering over and over under her breath, and wondered if she was praying. They rounded the corner and Kate gripped his hand so hard it hurt.

There was nothing in the playground.

Nothing on the ground beneath the gym block.

'Thank God,' Kate breathed. 'Thank fucking God.'

'Lizzie!' Jon shouted then. The strength of his voice over the silence was shocking. Kate squeezed his hand again and pulled herself closer to him.

He called again.

They waited for a response. Jon thought he could hear her.

'Lizzie!' he shouted. 'If you're here, please answer!'

Kate turned herself into Jon's arms and he wrapped his around her. 'Let's get out of here,' she whispered.

They turned to walk back to the car. Jon knew Kate was thinking about the night they found Anna, just as he was. This place wasn't Hula Hoops. This place, the darkened playground with the looming mass of the gymnasium, was the real thing. It was steeped in Anna, and her memory hung around it, sewed on like Peter Pan's shadow.

They climbed into the car, shut the doors and put their seat belts on.

'Now where?' Kate asked.

'Maybe we should check with my parents?' He prepared himself for Kate's incredulous surprise, but it was he who was surprised.

'Yes,' Kate said. 'She might well have gone there.'

They pulled up outside his parents' home. 'You stay here,' he said. 'I'll be a minute or two.'

'Hello, Jonathan, what are you doing here at this time?' His mother sounded weary. 'Are you here for Daniel? Because he went out for dinner. A girl, of course.'

Jon's flash of hope that Lizzie was sitting having a cup of tea with her grandmother, safe and sound and ready to come home with them, fizzled away and left him cold.

'No, I'm not here to see Dan,' he said. 'It's Lizzie. We don't know where she is.'

'What do you mean, you don't know where she is?'

'I think she might be with her boyfriend.'

'I didn't know she had a boyfriend.'

'Nor did we, not really. She and Kate had a row about it. Kate told her she couldn't see him. We think she's snuck out to meet him.'

'Why did Kate—'

'Not now, Mother. All we care about is making sure we find Lizzie safe.'

'Will you come inside? It's vulgar to talk on the doorstep like this. People will think you're one of those grubby men pushing tea towels.'

'I don't care what people think.'

'I do.'

'Look, I think we should keep looking for her. Will you call me if she turns up?'

'Of course,' she said.

Jon leant forward and kissed her. 'Are you OK?' he said, as he turned to go.

'I'm fine.'

'And Dad?'

'Yes, yes, he's fine. We're both fine. Now go, and please would you telephone when you find her? I won't be able to sleep until I know she's home.'

Jon nodded and ran back to the car.

He had only just turned out of their road when his phone rang. He glanced at his phone, desperate to see Lizzie's number on the tiny screen. It was his mother.

'I'm at the kitchen sink, darling, and I think I can see a light in the shed. Yes. Yes, there's definitely a light up there.'

Jon's heart jumped. He began to turn the car, holding the phone between his chin and shoulder. Kate pulled on his sleeve, mouthing urgent words at him. Jon waved at her to be quiet. 'Do you think Dad would have turned the light on?'

'He hasn't been out of bed today,' she said. 'I can't think who else would be up there.'

The Final Forbid

Lizzie and Haydn lay in each other's arms on the floor of the shed. Haydn held her tightly, her head on his chest, cheek resting on his hairless skin, and her stare held by one of the candles they'd relit. The flame danced a random dance. She was trying to spot a pattern, a repeat, but each duck and twirl was unique from the last, and she realized that even if the candle burnt for eternity, it would never duplicate its dance. This beautiful dance was only for her, the candle celebrating this love she'd found, her first, mighty in its perfection. It felt to Lizzie that the shed was the only place in the entire world, the entire universe, where she was allowed to be happy.

'I won't let her stop me seeing you,' she said, and turned her head to kiss him. 'I don't know what I'd do if that happened.'

'We could run away.'

Lizzie sat up on one elbow. 'Really? You'd do that?'

'Of course.' Haydn traced a finger down the side of her cheek, down her neck and over her shoulder.

'Where would we go?'

'I've got family in Leeds. And there's some mates in Manchester. We could go there for a bit. They'd be cool. We could get jobs.'

Lizzie was quiet. The thought was tempting: packing a bag,

running away – it sounded so romantic. But then there was school, her GCSEs, A-levels, her plans to go to university. She was considering reading Economics or maybe Engineering. And she'd miss her parents.

'I'm going to talk to them,' she said. 'You should come too. So they see how lovely you are.'

He kissed her shoulder, softly, suggestive in its lingering. She wrapped her arms around him.

Then there were noises outside, footsteps and low voices, coming closer, coming towards the shed.

'Blinking hell!' she whispered, grabbing her sweater.

She jumped on to her knees and blew out three of the candles. The one she'd been staring at refused to go out. It flickered backwards then defiantly jumped back to resume its endless dance. Lizzie left it and threw Haydn his trousers, and the two of them struggled into as many clothes as possible as the footsteps and the voices of her parents drew closer.

'Lizzie?' her dad called.

Lizzie looked at Haydn and put a finger up to her lips. He nodded slowly. She held her breath, hoping against hope that her dad wouldn't come in, knowing without doubt that he would. Sure enough, the door opened. Lizzie froze. Her heart thumped against her ribcage and sweat covered her half-dressed body.

Her dad and mum stood in the doorway, their faces lit by the dim orange light from the last candle. The darkness behind them was so black it looked painted.

'Thank God,' her mum said when she saw her. 'Thank fucking God.' Then she burst into tears and disappeared from the doorway, and Lizzie heard her crying grow to distraught sobbing. As she stared at her dad, feeling self-conscious in front of him, trying to pull her sweater down to cover herself more, she felt irritation towards her mum swell. Lizzie wasn't going to let her mum's pathetic histrionics get under her skin. She was allowed to see Haydn. It was her right to see whoever she wanted.

Her dad was shaking. 'Get dressed and get out here now,' he said.

Lizzie was annoyed to hear anger in his voice.

'No,' she said, and folded herself into Haydn's shoulder. He put an arm around her. She could hear his heart beating.

'Lizzie, we've been desperate with worry. Do you have any idea—' Lizzie's stomach turned over when her dad's voice broke with emotion, and was unable to finish his sentence.

'It's her fault!' Lizzie blurted. 'She thinks she can bully me into not seeing Haydn. And she's wrong. I love him and I'm not going to stop seeing him!'

Her dad turned his gaze on Haydn and Lizzie saw disgust. He looked at Haydn as if he were shit. Then he looked back at her. 'Yes, you are. From now on you are forbidden to see him.'

'Oh my God, what the hell is wrong with you both!' Lizzie screamed. 'Is this because you think he had something to do with Anna's death? It's bullshit! We're going away together. To get away from you! Tell them, Haydn. Tell them about Manchester!'

Haydn was quiet. He'd retreated into himself, hunched his shoulders and dropped his head.

'I love him!' she shouted. 'Why doesn't anybody care about that?' Lizzie threw her arms around Haydn, who felt rigid, his muscles tense, his breathing shallow. The next thing she felt was her dad, who grabbed her by the arms and began to pull her backwards out of the shed. Lizzie began to scream. She clung to Haydn as if he were her only hope for survival.

'No!' she shrieked. 'Don't! I want to stay with him! We're going to be together. We're going away. Haydn!'

Her dad began to uncurl her fingers from him.

'Haydn!' screamed Lizzie again, then she burst into tears. 'Don't let them take me away from you!' She tried to beat her father off her, hitting his arms and face with one hand while she grasped Haydn with the other. Then her mum appeared, and took hold of her free arm, while her dad concentrated on releasing her hold on Haydn.

'Don't let them do this,' Lizzie pleaded with Haydn. She stared deep into his eyes. 'I love you. We'll go to Manchester.' She began to sob. 'I don't care about school or anything. All I want is you.'

At last her parents succeeded in separating them. Her dad linked his arms around her waist and began to pull her backwards out of the shed while she continued to scream and kick.

'Drive the car round to this back gate,' he said to her mum. 'I don't want my mother seeing her like this.'

Lizzie kicked at her dad, and called out to Haydn again and again. Her dad held her firmly, his arms crossed over her body like a straitjacket.

'Haydn,' he called into the shed. 'I want you to go home. You are not allowed to see my daughter again. If you need to know why, you can ask your mother.'

'Don't do this, Dad! Don't do this to us. You don't understand. Please. I'm begging you. With all my heart. Dad, please! Why don't you get it? Why don't you? We love each other!'

Her dad ignored her. 'I'm going to call the police if you don't leave this house. Do you understand, Haydn?'

Haydn appeared at the doorway and looked briefly at her dad, avoiding her eyes.

'Don't call the police,' he muttered. 'I'm going.'

And then without even looking at her, he scuttled off into the shadows.

'No, Haydn!' she screamed.

Lizzie stared into the darkness and imagined her heart had liquefied.

She turned her head and glared at her dad, hating him more right then than she had thought possible. 'How could you!' she spat. 'You're just like her! I love him. He had nothing to do with what happened to Anna! I don't understand you. I've *never* been this happy and all you want to do is ruin it! You want to lock me up in that miserable, death-soaked house. I hate you! I hate you both.'

'You're right, you don't understand, you can't, but you cannot be involved with that family, Lizzie, and that's all there is to say.'

The car pulled up at the back gate, and she went with her dad as he led her along the overgrown path. She wasn't going to fight him any more. If she ran after Haydn they'd only come after her, and this would happen all over again, but in front of Mrs Howe, which would be even more hideous on all sorts of levels.

Her mum got out of the driver's seat and opened the back door, then climbed into the back seat and shuffled over to the far side. Then her dad put a hand on the top of Lizzie's head and bent her into the car as if she were a criminal. All she needed was handcuffs to complete the scene.

'I'll just go and tell Mother we're taking her home,' her dad said to her mum across her. 'I'll be a few minutes. Will you be OK?'

Her mum nodded in a weary, broken way that made Lizzie want to scream.

Lizzie sat on the seat, staring straight ahead of her, not bothered by her naked lower half that was peppered with goose bumps. Her dad closed the door and then turned the key in the driver's door and locked them in.

'We were so worried about you,' her mum said.

'Shut up,' Lizzie whispered. 'I fucking hate you. You're a fucking bitch and I fucking hate you.'

'Lizzie, you don't mean that. You don't—'

'Yes, I do! The only thing in this shit world that gives me pleasure is Haydn. You have no idea. You've never been in love like this. If you had then you'd understand, and you would never do this to us.'

Her mum was quiet.

Lizzie cast a glance at her quickly. She wasn't crying. She was looking out of her window, pinching her nose. Then she turned to face Lizzie and drew in a laboured breath. She dropped her head as if she had no strength to hold it up. When she managed to lift it again Lizzie saw in her eyes that there was no fight left.

'We don't want you to see Haydn because his father was having sex with your sister, and it's tearing us up.'

Monsters

Kate watched Lizzie's face crumple and realized her world was shattering. They had torn her apart from the boy she loved and then told her the truth about Anna.

'I'm sorry,' she said.

Lizzie shook her head violently, dislodging fresh tears. Kate was exhausted beyond repair, like she could curl up and sleep for a hundred years.

'No,' Lizzie said. 'You're wrong. It's not true.'

'I wish it wasn't, but it is. Rebecca had a film of them. I saw it with my own eyes.' She turned her head away from her daughter and stared out of the window into the darkness. 'God knows I wish I hadn't,' she said under her breath.

'No.'

'As far as your dad and I are concerned, it was abuse. A forty-eight-year-old headmaster had sex with a pupil of fifteen on school premises, and that man repulses us and we can't have you anywhere near any of his family because of what he did.'

Kate turned and stared out of the window again. She wondered how many monsters lurked outside the car. How many of the passers-by, ostensibly normal, innocent men and women, were actually monsters in disguise, people hiding secrets – child abusers, wife beaters, rapists, violent thieves, murderers. She tore her eyes off the darkness and turned in the seat towards her daughter.

'But how could he?' Lizzie stammered.

Kate didn't say anything.

'The way Mrs Howe was looking at me, and what she said about Anna, it all makes sense now,' she said. She shook her head and sniffed. 'She must blame Anna for him killing himself.'

'Anna isn't to blame. He was the adult and she was a child. Whatever she did, whatever she said to him, he should have said no. He killed himself because of what he did, not because of what she did.'

'The graffiti was right then, what it said . . . he . . .' Lizzie didn't finish her sentence. She collapsed against the side of the car, her face in her hands. 'But this doesn't have anything to do with Haydn,' she sobbed. 'It wasn't him, Mum. His father isn't him. Oh God, this hurts, Mum. It's hurting my tummy.' She bent over, gripping her stomach with her hands.

Kate reached over and rested a hand on Lizzie's lower back and gently rubbed a circle like she used to when the girls were little. Then she turned to look out of the window again and watched the monsters outside through tear-blurry eyes.

The Lost Watch

'She and Kate are waiting in the car,' said Jon. He felt as if he'd been battling in the trenches.

'Is she all right?' His mother was pale with worry. 'We heard the commotion.'

'She'll be fine. I need to get them home. I just popped down to tell you we were going; I didn't want you to worry.'

Dan was back, sitting in a chair in the corner of the kitchen holding a bottle of red wine and a full glass.

Jon nodded a terse greeting in his direction. 'Nice dinner?'

'She was dull; like eating with a stuffed fish.' He reached down to rest the bottle on the floor beside his chair. 'Only just arrived back. I can't believe I missed the show.'

'Daniel!' said their mother, before Jon was able to reply. 'And don't leave that bottle there, you'll knock it over when you get up.'

Just then his father wandered into the kitchen in his dressing gown. 'I heard burglars,' he said. His hands flapped frantically at his sides.

'No burglars, my darling. Just Jonathan,' his mother said. 'Let's get you back to your bed.'

'I heard them!' He sounded terrified. 'They were right outside my room.'

'There are no burglars, dearest. Come on, I'll take you up.'

'Up?'

'To bed.'

'Why should I go to bed?'

'It's night time. We all need to go to bed.'

'Don't speak to me like I'm a child! All I want is a glass of water and you're cajoling me like I'm a baby. And I've lost my watch. Someone stole it. How can I know anything if I haven't got my watch?'

Jon watched his mother take her husband's hand and stroke it. She reached into his dressing-gown pocket and pulled out a balled-up handkerchief. She took hold of one corner and gently shook his father's gold watch into her cupped hand.

'Here's your watch,' she said. 'I'll bring you up some water.'

Jon saw bewilderment cloud his father's face, and when his mother turned to lead him out of the kitchen he followed meekly.

'Do you know who I am?' Jon called out suddenly.

They stopped. His father turned and looked at him. His eyes seemed to search Jon's face.

'Do you know who I am?' Jon said again.

'What on earth are you doing, Jonathan?' asked his mother.

'I need to know if he recognizes me.' Jon couldn't keep the desperation out of his voice. He didn't know why it mattered, but at that moment he would have given anything for recognition to dawn on his father's face, for him to smile, and then to hear him say his name.

'He doesn't. You know that.' His mother was annoyed with him. She glanced at his father, whose hands had begun to flap at his sides again. 'You'll upset him.' She took hold of one of his father's jittery arms. 'Go back to Kate and Lizzie. They need you.'

Jon stared at the wasted, twitching figure of his father in his immaculate dressing gown. 'Yes. Yes, I'm sorry. I'm not thinking properly.'

He watched him shuffle out of the kitchen after his mother. When they reached the hall his father made to turn right towards the front door. His mother corrected him and led him the other way towards the stairs.

'I do know who that was,' he grumbled, as they began to climb the stairs. 'That was the bloody plumber who stole my gold watch.'

Jon and Dan were left in an uncomfortable silence. Dan leant down and picked up the bottle of red wine. 'You know, he hides that watch in his dressing-gown about fifteen times a day.'

Jon nodded and started walking towards the back door. Looking at his father, he wondered what the point was. Human beings live in the now, with a past made of memories and a future of hope. If a human being has no memories and no hope, and his now is less than decent, how can his existence be anything more than pointless?

'It's always wrapped up in that handkerchief. You'd think he might change the hiding place, you know, shake things up a bit.' Dan lifted his wine glass to his mouth, chuckling like a jolly Santa. 'Maybe tuck it into a sock, or stick it in the cistern or something.'

'You really are a wanker, aren't you?'

'Oh, don't be so sensitive. I'm joking. You know I am.'

'You're always *joking*. But your jokes aren't funny.'

'Where's Kiki? She would have laughed.' Dan stood up and stumbled to one side, steadying himself on the table. He laughed.

'You're drunk.'

Dan held up both hands. 'As charged. So where is she?'

Jon clenched his hands at his sides. 'Stay away from my wife.'

Dan's face scrunched up, and he looked at Jon out of one eye. 'What does that mean?'

'You know what it means. It means keep your bastard hands off my wife. I know what you want.'

'You do? And what exactly is it that I want?'

'You want Kate.'

Dan snorted with laughter.

'I've seen how you look at her.'

The smile fell away from Dan. 'Don't be so damn pathetic. Honestly, you're such a bloody wimp.'

Jon's temper flared. He knew he should walk away. Dan was drunk and antagonistic. He was trying to wind him up, and reacting wasn't going to help. He needed to get Lizzie and Kate home. Jon turned his back on Dan and reached for the back door.

'And anyway,' Dan said, 'if I wanted Kate I'd have her.'

Jon slammed his hand against the door and, swearing under his breath as his anger boiled over, he ran at Dan. He put his hands up against his throat and pushed him backwards until they rammed against the wall. There was a clatter of pans and utensils as the force of the impact brought down the shelf.

'You piece of shit,' Jon snarled into Dan's face. 'Kate's my wife. The mother of my children. She loves me. Not you.' He pushed his hands harder against Dan's throat. He watched as his brother's face began to redden as he struggled against his grip.

'Jon, stop it. I'm mucking about,' rasped Dan. 'I didn't—'

Jon pushed harder.

'She loves you,' Dan croaked. 'She told me.'

Jon loosened his grip, but didn't let go.

'What on earth are you boys doing?' It was their mother.

Jon and Dan locked eyes. Then Jon dropped his gaze, shook his head and let go. Dan bent over, coughing and rubbing at his neck. 'Fucking lunatic,' he whispered.

'How dare you fight in my kitchen,' said their mother. 'Did

you not just see your father? Do you want him to worry there are burglars again?'

Jon and Dan were quiet.

She breathed deeply. 'Take Lizzie home, Jonathan. Daniel, go upstairs to bed and sleep it off. Honestly, two grown men behaving like hormonal boys.'

'Sorry,' Jon and Dan mumbled.

Dan held his hand out towards Jon. Jon stared at it. He'd done that since he was six years old. It was all a show for their mother. Jon knew when he took his hand that Dan would squeeze too hard and maybe even wink if he was sure she wouldn't see. Jon took the hand and as he shook, he leant in to give Dan a hug and pat his back with his spare hand.

'If you touch my wife, I'll fucking kill you,' he whispered.

Stale Biscuits

'We hoped it might be a good time to talk.'

Rachel was on the doorstep, and behind her was the hunched figure of Rebecca, who was wearing a denim skirt above her knees with nylon tights and a faded Michael Jackson T-shirt. She looked terrified. Kate stepped immediately aside and opened her arm to let the two of them in. Rachel gently pushed Rebecca in before her and the girl shuffled reluctantly forward.

Kate left them in the living room and went into the kitchen. She opened the back door and called to Jon. He looked up from behind the upturned mower he was trying to mend. His shirt was rolled to the elbows and he had smudges of oil and dirt all over him.

'You need to come in!' she called.

'I won't be long,' he called back.

'Now, Jon. Rachel's here. With Rebecca.'

She closed the back door and flicked the kettle on, then opened the cupboard and scanned it for anything she might have to offer them. There was half a packet of digestive biscuits in the cupboard. They'd been there a while. She took the top biscuit, had a nibble and grimaced at its damp staleness. The next one down was just about passable, so she binned the two she'd tried and tipped the rest on to a small plate, then made a pot of tea, put four mugs, milk, sugar and the plate of old digestives on a tray. Her stomach fluttered with anxious nerves and she tried not to think about what Rebecca might be here to say.

Rachel and Rebecca were perched on the edge of the sofa. Neither spoke. Rachel sat with her knees together and her hands resting neatly in her lap.

'Jon will be here in a sec,' said Kate.

She sat on the armchair opposite the sofa, mirroring Rachel's pose. Nobody said a word. Rebecca sniffed quietly. Kate cleared her throat, then leant forward to pour four cups of tea.

'Would you like sugar?' she asked Rachel. Silly really, just filling air with words – she'd made her plenty of tea and coffee in the sixteen years they'd been friends. Rachel never had sugar. She didn't have a sweet tooth at all. She liked wine, cheese and, if she was treating herself, Walkers salt and vinegar crisps.

Rachel shook her head. 'Rebecca might like some sugar, though.' She turned to her daughter, who didn't move a muscle. 'Would you like sugar in your tea, Bec?'

Kate and Rachel stared at Rebecca for a few seconds. Then Rachel turned back to Kate and nodded. 'She'll have two, please.'

Kate held out the spartan plate of digestives and again Rachel shook her head. They sat without talking, Rachel and Kate easing the tension by sipping at their tea, and making a point of not watching Rebecca pull repeatedly at a loose string on the hem of her skirt.

'Hello, Lizzie,' Rachel said, over Kate's head. 'How are you?'

Kate turned around to see Lizzie at the door. Her heart sank. She'd forgotten she was upstairs. She tried to think of a way she could get rid of her. She had no idea what Rebecca might say, and it wasn't right for Lizzie to have to listen to things about

318

Anna that might shock or panic her, especially after the drama of last night.

Lizzie glanced briefly at Kate and then looked at the floor. 'Fine,' she said, in a voice that told them she was anything but.

Rachel put down her tea and stood. She went to Lizzie and hugged her tightly. Kate saw Lizzie hug her back, and was reminded once again how close they'd all been before Anna died.

'So are you two talking again?' asked Lizzie.

'Lizzie . . .' Kate said sternly.

'It's a good thing,' Lizzie said to Rachel. 'I've missed you.'

'I've missed you too, angel.' Rachel gave her another hug. Kate glanced uncomfortably at Rebecca, who sat like a statue on the sofa.

Jon came in and mumbled a hello to Rachel. He kissed her awkwardly on the cheek and then shuffled past her and stood, silent, by the coffee table.

'So what's going on?' said Lizzie.

The adults exchanged looks.

'Rebecca needs to talk to us, Lizzie,' said Kate. 'I don't think you should be here.'

'Why not?' Lizzie crossed her arms. 'If it's something to do with my sister then I want to hear it. I've had just about enough of being kept in the dark.'

'But Lizzie, it might—'

'I think Lizzie should stay,' Jon interrupted. 'She's right; there've been enough secrets.'

'Rachel?' Kate asked.

'I think it'll be fine,' Rachel said. 'She's nearly the same age as Bec, after all.'

Rebecca looked quickly up and then back down at her hands.

'So, Rebecca and I talked last night,' said Rachel, as soon as they

319

had all sat down. 'She's upset. Really upset. I know you said she was, Kate, and you were right. I didn't realize quite how Anna's death had affected her, and she finds it very difficult to talk about what happened.'

Rachel reached out and took Rebecca's hand in hers.

'Rebecca?' Rachel said gently.

Rebecca looked at her mother, who smiled and gave an encouraging nod. They waited. Kate cast a glance at Jon, who was staring at the plate of digestives.

'Rebecca said it was Anna who made her film them,' said Rachel.

'No.' Kate shook her head against the implication of those words. 'That's crazy. Why would she want—'

'I think you should try to listen, Kate,' Rachel said. 'You wanted to hear what Rebecca has to say, but if you don't want to, if it's too hard, then maybe we should leave.'

'Of course I want to hear what she has to say, but not if it's just a load of lies.'

'You always say I'm lying,' said Rebecca. Her words were so quiet she was scarcely heard, but nonetheless the room stilled. Rebecca stared right at Kate. 'And I'm not lying to you. It was Anna that made me film them.'

The sincerity in Rebecca's voice stabbed at Kate, and she wondered if she really did want to know the secrets that lurked in the girl's Pandora's box.

'At first I said no, but she went on and on about it. She even said I couldn't be a proper friend if I didn't.' Rebecca was blinking back tears, tipping her head back as if trying to stop them rolling down her face. They fell anyway. Rachel stroked her knee and took a tissue from her bag, which she passed to Rebecca who took it but didn't use it. 'So we bunked off school and went to her gran's house and she told me to hide in this bush thing and then said to wait, and that I needed to be completely quiet and she would be back soon, with him. She was meeting him in his car by the park. I was worried someone would come out of the house, but she said nobody ever did because her grandad was ill and her gran never came up there. She opened this small window and told me where to point the phone and then she said to film them, but not until they were actually doing it. She didn't need the bit with clothes on. That wasn't any use, she said.'

Kate blinked hard and stared at the ceiling above them. She found a crack and followed its meandering line from one side of the room to the other.

'Why was it no use, Rebecca?' Jon sounded so cool.

There was a long pause.

'Rebecca,' said Rachel, as composed as Jon. 'You need to tell Kate and Jon what you told me.'

'Can you remember why she wanted you to film her and Dr Howe?'

The softness of the two adult voices made Kate nauseous and she gripped the seat cushion hard.

'For Mrs Howe.'

'What?' Kate's voice burst out. 'That woman was involved? How? How was she involved?'

'She was sort of involved, I mean . . . not with the film . . . it was Anna. She wanted Mrs Howe to . . . um, know . . . she thought she could make him leave her if Mrs Howe saw them, you know, doing it.' Rebecca closed her eyes and shook her head as if she couldn't make sense of herself.

'Kate,' said Jon. 'You need to keep calm; you're flustering her, and we need to hear what she has to say.' He turned back to Rebecca. 'It's OK, Rebecca, nobody here is angry with you in any way, but I need to get this straight. Anna wanted proof of the relationship to blackmail Stephen Howe into leaving his wife.'

Rebecca thought for a moment or two before nodding her head. 'Waiting for them was horrible. She was ages. Way more than an hour, and it was really uncomfortable. There were sticks scratching me and insects everywhere, and all I could do was think about what she had told me to do. It made me sick. I was actually sick into my mouth. I nearly left then, but just as I was trying to get out of the bushes without getting even more scratched, I heard them. So I kept quiet while they went into the shed.'

Kate glanced at Lizzie and saw her horror. 'Lizzie,' she said. 'Would you like to leave? We could leave Dad to talk to Rebecca and I'll come and keep you company upstairs.'

Lizzie pursed her lips and shook her head.

'Go on, Rebecca,' said Jon.

'Well, I did what she told me. I watched them through the crack in the window until they started, you know, doing it, and when they did, I pressed record and stuck my phone through the gap. I looked through the window and tried to make sure that the phone was pointing in the right place. Anna said she would move about so that the film would get them in different positions and that's what she did, because I saw her looking at the phone and then making him change what he was doing.'

Rebecca's nerves seemed to have lessened and she now spoke freely and methodically, recalling each piece of information without cadence, as if badly reciting a poem.

'I thought he'd see me, and while I was holding the phone I couldn't stop shaking, because I suddenly thought about what would happen if he did. Dr Howe doesn't like me at all – I'm always in trouble – and I thought filming him like that with Anna would really make him hate me, and I'd definitely get excluded from school, and all I could think about was how I'd tell my dad,' she looked at Rachel, 'because he gets really cross about me getting into trouble at school.' She looked back at her hands. 'Anyway, I had to make sure I didn't shake too much and jiggle the phone. I was sure afterwards I hadn't done it right, and I'd recorded the wrong place, like the wall or something, but when we looked at it, it was fine. She was really happy.'

Rebecca was quiet for a while. Everyone else was silent too; Kate couldn't even hear breathing.

Rebecca took a sudden long, deep breath in. 'Then we set up an email account and wrote an email with the film attached that said if he didn't leave his wife then she would post it on the internet.'

'On the internet?' asked Jon.

'YouTube,' said Rebecca. 'Even though I told her YouTube wouldn't let it on because they don't allow full-on sex. But she said it didn't matter because he'd leave his wife anyway just at the thought, and if he didn't, and YouTube wouldn't take it, then there was always RedTube, which does porn and stuff, or we could fix a viral email, which would be worse anyway because it would go global in a day.'

Though Kate didn't really know what Rebecca was talking about, and from the look on Jon's face he didn't either, she got the general gist and her stomach turned over.

'Anna thought it was funny. She was laughing when we attached the film, so much she was crying. She was like, "*Oh my God*, he is going to totally flip when he sees this." She was sure he'd leave Mrs Howe, and then I asked her if she really did love him, and she sort of went quiet and then nodded and smiled and said, "Yes, I really, really, do." And she was laughing and saying, "Oh my God, I love him!" And then she was about to send the email and I said "Are you sure", and she sort of raised her eyebrows and giggled and then pressed send.' Rebecca paused. 'The look on her face was like, "Shit, what have we done", and then she just started laughing like she was never going to stop, and it was really weird because I felt sick and really scared but I started laughing too, but maybe that was because I was so nervous and stuff.'

Rebecca was picking at her tights. She'd made a small hole in them, which she hooked her finger through, then pulled and pulled to make the hole bigger until most of her knee began to show through. Rachel reached over and stilled her hand.

'She said we had to sit and wait for a reply. But I said that it was the weekend, and maybe he wouldn't get his emails because it was his school email address. She said we should text him and tell him to look at it. Then she just grabbed my phone which was right by the computer, and, well, she texted him.'

Rebecca took a shattered breath.

'How did she know his number?' Lizzie's voice was flat and controlled.

Rebecca looked at her and shrugged. 'She just did. She knew it off by heart. Anyway, my phone rang about ten minutes later. It wasn't a mobile number, it was a landline, a number I didn't recognize, but I answered it anyway, you know, without really thinking, and it was Mrs Howe. She didn't ask for Anna, she just started shouting at me. She said I was a bitch and she swore and said she would kill me when she got her hands on me. She actually said that. That she would kill me. I tried to say I wasn't Anna, but I couldn't get any words in because she was screaming so much. I looked at Anna and she was trying to ask me who it was and then she just snatched the phone from me and she started shouting back. She told Mrs Howe that she was a cow and that Dr Howe was going to leave her because he said she was no good at sex,' she paused and shook her head, 'well, loads of other stuff like that.'

Kate wished Lizzie wasn't there. She wished she didn't have to hear about Anna this way. She wished she could remember her, untarnished; she wished that for all of them.

'When she put the phone down I was really scared. I told her we shouldn't have done the film and that it was a stupid idea, but she said I had to realize this was real life and this sort of thing happened all the time. She said she wasn't scared, and she meant it. Nothing scared her. *Ever.*' The admiration in Rebecca's voice rang clear as a bell.

Kate closed her eyes. Nothing ever used to scare her, either. Not when she was young. Not until she realized how much there was to be scared of.

'What happened then, Rebecca?' coaxed Jon.

'Dr Howe called Anna's phone.'

She stopped speaking and pulled more at the hole in her tights. Rachel took hold of her hand.

'He basically told her it was over.'

'What did Anna say?'

'Oh my God! Crazy things. And all this mad swearing and shouting and stuff. It was the headmaster! And when she put the phone down she was like, "Yeah, well, we'll see about that." She said he was lying, there was no way he could love Mrs Howe more than her and that she'd show him that, make him realize what he wanted. She said she knew he loved her. So anyway, then Mum comes up and asks if we're coming down for supper.' Rebecca looked at Rachel and a weak smile flashed across her face. Rachel stroked her hand against Rebecca's and smiled back.

'Keep going. You're doing fine,' she said.

'Anna told Mum she wasn't feeling well. Mum asked if she wanted to go home, but she said she probably just needed a lie-down. Then Mum went downstairs.' Rebecca coughed and shifted position on the sofa. 'Anna started saying the best way to get Dr Howe back was to make him jealous. She said that he was always going on about how jealous he was when he saw her with other boys. Most of all with Haydn. That's why she used to hang out with Haydn, because Dr Howe would get annoyed and stuff and then be major desperate to, well, you know.'

Kate glanced at Lizzie, who was staring at her knotting fingers.

'She said she loved doing it with him afterwards.' Rebecca looked up at Rachel briefly, but Rachel didn't make eye contact. 'So she rang Haydn and told him to meet her. She laughed and said it was like asking a kid if he wanted chocolate. He jumped at it. She said she would call Dr Howe later and tell him she didn't love him any more and had decided to start with Haydn, and that would make him come begging on his knees. Then I went for supper and she stayed in bed. When I came up she was all dressed and ready. She told me to put pillows under my bed and we'd sneak out. She told me it would be fun, we were going up to the gym block roof to drink and she said I'd enjoy seeing Dr Howe's face when he found her and Haydn together. She said she might even do stuff with Haydn to really wind Dr Howe up. I said I didn't want to go. All I could hear was Mrs Howe shouting. I . . . I was scared . . . of what she'd said to me. I asked her again and again not to go. I even said I'd tell my mum, which made her sulky with me. She said if I told anyone she'd hate me for ever. So I promised I wouldn't. "Swear it, Bec," she said, "swear you won't tell." So I swore. Then she asked me again if I'd go too. She said it would be much better with me there. But I said I didn't want to. I felt really guilty; I knew she thought I was being a rubbish friend.' Rebecca's voice cracked.

Hearing Rebecca talk was difficult. Watching her struggle, fidgeting, her foot tapping fretfully against the base of the sofa, the obvious pain she was feeling as she remembered the conversations she had with Anna that night. Through Rebecca's recollection Kate saw an Anna she didn't recognize, playing a game she should never have played, and she wondered with every syllable what she could have done as a mother to stop it.

'I got into bed and read and Mum came in to check on Anna. Anna pretended she was asleep. Then Mum went downstairs and turned the telly on and a bit after that Anna got up. I didn't say anything, and she didn't either. Then she opened the door and went out.' Rebecca looked up at Kate, and then at her mother. 'I should have stopped her, shouldn't I?' Tears began to stream down her cheeks. 'If I'd stopped her then she'd still be here.' She looked up at the ceiling and put the flats of her hands against her face.

Kate winced at the desolation in Rebecca's voice. She stood up and walked over to her. She rested her hand against the side of Rebecca's hot, tear-wet cheek. Rebecca lowered her hands and stared at Kate, who leant forward and kissed Rebecca's forehead. When Rachel took Kate's hand and squeezed it, she had to fight hard to keep her own tears back.

'I'm sorry I told you about them,' Rebecca whispered. 'Mrs Howe said I was a selfish little girl who only thought of myself and didn't think about your and Jon's feelings.'

'She said what?' said Rachel.

Kate stepped back in shock and sat down on the edge of the coffee table. 'When did she say that?' she asked.

'She asked me to come into her office. It was after the memorial. I didn't want to go, but I had to because she's the deputy head. She closed the door and then she told me I was meddling with things I didn't understand. "If you mention this disgusting business to anyone, or if I see you talking to Mr or Mrs Thorne, I'll make your life a misery." And then she asked me if I had any more copies of the film. I said I didn't, even though I had it on my phone and you can easily get it off the email account we used.' And now Rebecca burst into tears and drew her arms around her body, and looked to Kate as terrified as she had been the day they talked outside the school. 'Then she said if I knew what was good for me I'd keep my mouth shut.'

'She threatened you?' gasped Rachel. 'But she can't do that. Oh, sweetheart, come here.' And Rachel folded her into a strangling hug, stroking her hair and rocking her gently. 'It's all right, Bec. It's OK.'

Kate rubbed Rebecca's knee. 'She's wrong, sweetheart, you did the right thing to tell us.'

Kate glanced across at Lizzie. She was sitting ramrod straight with her head set and eyes fixed ahead. Her hands lay flat on her knees, which were pressed together. She looked so grown up. Kate saw a lot of Jon's mother in her. It wasn't a likeness she'd noticed before, but it was there: beneath the freckles, the flyaway hair and the pale slightness, was her grandmother's resolute stare, the stoic quietude and the tumble of thoughts hidden behind a steely mask.

The Wasp Apothecary

Lizzie sat on her bed and stared out of the window at the glorious weather. It was a spectacular afternoon. The sun was making fun of her.

'Bloody sun,' she muttered, and stood up to pull the curtains together, poking her tongue out at it before shutting it out.

Her mum knocked on the door and then came in with tea and toast. They didn't speak. They didn't even look at each other. She waited until she'd left, then picked up a triangle of buttery toast. She went to take a bite, but she didn't really feel like it so threw it back on to the plate untouched. She slumped backwards on her bed. A few moments later she leant forward and grabbed her phone. She stared at it. After a hesitation, she turned it on. There were thirteen missed calls and seven texts from Haydn. She threw the phone down on the bed and leant against the wall. Then she groaned and gently banged her head twice, and then in one swift movement, before she had time to rethink, she pulled up an empty text window, typed and pressed send.

Did you know about anna and your dad???

She stared at the phone, but instead of the bleep of the text she expected, it rang.

'Yes,' was all he said.

'Why didn't you tell me?'

'How could I?'

Lizzie bit her lip.

'What would I say?' he said. 'If you knew what he—'

'How did you find out?'

'Why do you need to know?'

'I just do, OK!'

'Look, I heard my parents fighting, heard what they were saying. It made me sick what he did. You asked why I hated him so much, well, now you know.'

'Did you say anything to Anna?'

He didn't reply.

'Rebecca was here. She told us things.' Lizzie paused. 'Anna wanted your dad to leave your mum and be with her. Did you know that?'

Just silence.

'Haydn? Did you hear me?'

'No, of course I didn't know. How would I? I only knew about them because I heard them arguing. I just told you that.'

'I still don't know why you didn't tell me. This is so major.'

Just silence.

'Haydn!'

'I was scared, all right!'

'Scared of what, for God's sake?'

'Of . . . of . . . I don't know of what. Of what you'd say. Of you hating me.'

Lizzie shut her eyes and began to chew on her bottom lip.

'I love you, Lizzie. So much my heart feels like it's exploding.'

He waited for her to say something, but she didn't.

'I was scared you'd leave me.'

'Well, you know what?' she said. 'Sometimes you just have to

face up to what scares you. Knowing you kept this from me . . .'
She hesitated. 'I don't know. I just need to work it all out.'

Then Lizzie hung up and turned her phone off so he couldn't
call her back. It was as if there were an enormous heap of poisonous bricks in her stomach. She loved him so desperately, but she
totally understood why her parents couldn't stand the thought of
them together. If she was brutally honest, she wasn't sure she could
stand the thought either. She put her head in her hands and tried to
think. She pictured him carefully: hair over his face, slightly lopsided grin, beautiful blue eyes locked on to hers in those moments
before he kissed her, the way his skin felt, his smell, the way he
put his lips to the tip of her nose as light as a tiny butterfly. How
was it fair for him to be held responsible for his father's actions?
Was it his fault his mother hated Anna so much? Of course not!
How could it be? It was like her mum said: he was the child, just
like Anna, vulnerable and unable to manipulate events in the adult
world. She saw his face smiling as he showed her his candlelit fairy.
She couldn't love anybody more, and she needed him. Her body
began to ache. None of it was his fault!

She tried to think back. Imagined him telling her about Anna.
At the memorial. Then in the cemetery. In the street when he
freaked out. In the shed before they made love. What would she
have said? What would she have done?

It was then that she heard the buzzing.

She opened her eyes and sat up. It was a wasp, buzzing and tapping as it bashed itself against the window. She felt herself go cold
and a sweat grew on the back of her neck. She reached for her bag
on the desk and clutched it to her, easing herself off the bed. With
her eyes fixed on the wasp she slowly and carefully reached for the
window catch. She held her breath, unlocked the window, slid the
bottom half of the sash window upwards. Then she sat back on

the bed and waited for it to find its way out of her room. But the stupid thing couldn't work it out. It crawled around on the pane, and every now and then it would drop in the air and fall down the window, but not far enough to find its route out. Lizzie watched as it fought desperately to escape, hurling itself against the glass, confused and cross. She wished Haydn was with her; he'd get rid of it. She remembered the way he'd slapped his hands together in the cemetery, killed that wasp without being hurt, how brave he was, how safe she felt whenever he was around, how little she thought about bees and wasps and hornets.

How can you be so critical of Haydn's fears, she thought, *if you're so vulnerable to your own?*

And it was a lot of things that scared her, not just bees. She was scared of noises in the house, upsetting her parents, missing hockey, Dalston station, Mrs Howe in the dark, the spot on the mantelpiece where Anna's urn had stood. She was scared of bloody everything, and what good did it do her?

Lizzie stood up and put her bag on the bed. Then she took a step towards the window. All she had to do was bang the wasp quickly. Haydn hadn't been stung. He'd just clapped his hands and killed the wasp. It was easy.

This is your chance, she thought. *If you do this you don't need to be scared of anything again.*

'Be brave,' she whispered. 'Be really brave.'

She took three deep breaths and reached her hand out towards the wasp. Sweat rose up her neck and across her forehead, and she began to feel faint as her head swam. She thought of Haydn, lifted her hand, shut her eyes and slammed her hand on to the window, squashing the wasp against the glass.

The sting fired up her arm.

'Oh my God,' she whispered.

She lifted her hand away from the window and the half-dead body of the wasp fell on to the sill, its legs scrambling helplessly, its wings buzzing irregularly against the paintwork.

She looked down at her hand and saw the deep purple mark where the sting had punctured her skin. She clutched her throbbing hand to her chest. Her throat was already tightening as it swelled with the poison. Her mind seemed to drift away from her body, and then Lizzie thought about trying to reach for her bag. Her knees buckled. She fell on to the carpet. She needed a shot of adrenalin, but she realized she'd floated too far from her body to make herself move. She thought of her bag lying on the bed and tried to sit up. She caught a glimpse of it before it faded away like a mirage in the desert. Then she was aware of herself lifting upwards, like an astronaut weightless in space. She looked down and saw her body collapse backwards. Her reddened hand fell across her chest and her legs were splayed uncomfortably. She looked at the window sill. The wasp was dead now, its tiny black corpse curled up, still. She looked back at herself and was surprised to see how tranquil she looked considering how hard it was to draw breath, that iron-fisted hand tightening fraction by fraction around her lungs, squeezing the oxygen out of them, turning her lips and the tips of her fingers the purple of blueberries.

Then the door opened. It was her mum. When she saw Lizzie on the floor she dropped to her knees beside her suffocating body. Then she screamed. It was the same scream she'd screamed when she answered the phone the night Anna died. Lizzie's blood froze.

Her mum gathered Lizzie's limp body in her arms and held her tightly. Lizzie saw her own head flop backwards, the blueberry lips a fraction open. Her mum kissed her over and over, and tears fell from her eyes that cooled her burning skin. She could taste their saltiness even from way up where she was. Then her mum began to shout for help. She tipped her head back and opened her mouth and bellowed, at least she looked like she was bellowing, because although Lizzie could read her lips and make the words out she could no longer hear any actual noise, it was like her ears had been stuffed with cotton wool. Her mum looked right up at her then. Lizzie smiled but her mum didn't see her, she just called out for someone to do something.

There's not much I can do from up here, Mum, Lizzie tried to say. But she couldn't make her mouth work and the words didn't come out.

Lizzie started to point frantically at the bag on her bed, but her mum just closed her eyes and rocked Lizzie's stifled body.

Then there was someone else at the door. *Oh my God. Haydn!*

Lizzie waved at him, but he was only looking at her empty body as it struggled to breathe on the carpet below. She watched him step closer to her. Her mum went crazy then. She screeched and started to beat him away, while curling Lizzie away from him behind a protective shoulder.

Lizzie tried to shout at him to tell him the bag was just there on the bed, but still nothing came out. He took his phone out of his jeans pocket and dialled. His lips moved, but of course she couldn't hear a word. It was so peculiar to watch them like this, from up where she was, like two characters on a muted television screen. Then suddenly Haydn saw the bag. He grabbed it.

Clever Haydn, she thought. *Clever, clever Haydn.*

He fell to his knees and emptied the contents all over the carpet like he was searching a stolen handbag. He shouted at her mum, but she didn't respond. Maybe she couldn't hear him either. Haydn shook her shoulder, thrust a handful of the pills and syringes that lay scattered on the floor out towards her, right under her nose. He didn't know what to do.

Oh, Haydn, Lizzie tried to shout, *there's a piece of paper, a folded one. It's got instructions on it. Can't you see it?*

Haydn shook her mother again, harder this time. At last her mum seemed to get it. Lizzie watched her eyes focusing on the syringe. She held Lizzie's body tight to her chest with one hand and with the other pointed quickly. Then she looked at Lizzie's face and cried out. She slid her fingers between the freezing-looking lips and tried to make room for air to pass around the tongue, which was so swollen it nearly filled her mouth. She saw her mum's lips moving, but she was so far away from her now, out of the room and through the roof, and it was hard to make out the words. She definitely said *I love you*, and then *please don't die, please don't die*, but then she started to mumble, which was impossible to read.

Lizzie looked back at Haydn. He had the syringe. He spoke to her mum. She didn't respond. He took her face in his hands and turned it towards him. Then he spoke again, slowly and clearly.

'What do I do?' he said. 'You have to tell me what to do.'

Even from where she was, high up in the sky with the clouds, she could see her mum's eyes lock on to Haydn for a second time. She spoke to him, and Haydn nodded and tipped the syringe upwards. He tapped it with a finger. Lizzie was amazed how perfectly she could smell the old tobacco on that finger.

She winced as Haydn jammed the needle into her body on the floor and watched the syringe depress. The clear liquid powered into her bloodstream and began to shoot around as each pump of that slowing heart pushed the adrenalin to the outer reaches of her feeble body. Then she felt herself falling downwards, out of control, like an enormous ball that had reached the height of its bounce and was coming back down. As she neared her body she picked up speed. Sound returned, slowly at first, then loud as anything. Her head began to pound. She heard her mum crying. She felt hands around her body. Kisses all over her face. She heard Haydn panting next to her. She was aware of his exhausted body shivering with effort and emotion. She twitched her fingers just to see if they still worked. Her mouth loosened and the fist around her lungs at last began to ease its grip. She tried to open her eyes, but they seemed to be nailed shut.

Then she heard people in her room, strangers with serious voices, the static crackle of a radio, hands that weren't her mother's all over her. Then straps and wires, something placed over her mouth and nose, and the cool, smooth breaths that followed. Footsteps thumped heavily on the stairs. A man said her name. She heard someone talking behind him.

'Mum . . .' Her voice struggled out in a whisper and the last thing she heard before she gave in to the blackout was her mother's strangled cry of relief.

Freesias and Roses

Kate stared at the grey liquid in the polystyrene cup she held. It had long turned cold, and the familiar disc, synonymous with the countless cups of untouched tea of the past year, floated listless on its surface.

The hospital waiting room was quiet. It was Saturday and hot, not blistering, but easily warm enough for T-shirts and shorts. Kate imagined most people would be lighting the barbecue or mowing the lawn or filling paddling pools, enjoying this beautiful gift of a day.

Watching Lizzie dying in her arms, her lips losing colour, her mouth, throat and tongue swelling before her eyes, left her drained of everything. Numbed. She thought she'd lost her. Another dead daughter.

And all she did was watch.

She shuddered when she thought about Haydn, about what might have happened if he hadn't turned up, if he hadn't run all the way from his house to theirs when Lizzie had hung up on him. What if he'd been too worried about bumping into Kate? What if he hadn't loved Lizzie enough to fight to see her? And what would have happened if she'd remembered to put the latch on the front door, or he'd stopped at the newsagent for gum or cigarettes

337

and arrived five minutes later to find Lizzie lifeless and cooling, her heart stilled?

Kate was aware of somebody sitting down beside her. She glanced up. It was Barbara. Kate was shocked by how different she looked that day. The glamour had left her. The snow-white hair that used to sit immaculate, with every silken hair brushed and set in place by the tortoiseshell comb, was dishevelled and without its lustrous shine. Her skin hung in loose grey folds and her eyes were rheumy, rimmed red with tiredness. Kate looked down at the cup of cold tea.

'How are you?' her mother-in-law asked.

Kate nodded and tears brewed.

Barbara rested a hand on Kate's knee.

'Don't say anything nice,' Kate said quickly. She bent to put the polystyrene cup at the foot of the chair. 'If you do I'll cry, and I don't deserve to cry.'

Barbara didn't reply.

'I couldn't help her,' whispered Kate. 'I did nothing. If Haydn hadn't arrived, I . . . I . . .' Kate shook her head. 'She would have died, Barbara. I'd have let her die, like Anna.'

Barbara tutted. 'You have absolutely no idea what you would have done. It was a matter of minutes. You would have got it together. You would certainly have called the ambulance. And I'm convinced you would have reached for that syringe within moments. You were dealing with the shock of finding her. You can't be so hard on yourself. And anyway,' she said, 'he *did* arrive. And thank God he did. That boy, by all accounts, is a hero.'

Kate nodded. Haydn's rational calm had saved Lizzie. His enduring love had brought him to her in her time of need. He was her guardian angel, and Kate owed him everything.

'I'm sorry,' said Kate.

'I told you, you have nothing to be sorry for. Everybody reacts differently in an emergency, and given what you've been through . . . well, let's just say it was a miracle you were able to tell the boy what to do with that needle.'

'I mean, I'm sorry to you. For how I behaved at Anna's funeral. And since.'

'There's no need to talk about it,' said Barbara. There was a level of emotion in her words that tore Kate in half.

'I want to,' struggled Kate. 'It's important. I need you to know I'm sorry. Anna's death has unravelled me. I'm so eaten up by it I can't see anything else.' Kate rested her head in her hands and sighed. 'I miss her so much, Barbara. Every day, every minute, I miss her. Some days I wake up without the pain in my stomach, thinking everything's fine, and then it hits me like a shovel in the face and I remember she's not in her bed and I'm never going to be able to feel her again, or kiss her, or smell her, and this horrific deprivation smothers me.'

'She was a special child, Kate. And so like you.' Kate looked sideways at Barbara, who smiled. 'Wasn't she? Like you in every way.'

Grown in a Petri dish, Jon used to joke. A doppelgänger. A clone.

'All passion and vitality,' said Barbara. She patted Kate's knee. 'Beauty inside and out. It spilled out of her. But my goodness, there's a wicked streak to you both.'

Kate nodded. 'And then my good girl Lizzie, like Jon.'

Barbara smiled again. 'Yes, Lizzie so like Jonathan.'

Kate had a picture of Lizzie and Jon together. They were in the kitchen making sandwiches. They held their knives the same way, stood the same way, their shoulders hunched just a little, taking the business of making lunch so seriously. They both cut the crusts off, as finely as possible so as not to waste too much bread. She and Anna wouldn't even get a plate out; they'd just grab a slice of bread and a bit of ham from the fridge, fold the two together and take a bite whilst they kicked the fridge door shut. Lizzie and Jon, though, would sweep the crumbs off the worktop, put their knife in the dishwasher and their plate on the table before sitting down to eat. They were both so desperate to please, needing to do the right thing, so conventional, loyal, with such a powerful sense of right and wrong, the moral and immoral.

'When Jon first met you he was so overwhelmed he used to make me talk to him for hours on end to try and make sense of what he felt. Then he'd tell me everything funny that you said, what you did, even what you ate or drank. Of course, I'd pretend I wasn't interested, that I *disapproved* of you.' She smiled.

'And did you?'

'Disapprove of you?'

Kate nodded.

'A little. I'm a dreadful snob.' She lifted her hand off Kate's knee and took her hand. Then she squeezed it. 'But I could see that as far as he was concerned you were the one, and that was obvious from the first day he brought you home.' Barbara sighed deeply. 'He loves you very much.'

There was a maternal pleading, a protectiveness, in Barbara's words that sent a wave of guilt surging through Kate.

'I love him too. It's just . . .' She tailed off as she tried to work out exactly what had happened to that enviable love. 'I seem to have forgotten what to do with love. I feel spent, like an empty shell, dead, if you like. It was only when I was holding Lizzie, when I thought I'd lost her too, that I realized how much love I was still capable of feeling.'

'I understand that more than you would imagine.' Barbara's voice stumbled.

Kate looked at her, but her mother-in-law made a point of looking away. Barbara brushed her hands repeatedly up and down her lap, desperate to regain control of her emotions. Kate suddenly felt very close to her. The last time she had felt like this towards her was the day before the funeral. Kate was supposed to be doing the flowers. It was a job she was determined to do. It seemed right for her to do it for Anna, to make the place look fresh and young. But faced with her living room full of flowers, all of them cut in their prime, she had folded, backed away into the kitchen and collapsed. By chance Barbara arrived at that very moment and found her trembling on the floor. She sat with her and held her hand and waited patiently until her shivering sobs stopped. Then she led her into the living room to the buckets of freesias and roses in pinks, purples and whites, their sweet scent filling the room, and the two of them stood shoulder to shoulder in silence and arranged the bouquets and vases.

'You're a special person, Barbara.'

Barbara shook her head. 'No. Not special at all.' She looked at Kate, and Kate saw a deep sadness in her.

'What's wrong, Barbara?'

She didn't reply.

Kate rubbed her lower back. 'It's OK,' she soothed. Then she put her arm around her mother-in-law's shoulder and drew her in. 'What you do with Peter, it's amazing. But you need help. You have to ask us for help. Jon finds it hard, but he means it when he says he'll help. All you have to do is give him some guidance. He's not sure about it. Seeing Peter like this unnerves him. It's been a rough year – neither of us have been any use to anyone, least of all ourselves. But we are here.'

Barbara looked at her and smiled. 'I know you are.' She patted Kate's knee. Kate took hold of her hand and squeezed it. At the sound of footsteps she turned to see Jon, and caught his happy surprise at the sight of his mother and wife holding hands.

Barbara straightened her back and let go of Kate. She smoothed her skirt. 'Jon, darling, would you mind dropping me home? I should get back to your father.'

'Of course,' he said. 'I'd love to.'

An Important Smile

Jon stood next to Kate in the doorway of Lizzie's room watching her sleep. The bedside lamp threw a warm glow across her face. Kate had tucked the covers around her body so she was snug and warm, cocooned in the safety of her bed. The carpet was vacuumed and a small vase of pink roses sat next to a giant tin of Quality Street on her desk.

Jon would know when she was better because she'd start to rifle through the chocolates for the Golden Pennies. It was a standing joke. Whenever Quality Street came into the house, Christmastime generally, he and Lizzie would declare war on each other and the Golden Pennies were the booty. When one of them opened the tin and found the last penny stolen, the loser would bow in mock deference to the other. Jon had once found Lizzie sitting behind the sofa, aged eight, with a fistful. She was carefully unwrapping one at a time, popping it into her mouth and then starting on the next. Beside her was a neat stack of wrappers, flattened and piled perfectly in line.

'Thank God she's OK,' whispered Kate. 'What would we have done? How would we have coped?'

'I don't know,' said Jon in a matched whisper. He had spent the day in a daze, wrestling constantly with that same haunting thought: *how would we have coped?*

He wasn't there when it happened. He was at the hardware store trying to find a piece of rubber tubing to fix the water butt. It was all part of his new idea to collect grey water from the baths and sinks to water the plants. That morning he'd woken and resolved to finish the project. He was desperate to give himself something to do, something to think about other than his collapsing marriage and Stephen Howe and the look of hatred that Lizzie had given him as he tore her off Haydn, but of all the times to be away from the house, pointlessly trawling aisles and aisles of plumbing paraphernalia . . .

He arrived home to the ambulance pulled up outside his house, the front door open, paramedics talking urgently. His heart stopped when the stretcher came through the front door. Kate followed after, her face stricken and puffy from crying. Then came the Howes' son.

Lizzie.

There was a blanket over her, a drip in her arm and an oxygen mask covering her face. Her skin was a bluey-white, apart from one exposed arm, which was inflated to the point of rupture and as red as a telephone box.

Jon grabbed the closest paramedic. 'What happened?'

No answer, just a concerned face monitoring the mobile drip. He grabbed at Kate. She had a foil blanket around her shoulders. She looked dazed, shattered. It terrified him. His stomach soaked with dread and bile swelled.

'She's OK,' she said then. 'It was a wasp. But she's OK.'

He watched them load Lizzie into the ambulance, motionless, poisoned and swollen, and felt the floor beneath him begin to crumble.

Now the drama was over and she was safe, her recovery certain, with no ifs or buts. All she needed was sleep. Kate's hand reached for him and she laced her fingers through his. He held his breath. He didn't speak; he couldn't risk it. It was an almost perfect moment, the two of them together, watching their precious daughter breathing steadily in the warmth of her bedroom.

They stepped away from the door and Kate pulled it to. She looked up at him. She wore jeans and a crumpled T-shirt, and her hair, which needed washing, was tied up in a hasty bun. Without any make-up and after weeks and months of trauma, her skin was pale and her eyes ringed with dark. Her eyebrows, which had always been neatly plucked, were unruly, with stray hairs peppering the space between. His heart began to hammer just as it had the first time he saw her across the room at a crowded, sweaty party.

And then, right there outside Lizzie's room, she smiled.

The smile was unforced and honest, and he drew it into his suffocating body like oxygen. Her hands went up to his face and rested gently on his cheeks. She pulled him towards her and he closed his eyes. Then he felt her lips on his. Her hands ran down his arms and her fingers linked into his. She kissed his neck, under his chin. He allowed his head to tip ever so slightly, unsure, not wanting to give in to the surges of lust that fired inside him, not wanting to scare her away. She stopped. He opened his eyes, worried he'd ruined it. The smile had gone. Her face was serious and her eyes glistened with a film of tears. She pulled him with one hand towards their room. She sat him down on the edge of their bed. Then she sat next to him. Then she lay backwards and pulled him with her. He felt as if this were the first time: nerves, fear, exhilaration. She rested her head on his chest and slid a hand inside his shirt. Her fingers moved just a little, stroking his skin so lightly.

'I thought you were leaving me,' he said.

'How could I do that?' she whispered. 'You're the father of my children.'

'That's no reason to stay.' He hated himself for saying it. He would have imagined he would stay with her whatever she said, take whatever of her she was prepared to give, but if all she saw was Lizzie and Anna he knew it couldn't work.

'That's not why I stay. I stay because I love you,' she said then. 'I've loved you from the first moment I saw you.'

Jon shook his head. 'That's not true.'

'What do you mean?'

'I stole you.'

'Stole me?' She looked incredulous. 'How on earth did you steal me?'

'I told you Dan wouldn't be faithful. I pursued you, bullied you into dinner when you were upset about Dan. I remember. I remember thinking, what kind of man does this to his brother?'

Kate sat up and faced him. Her brow was furrowed with frustrated disbelief. 'You don't know what you're talking about. I wanted you from that first conversation. You, in that tweed suit! You were so different from everyone else. Clever and funny. And so intense. Dan meant nothing to me. I would have taken you home that night, but it was his birthday, remember?' She nudged him. 'What kind of girl dumps the birthday boy for his brother? For goodness' sake. I had to pretend I was upset about Dan and that tart from the sculpture class. I'm not stupid, you know. Dan and I would have lasted about five minutes. I mean, what good is he for me? Christ, one night with the idiot and I'm taking drugs and vandalizing houses.' She shook her head. 'It's you, Jon, you I've always loved.' She paused. 'But you can't ask me to separate you from my children. I can't do that. You gave them to me. It's been such a tough time for both of us, and I know the way I've handled myself has made it so hard for you. But that's me and, you know, that's why I need you. These last few days, the fog

346

seems to have lifted a little, and I've been doing a lot of thinking. I feel like I've turned a massive corner. I think things are going to improve. I really feel that. But I can't promise I'm not going to break again. I can't promise it's going to be easy.'

Jon put his arm across Kate and rested his forehead against hers.

'We lost one of the two most important things in our lives,' she whispered. 'We'll be sad about that until we die. That sadness is a part of us now. She will never leave me, and she'll never leave you. But I won't give up on us, on this family.' She paused to gather herself. 'And you can't give up on us either.'

Jon tilted his head to kiss her. She kissed him back, and then he felt her hands unbutton his shirt. She bent and kissed his chest. Then he felt her hesitate and her body braced. He heard her draw a difficult breath.

'No,' he said. 'It's not the right time.'

'Yes,' she said. 'It is.'

Suspicions

Lizzie was still in bed. It was ten thirty and she was reading. She was glad of the rest. Getting her head around Anna and Dr Howe and what Rebecca had told them had left her in pieces. And she knew her parents were totally shattered too. It was like they'd been in a plane crash and only just survived. Her dad looked especially dreadful. She'd never seen him so thin and tired. He looked at least sixty, and normally he didn't look close to that.

Lizzie tried desperately hard to keep focused on her book. She didn't want to think about anything to do with Anna, but it was impossible. The more she tried to concentrate on the words, the more they seemed to blur and swim. She had to keep squeezing her eyes shut really tight, then rereading sentences she'd just read. But she just kept hearing Rebecca's voice. She shook her head and reread her last page.

When Lizzie heard her mother's footsteps on the stairs, she folded the corner of her page and put the book on her desk. Her mum knocked once and came into her room with a glass of Ribena that clinked with ice cubes.

'I thought you might like a drink.'

'Thanks,' said Lizzie.

Her mum put it on the desk and then straightened her sheets.

'Lean forward a sec,' she said. She plumped the pillows, then smiled and picked up the empty cereal bowl and Lizzie's half-drunk mug of tea.

'Your uncle's flying back to New York this afternoon, and your dad's leaving work early to drive him to the airport. I'm going round in a bit to say goodbye and take a lasagne over for your grandparents. Do you want to come?'

Lizzie suddenly felt guilty remembering that she never made it round to see her grandpa on his birthday, and nodded.

'Lovely. Dan will be pleased, and I know your gran will be over the moon to see you,' her mum said. 'Get yourself dressed and when you're ready, we'll go.'

On her way to the bathroom, Lizzie passed the stairs up to the attic and smelt the strong reek of oil paint and white spirit. She loathed the smell. It reminded her of her mum crying. She hadn't been up there. Not since Anna died. At first it was because her mum hadn't let her. The door was always locked, whether her mum was painting or not. And then, as the months progressed and Lizzie was forced to endure the noises coming from above her room, the sobbing, banging and thrashing that sometimes went on all night, it became a place she wouldn't go near, even if she was welcomed with open arms.

Lizzie listened for her mum downstairs. The vacuum cleaner was on. She peered up at the studio door and hesitated. Then, with another quick check for the sound of the vacuum cleaner, she took a couple of steps. She hesitated again, rubbing her hand and arm which were still tingling painfully from the wasp sting, then she took another few steps until she was standing at the door. She reached out and opened it and, without going in, stared into the room. Sunlight flooded it through the two large roof lights. The room was cleared. The tubes of paint were lidded and in a neat row on the table in the corner, like the dead after a massacre line the side of a road. The palettes were stacked and the paint-smeared jars were empty of spirit. It was remarkably restful up there, nothing like the dark place of misery and emotional torture she'd imagined.

She stepped inside. There were canvases of all sizes stacked in horizontal piles against the walls around the room. The first picture in each stack, and there were maybe fifteen stacks, was a different depiction of Anna. Lizzie knew without looking that the other canvases, the ones she couldn't see, were all of Anna too. She did a quick calculation. What was it? A hundred, more like a hundred and fifty, paintings of her sister? Lizzie felt suddenly uneasy, trespassing on her mum's secret psychosis, witnessing a side of her she shouldn't see. Cautiously she began to look through them. Though some were better than others, each one seemed to have something about it. There was her defiance, perfectly captured in the set of her mouth as a teenager; her wide, enthusiastic smile as a toddler; grace and sensuality in a study of her hand, painted open, palm up as if it belonged to a goddess who proffered a heavenly peach.

She looked up and noticed the painting on the easel in the corner of the room beneath the slope of the roof, and her breath caught in her throat. It was phenomenal. It was Anna, smiling, her head tipped back as if she were about to laugh. It was as if Anna were right there in the studio with her. Lizzie walked up close to the painting, her arms crossed, leaning lightly away, drawn by the picture but at the same time wary of it. She uncurled an arm and slowly reached out to touch the tips of her fingers to the side of Anna's face. As she touched the painting, her whole body began to ache with missing.

Then she saw Mrs Howe. She was sitting in that armchair in the dark, her face twisted with loathing and hatred, calling her sister a slut. She heard Rebecca's fearful voice telling how Mrs Howe had threatened her. Her head began to turn over and over as thoughts battled and jostled, her mind beavering away, fingering through the facts, the motives, piecing it all together, puzzling.

'Lizzie!' she heard from downstairs. 'We should leave!'

Lizzie took one last look at the painting of her sister. 'Did she?' she asked Anna softly. 'Did that woman do it?'

'Great,' her mum said when she came into the kitchen. 'Shall we go?'

'Mum,' she said, catching her breath a little.

'Yes?'

'We haven't really spoken about what Bec said.'

Her mum hesitated. 'No,' she paused. 'Do you want to?'

'Do you think Mrs Howe did something to Anna?' Lizzie could tell by the shock on her mum's face that she wasn't expecting her question.

Her mum sat at the kitchen table and stretched her arms out in front of her. Lizzie pulled out a chair and sat too.

'Mum?'

Her mum turned her head to face her. She looked sad again, as if she might cry. Lizzie would normally have felt guilty, but she didn't feel guilty; she wanted to know what her mum thought. Her suspicions, her conclusion, ate away at her. It had been since Rebecca talked to them. It made perfect sense to her. Too much sense, so that she was incapable of seeing any other way. It was all far too convenient. Anna sleeping with Dr Howe, trying to get them to break up, saying the things she said to the woman, the Howes the first on the scene.

'No, darling,' her mum said. 'I don't think that.'

'She was so angry with Anna. Those things Rebecca said . . . how livid she was about Anna and him. Then the blackmail. She said she was going to kill Rebecca when they sent the film. Bec said that. What if she went up on the roof and *pushed* Anna?'

Her mum took her hand. 'Sweetheart, this whole business has been so traumatic for all of us. Really, it has. But you can't say things like that. You can't go around saying Angela Howe murdered Anna. You can't even *think* it. There's no evidence—'

'But didn't you hear what Rebecca said? How angry she said Mrs Howe was? Then Mrs Howe was there minutes after she died. What if they lied? What if she was there when Anna was still alive? It can't be a coincidence. I don't believe it.'

'Look, Angela was at the school because Haydn called her. He asked her to come, because he was worried about what Anna was doing. There is no reason not to believe her.'

'What about her telling Rebecca not to tell anyone? She said she'd make her life a misery.'

'Just because she doesn't want anyone else to know about her husband and one of his pupils doesn't mean she is a murderer.'

'But Mum,' Lizzie pleaded. 'She was so angry. You didn't see her. I did, and she definitely looked like she wanted to kill someone. And you should have heard the way—'

'I've seen her angry too. But there's getting angry and then there's killing someone.'

'But *you* got angry and hurt Rebecca, and you're not half as loony as Mrs Howe.'

Her mum pursed her lips and looked down at her hands, and Lizzie immediately wished she hadn't mentioned the thing with Rebecca.

'Listen,' her mum said gently. 'The woman's husband was having sex with a child at his school, there was a film Anna threatened to show everyone, then he kills himself. This kind of stuff will make her desperate and unhappy, and yes, angry. But it doesn't make her *bad*. Do you understand that, Lizzie? Angela Howe is not a murderer.' She paused. 'In the last few weeks you've been through so much, and lots of it is difficult for you to understand.'

Lizzie opened her mouth to protest, but her mum was quicker.

'My behaviour at the memorial, you falling in love, all the fighting and the things you heard about Anna and Dr Howe. Then you were stung. All this will interfere with your judgement, the way you see life.' Her mum shuffled her chair closer to Lizzie so their knees were touching. Then she took hold of her hands. 'Look at me.'

Lizzie stared at the fruit bowl on the table as tears welled in her eyes.

'Please, Lizzie, look at me.'

She lifted her gaze from the fruit bowl and drew in a deep breath. She turned her head to look at her mum. Her mum smiled.

'There is no evidence to suggest Angela hurt Anna, and so the police won't reopen the file.' She looked at Lizzie and raised her eyebrows, looking for confirmation that Lizzie understood. 'Lizzie?' Her mum lifted her chin so she was forced to make eye contact. 'Angela Howe did not push Anna off that roof. She fell. I know it's hard. God knows I find it hard myself, but that's what we have to believe.' Her mum pulled her in for a hug. 'These last weeks have shown me that blame and anger and self-pity, they aren't healthy things to feel.' She kissed the top of Lizzie's head. 'Anna fell,' she whispered. 'It was an accident.'

Lizzie stared at her mum.

'OK?' her mum said. 'Lizzie, I want you to say you understand.'

Reluctantly, Lizzie nodded.

The Tortoiseshell Comb: Part Two

Kate shook as they drove over to Jon's parents' house; trying to stay calm and address Lizzie's fears without letting on that she had her own suspicions had been almost impossible. There was so much of her that wanted to jump up and cheer.

At last! Someone believes me. Someone else believes that Anna didn't fall off that roof.

But she had to be the parent. She had to do what was best for Lizzie.

They stood on the doorstep and rang the bell. Barbara opened the door, but only a crack. She peeped through the gap, and when she saw who it was, she neither smiled nor opened the door.

'You've come for Daniel.'

'And we brought you a lasagne,' said Lizzie before Kate could speak.

Barbara still didn't open the door.

'Can we come in?' Kate asked.

Barbara looked hesitant, but then she stepped back and disappeared. She left the door ajar. Kate and Lizzie exchanged looks, and then Kate pushed the door open.

They walked into the hall and found Barbara with her back to them just in front of the door into the kitchen.

'I haven't had time to tidy, I'm afraid,' she said weakly.

'Is Jon here yet?' Kate asked.

Barbara shook her head and walked into the kitchen.

Kate followed her. 'He'll be here soon.'

The kitchen was in a state, with crockery and pans stacked in the sink, clothes heaped up on the table; a pile of Peter's books and papers had fallen like a demolished tower block, throwing itself across the floor, which itself needed a sweep and a mop.

Suddenly, Barbara began to shake, almost as if she were having convulsions. 'I can't. I can't. I . . . I . . .'

Kate went to her side and put her arm around her shoulders and gently shushed her.

'Lizzie, darling,' she said. 'Will you make Granny a cup of tea with some sugar in it?'

Kate moved Jon's mother over to one of the chairs at the table and sat her down. She noticed her eyes, red from crying some time earlier, with bags beneath them like deflated grey balloons. There was no tortoiseshell comb and her hair was loose, unbrushed and unruly. She looked like a mad, exhausted *Macbeth*ean witch. Kate went to the living room and grabbed a crocheted blanket off the sofa, which she took back to the kitchen and wrapped around Barbara's shoulders. Then she knelt beside the chair.

'Is everything OK with Peter?' she asked.

There was no reply.

'Barbara—'

The doorbell rang.

'Lizzie, can you get that? It'll be your dad.'

Kate stroked her mother-in-law's knee.

'Is she all right?' he said as he came in.

Kate looked up at him. 'Maybe you should check on your father?'

355

Jon didn't move.

'Jon, I think you should make sure everything's OK upstairs.'

The first thing he noticed was the mess in his parents' room. There were clothes everywhere, empty teacups, a plate with a half-eaten piece of toast on it. The curtains were drawn and it smelt musty. It was a shock. His mother was someone who colour-coordinated the towels in the airing cupboard, who always opened the curtains in the morning and spent considerable time arranging their folds until they were just so.

His father lay in his bed, the bedside light was on and the covers were crumpled loosely around his body. His withered arms lay close to his sides, and his eyes were closed, mouth slightly open. Jon wondered if, finally, his father had passed away. He certainly looked like a corpse, thin and drained of colour. Jon leant close to him and turned his ear towards his father's mouth. There was a faint rasp of life; Jon pulled back. He was sleeping, peaceful, breathing invisibly, his wasted body housing a wasted brain, a brilliant mind that, with the callous march of time, had atrophied such that he hid his watch fifteen times a day and needed help to take a crap.

'She's been crying at night,' said Dan's voice from behind him. Jon turned. His brother stood in the doorway. He wore tracksuit bottoms and a T-shirt. His hatless head was more balding than Jon remembered, and he hadn't noticed so many wrinkles before. 'She goes downstairs and cries. Not loudly, mind; whimpering, really. I went down to her the first night I heard her. It was maybe three or four nights ago. I'd needed a pee. Anyway I went to see if she was OK, but she shouted. Told me to leave her alone. That she didn't need fussing over.' Dan laughed nervously. 'I thought maybe he'd died, you know, because she doesn't cry. And my first thought was thank God. Thank God he's dead.'

Dan sounded incredulous, shamed even, by his statement, but for once Jon didn't point the finger. He looked at the floor, noticing his mother's hair comb half hidden beneath the bed. The mother-of-pearl glinted green and purple like treasure on the sea bed. He picked it up, put it on the bedside table and then stood and turned to go out of the room, waiting for Dan to go first rather than pushing past him.

In the kitchen Lizzie was sitting next to her grandmother and they both held cups of tea. His mother looked up when he and Dan came in.

'Lizzie made me tea.' She smiled. 'She's a good girl.'

'Are you feeling warmer now?' Kate asked.

'Much, thank you. How ridiculous to be so cold in the summer. Honestly, old age.' She turned to Lizzie. 'You make the most of being young, my darling. It's over in a flash.' Her face fell. 'I'm finding this terribly hard,' she said. 'Too hard. I . . .' she hesitated. 'You know,' she paused a bit. 'When I first met him, wow, he was quite something. Like no other man I'd ever come across. To this very day he's the most intelligent person I've had the privilege of meeting. He questioned everything. He read everything. You could ask him about anything and he'd have an opinion, and not just any old opinion, but a coherent, knowledgeable opinion that demanded one listen.'

She looked up at Jon and then at Dan. 'Can you imagine what it feels like to have that sort of mind then find yourself unable to remember the days of the week?' She rubbed her lap with the flats of her hands. 'The disease is becoming a living death. It's like he's dissolving in front of my eyes. He's almost completely incontinent and recognizes me only intermittently. Everything about him is different. It's like living with a stranger, and every day I mourn the man I used to know. It's like he's been possessed.' The effort she had to muster to keep her emotions at bay was clear. 'The doctor told me it was like looking after a child. He was trying to be sympathetic.' She shook her head and rubbed the flats of her hands down her lap a couple of times. 'Well, it's nothing like looking after a child! With a child you watch them learn and develop skills. You see them grow in body and mind, but with Peter all I see is him falling apart in front of me—' Her eyes had filled with tears, and she broke off for a moment until she had composed herself. 'The illness has no regard for the man Peter was. I can't sleep with the worry. I worry about our finances, about loneliness, how I'll cope further down the line. I worry I missed Anna's memorial. How could I do that?'

Jon glanced at Kate, but her eyes stayed fixed on his mother.

'He needs so much care, and I'm weak with tiredness. I can't keep up with the housework and I haven't had a bath in days. I even went to the doctor last week to see if there was some sort of tonic I could take to boost my immune system. The silly man suggested anti-depressants. He said they would help.' She paused and shook her head scornfully. 'How on earth would they help? Would the pills wash him? Change wet bedsheets and soiled underclothes?' She closed her eyes, her hands rubbing down her lap over and over. 'I spoke to Peter last night about a nursing home. I told him I'd been looking on the interweb and found some quite respectable places. One has an ornamental pond where the residents take afternoon tea, and he loves water. But he got upset, scared, he . . .' She took a deep breath. 'Well, he became so agitated he raised his hand to me.'

'Oh, Granny,' said Lizzie.

'Don't you worry, my darling,' she said, suddenly sounding

stronger. 'These old bones can survive a knock or two. Goodness me, but he was upset. And then I got so angry with him. Suddenly. It hit me like a steam train. Anger and frustration and so much resentment. I shouted at him and told him to leave me alone. Didn't he understand what I was doing for him? Didn't he see how hard it was? How dare he make me feel so worthless! Such a damn failure. I shouted terribly and he crumbled like a terrified child, but I kept on. I told him how unfair it was. This wasn't what I planned for my life. I've spent my whole life caring for children, and now him. I told him I wanted my life back.' She stopped, her head dropped, and she was quiet for a moment or two. 'Then I walked out and left him. I went out of the front door, but as soon as I was on the doorstep, as soon as the breeze hit my face, I realized I had nowhere to go to. My life is with him. For better or worse. This is my lot and I knew I couldn't leave, and I knew I could never put him in one of those dreadful places with people who don't love him. How can you clean diarrhoea off a man if you don't love him? The thought that he would be shut in a room, alone and unloved . . .'

Then her face shattered like a stone might shatter a pane of glass, and tears began to tumble down her cheeks. She rubbed her lap faster, desperate to regain her composure. 'I even thought about . . .' She stopped talking and shook her head. 'I was . . . lying next to him . . . and he was barely breathing. It was as if his body was only just holding on to life. So I got up and I kissed him, and I told him how very much I loved him and that I would see him soon, and then . . .' She paused as crying swamped her words. 'I took hold of my pillow . . . and I held it above his face.'

Jon felt his stomach cave in.

Kate reached for Lizzie's shoulder.

'I couldn't do it,' she whispered. 'I just couldn't.' She looked up at her family. 'You're shocked, aren't you? I can see by your faces. You're asking yourselves how I could have even *thought* such a thing. What kind of person it makes me.'

'It makes you a very normal, very human kind of person,' said Kate, without a hint of blame or shock. She knelt. 'Barbara, you don't have to do this alone. You have us. We've been distracted, not thinking about you, and I am so sorry. We're your family. We're Peter's family.' Jon felt a tremendous rush of love for her. 'We'll get the house organized and bring you food. We'll help every day. And if that's not enough, if it's still too much, he can come and stay with us.'

'But you've so much on your plates,' his mother said. 'It's not fair; you're both exhausted. You've had such a dreadful time recently. I know there are things you're not telling me to do with Anna. And Lizzie. It's Lizzie who needs your time and support. Not me.'

'I could move back,' said Dan. They all looked at him. 'I could come home and help. To be honest, I'm finding the whole New York thing rather dull now.'

'That's very kind of you, Daniel,' his mother said fondly. 'Thank you. But you are a disaster area. You can't even look after yourself, let alone your father.'

Jon and his brother exchanged a brief flash of understanding.

'You know, Mother, there are lots of options,' said Jon. 'And we can help you decide which is the best.'

'And if he needs to come and live with us, even for a short time, if you need a break or something, there's Anna's room,' said Kate, her voice a little strained.

Jon thought of their daughter's room, just as she'd left it, and imagined them packing her things away, taking her toys off her bed, the make-up and jewellery off her dressing table, in order to move his father in. He reached for Kate and pulled her hand to his mouth and pressed it against his lips.

'For now, though, I think Jon should take Dan to the airport while Lizzie and I stay here and tidy up a bit. We're going to run you a nice warm bath, and you're going to wash your hair and have a soak.'

As Jon and Dan were leaving the house, Jon kissed his wife. 'Thank you,' he said. 'I love you.'

'I love you, too.'

'I won't be long. I'll drop him at Heathrow and turn right around.'

'OK,' she said. 'But we'll be fine.'

'I know.' He walked out of the house and down the steps. Then he remembered the tortoiseshell comb. 'Her comb is by the bed. Maybe she'd like to wear it.'

The Girl in the Cage: Part II

Lizzie and her mum worked quickly in the kitchen. It didn't take too long, and though she wasn't a massive fan of housework it felt great to be helping her grandmother. Seeing her so upset had shocked her because as far as she was concerned, the woman was made of rock. When Lizzie was seven Anna told her that their granny would never die because she was a white witch. Lizzie believed her, of course, and they used to spend hours poring over photo albums and picking out pictures of their grandmother that clearly showed she hadn't aged a day in decades.

'And that hair?' Anna had said. 'Only a real witch can have hair that long and white.'

Lizzie sprayed Pledge on the cleared table and polished in big sweeping circles. She was glad her grandmother was clean and dressed again, and her hair had lost that crazy bedhead look. It hadn't suited her.

'Have you spoken to Haydn since you came out of hospital?' her mum asked suddenly.

Lizzie's heart skipped. 'Um, no,' she said.

'Maybe you should.'

Lizzie nearly choked in surprise, and she stopped polishing.

'I thought you didn't want me anywhere near him.' She couldn't stop her heart thumping against her chest.

'He saved your life.' Her mum turned on the tap and squeezed some washing-up liquid into the sink.

'But you said—'

'I said many things, Lizzie, but we owe him a lot. And at the very least I think it's right you thank him.' Her mum said the words as if she were rehearsing them for a play.

Lizzie nodded. 'I would like to do that. I'd like to thank him.'

Her mum tried to smile.

Lizzie put the polish and duster on the table. 'Can I call him now?'

Her mum looked reluctant, nervous even, but nodded.

Lizzie went through to the living room and then turned her phone on. There were dozens of missed calls from Haydn and four texts.

Call me asap :L xx

I need to talk to you!!! :s

Please Lizzie my hearts breaking :((x

Lizzie you have to call me

She sat on the sofa and laid her head back and closed her eyes. Just those four texts filled her with glorious thoughts of him. But then, as easily as those things came into her head, so did the nasty stuff. Was this how it was always going to be? Her thoughts of Haydn forever tinged sour by spiking imaginations of his perverted dad and murdering mum?

She picked up her phone and took a deep breath. Then she hesitated, resting the phone against her mouth, her mind turning over and over.

No, she thought. *You have to.*

He answered the call before the first ring had finished.

'Lizzie?' Just hearing his voice sent shivers down her spine.

'Hi.'

'I've been trying to get hold of you.' He sounded desperate. 'I called you loads.'

'I know. My phone was off.'

'We're leaving.'

'What do you mean, leaving?'

'Me and my mum.'

'Leaving where?'

'Here. London. We're going to stay with my nan in Leeds.'

'Leeds! Oh my God. How long for?'

'I don't know. Mum says she can't live in London any more.'

'When are you going?'

'She packed last night. We're leaving this afternoon. I've been trying to call you.'

Lizzie felt sick.

'I want to see you,' he said.

'OK,' she whispered.

'I'll come to yours, if that's all right. I'll get Mum to pick me up on the way.'

Lizzie tried to say OK again, but she couldn't speak because she was crying.

'Lizzie?'

'Yes,' she managed. 'I'm at my grandmother's. I'll leave now.'

'I'll be there soon.'

Lizzie wiped her eyes with the back of her hand. Then she thought of Angela Howe. There was nobody in the world she hated more. 'I don't want to see your mum.'

'No, OK.'

Lizzie chewed on her lip to stop from crying.

'Lizzie?' he said.

'Yes?'

'I love you.'

Lizzie hung up and then burst into wretched sobs.

'Sweetheart?' Her mum sat down beside her and rested a hand on her knee.

'He's leaving, Mum. She's taking him away from me . . .' She sniffed. 'They're going to Leeds . . . this afternoon.'

Her mum hugged her tightly, resting her chin on the top of Lizzie's head.

'He wants to say goodbye to me. Is that all right?'

'Of course.'

'I said I'd meet him at home. I don't want to see her.'

Her mum let go of her and sat back. She carefully stroked her hair out of her face and tucked it behind her ears. 'Do you want me to drive you?'

'No, you finish with Granny. I'll walk.'

'OK,' said her mum. 'I won't be long.' Then she hesitated. 'I won't disturb you when I come in.'

Lizzie flushed red.

She ran most of the way home, stopping to walk a bit when the air in her lungs burned too much. She felt like the desperate heroine in a tragic love story, running through the streets to get to her lover, bumping shoulders with people, dodging dogs and bikes and bins. She half expected him to be waiting on the step when she got there, and when she saw he wasn't she was a little disappointed. But then again, she was hot and sweaty, dirty from cleaning her grandmother's house; it was probably better she cleaned herself up before he got there.

She flew up the stairs two at a time and flung herself under the shower, then got dressed and dried her hair. She smoothed the flyaway strands down and put some mascara on. Her stomach twisted

365

with nerves and dread; she felt as if she were making herself pretty for her own funeral. When she was finished, he still hadn't come. She looked at the clock. It was nearly three. If he was leaving that afternoon there was hardly any time left; he had to be here soon. Her tummy teemed with nerves.

Hurry up, she thought, *where are you? We've so little time.*

She went into the living room to peer out of the window for the umpteenth time. She pressed her forehead against the glass and waited as time sloped past with hours for seconds. She remembered her grandparents' shed. It was the last time they'd been together, not including when she was stung. She winced as she remembered her dad pulling her off him. She hoped she hadn't made a mistake and tried not to think of her mother, who was surely worrying right now.

Please, she thought, *please let everything be all right between us.*

She needn't have worried. When he finally appeared, her heart leapt and she squealed with joy as she jumped up.

'Haydn, Haydn, Haydn,' she whispered, and ran to the front door. She flung it open and jumped into his arms, kissing him all over his face and neck.

He grinned and stroked her face with the back of his hand as he kissed the tip of her nose. She turned her head enough to kiss his wrist, but as she did, she tasted the metallic tang of blood. She took hold of his arm and looked at his wrist. A smattering of dried blood was visible below the line of his sleeve. He tried to pull away, but she held on and pushed his sleeve up his arm.

'Haydn!' she gasped. 'What have you done?'

There were new cuts. Lots of them. Parallel lines of dried and drying blood doodled into his scarred skin, with the skin between inflamed and red. She touched her fingers over the cuts, then looked up at him and saw his eyes fill with tears. She lifted her hand and placed her palm on his cheek.

'I thought you said you'd stopped doing that to yourself.'

'I had,' he said, pulling his sleeve down over his wrist to cover his arm. 'It's just, I don't know, finding you on the floor like that, all blue, and you couldn't breathe. I thought you were going to die.' He took her hand and turned it over, then touched the small brown dot where the wasp had stung her. Her hand was still swollen, tight and red, and when he stroked her it tingled as if a thousand tiny needles pulsed against her. 'If you'd died, Lizzie, my life would have been over. But you didn't die. And I've never been so relieved and happy and, I don't know, God, just so fucking grateful about anything ever.' He reached for her hand and pulled it up to his mouth and kissed her.

They pressed their foreheads together. She closed her eyes and breathed in the delicious, sweet smell of cigarettes and chewing gum on his warm breath.

'Don't leave me,' she whispered.

'I have to.' Haydn squeezed her hands. 'She's selling the house.'

'But what about Manchester? We could still go.'

'I can't do that to her.' He shook his head. 'I can't leave her. She needs me.'

Lizzie felt a smack to her gut. 'But I need you too.'

They stared at each other, his eyes flicking over her face, taking her in.

The sound of a car horn made her jump.

'That's her,' he said.

'No,' she breathed. 'Not now.' She glanced over his shoulder at their car, which had pulled up on the opposite side of the road, its roof rack piled high, the load covered by an electric-blue tarpaulin and lots of yellow bungee cords.

Her stomach clenched; this couldn't be happening.

'Oh, God,' Lizzie whispered, tucking herself tighter into Haydn. 'She's got out of the car.' She gripped his shirt with both fists.

'Haydn!' called Mrs Howe. 'It's time to get in the car.'

He turned and nodded at her. 'Just a few minutes!' he called.

Then Lizzie flung her arms around him. 'When everything's calmed down,' she said, 'when all this has gone away, we'll be together, won't we?'

He kissed the crook of her neck. 'Yes.'

'And you'll phone me?'

He nodded.

'And text?'

'Every day.'

'Haydn!' his mother called. 'Come on!'

'I'm coming!' he shouted back, without taking his eyes off Lizzie.

'I can't believe this is it.' She felt as if her heart were being cut out of her chest. Then, from over his shoulder she saw Mrs Howe crossing the road and walking towards them. Her heart missed a beat and she pulled him close again.

'Your mum's coming,' she whispered.

Mrs Howe was wearing jeans and trainers and a navy sweater. Lizzie had only ever seen her in knee-length skirts and stiff-collared shirts.

'Please, Haydn!' she said as she reached the gate. 'You've had enough time.'

Lizzie started to cry. 'Don't go. You can't,' she said, stumbling over the words. 'I can't think what I'll do.'

'I'll call you when we get to my nan's.' He touched her teary cheeks with his sandpaper fingers. Then he reached into his back jeans pocket, and with his other hand took hers. He leant in to kiss her, and as he did he closed her fingers around something. She knew without looking it was his iPod. 'I've put songs on it for you. And our playlist, the one from our first time, it's on there too.'

Lizzie sniffed and tried to smile through her tears.

'And there's something else.' He handed her a folded piece of paper. She opened it. It was Anna's drawing of the crouching caged angel. A lump formed in Lizzie's throat. 'You know, she talked about you all the time,' he said. 'When she gave me this drawing I remember what she said. She said she was jealous of how sorted you were, of how you knew exactly what you wanted and how you didn't care what people said or thought, and how you knew who you were. She said you were truly free. She said you were amazing, and she was right. She loved you loads, Lizzie. Like I do.'

'Haydn, we have to go.' Mrs Howe was standing right next to them.

Lizzie turned her head to look at Mrs Howe. She hated her so much. She'd never known a feeling like it; it burnt inside her like caustic acid.

'There's no need to glare at me like that, Elizabeth,' Mrs Howe said.

'Why shouldn't I?' said Lizzie. 'I hate you.'

'Come on, Haydn.' Mrs Howe jerked her head in the direction of her car. 'We've got a long journey ahead of us.'

'You know,' said Lizzie. She stood as tall as she could and narrowed her eyes. 'I know why you're leaving.'

'Lizzie, I've got to go,' said Haydn, quickly. 'I'll text you on the way, OK?'

Lizzie ignored him. 'You're leaving because of Anna.'

'Because she destroyed our lives, you mean? Yes, Elizabeth, you're right. That's exactly why we're leaving.'

Lizzie balled her fists and needled her eyes into Mrs Howe. 'She didn't destroy *your* lives. You destroyed *hers*! And ours.' Her voice quivered as she fought to keep her words steady. 'I know what you did to her.'

Mrs Howe's face darkened. Lizzie swallowed and stepped backwards a fraction. Mrs Howe crossed her arms and briefly allowed her eyes to leave Lizzie before fixing them on her again.

'Oh really? And what exactly do you think I did?'

'You pushed her.' Lizzie's heart thumped so hard it threatened to smash its way out of her body. Mrs Howe's face fell. The anger slipped away, wrong-footed, it seemed, by the accusation. 'Didn't you, Mrs Howe? You pushed her off the roof and killed her. Rebecca told us what Anna wanted. I know you saw the film, and got so cross you told Rebecca you'd kill her. I know you screamed at Anna and she said stuff to you. And then Haydn called you and said they were on the roof. And it was just too tempting, wasn't it?'

'Lizzie, be quiet,' said Haydn. 'Please. Just leave it. You don't know what you're talking about.'

He grabbed at her, but she yanked her arm out of his grip and stepped up close to Mrs Howe. 'You went up there and saw her on that wall and you pushed her, didn't you?'

'Lizzie, stop it! You're wrong. I told you what happened. It had nothing to do with Mum. Anna fell. I saw her fall.'

'No!' screamed Lizzie. 'She pushed her!'

'Lizzie,' said Mrs Howe, her voice suddenly gentle. 'Please don't do this. I didn't hurt Anna. I didn't—'

'You couldn't stand it, could you?' Lizzie shouted then. 'He loved Anna so much more than he loved you! You knew you could never compete with her, didn't you? You knew that he'd always love her more—'

'Lizzie!' It was her mum. Kate shut the car door and marched up the path, pushing past Angela. When she reached Lizzie she put a hand on her shoulder. 'What's going on here?' she asked firmly. Lizzie suddenly felt faint from all the adrenalin and emotion surging through her body. She grabbed her mum's arm to steady herself.

'Nothing,' said Angela, flatly. 'Nothing is going on. Haydn and I are just leaving.'

'She did it, Mum. She killed Anna!'

Her mum sighed. 'Darling, we spoke about this.' She turned to Angela. 'I'm sorry,' she said, though her voice had hardened and Lizzie saw that she wasn't looking Mrs Howe in the eye. 'It's all been very stressful for Lizzie. She's had so much happen.'

'But Mum—'

'No buts, Lizzie. This is over.'

Lizzie felt as if she were dissolving. She looked at her mother, desperate to convince her of what she knew was the truth. 'Mum,' she begged. 'Please listen to me.'

Her mum shook her head and pulled her into a tight embrace. She rested her chin on Lizzie's head. 'You know,' she breathed, 'I can see her right now. She's dancing. Twirling around and around.' Lizzie could see her too. Her shining hair was flying out behind her, her hands and arms outstretched, graceful like a ballerina's, her fingers long and delicate and angled so that the moonlight in which she danced flowed over her and fell like raindrops off them. 'Lizzie, sweetheart, we can't do this any more,' her mum whispered. 'We have to let this go. We have to move on. It's time, darling. It's time for us all to move on.'

Lizzie knew she was right. Feeling her mother holding her, her arms wrapped around her, her smell so comforting and familiar, she knew she was right, but it meant that they would never know exactly what happened on that roof, and that was something they were all going to have to accept. If not, it would destroy them.

'Lizzie, I have to go now,' said Haydn from behind her.

Lizzie didn't move. Instead, she clung to her mother even tighter and closed her eyes.

She listened to their footsteps move away; she heard them crossing the road, the car doors opening and shutting, and a few moments later, the car engine. Her stomach turned over.

'No,' she said, suddenly pushing away from her mum and running down the path. 'Wait!' she shouted. 'Wait!'

But the laden car had already pulled out and was driving down the road. As she ran, she began to panic. She didn't want to leave him like that. She didn't want that to be their last memory. She stopped and watched the car driving away from her. Her heart sank and she dropped her head. When she looked up, however, she saw the car had stopped. She broke into a run. As she reached Haydn's window, he lowered it. He was crying, his face blotched red. She reached through the window and wiped his tears with her hand and then she leant in to kiss him.

'I will never forget you,' she said. 'I'll never forget what you did for me, Haydn. I needed you and you came for me.'

Then she stepped away from the car and smiled at him, and though it felt like her insides were being ripped out of her as she watched his car turn off their street, she had a good feeling too, because she knew that somehow life was going to be a little bit better now.

Almost a Year After

'When my dad suggested I read the eulogy today I told him I didn't think I'd be able to. It wasn't the thought of standing in front of you all in church that so terrified me, it was the daunting task of making sure I did justice to my grandmother's life. She was a formidable lady, with tremendous traits and attributes, and to give her the credit she deserves is something I was unsure I'd be able to do. My dad told me not to think about it like that. He reminded me that everybody attending the service would have their own memories of my grandmother, and that if I spoke to you all about what she meant to me and expressed my love for her, then you would all be able to identify with my sentiments and share in my remembrance of her. He said this was all I needed to do.'

Lizzie smiled at Jon, who smiled back and nodded.

'My grandmother touched many lives and was an inspiration to many people. I know she was to me. News of her illness came as a massive shock to all of us. Our family were just recovering from a traumatic year following Anna's death, and to be hit with more devastating news was unbearable. I felt as if my world was collapsing.'

Lizzie paused and took a couple of deep breaths as she felt the threat of imminent tears. She didn't want to cry. Her grandmother wouldn't have cried. She would have stood straight and read clearly. Lizzie squared her shoulders and ran her eyes over the congregation.

'Just days before she finally lost her arduous battle with cancer, a battle she fought with the stoic bravery that typified her, she gave me the tortoiseshell comb that I'm wearing today.'

Lizzie stopped speaking and turned her back towards the congregation to show them the comb with a quick bobbed curtsey. A quiet rumble of laughter rang around the church.

'She wore this comb in her beautiful hair every day that I knew her. And that day, she took my hand in hers and told me she was giving me this comb as a reminder that life is for living, that it was a magnificent collection of fleeting moments and that each of these moments is as precious as the next and should be embraced. We spoke about Anna, my beloved sister, and she said that though I would always miss her, I must never let her memory, or indeed the memory of any of our deceased loved ones, interfere with these moments. She took both my hands and told me to grab every opportunity that showed itself; she told me to keep learning, to keep reading and improving my mind, and never assume that I knew anything wholly. She said that intelligence is a gift. My grandmother was a strong woman, opinionated and bright. She didn't like asking for help, but at the same time she was a selfless and compassionate human being, demonstrated so clearly by the unrelenting way she cared for and loved my grandpa. She was loyal, principled and determined, and I pray these are qualities I have inherited. She also had the capacity to give and receive great love, and this is something we must all strive to achieve. I am thankful, as I hope you are, for the privilege of knowing someone as special as my grandmother.'

Lizzie looked at the sea of faces in the church, then settled on her mum and dad. She watched her mum holding her grandpa's hand, his knees covered by a new tartan blanket.

'Well done,' her mum mouthed.

Lizzie smiled.

Then she turned and stepped down from the lectern. She paused briefly in front of the glorious portrait of her grandmother. It was still wet. Her mum had only finished it in the early hours of that morning. She had worked on the painting day and night for six days. It was a triumph and, at that very precious moment in time, Lizzie was the proudest daughter in the world.